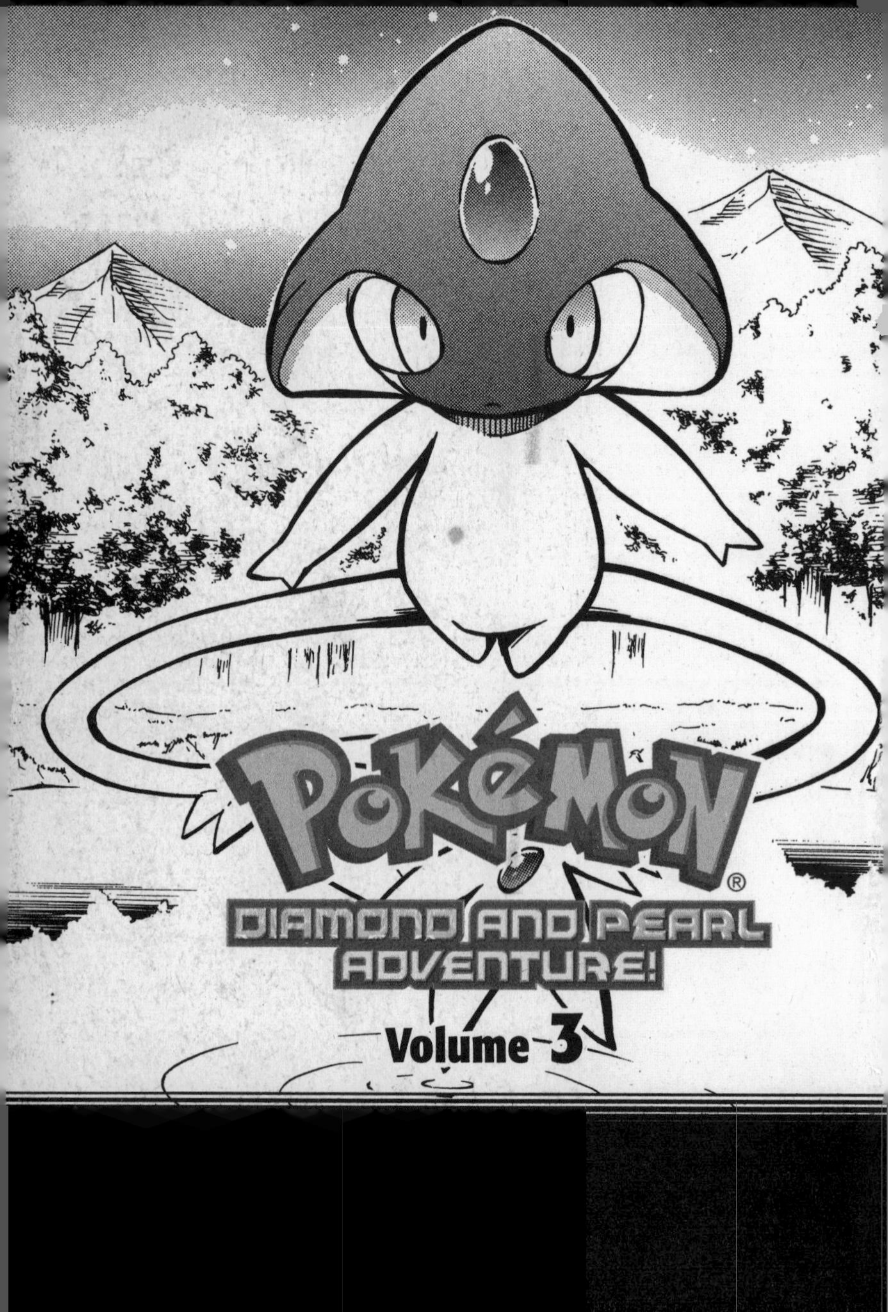
POKÉMON®
DIAMOND AND PEARL ADVENTURE!
Volume 3

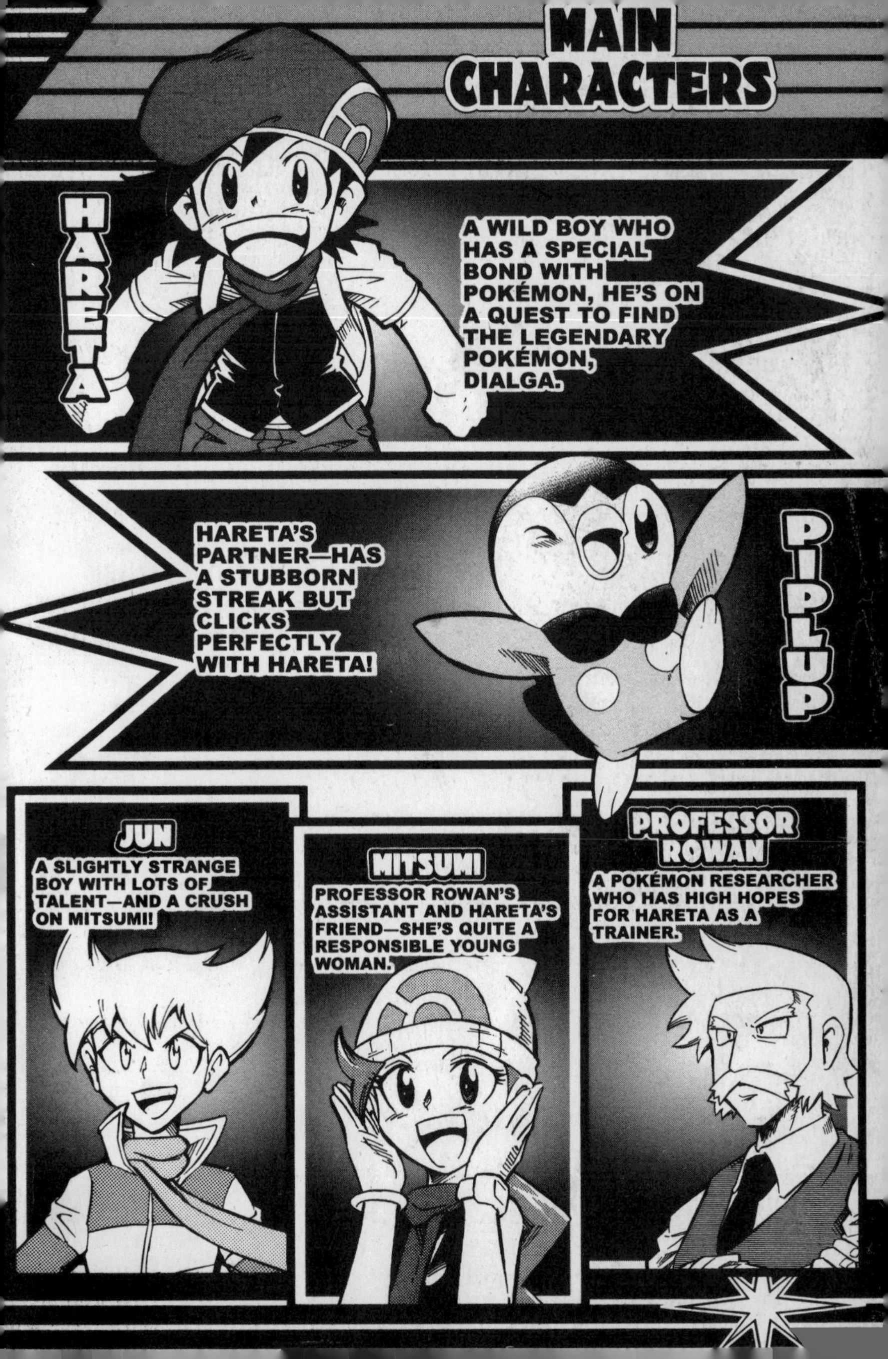
MAIN CHARACTERS
HARETA
A WILD BOY WHO HAS A SPECIAL BOND WITH POKÉMON, HE'S ON A QUEST TO FIND THE LEGENDARY POKÉMON, DIALGA.
PIPLUP
HARETA'S PARTNER—HAS A STUBBORN STREAK BUT CLICKS PERFECTLY WITH HARETA!
PROFESSOR ROWAN
A POKÉMON RESEARCHER WHO HAS HIGH HOPES FOR HARETA AS A TRAINER.
MITSUMI
PROFESSOR ROWAN'S ASSISTANT AND HARETA'S FRIEND—SHE'S QUITE A RESPONSIBLE YOUNG WOMAN.
JUN
A SLIGHTLY STRANGE BOY WITH LOTS OF TALENT—AND A CRUSH ON MITSUMI!

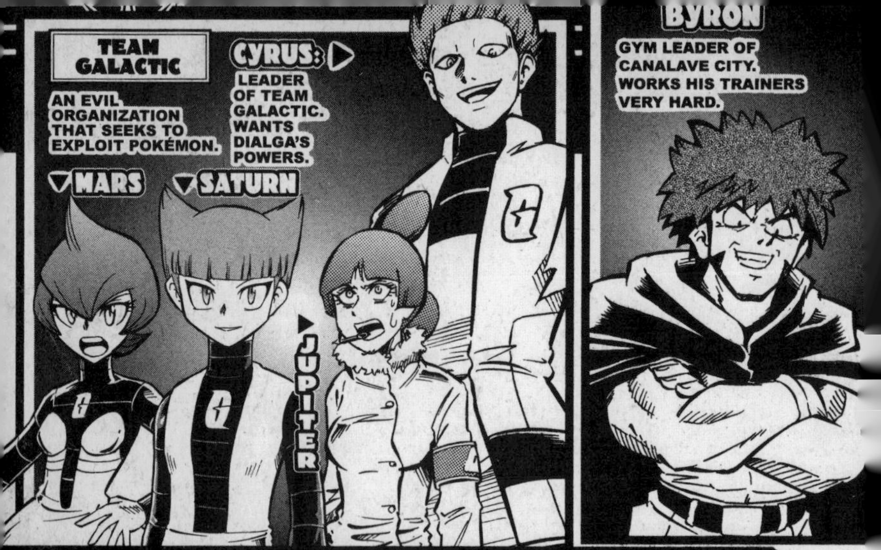
BYRON
GYM LEADER OF CANALAVE CITY. WORKS HIS TRAINERS VERY HARD.
TEAM GALACTIC
AN EVIL ORGANIZATION THAT SEEKS TO EXPLOIT POKÉMON.
CYRUS:
LEADER OF TEAM GALACTIC. WANTS DIALGA'S POWERS.
MARS
SATURN
JUPITER

THE STORY SO FAR

Hareta, a boy with a special bond to the hearts of Pokémon, and Mitsumi continue their quest to find Dialga, the Pokémon master of time. Three special Pokémon are the keys to finding Dialga. As soon as Hareta and the others discover this fact, they are defeated by Cyrus—the leader of Team Galactic—who is also after Dialga. As Hareta begins his training, disaster hits Sinnoh...

TABLE OF CONTENTS

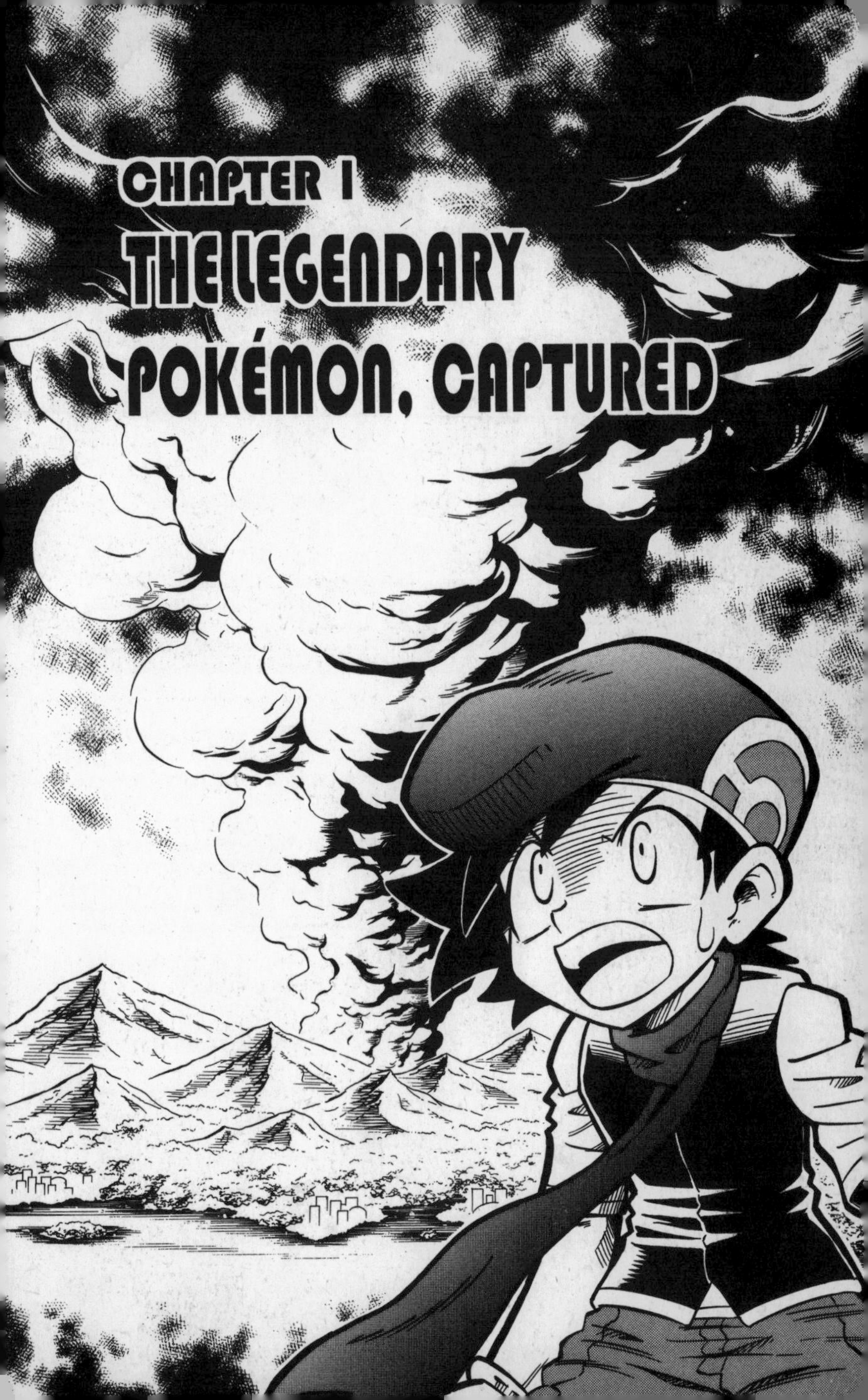
CHAPTER 1
THE LEGENDARY POKÉMON, CAPTURED

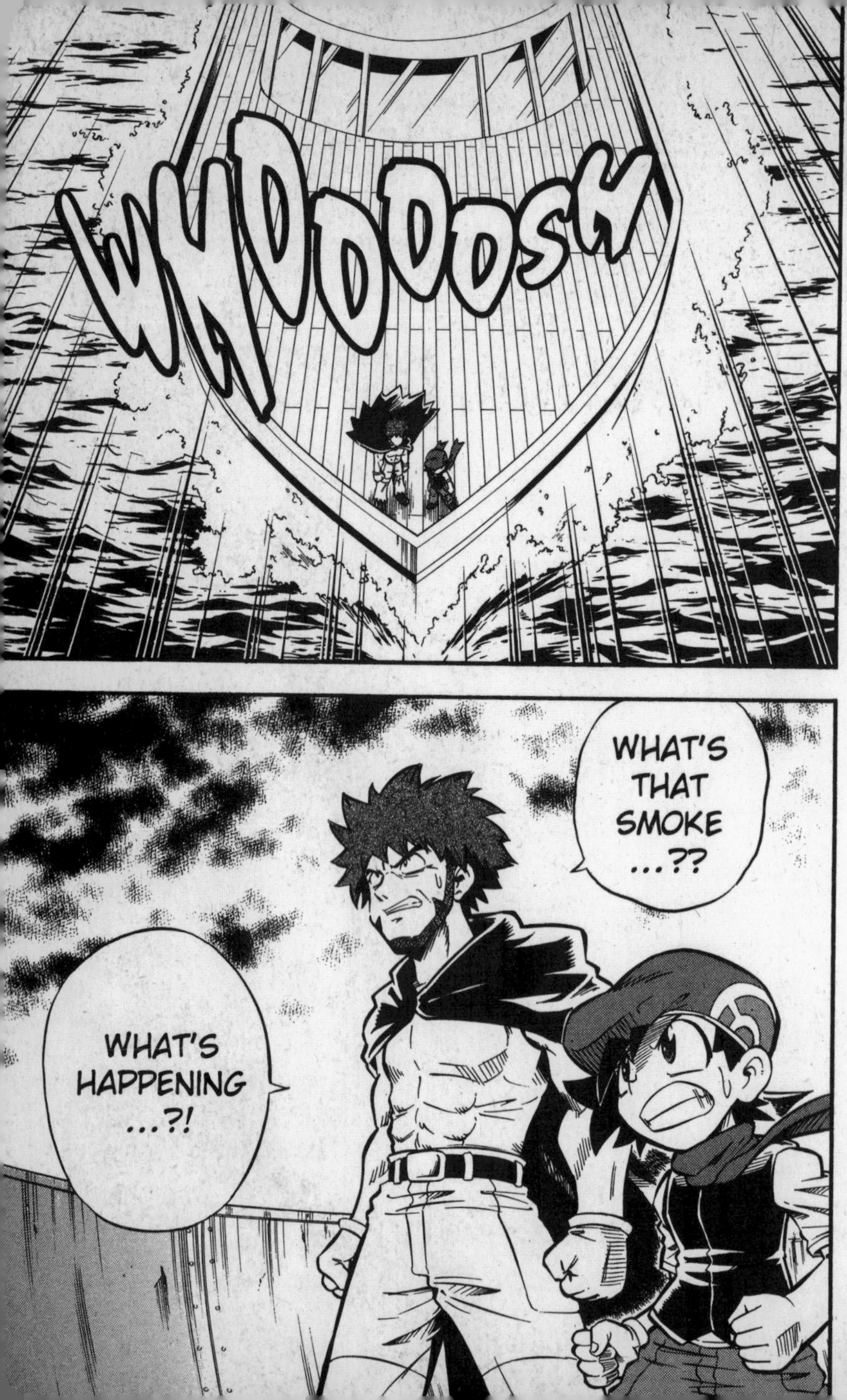
WHOOOSH
WHAT'S THAT SMOKE ...??
WHAT'S HAPPENING ...?!

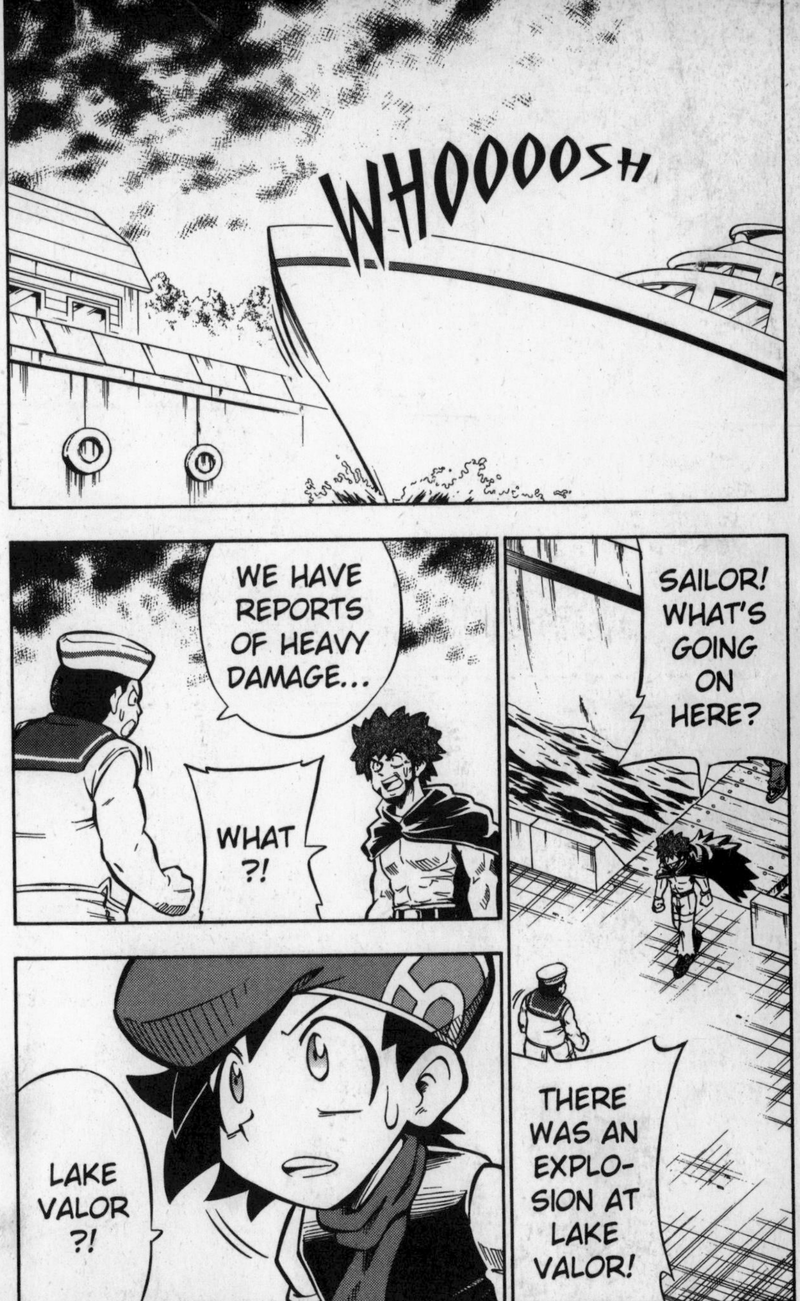
WHOOOOSH
SAILOR! WHAT'S GOING ON HERE?
THERE WAS AN EXPLOSION AT LAKE VALOR!
WE HAVE REPORTS OF HEAVY DAMAGE...
WHAT ?!
LAKE VALOR ?!

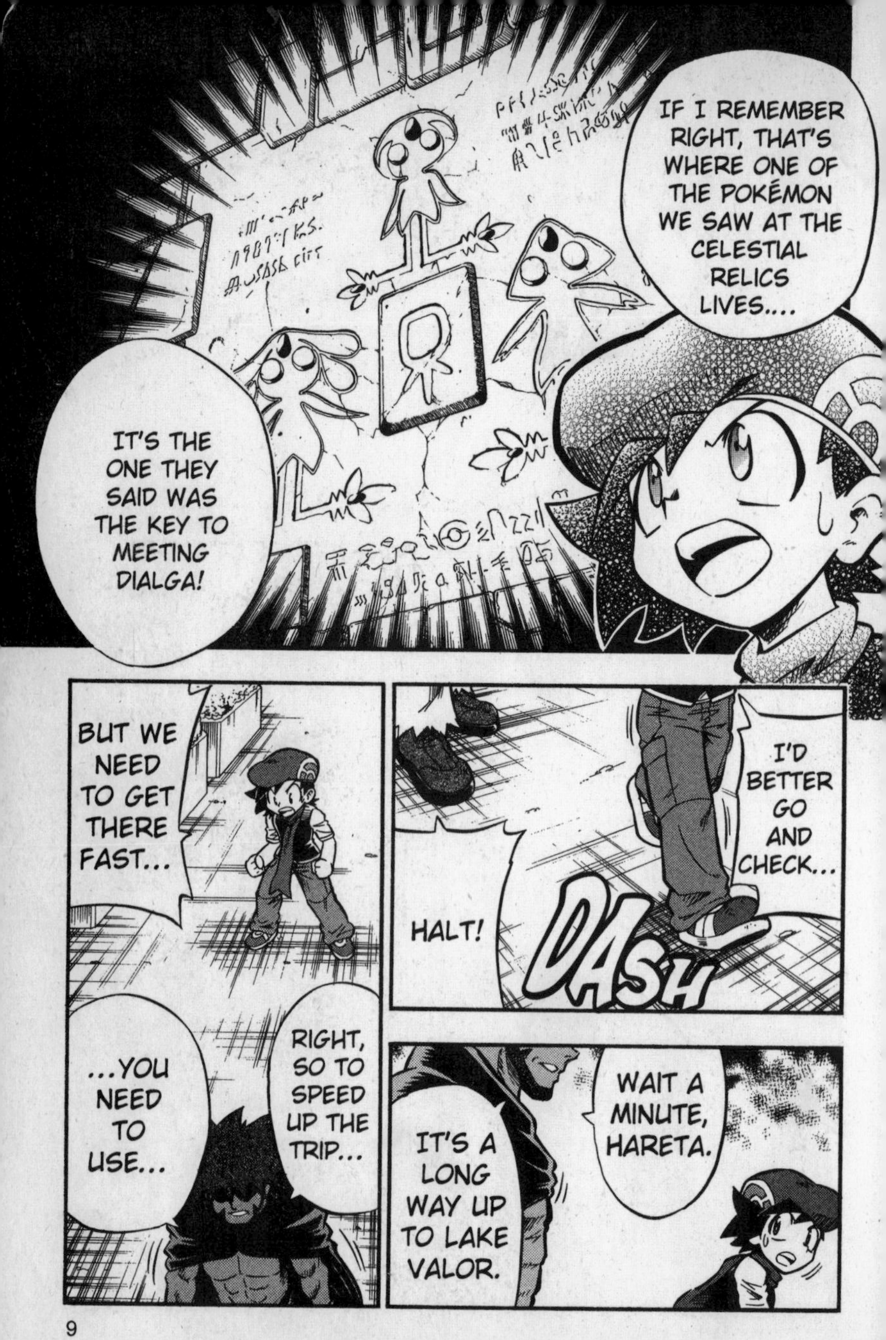
IF I REMEMBER RIGHT, THAT'S WHERE ONE OF THE POKÉMON WE SAW AT THE CELESTIAL RELICS LIVES....
IT'S THE ONE THEY SAID WAS THE KEY TO MEETING DIALGA!
I'D BETTER GO AND CHECK...
DASH
HALT!
BUT WE NEED TO GET THERE FAST...
WAIT A MINUTE, HARETA.
IT'S A LONG WAY UP TO LAKE VALOR.
RIGHT, SO TO SPEED UP THE TRIP...
...YOU NEED TO USE...

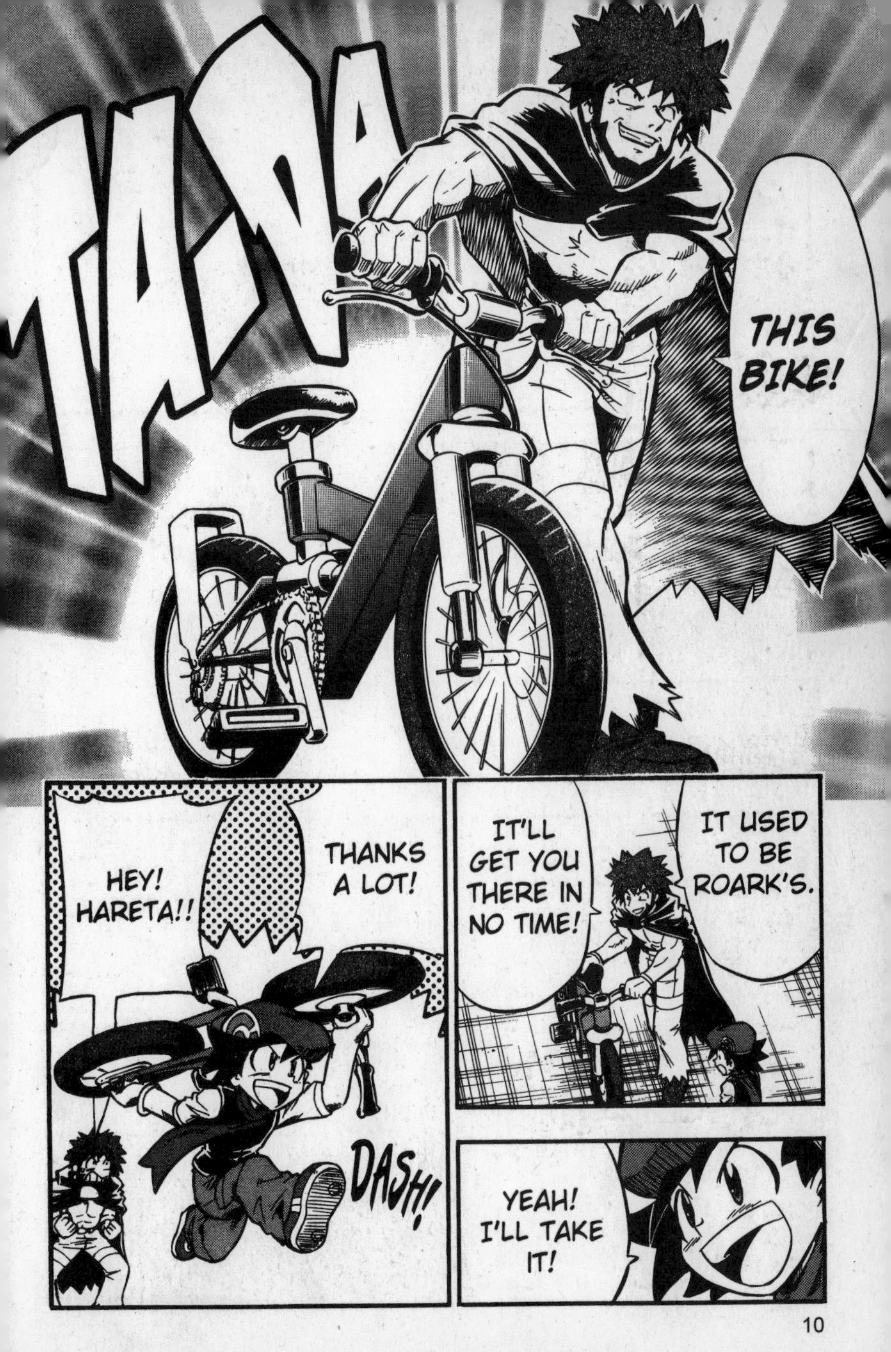
THIS BIKE!
TA-DA
IT USED TO BE ROARK'S.
IT'LL GET YOU THERE IN NO TIME!
YEAH! I'LL TAKE IT!
THANKS A LOT!
HEY! HARETA!!
DASH!

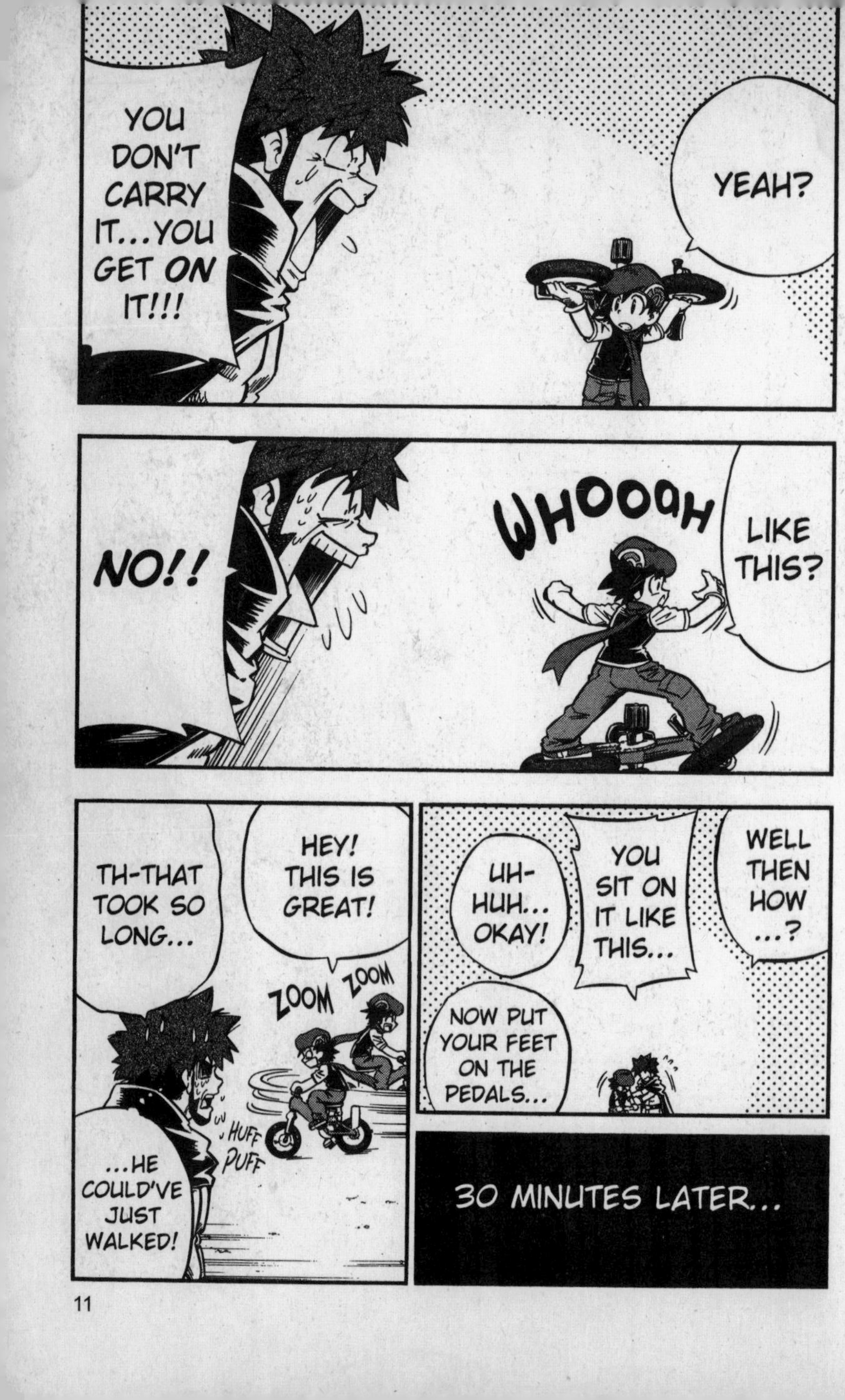
YEAH?
YOU DON'T CARRY IT...YOU GET ON IT!!!
LIKE THIS?
WHOOOAH
NO!!
WELL THEN HOW ...?
YOU SIT ON IT LIKE THIS...
UH-HUH... OKAY!
NOW PUT YOUR FEET ON THE PEDALS...
30 MINUTES LATER...
HEY! THIS IS GREAT!
TH-THAT TOOK SO LONG...
ZOOM ZOOM
HUFF PUFF
...HE COULD'VE JUST WALKED!

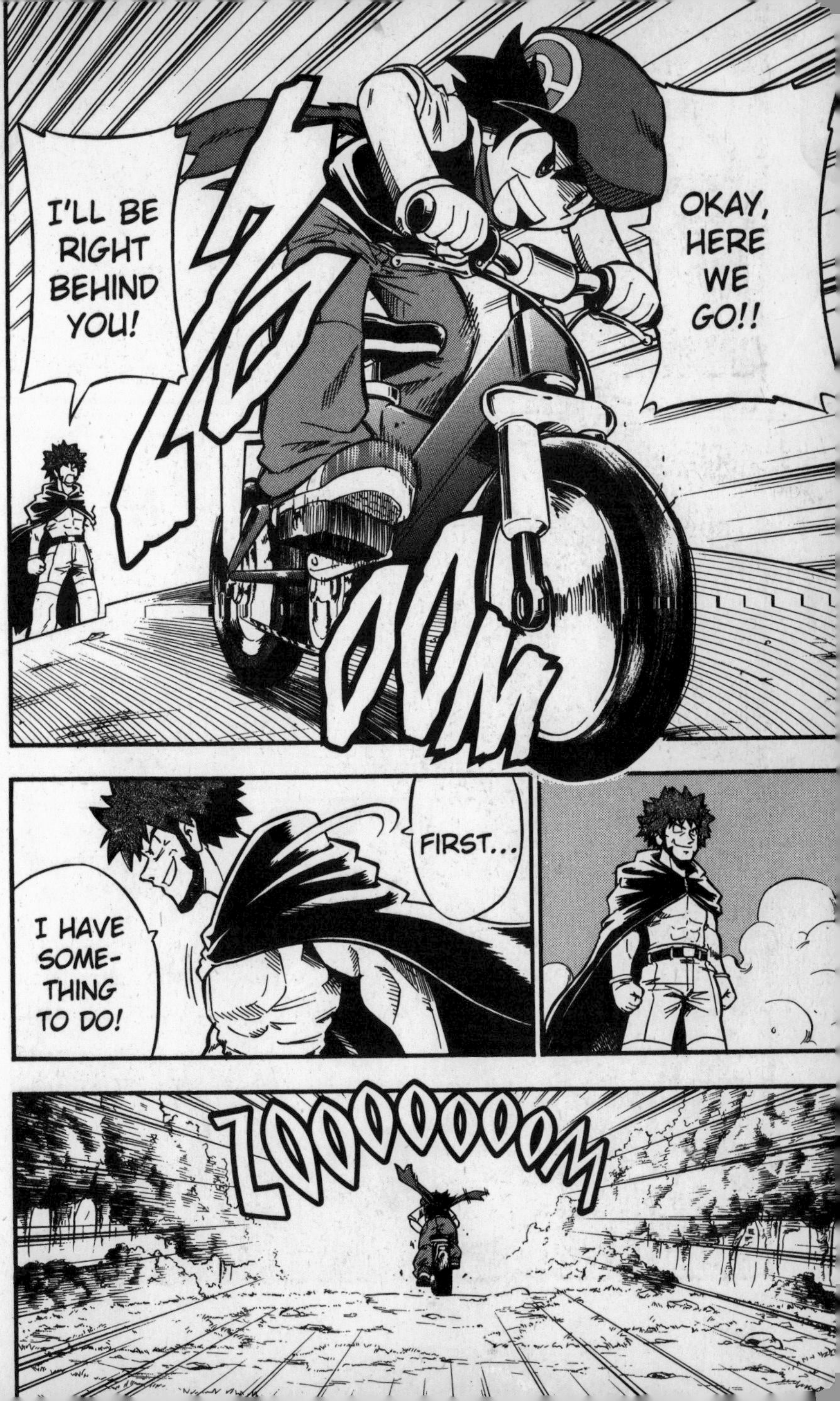
OKAY, HERE WE GO!!
ZOOM
I'LL BE RIGHT BEHIND YOU!
FIRST...
I HAVE SOME-THING TO DO!
ZOOOOOOOM

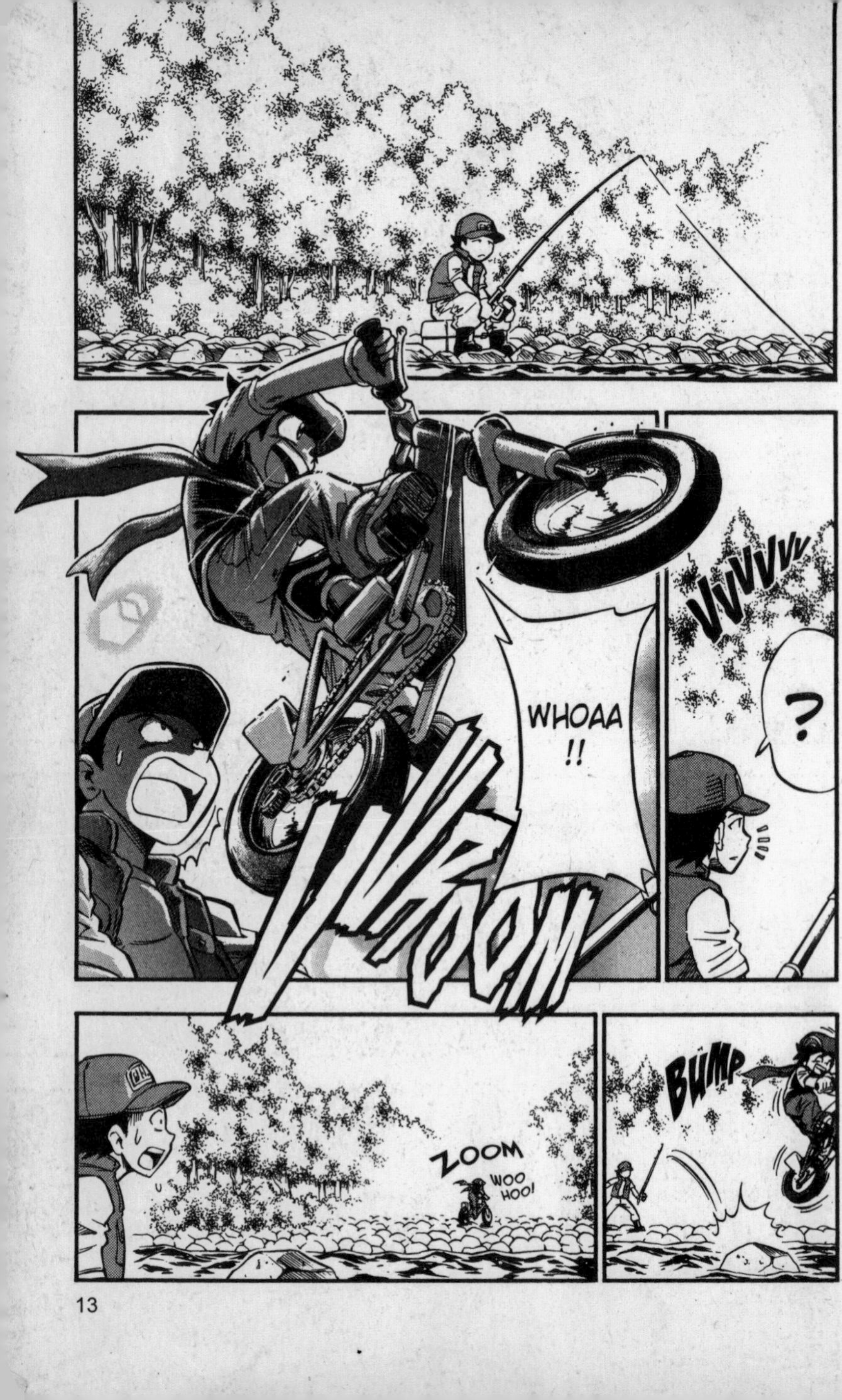
VVVVVV
?
WHOAA !!
VROOM
BUMP
ZOOM
WOO HOO!

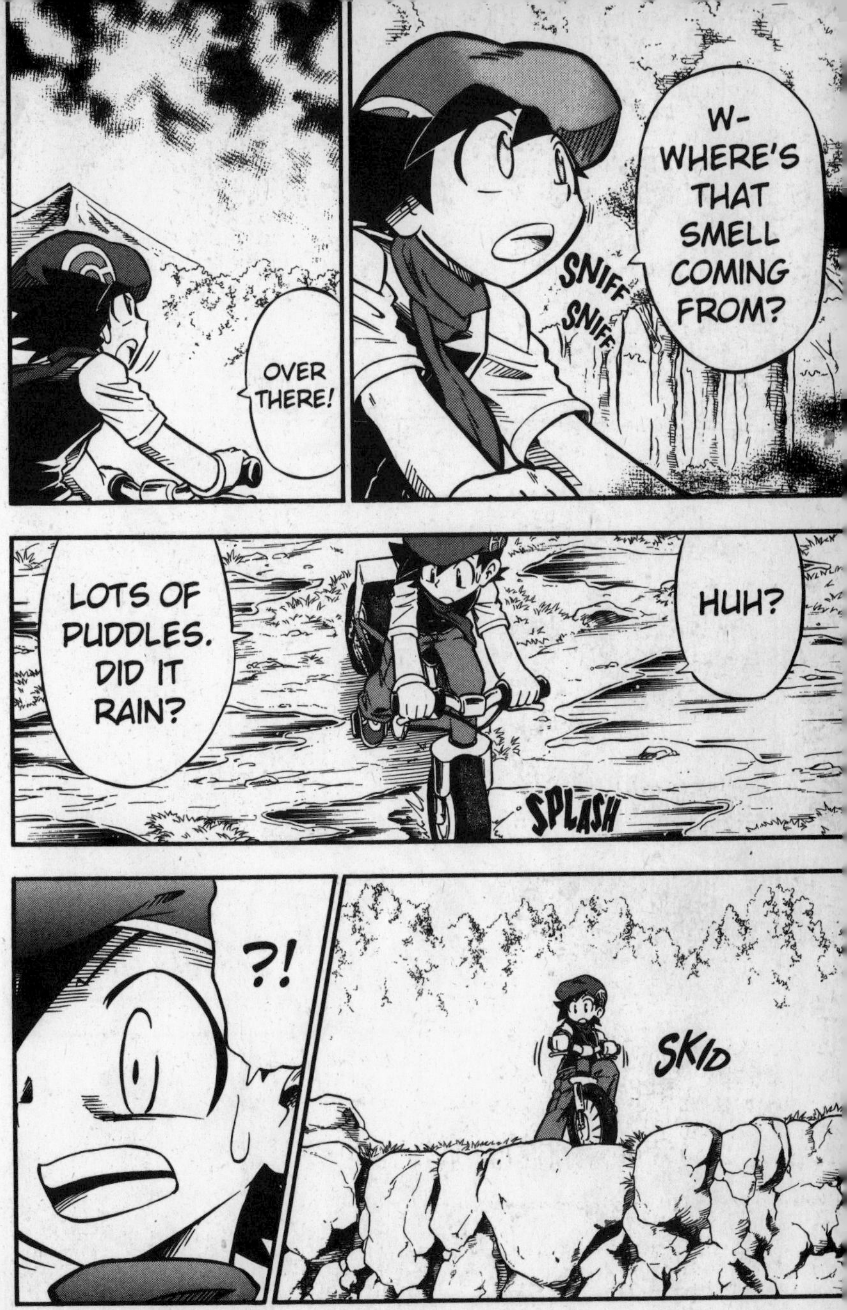
W- WHERE'S THAT SMELL COMING FROM?
SNIFF
SNIFF
OVER THERE!
HUH?
LOTS OF PUDDLES. DID IT RAIN?
SPLASH
SKID
?!

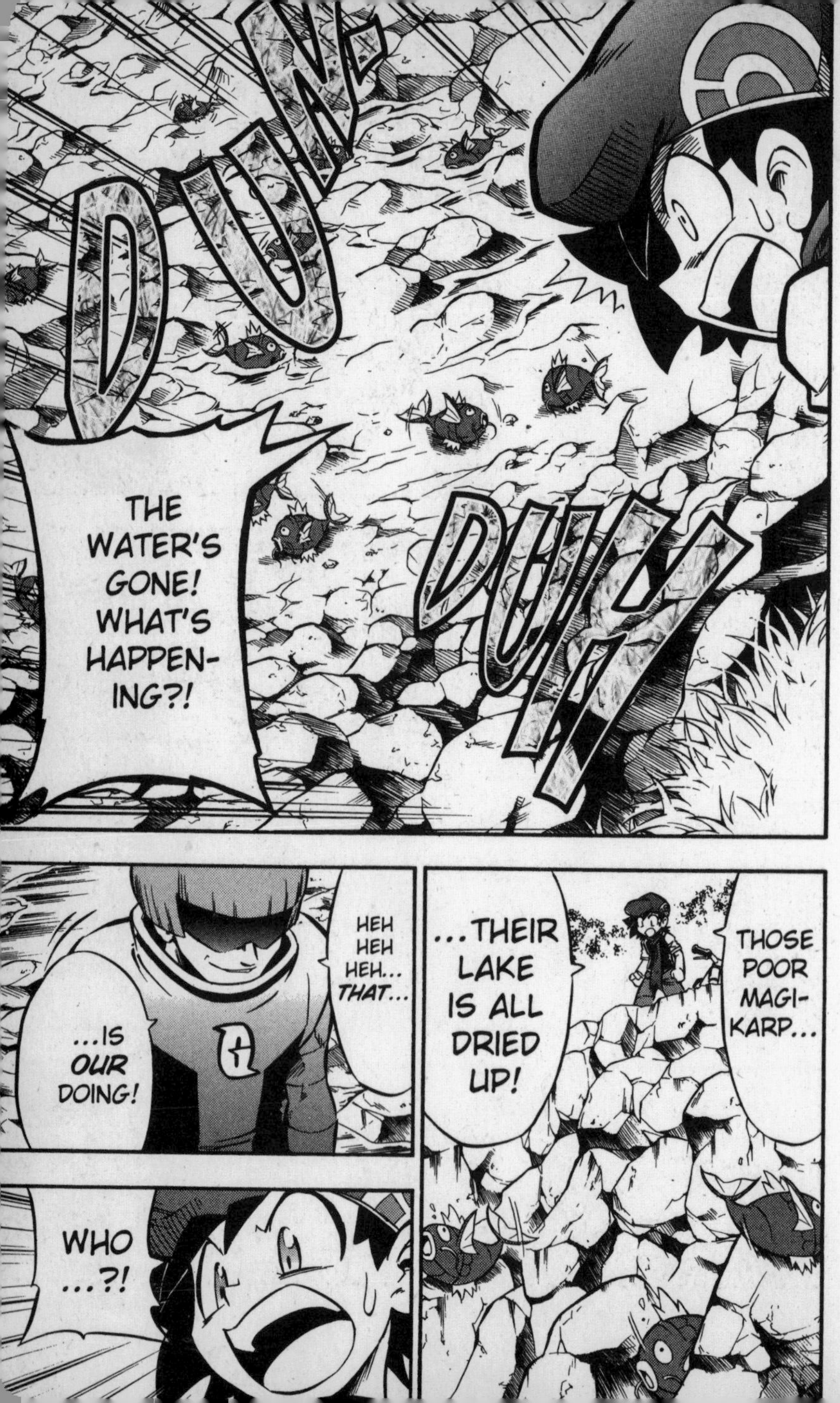
THE WATER'S GONE! WHAT'S HAPPEN-ING?!
THOSE POOR MAGI-KARP...
...THEIR LAKE IS ALL DRIED UP!
HEH HEH HEH... *THAT*...
...IS **OUR** DOING!
WHO ...?!

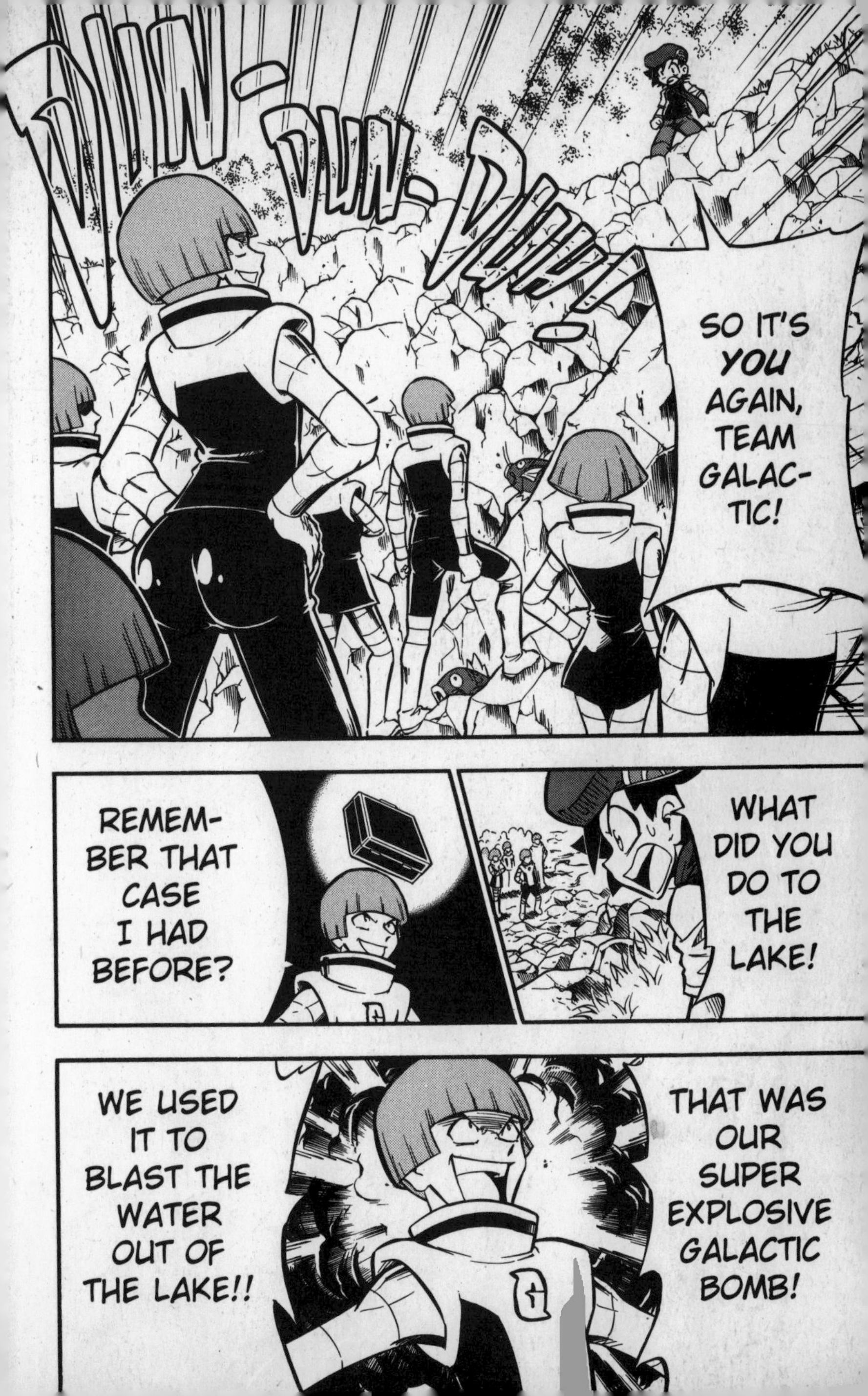
DUN-DUN-DAH!
SO IT'S *YOU* AGAIN, TEAM GALACTIC!
WHAT DID YOU DO TO THE LAKE!
REMEMBER THAT CASE I HAD BEFORE?
THAT WAS OUR SUPER EXPLOSIVE GALACTIC BOMB!
WE USED IT TO BLAST THE WATER OUT OF THE LAKE!!

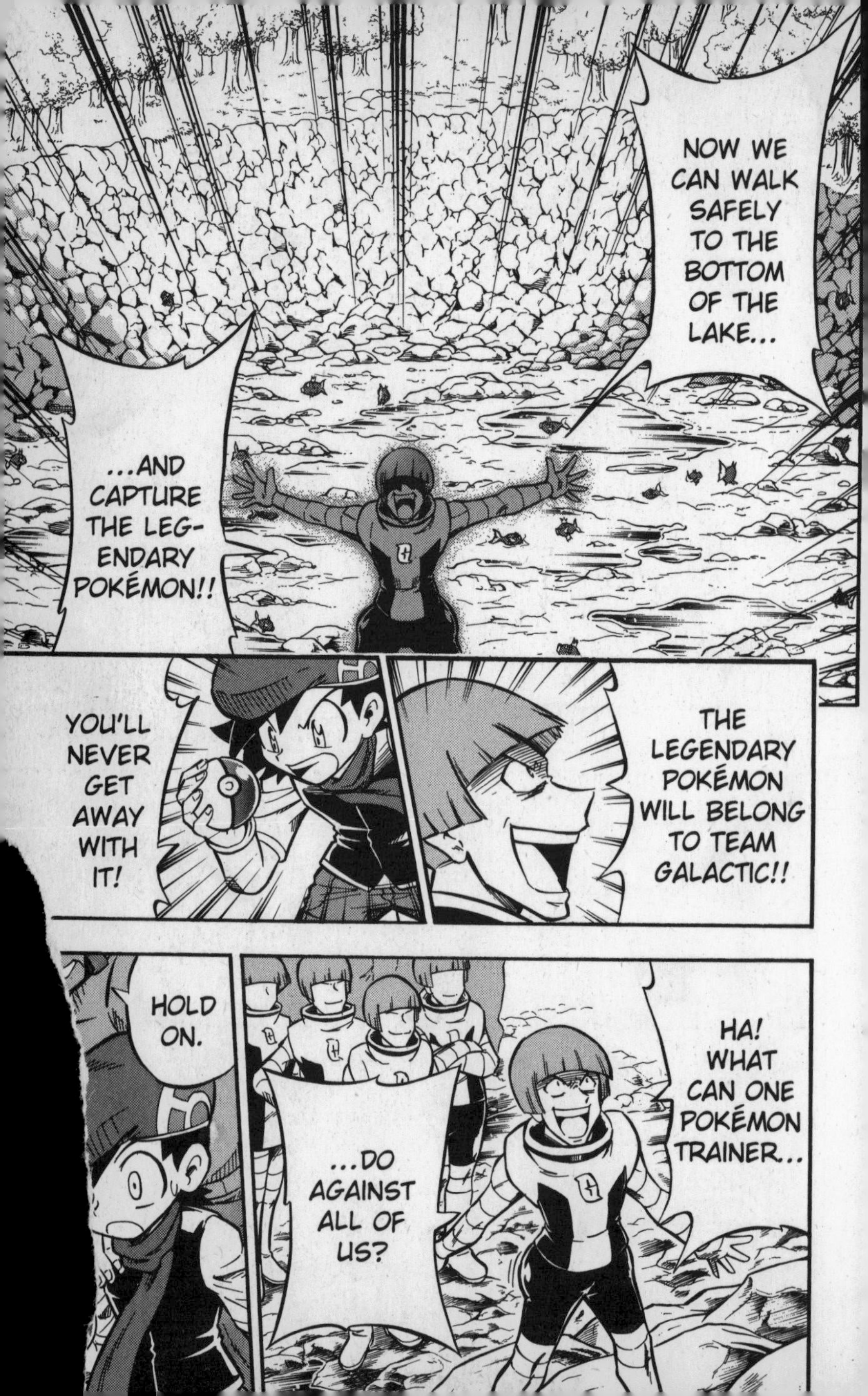
NOW WE CAN WALK SAFELY TO THE BOTTOM OF THE LAKE...
...AND CAPTURE THE LEGENDARY POKÉMON!!
THE LEGENDARY POKÉMON WILL BELONG TO TEAM GALACTIC!!
YOU'LL NEVER GET AWAY WITH IT!
HA! WHAT CAN ONE POKÉMON TRAINER...
...DO AGAINST ALL OF US?
HOLD ON.

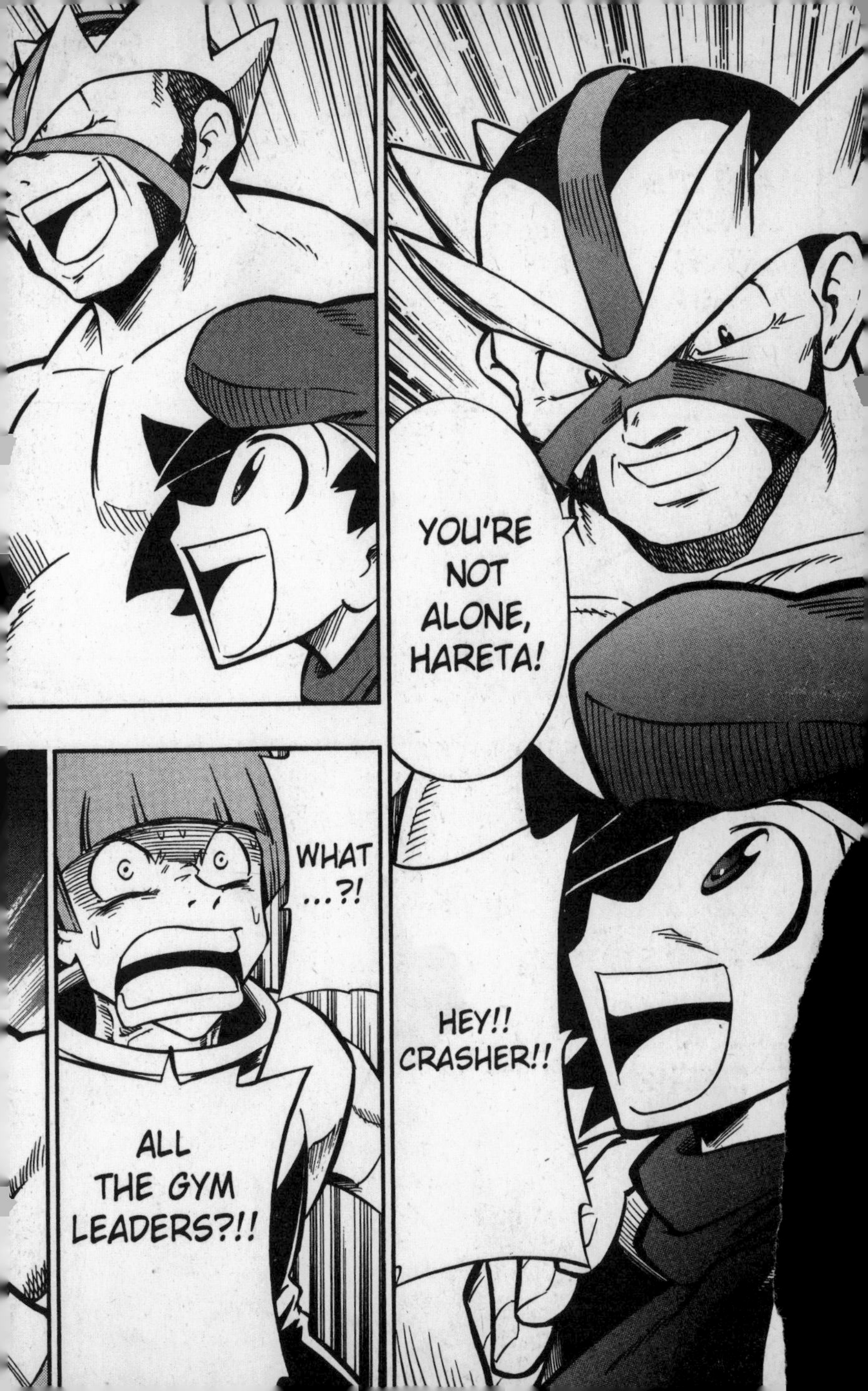
YOU'RE NOT ALONE, HARETA!
HEY!! CRASHER!!
WHAT ...?!
ALL THE GYM LEADERS?!!

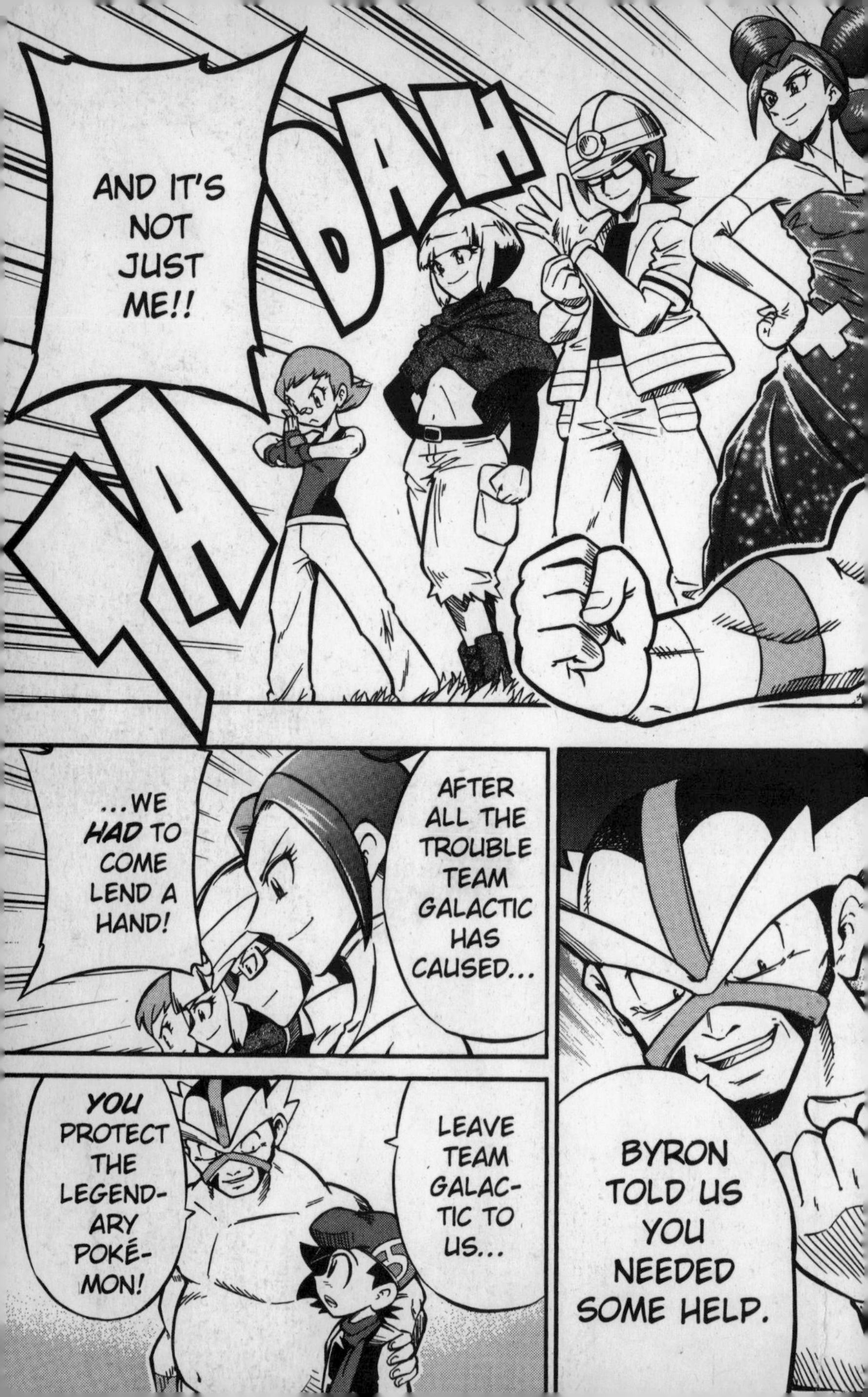
AND IT'S NOT JUST ME!!
TA DAH
BYRON TOLD US YOU NEEDED SOME HELP.
AFTER ALL THE TROUBLE TEAM GALACTIC HAS CAUSED...
...WE *HAD* TO COME LEND A HAND!
LEAVE TEAM GALAC-TIC TO US...
YOU PROTECT THE LEGEND-ARY POKÉ-MON!

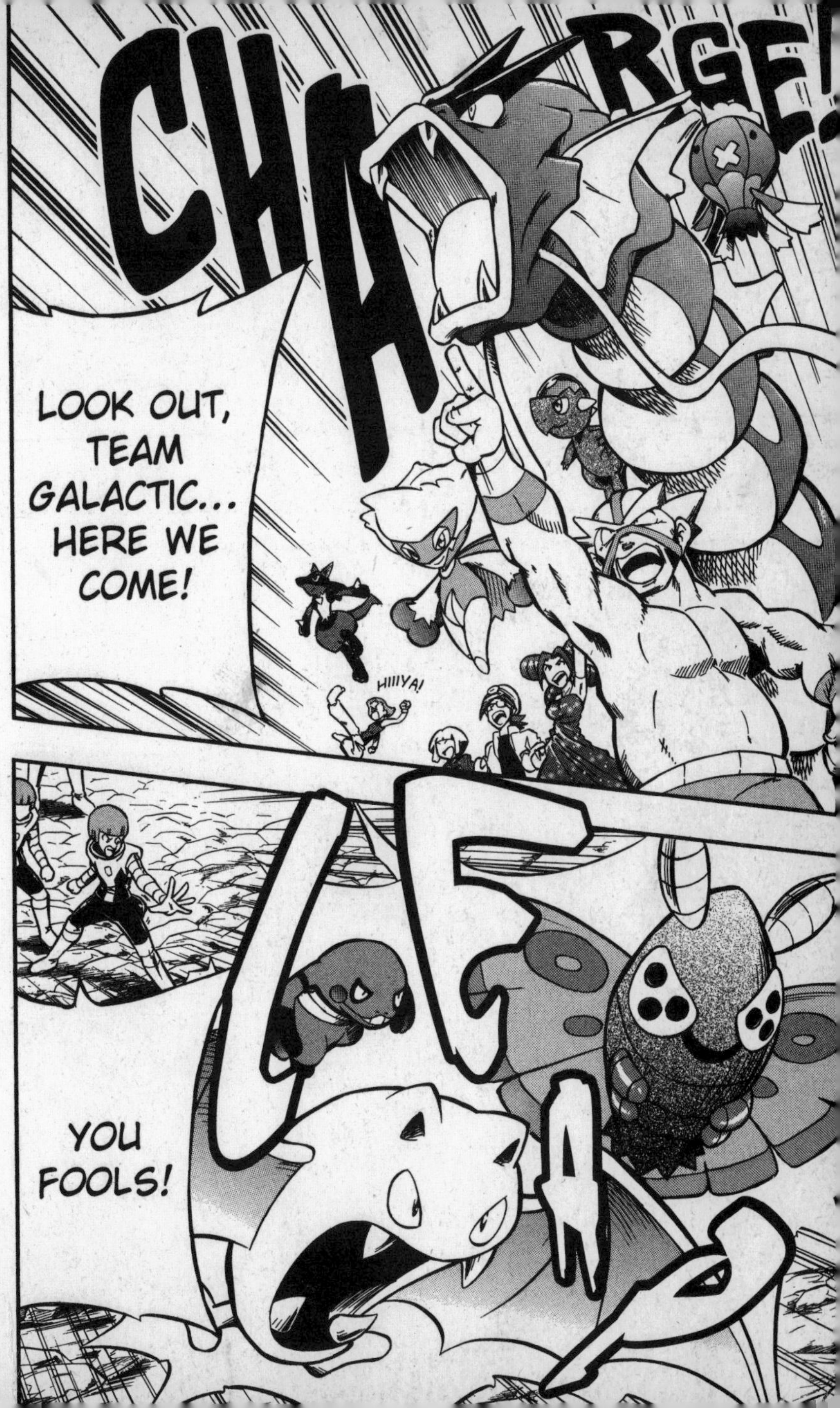
CHARGE!
LOOK OUT, TEAM GALACTIC... HERE WE COME!
HIIIYA!
YOU FOOLS!

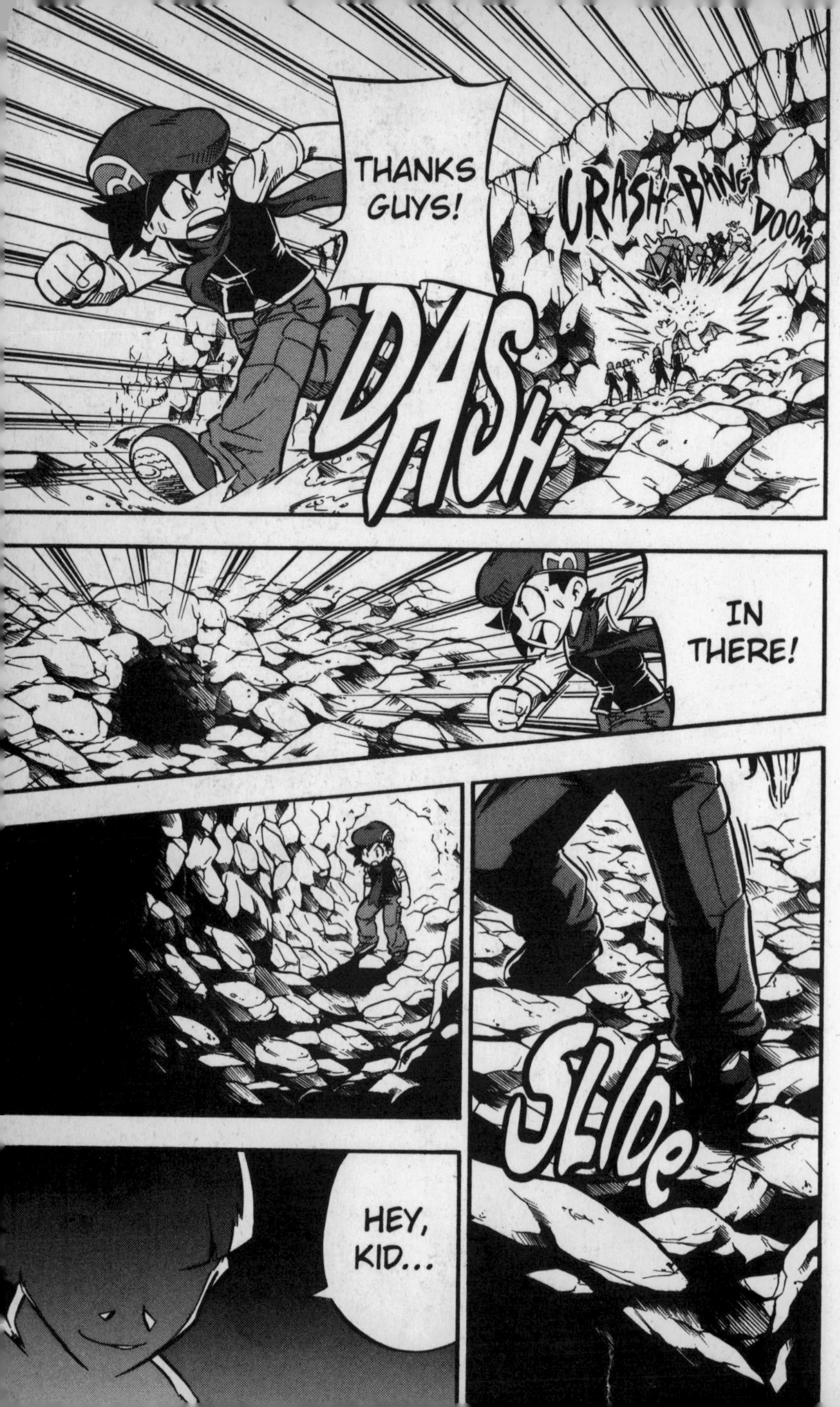
CRASH BANG DOOM
THANKS GUYS!
DASH
IN THERE!
SLIDE
HEY, KID...

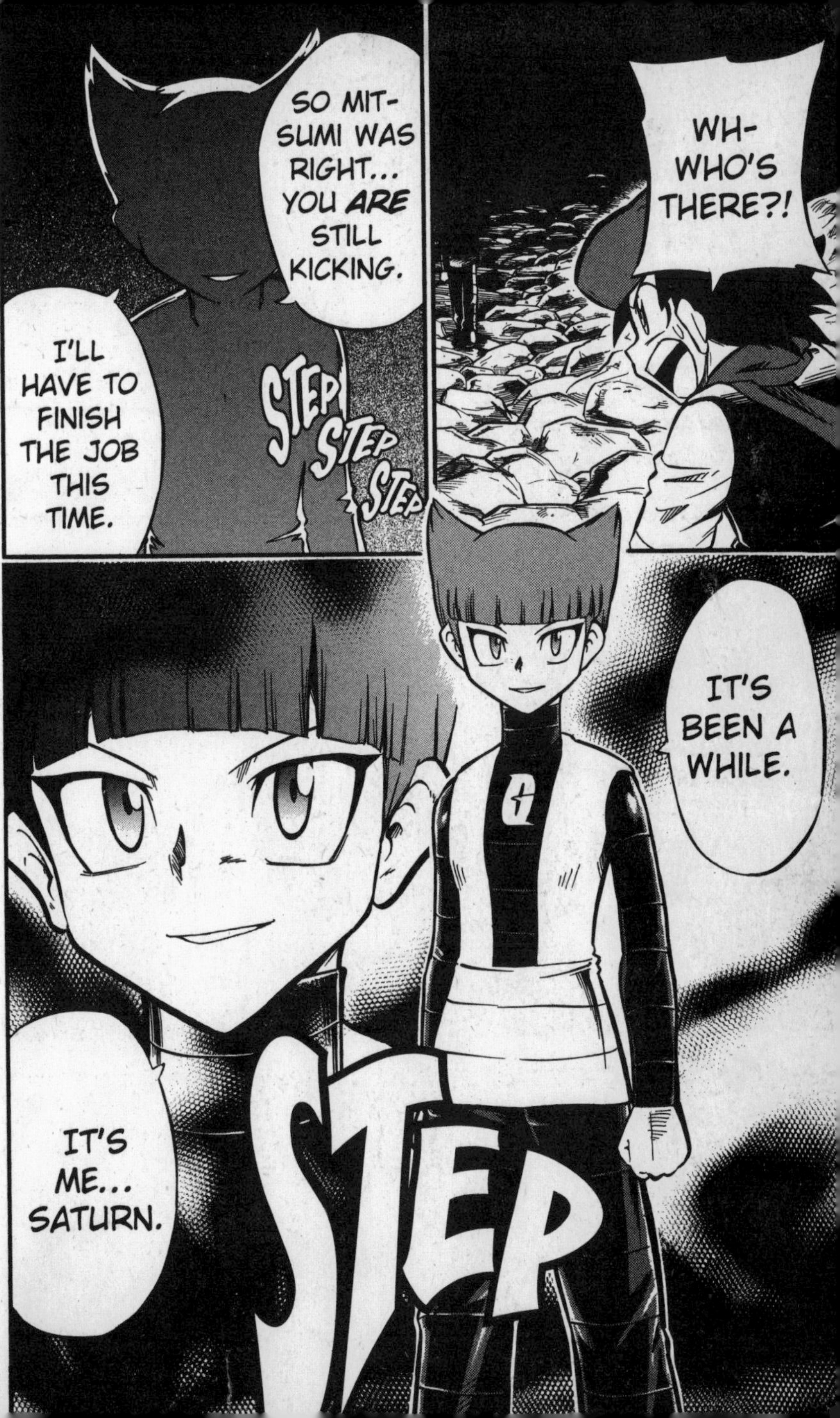
WH- WHO'S THERE?!
SO MIT-SUMI WAS RIGHT... YOU *ARE* STILL KICKING.
STEP STEP STEP
I'LL HAVE TO FINISH THE JOB THIS TIME.
IT'S BEEN A WHILE.
STEP
IT'S ME... SATURN.

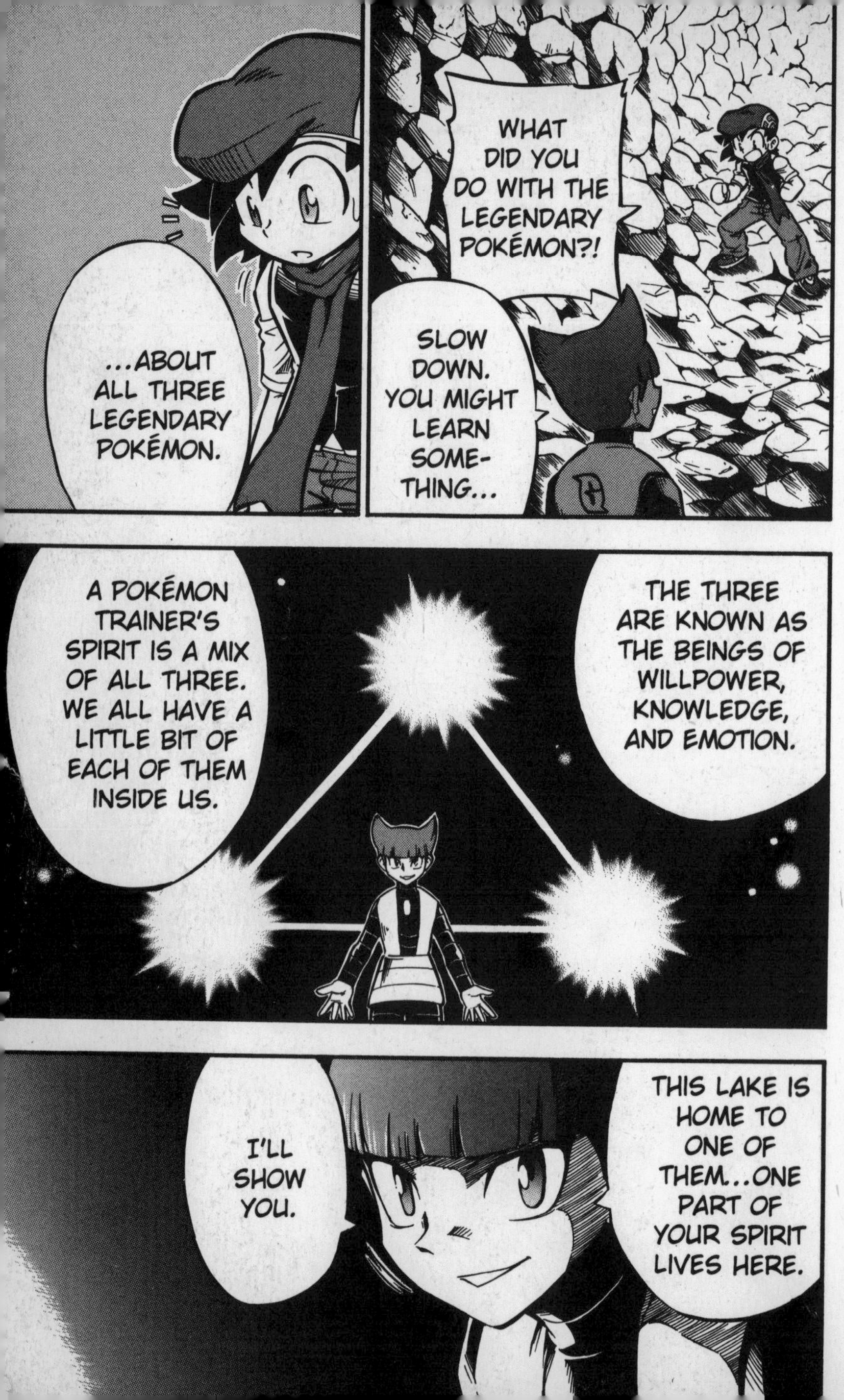
WHAT DID YOU DO WITH THE LEGENDARY POKÉMON?!
SLOW DOWN. YOU MIGHT LEARN SOME-THING...
...ABOUT ALL THREE LEGENDARY POKÉMON.
THE THREE ARE KNOWN AS THE BEINGS OF WILLPOWER, KNOWLEDGE, AND EMOTION.
A POKÉMON TRAINER'S SPIRIT IS A MIX OF ALL THREE. WE ALL HAVE A LITTLE BIT OF EACH OF THEM INSIDE US.
THIS LAKE IS HOME TO ONE OF THEM...ONE PART OF YOUR SPIRIT LIVES HERE.
I'LL SHOW YOU.

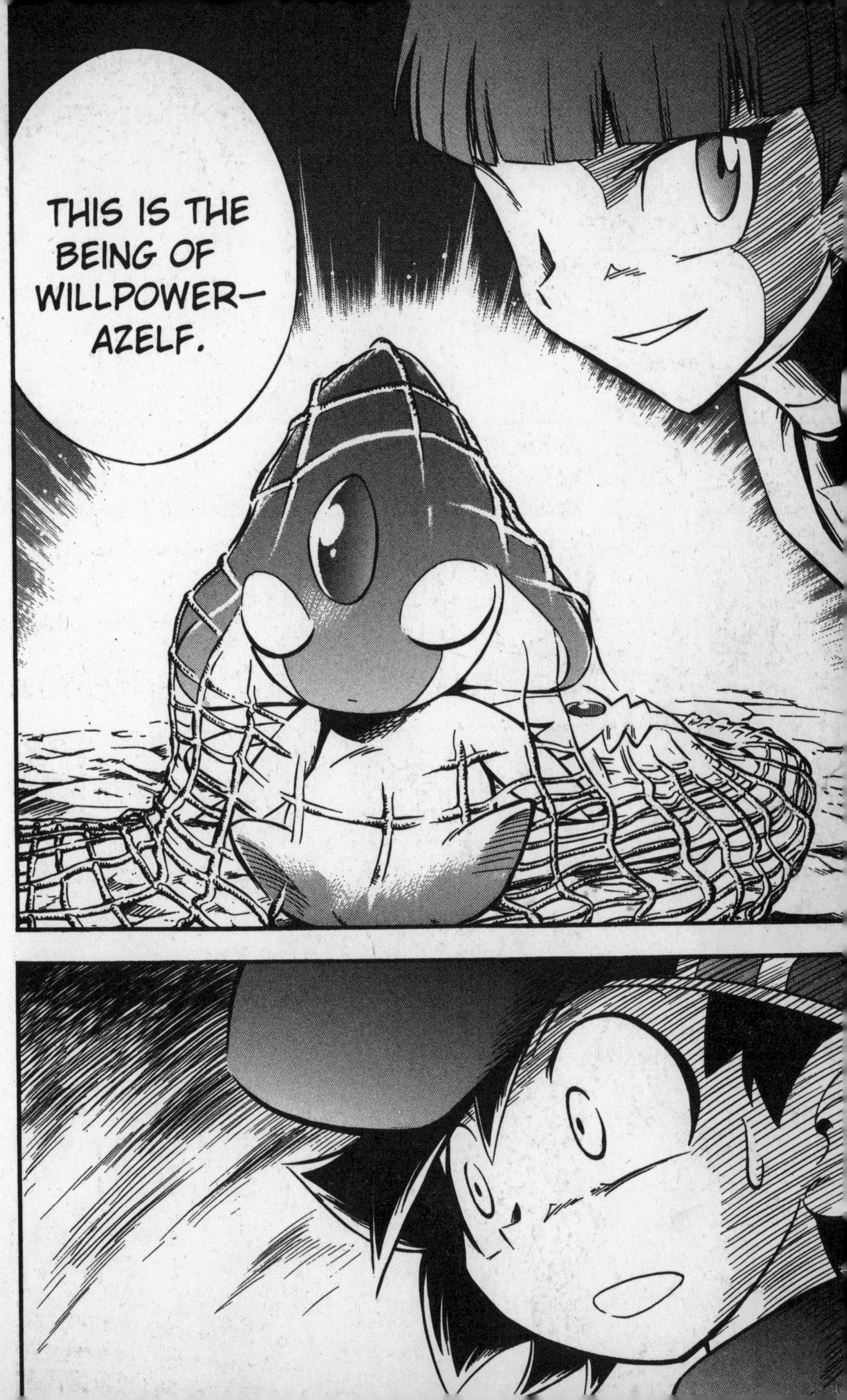
THIS IS THE BEING OF WILLPOWER—AZELF.

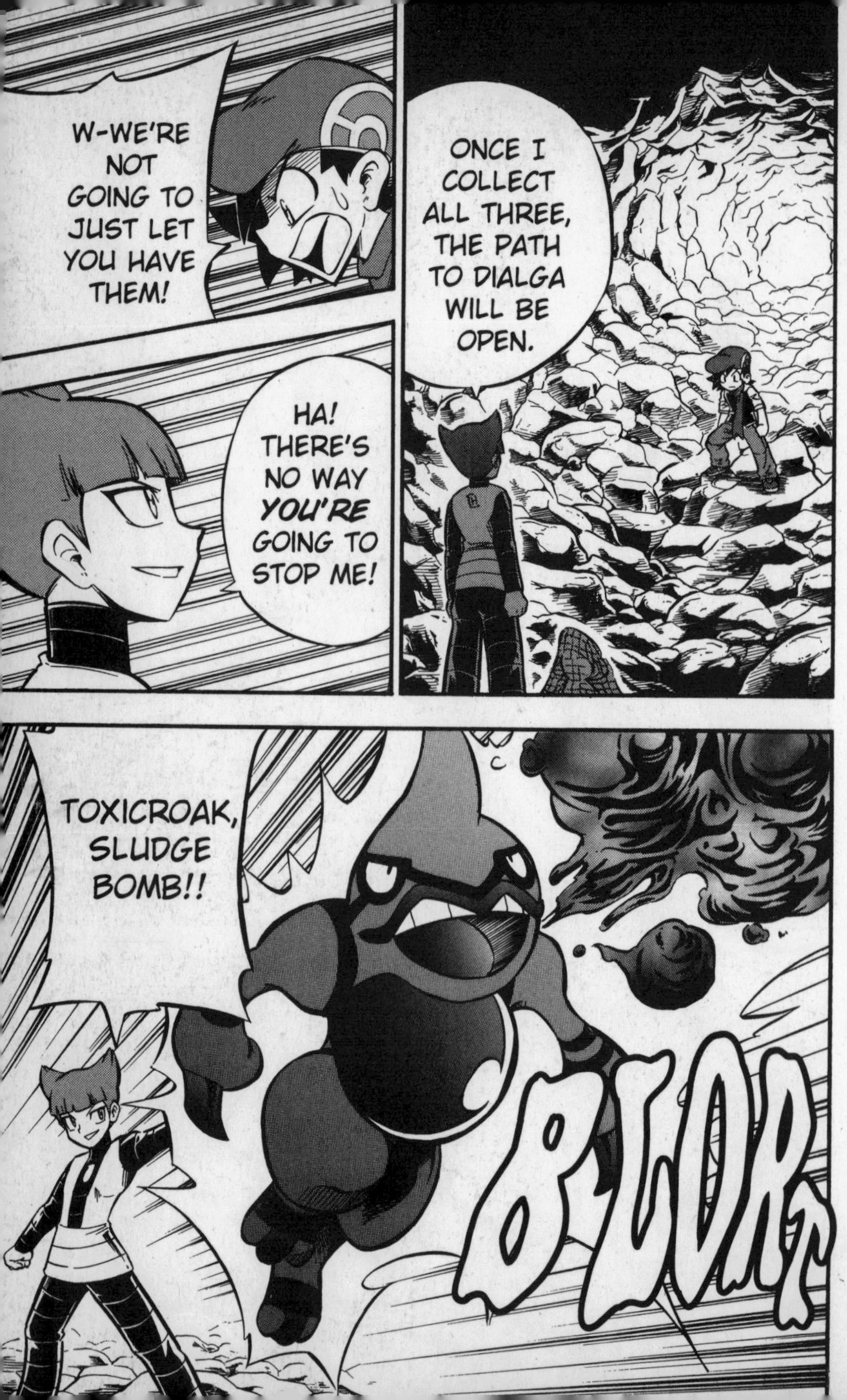
ONCE I COLLECT ALL THREE, THE PATH TO DIALGA WILL BE OPEN.
W-WE'RE NOT GOING TO JUST LET YOU HAVE THEM!
HA! THERE'S NO WAY *YOU'RE* GOING TO STOP ME!
TOXICROAK, SLUDGE BOMB!!
BLOP

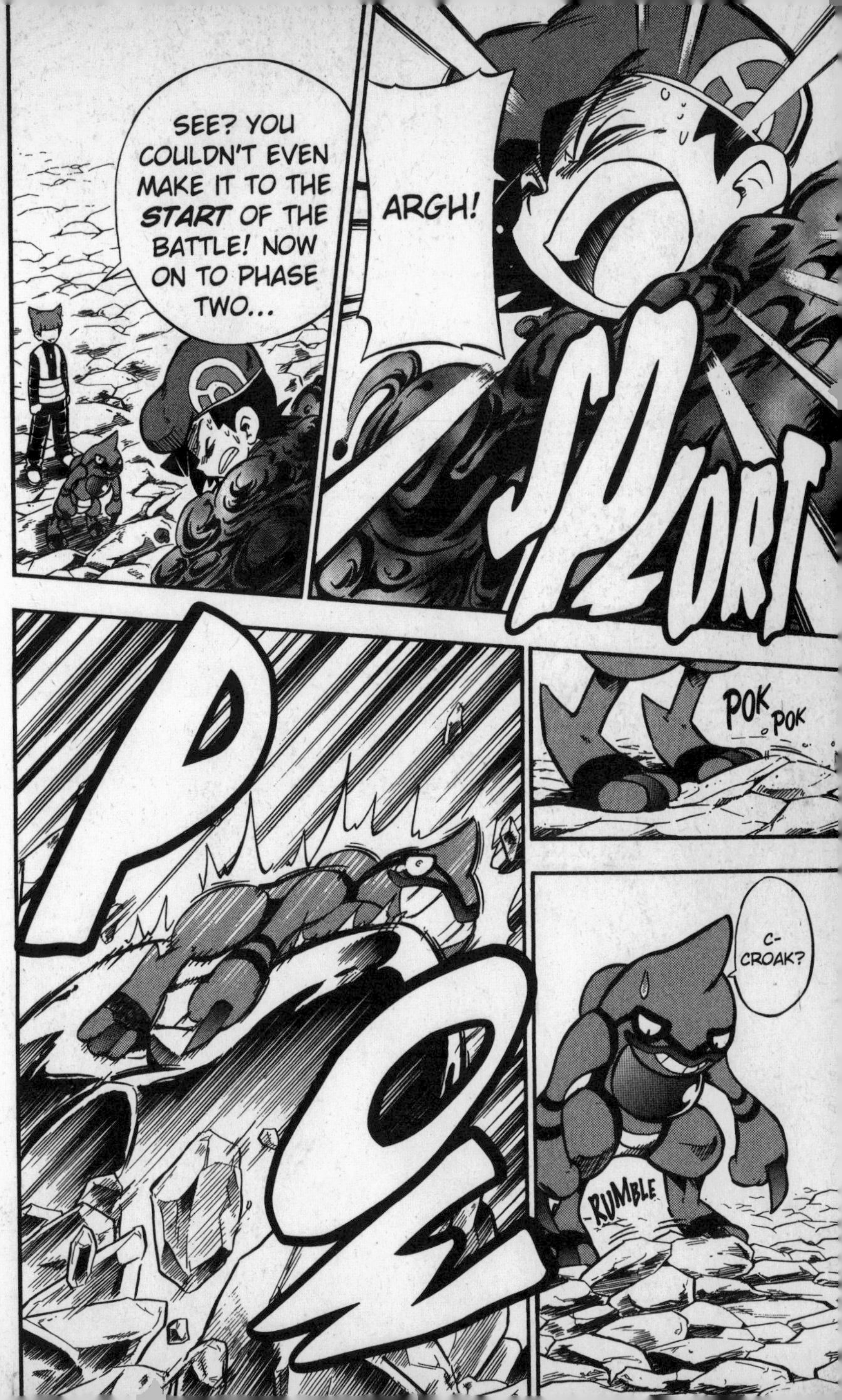
ARGH!
SEE? YOU COULDN'T EVEN MAKE IT TO THE START OF THE BATTLE! NOW ON TO PHASE TWO...
POK POK
C-CROAK?
RUMBLE

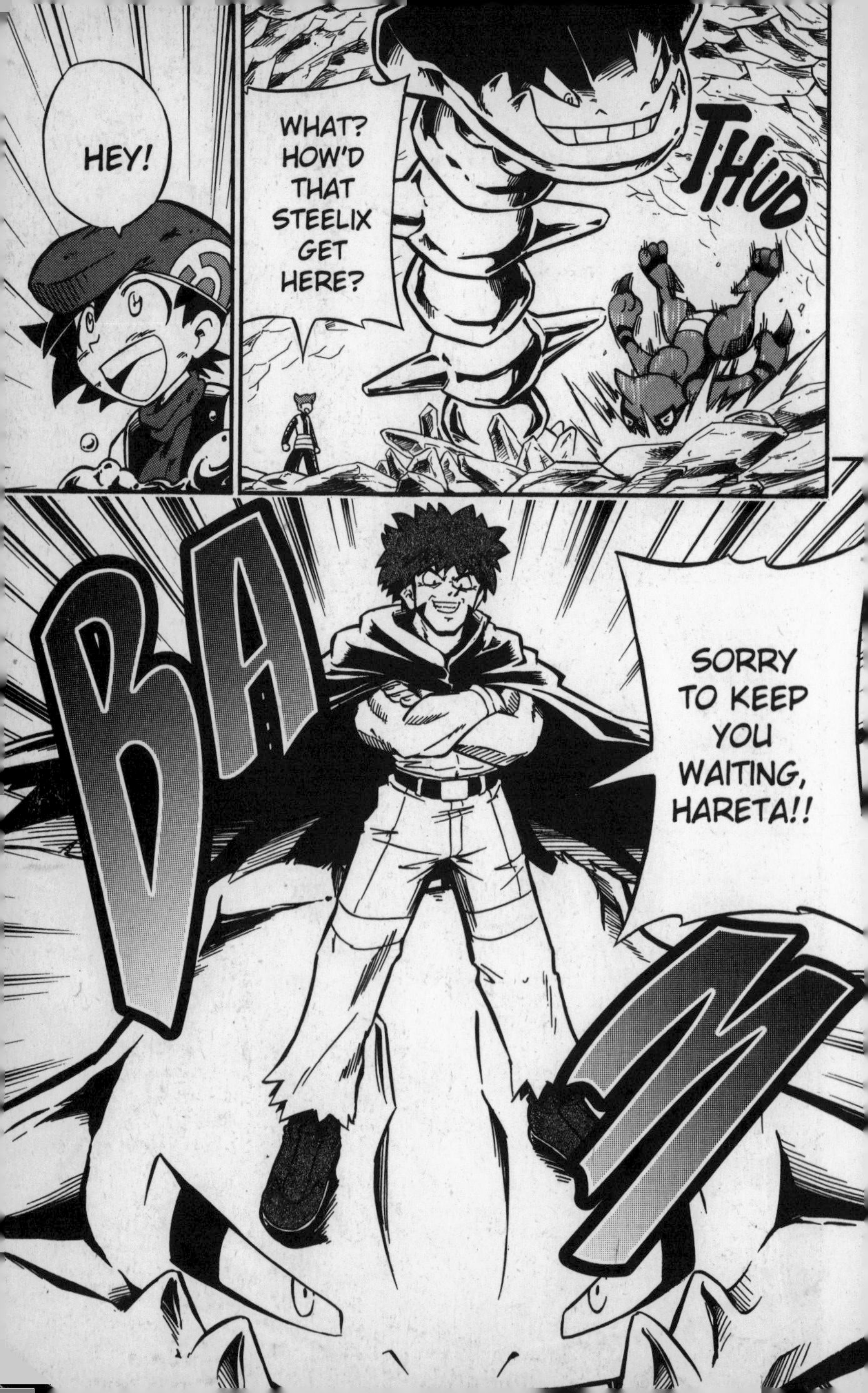
THUD
WHAT? HOW'D THAT STEELIX GET HERE?
HEY!
SORRY TO KEEP YOU WAITING, HARETA!!
BAM

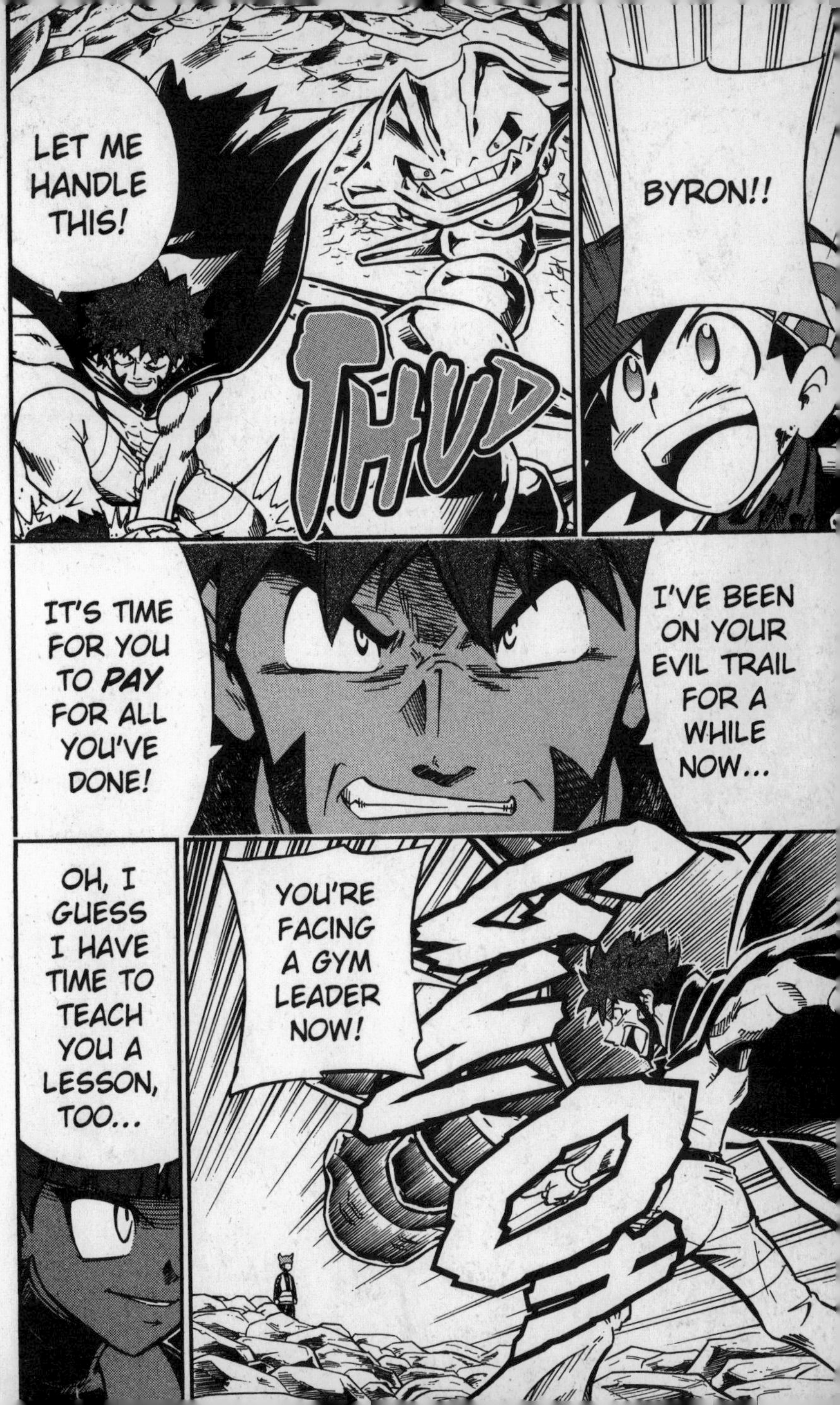
BYRON!!
LET ME HANDLE THIS!
THUD
I'VE BEEN ON YOUR EVIL TRAIL FOR A WHILE NOW...
IT'S TIME FOR YOU TO *PAY* FOR ALL YOU'VE DONE!
YOU'RE FACING A GYM LEADER NOW!
OH, I GUESS I HAVE TIME TO TEACH YOU A LESSON, TOO...

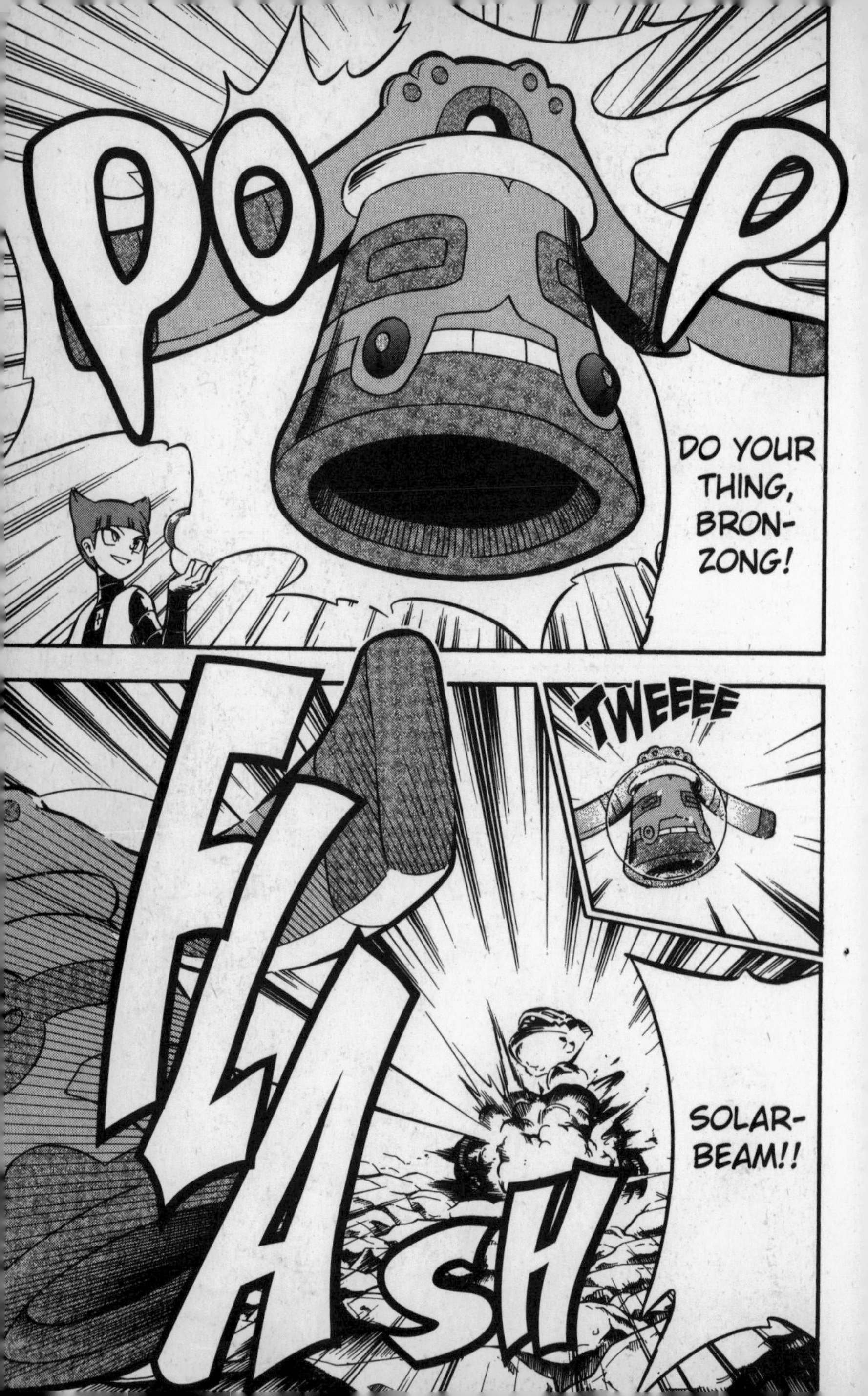
DO YOUR THING, BRON-ZONG!
POP
TWEEEE
SOLAR-BEAM!!
FLASH

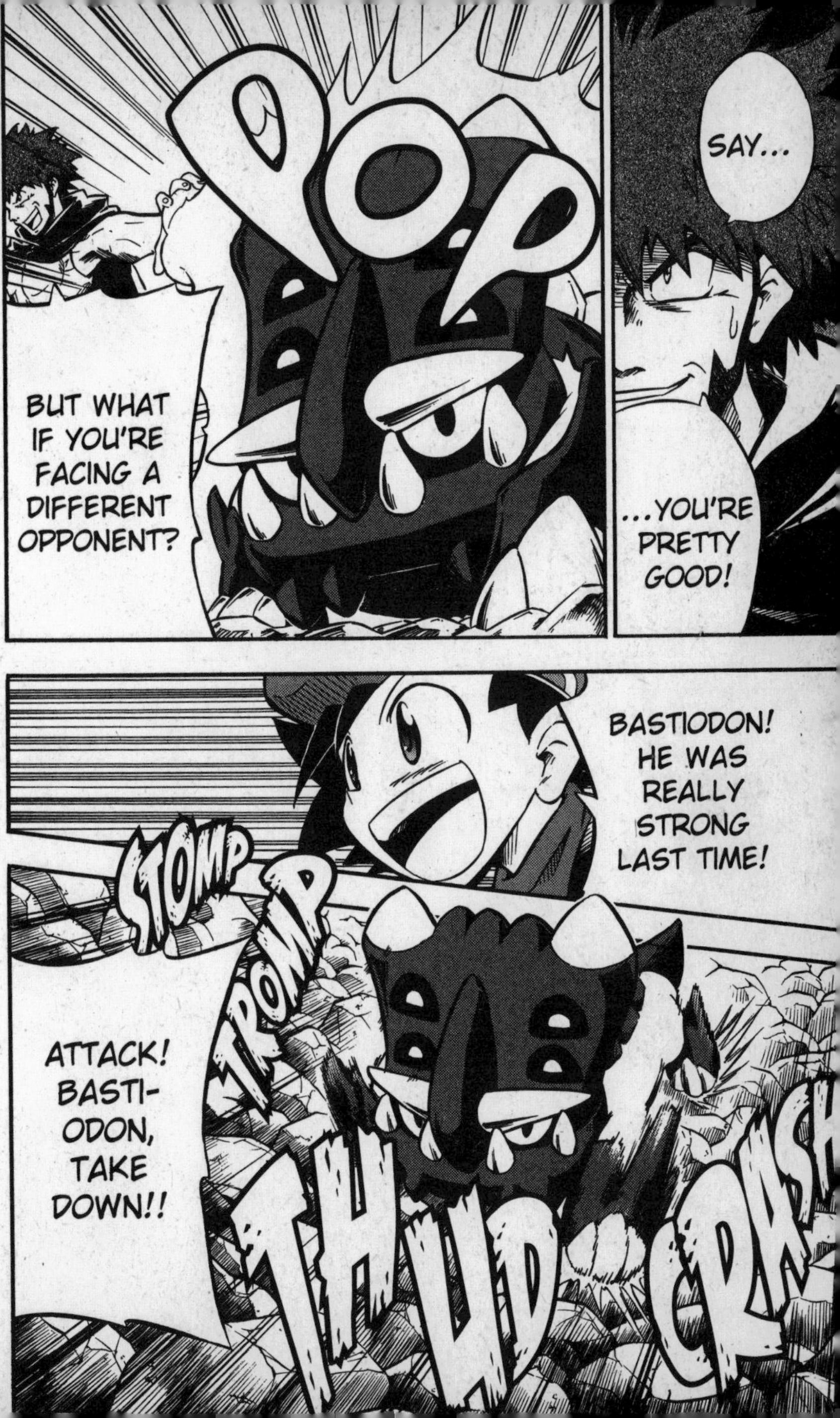
SAY...
...YOU'RE PRETTY GOOD!
POP
BUT WHAT IF YOU'RE FACING A DIFFERENT OPPONENT?
BASTIODON! HE WAS REALLY STRONG LAST TIME!
STOMP
TROMP
ATTACK! BASTI-ODON, TAKE DOWN!!
THUD
CRASH

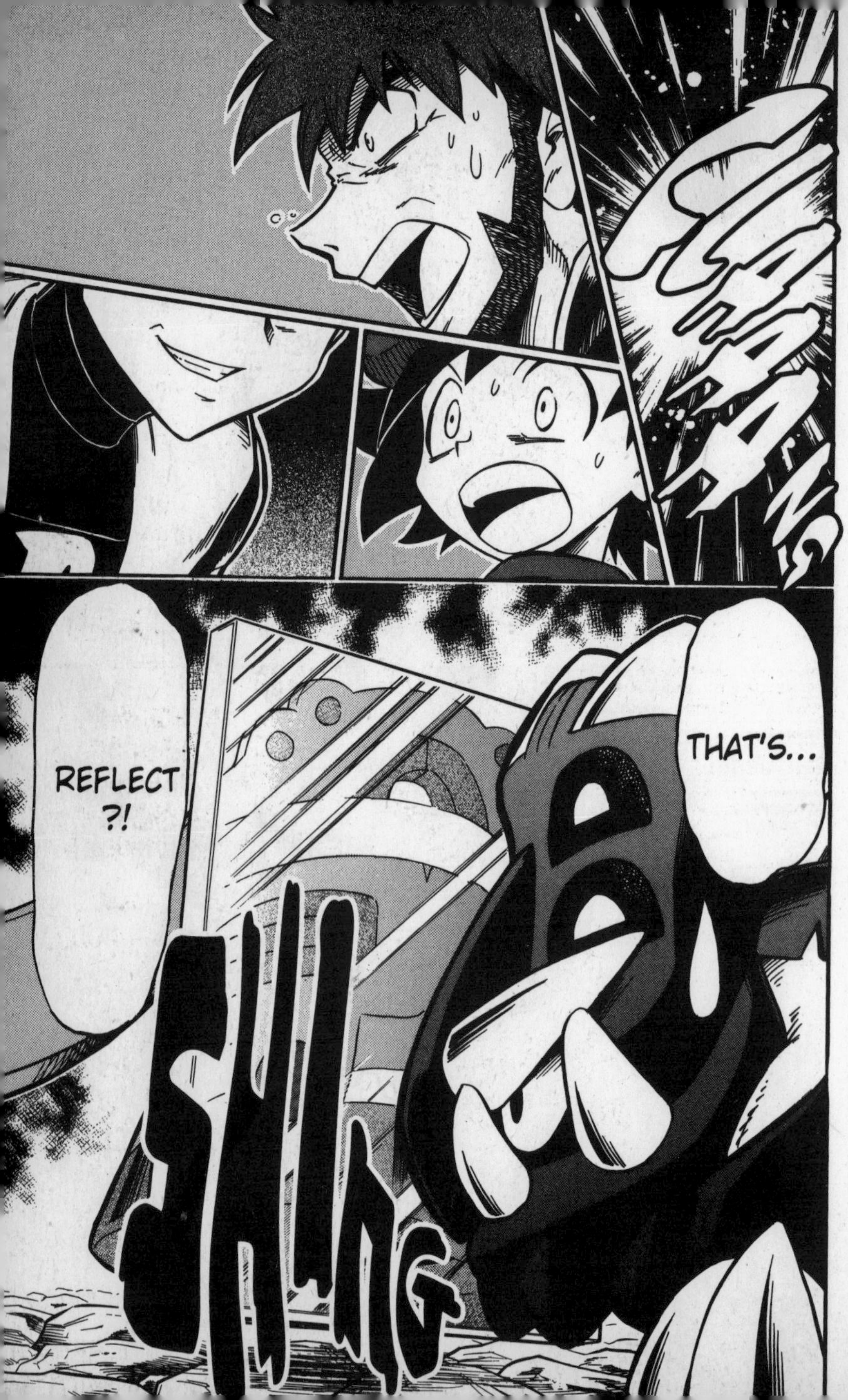
THAT'S...
REFLECT ?!

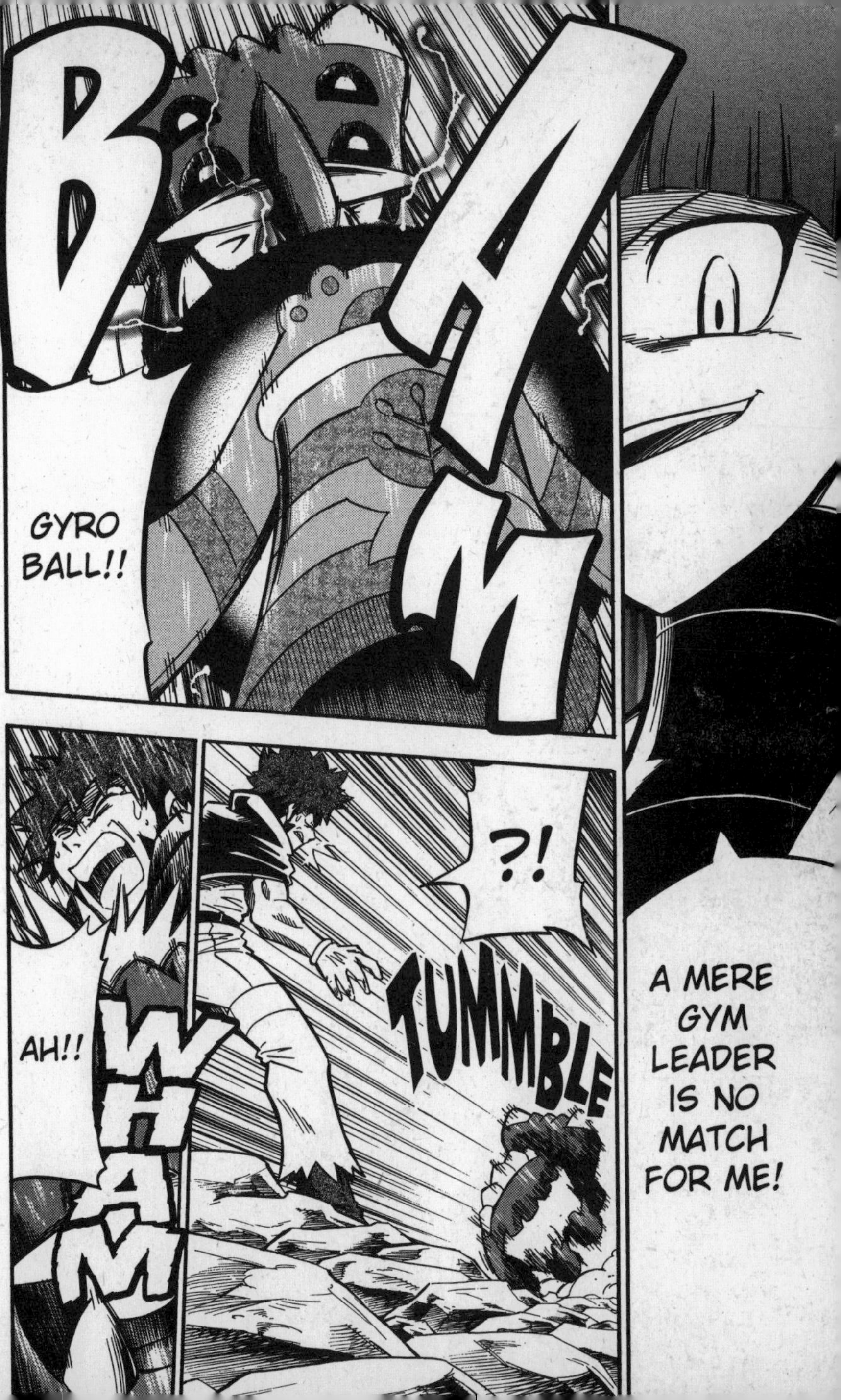
A MERE GYM LEADER IS NO MATCH FOR ME!
BAM
GYRO BALL!!
?!
TUMMBLE
AH!!
WHAM

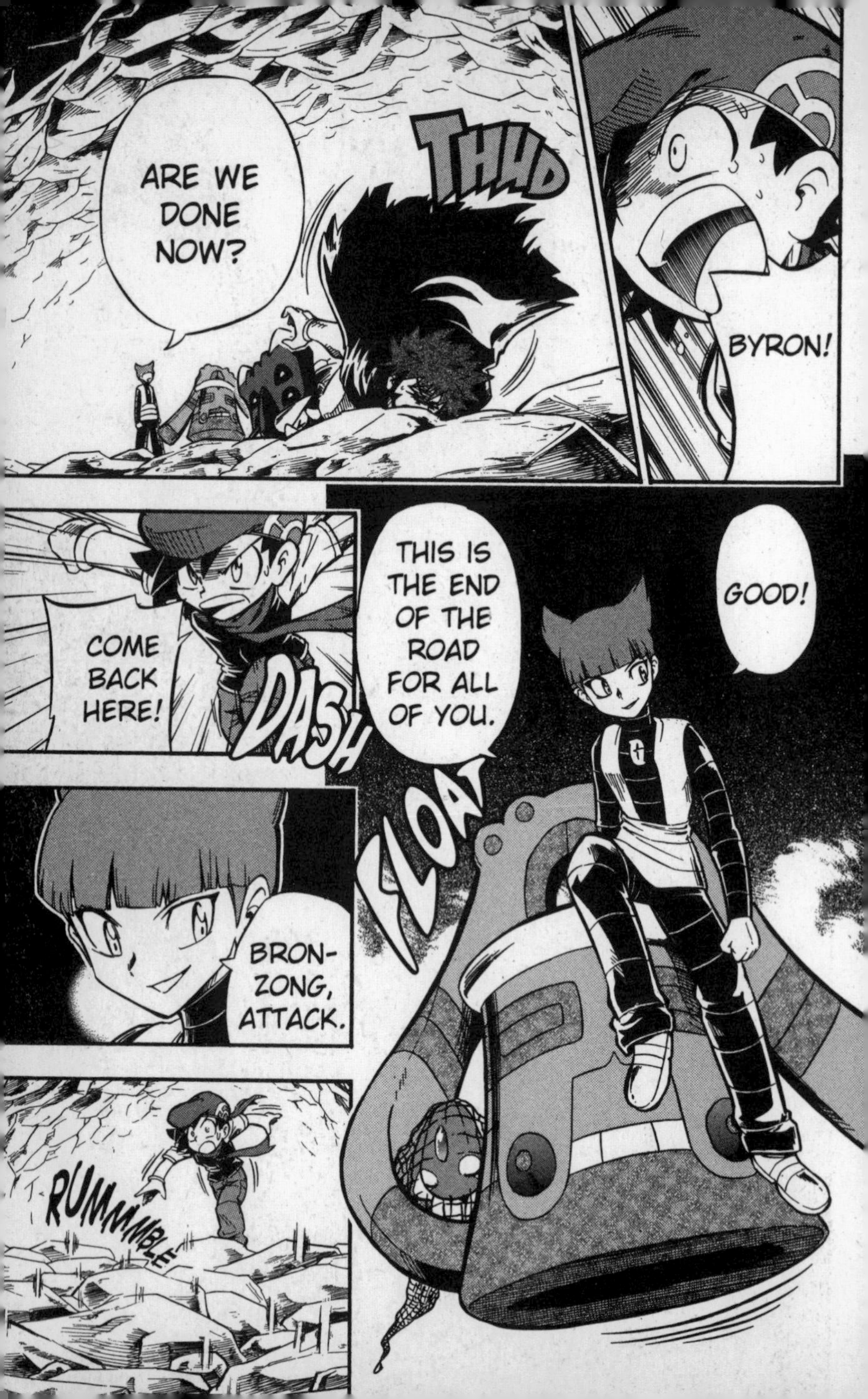
BYRON!
THUD
ARE WE DONE NOW?
GOOD!
THIS IS THE END OF THE ROAD FOR ALL OF YOU.
FLOAT
COME BACK HERE!
DASH
BRON-ZONG, ATTACK.
RUMMMBLE

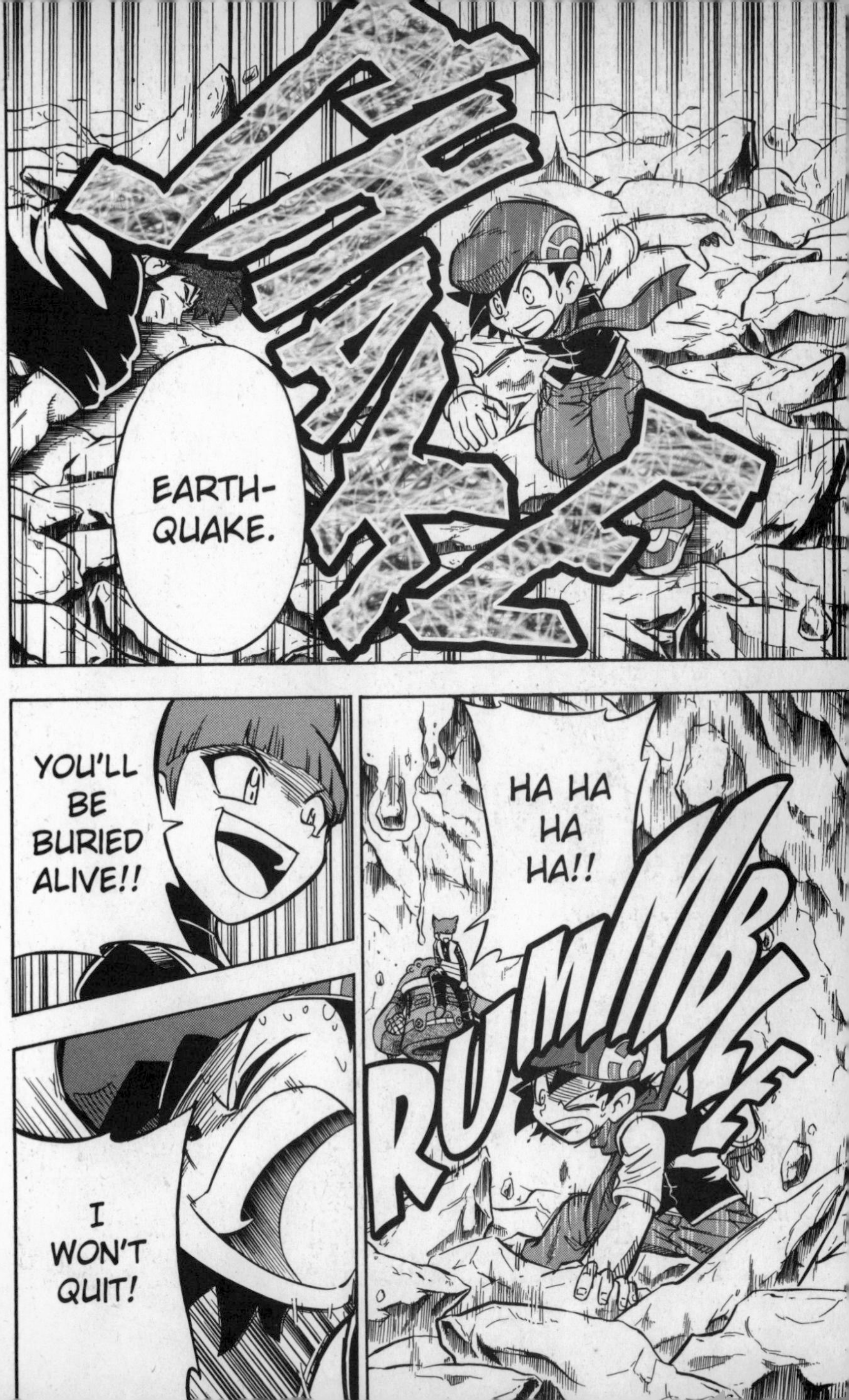
EARTH-QUAKE.
HA HA HA HA!!
RUMBLE
YOU'LL BE BURIED ALIVE!!
I WON'T QUIT!

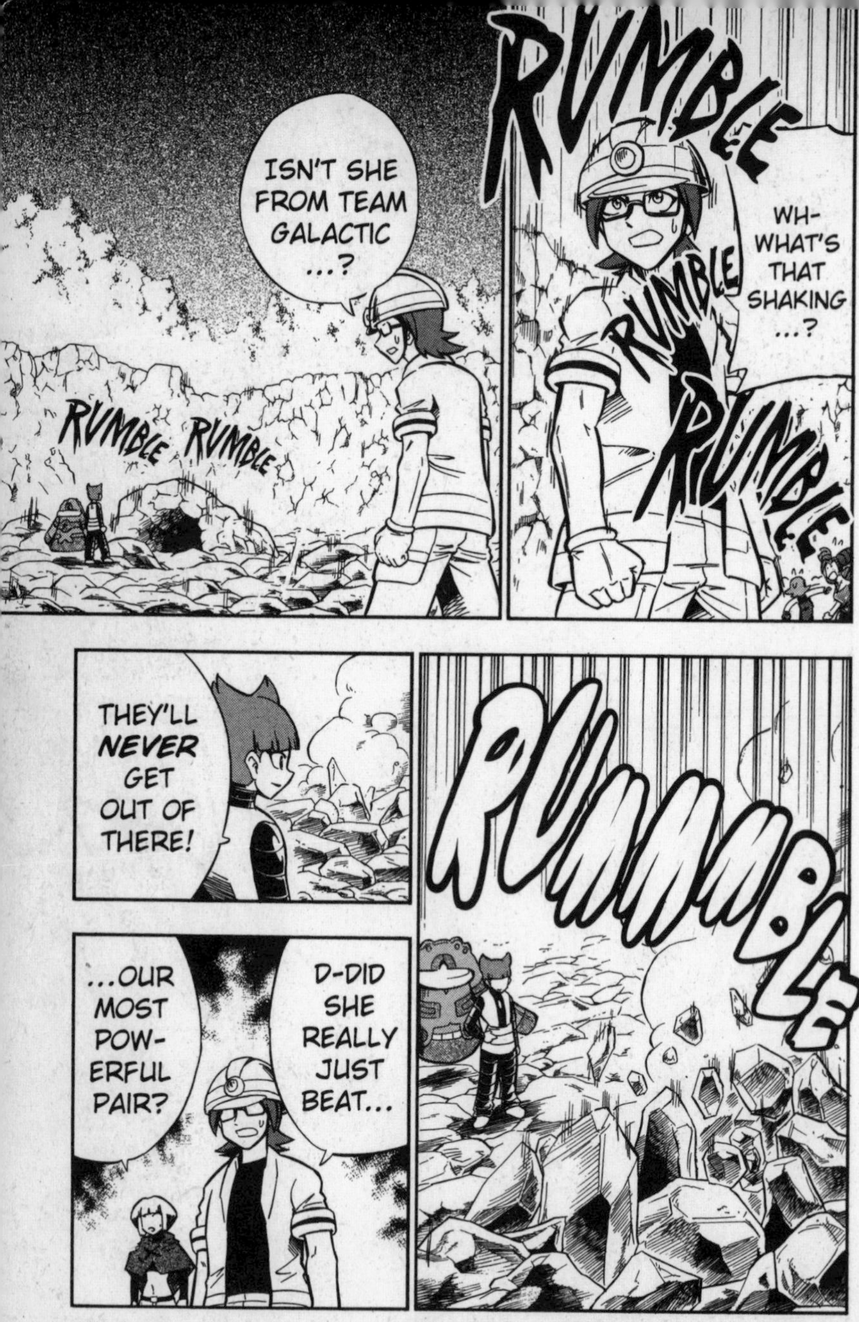
RUMBLE
WH-WHAT'S THAT SHAKING ...?
RUMBLE
RUMBLE
ISN'T SHE FROM TEAM GALACTIC ...?
RUMBLE
RUMBLE
RUMMMMBLE
THEY'LL ***NEVER*** GET OUT OF THERE!
D-DID SHE REALLY JUST BEAT...
...OUR MOST POW-ERFUL PAIR?

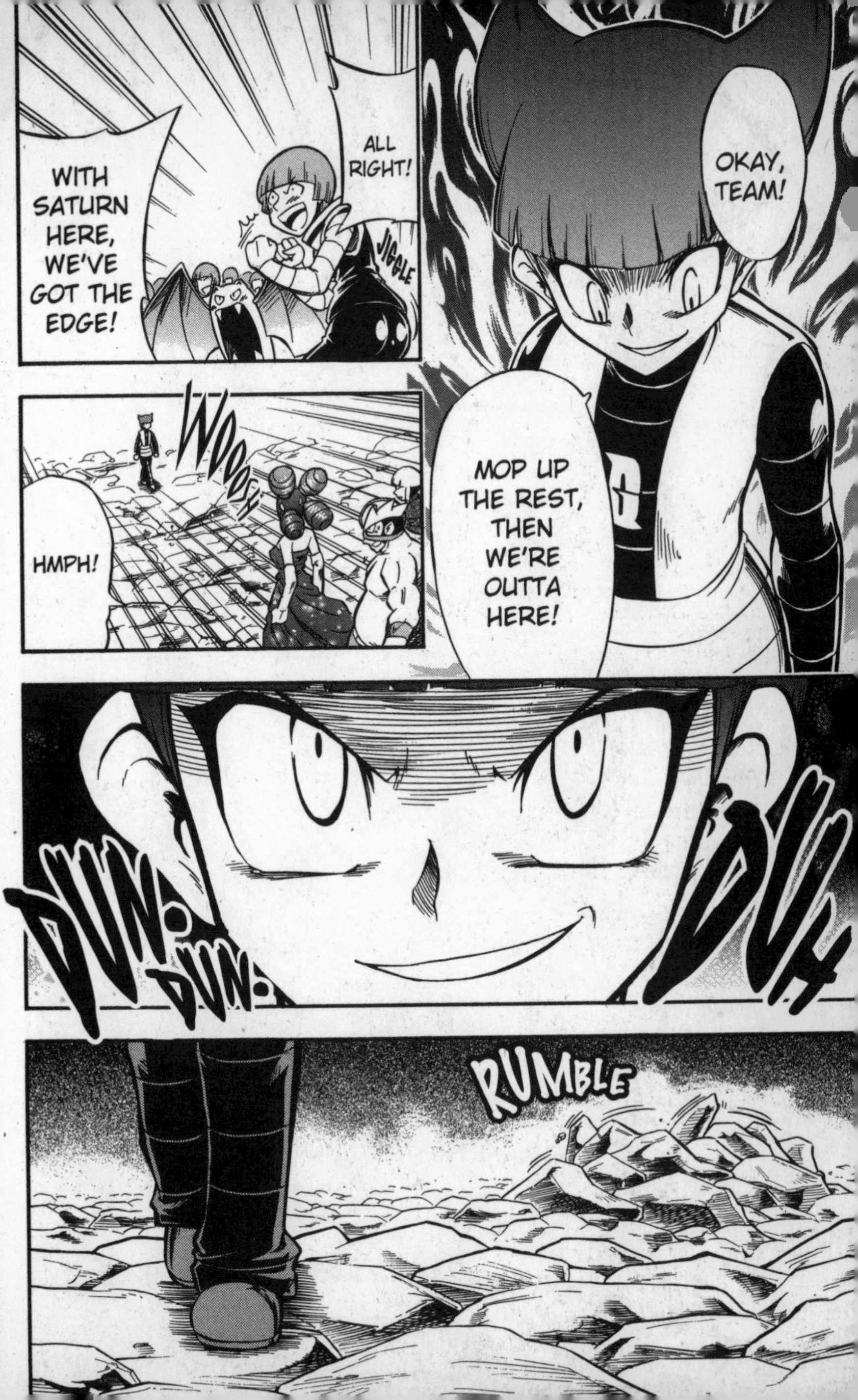
OKAY, TEAM!
MOP UP THE REST, THEN WE'RE OUTTA HERE!
ALL RIGHT!
JIGGLE
WITH SATURN HERE, WE'VE GOT THE EDGE!
WOOOSH
HMPH!
DUN
DUN
DUN
RUMBLE

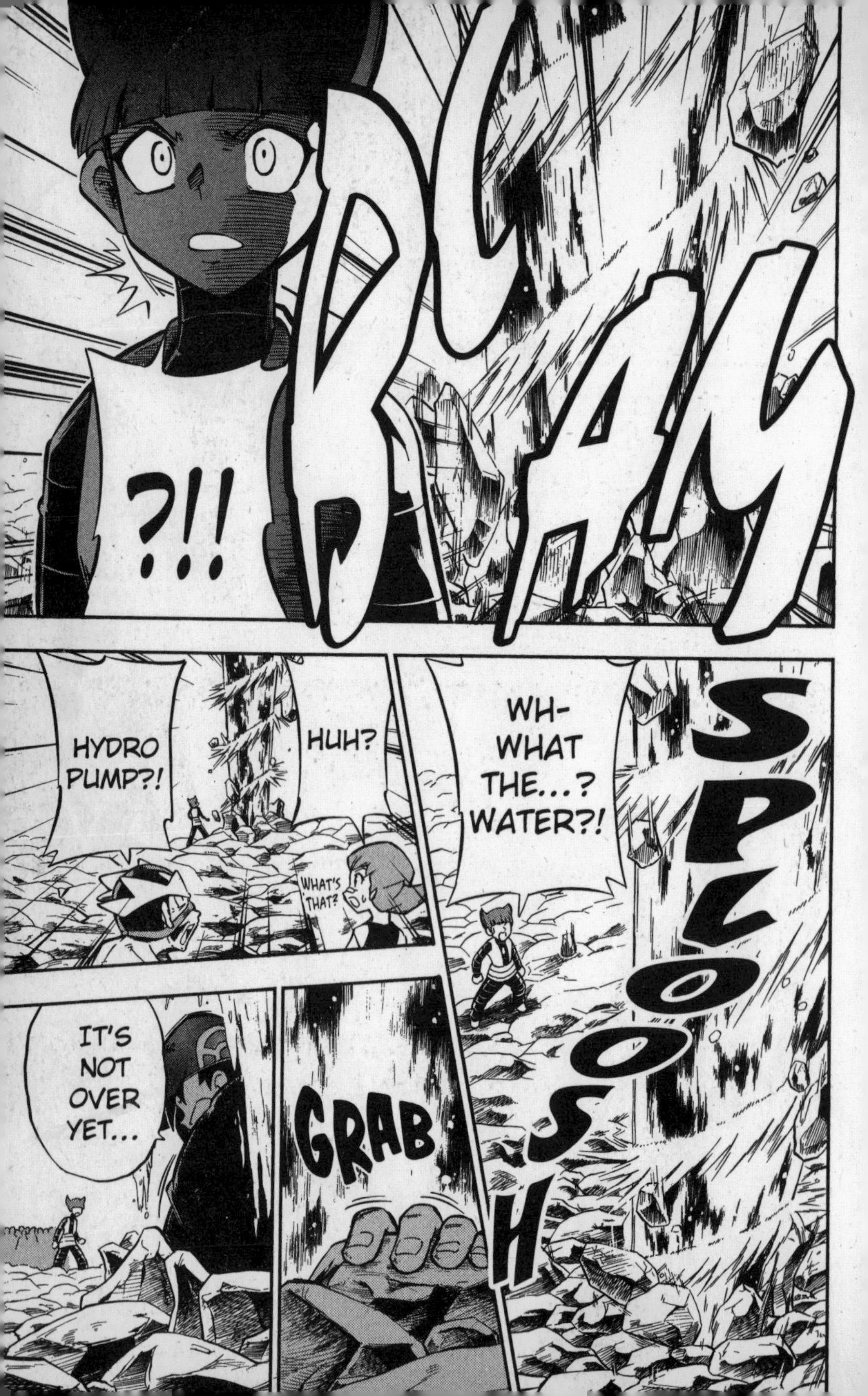
?!!
WH- WHAT THE...? WATER?!
SPLOOOSH
HUH?
HYDRO PUMP?!
WHAT'S THAT?
GRAB
IT'S NOT OVER YET...

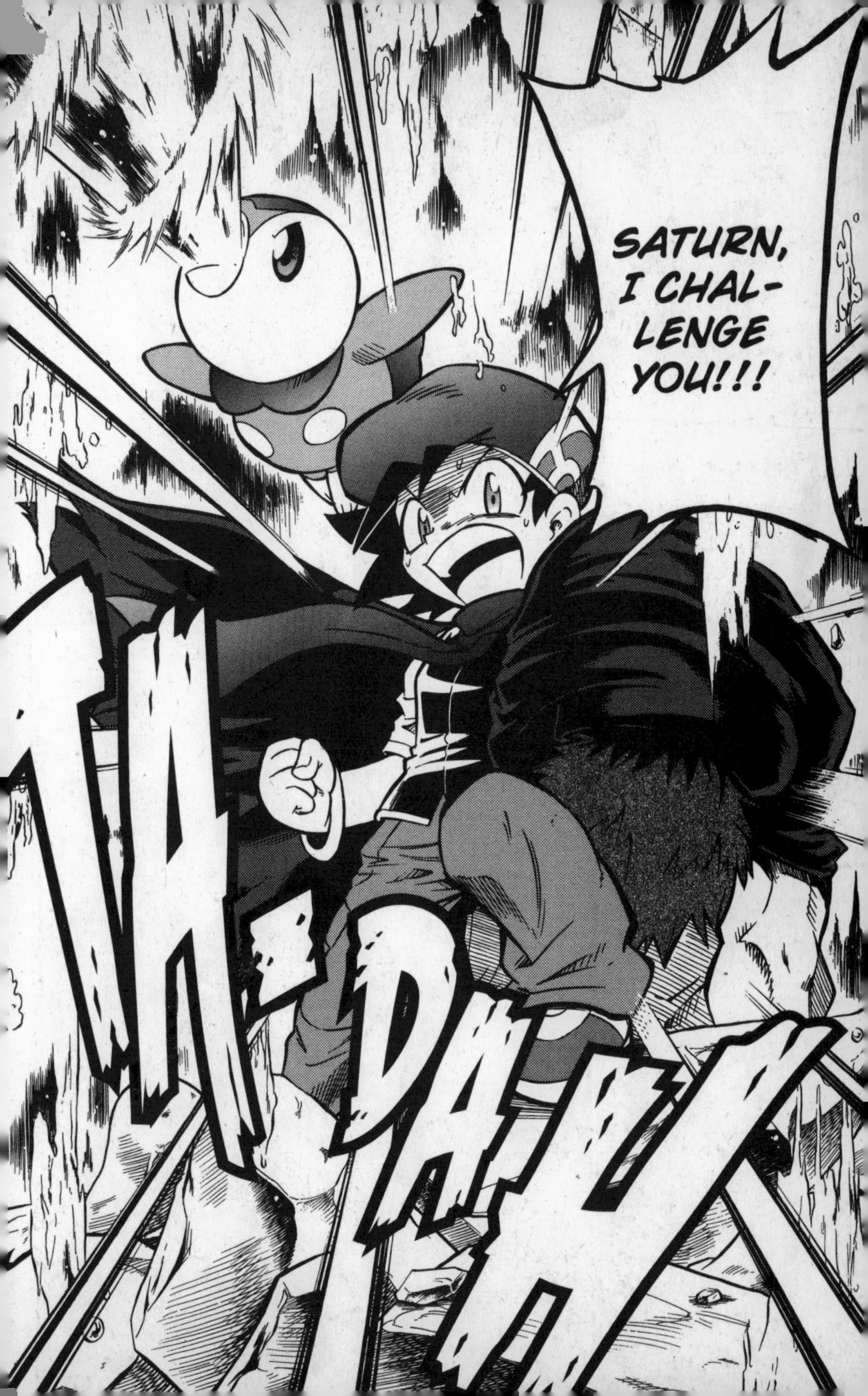
SATURN, I CHAL-LENGE YOU!!!

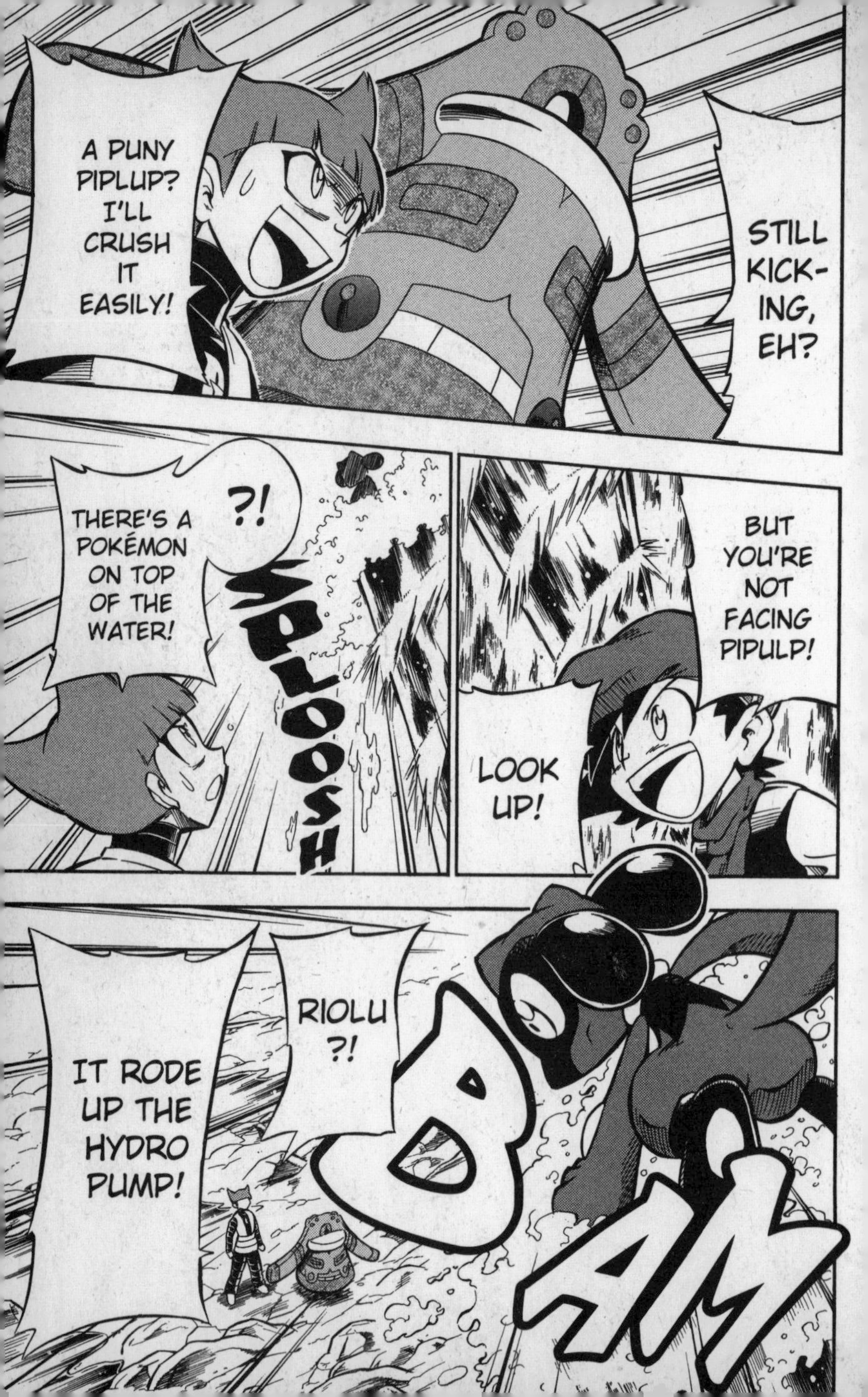
STILL KICKING, EH?
A PUNY PIPLUP? I'LL CRUSH IT EASILY!
BUT YOU'RE NOT FACING PIPULP!
LOOK UP!
SPLOOSH
?!
THERE'S A POKéMON ON TOP OF THE WATER!
BAM
RIOLU ?!
IT RODE UP THE HYDRO PUMP!

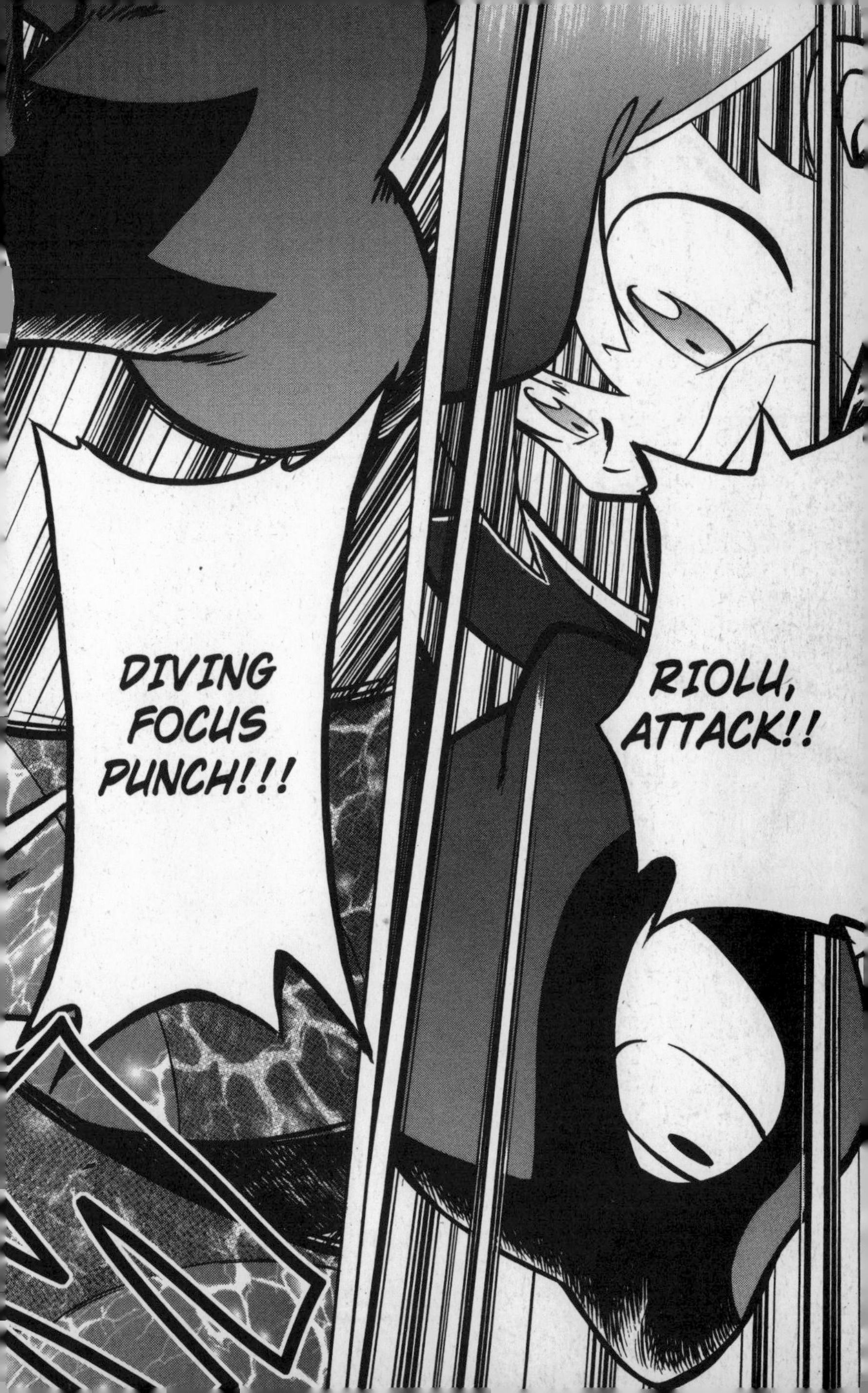
RIOLU, ATTACK!!
DIVING FOCUS PUNCH!!!

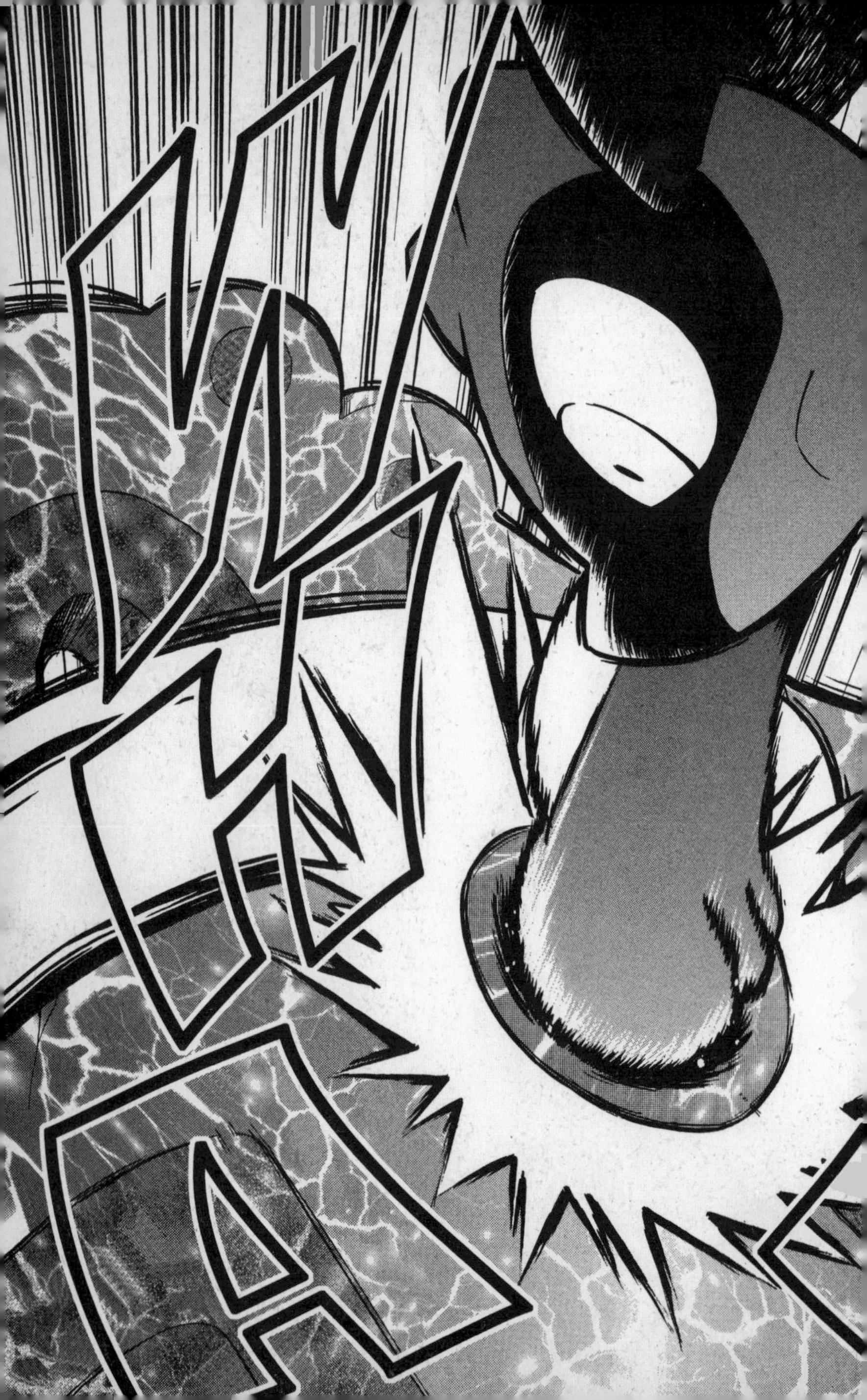

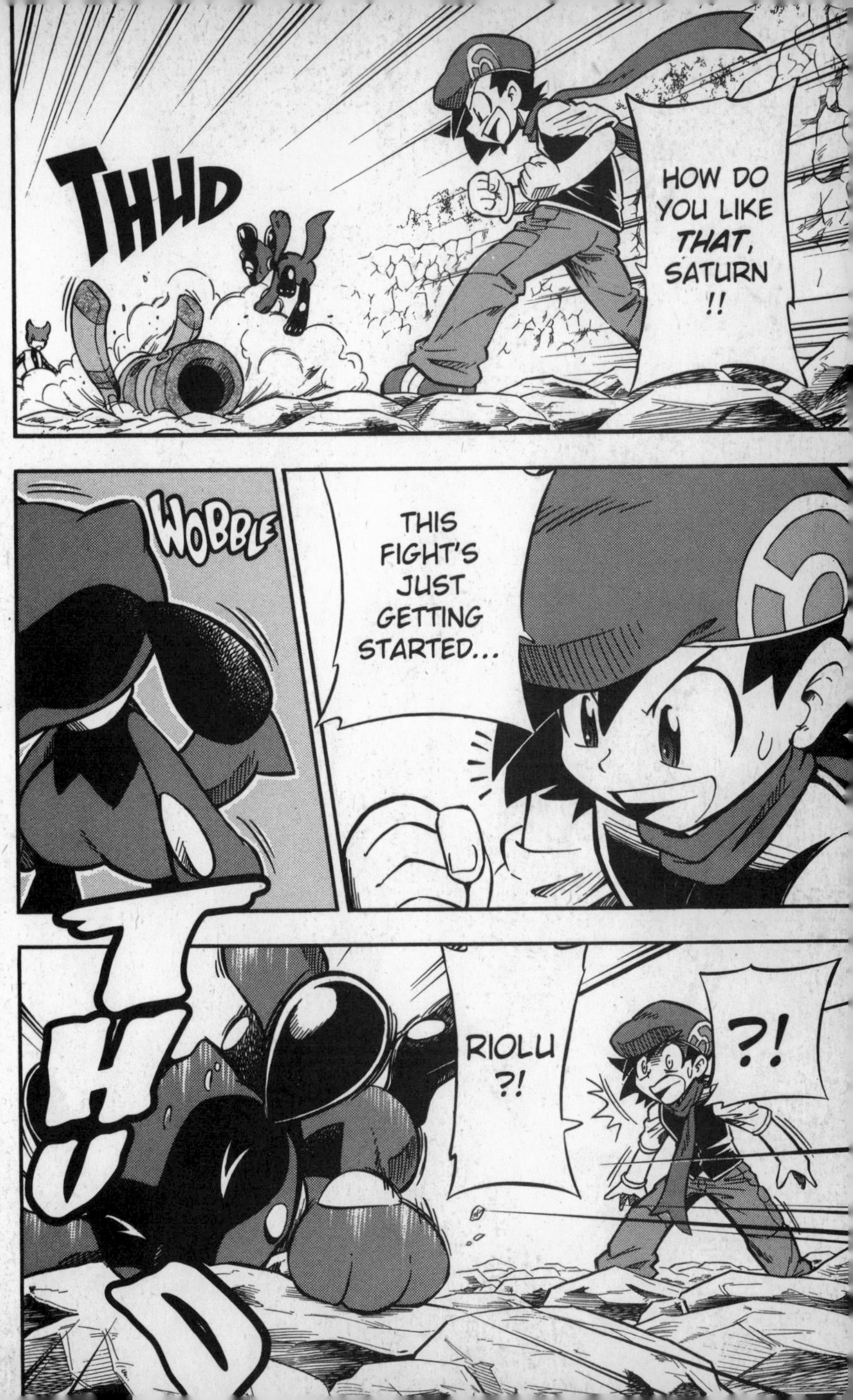
THUD
HOW DO YOU LIKE *THAT*, SATURN!!
THIS FIGHT'S JUST GETTING STARTED...
WOBBLE
?!
RIOLU ?!
THUD

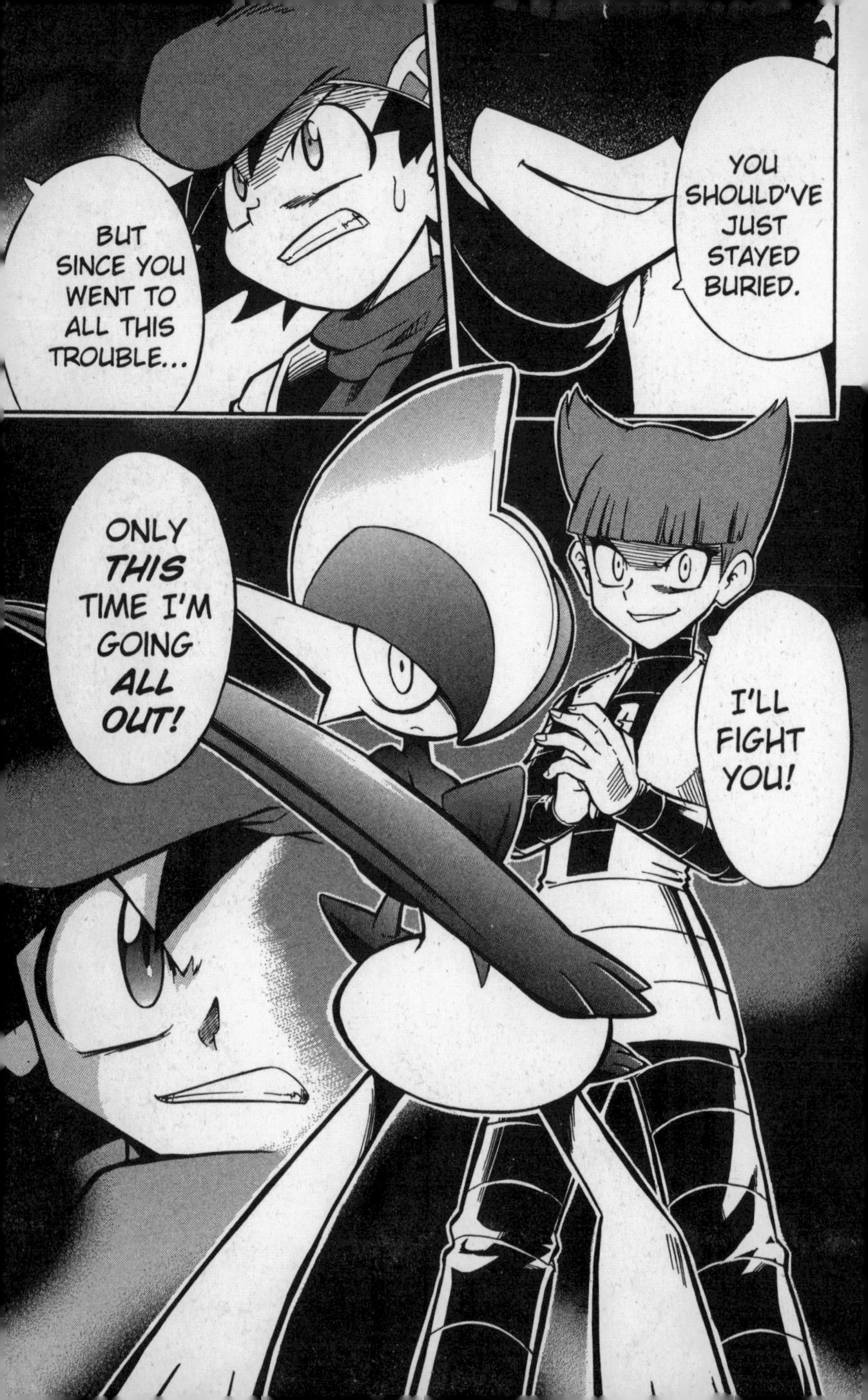

YOU SHOULD'VE JUST STAYED BURIED.
BUT SINCE YOU WENT TO ALL THIS TROUBLE...
I'LL FIGHT YOU!
ONLY *THIS* TIME I'M GOING *ALL OUT!*

CHAPTER 2
A BATTLE OF WILLS

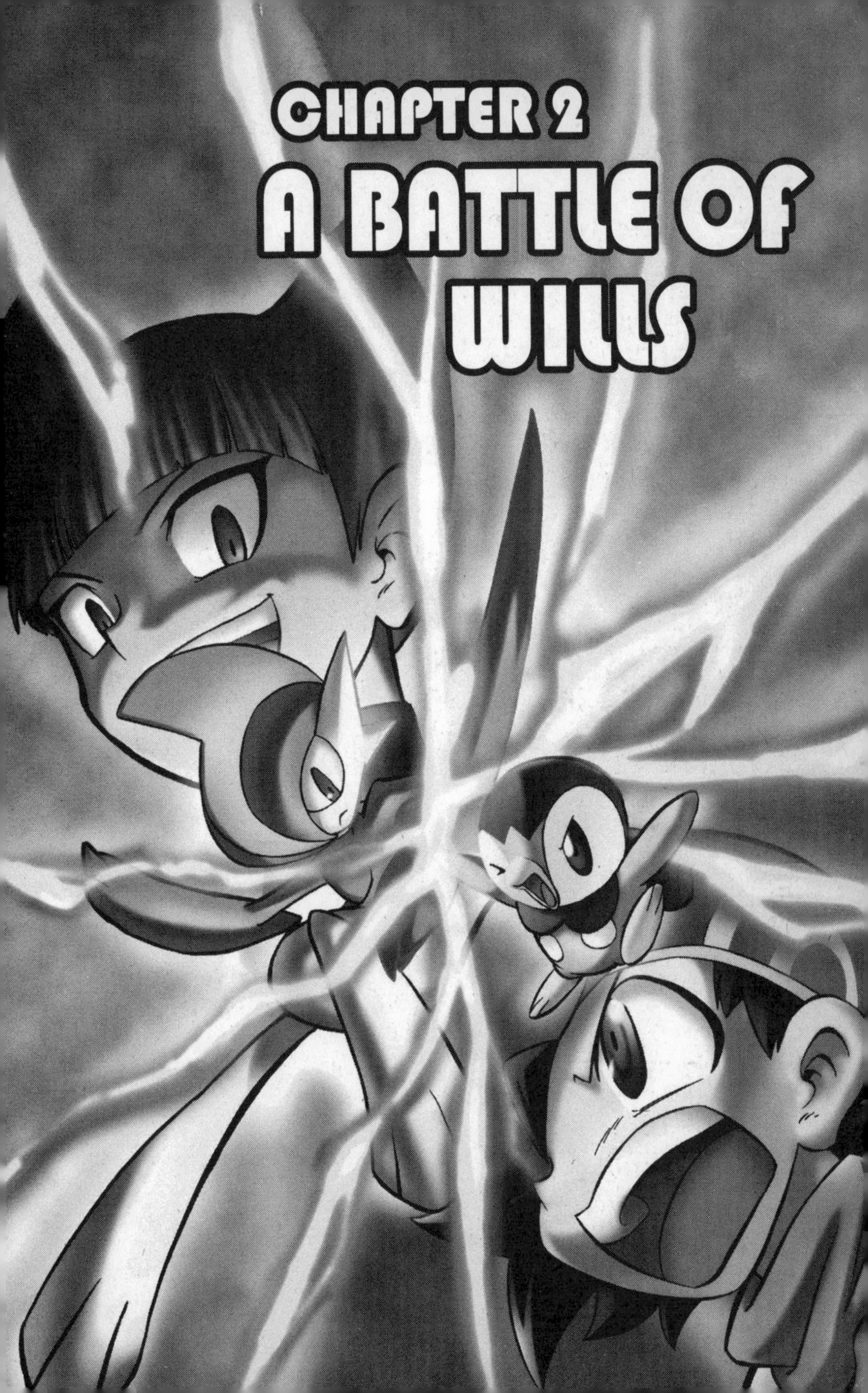

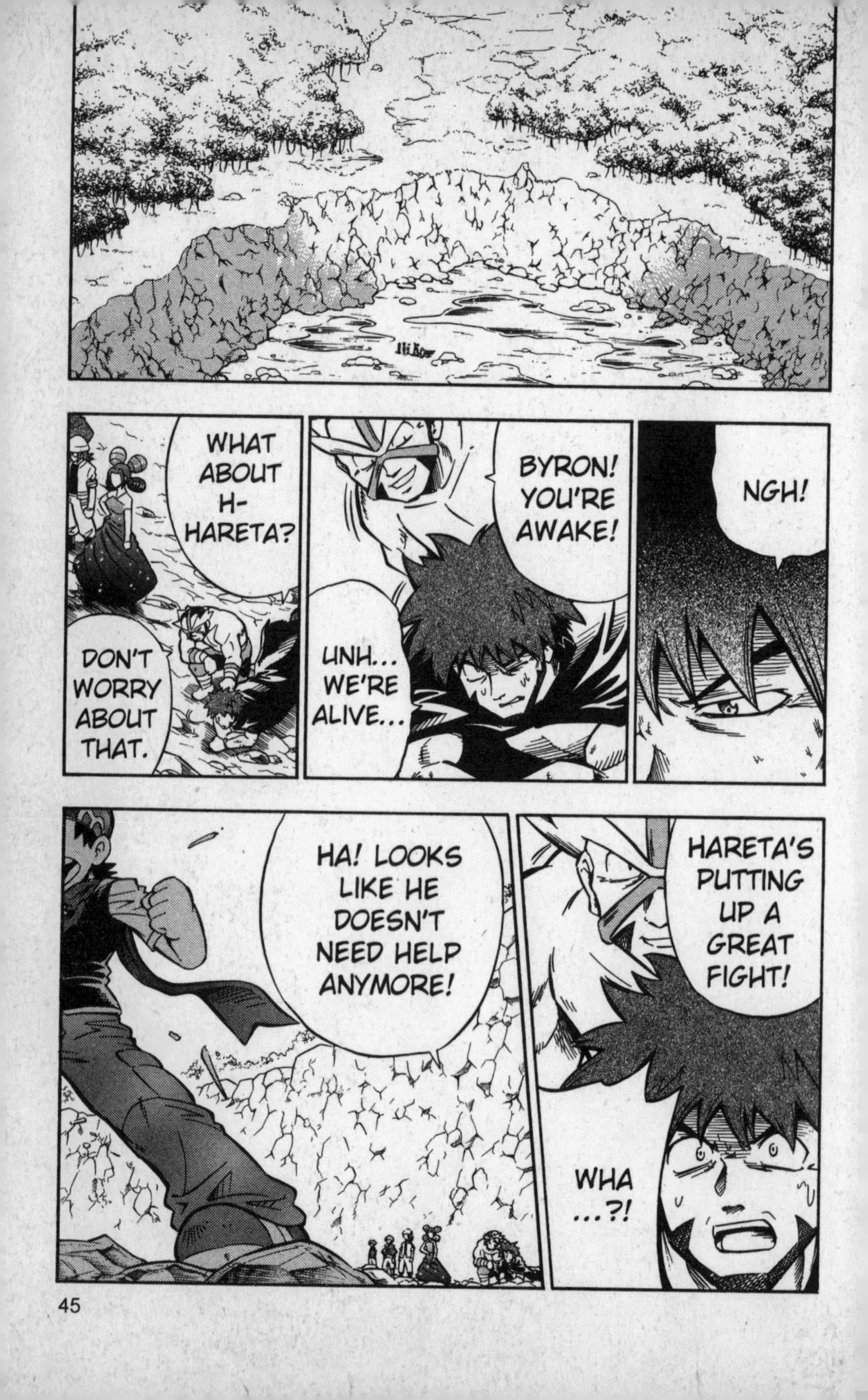
NGH!
BYRON! YOU'RE AWAKE!
UNH... WE'RE ALIVE...
WHAT ABOUT H-HARETA?
DON'T WORRY ABOUT THAT.
HARETA'S PUTTING UP A GREAT FIGHT!
WHA ...?!
HA! LOOKS LIKE HE DOESN'T NEED HELP ANYMORE!

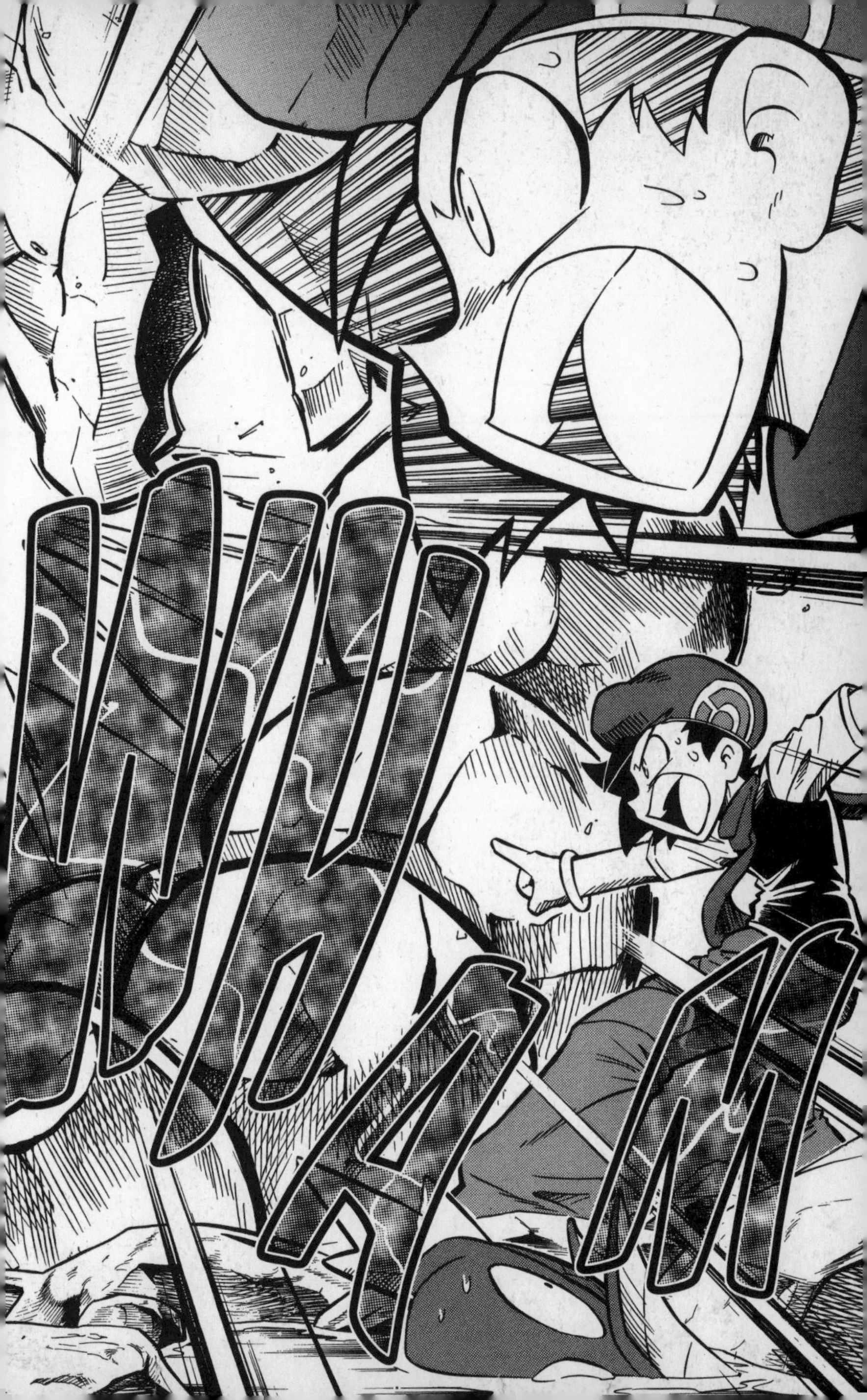
WHAM!

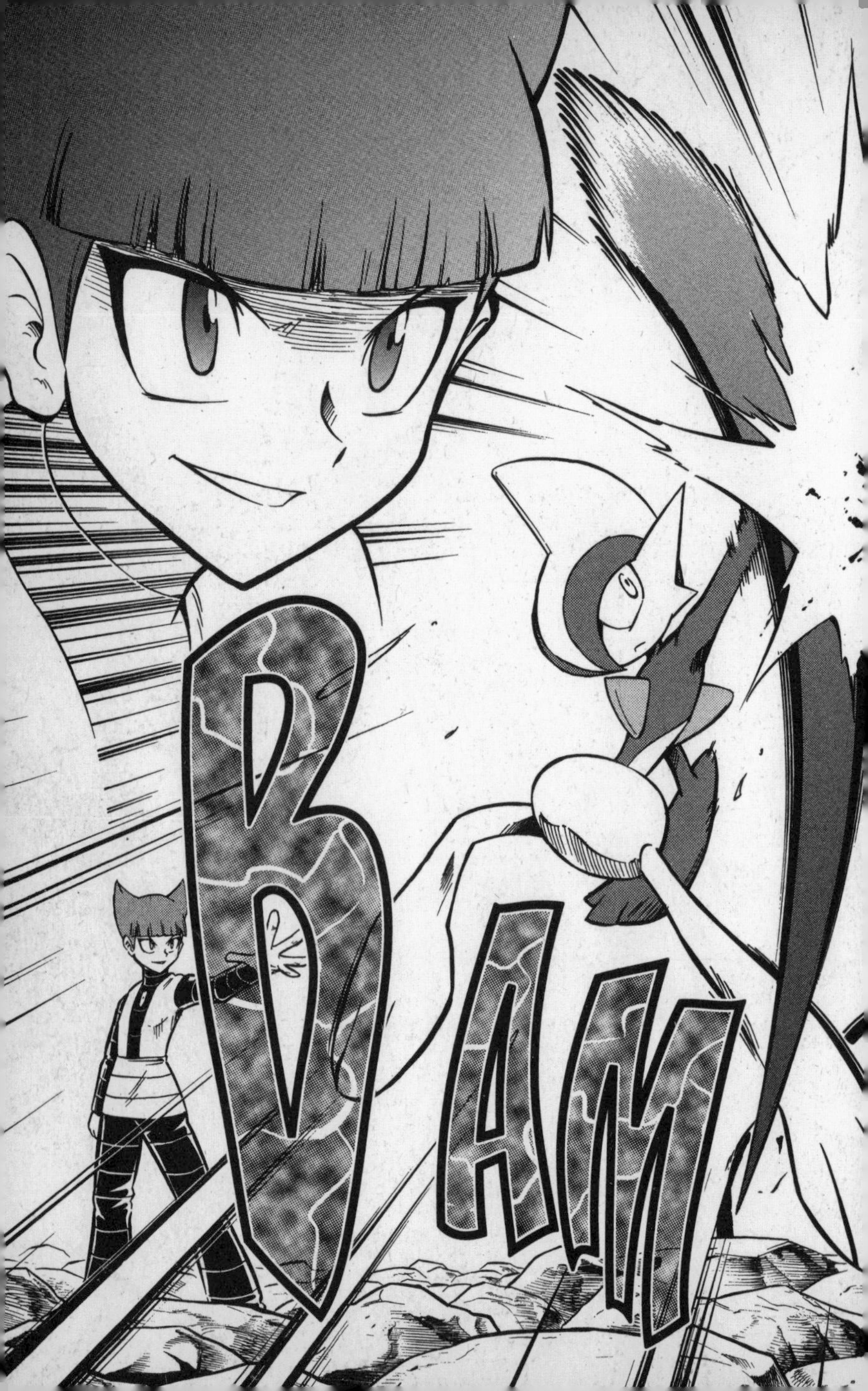
BAM

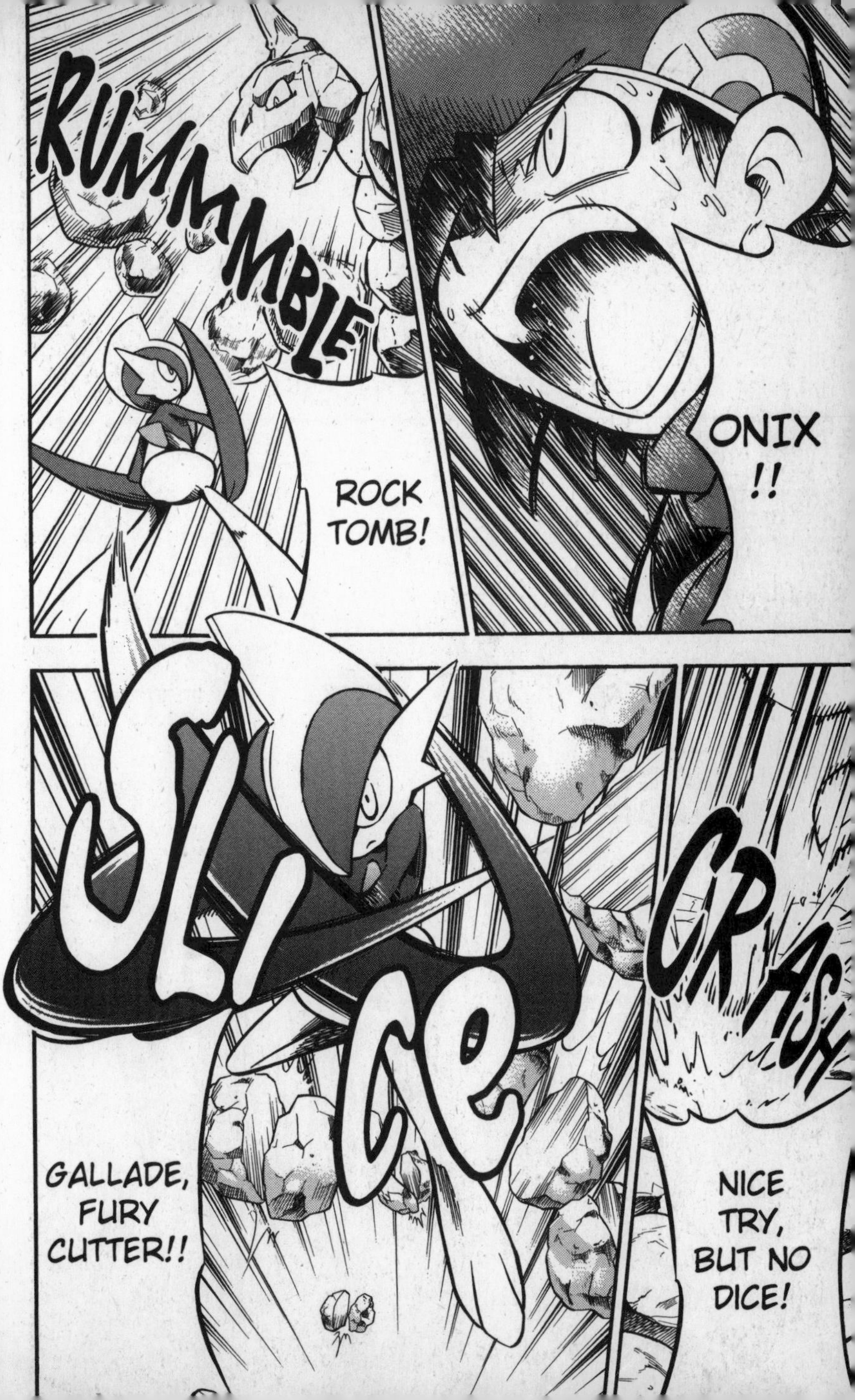
ONIX !!
RUMMMBLE
ROCK TOMB!
CRASH
NICE TRY, BUT NO DICE!
SLICE
GALLADE, FURY CUTTER!!

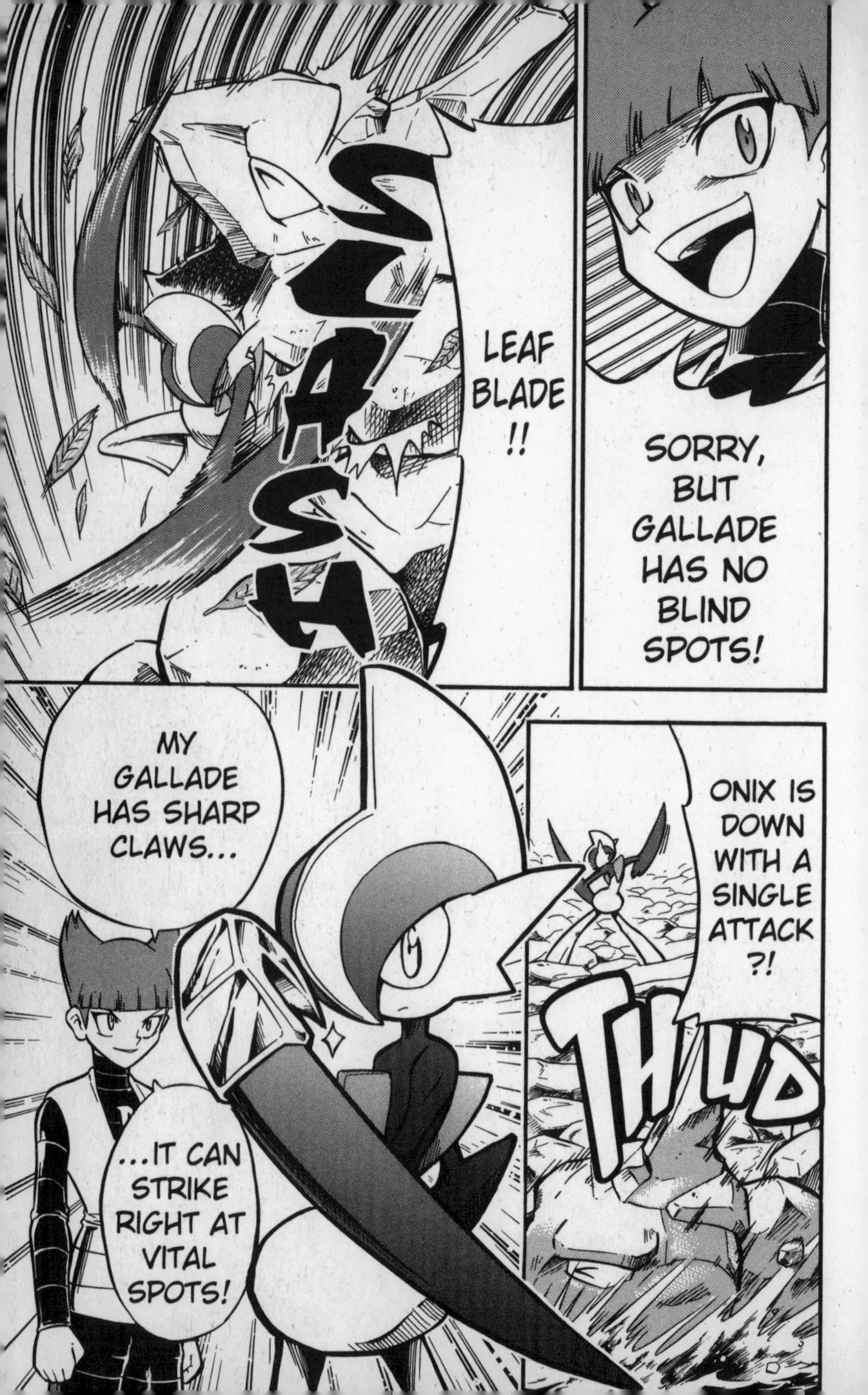
SORRY, BUT GALLADE HAS NO BLIND SPOTS!
SLASH
LEAF BLADE !!
ONIX IS DOWN WITH A SINGLE ATTACK ?!
THUD
MY GALLADE HAS SHARP CLAWS...
...IT CAN STRIKE RIGHT AT VITAL SPOTS!

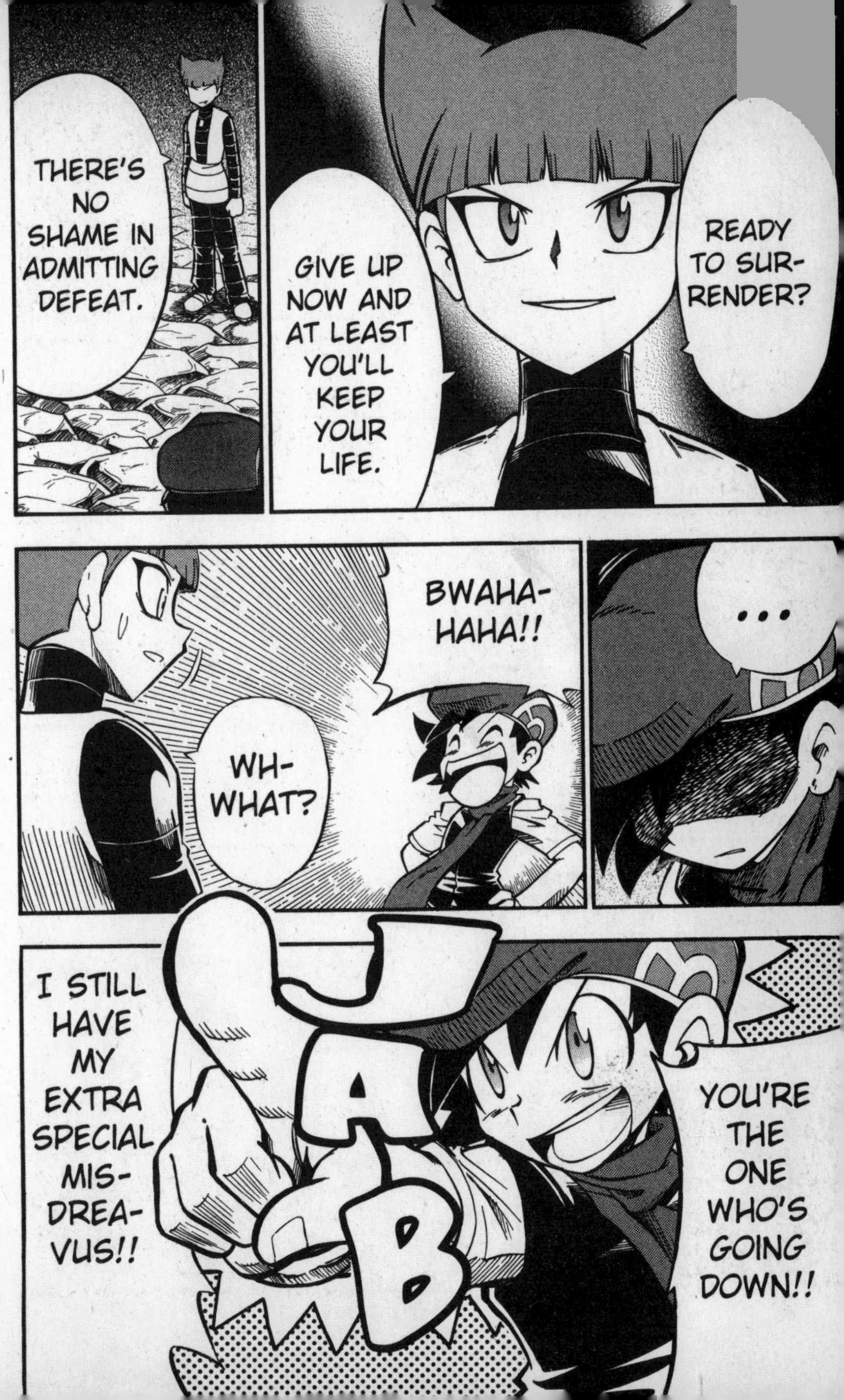
READY TO SUR-RENDER?
GIVE UP NOW AND AT LEAST YOU'LL KEEP YOUR LIFE.
THERE'S NO SHAME IN ADMITTING DEFEAT.
...
BWAHA-HAHA!!
WH-WHAT?
YOU'RE THE ONE WHO'S GOING DOWN!!
JAB
I STILL HAVE MY EXTRA SPECIAL MIS-DREA-VUS!!

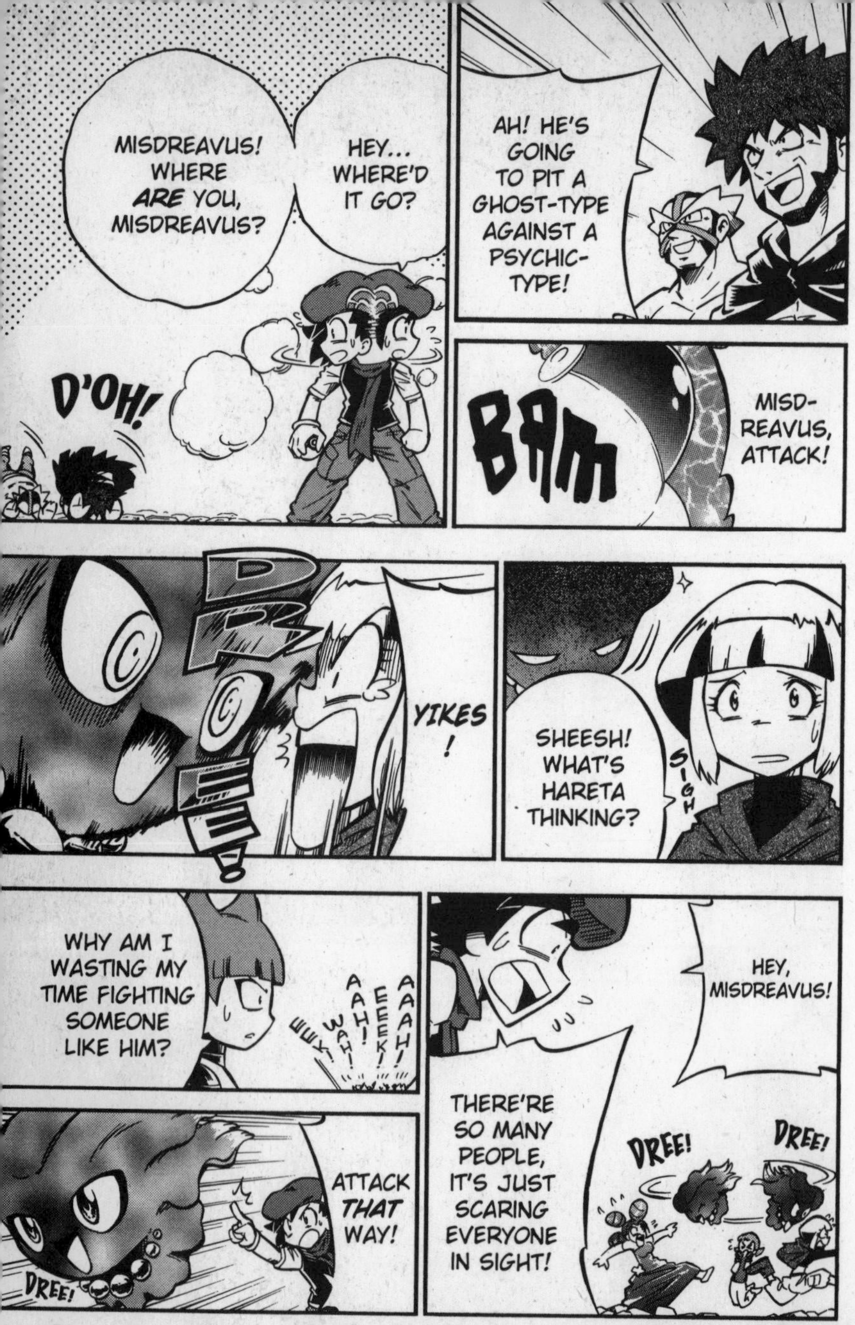
AH! HE'S GOING TO PIT A GHOST-TYPE AGAINST A PSYCHIC-TYPE!
MISD-REAVUS, ATTACK!
BAM
HEY... WHERE'D IT GO?
MISDREAVUS! WHERE ARE YOU, MISDREAVUS?
D'OH!
SIGH
SHEESH! WHAT'S HARETA THINKING?
YIKES!
DREE
HEY, MISDREAVUS!
THERE'RE SO MANY PEOPLE, IT'S JUST SCARING EVERYONE IN SIGHT!
DREE!
DREE!
WHY AM I WASTING MY TIME FIGHTING SOMEONE LIKE HIM?
AAAAH!
EEEEK!
WAH!
EEK!
ATTACK THAT WAY!
DREE!

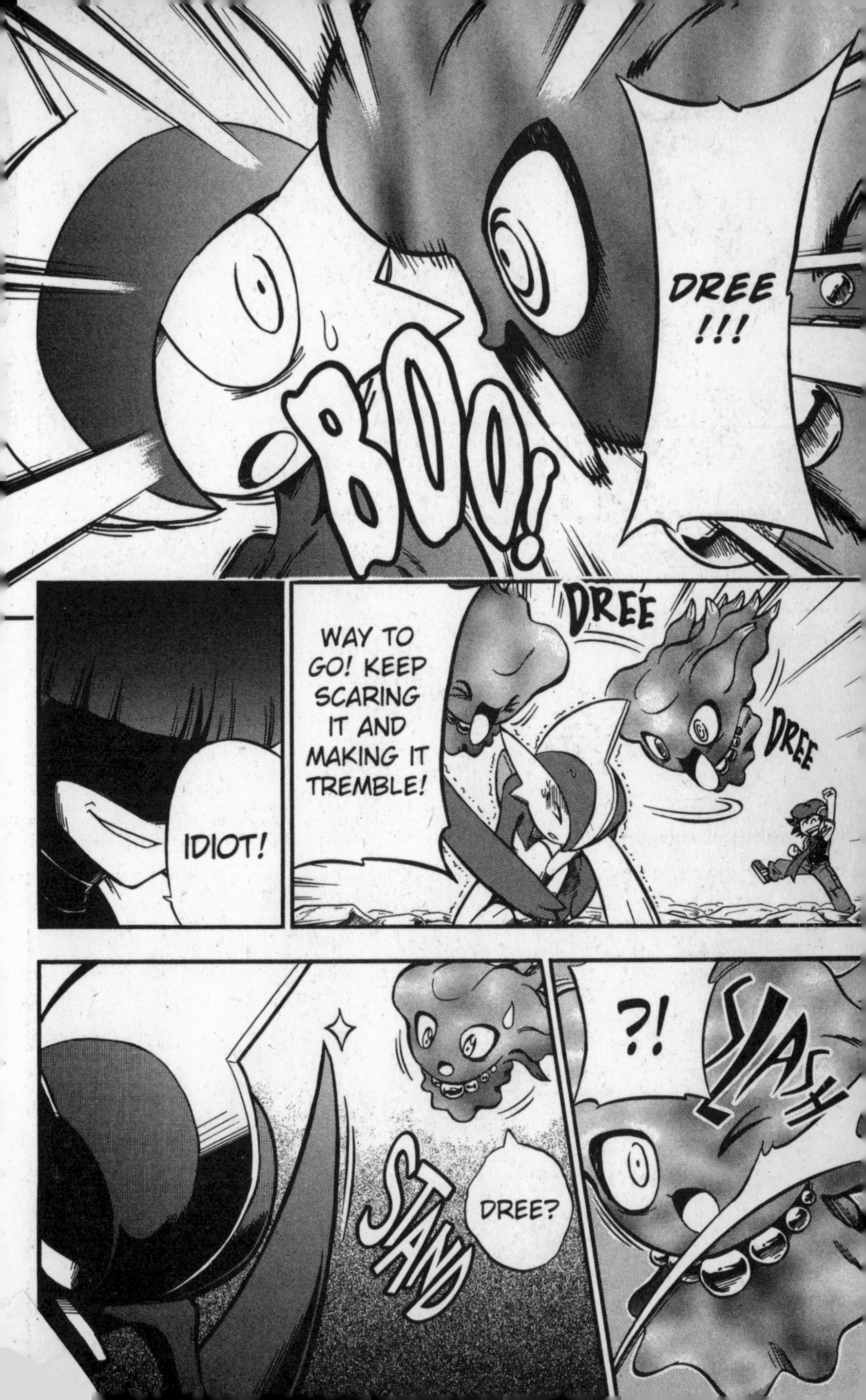
DREE !!!
BOO!
DREE
DREE
WAY TO GO! KEEP SCARING IT AND MAKING IT TREMBLE!
IDIOT!
?!
SLASH
DREE?
STAND

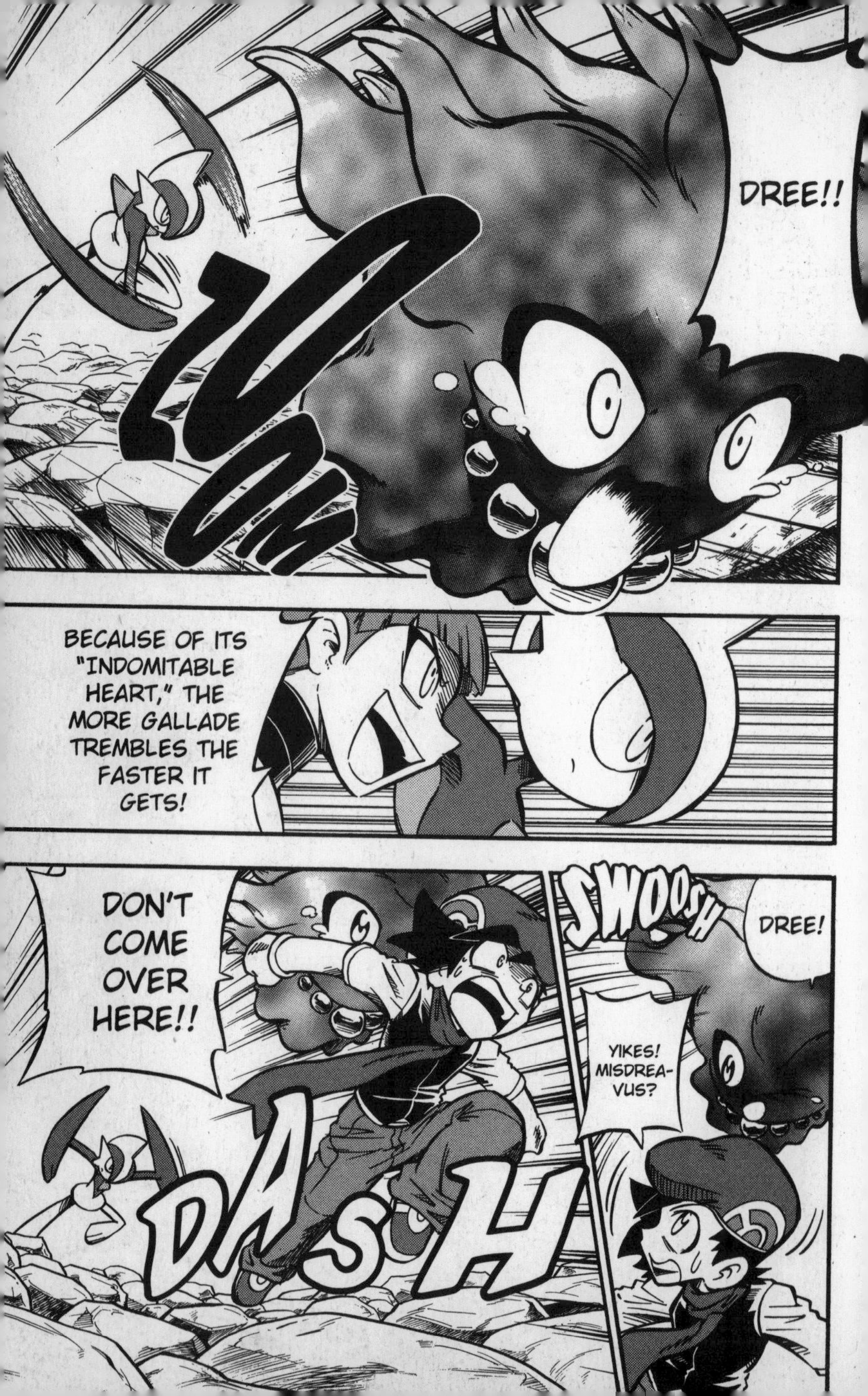
DREE!!
ZOOM
BECAUSE OF ITS "INDOMITABLE HEART," THE MORE GALLADE TREMBLES THE FASTER IT GETS!
SWOOSH
DREE!
YIKES! MISDREAVUS?
DON'T COME OVER HERE!!
DASH

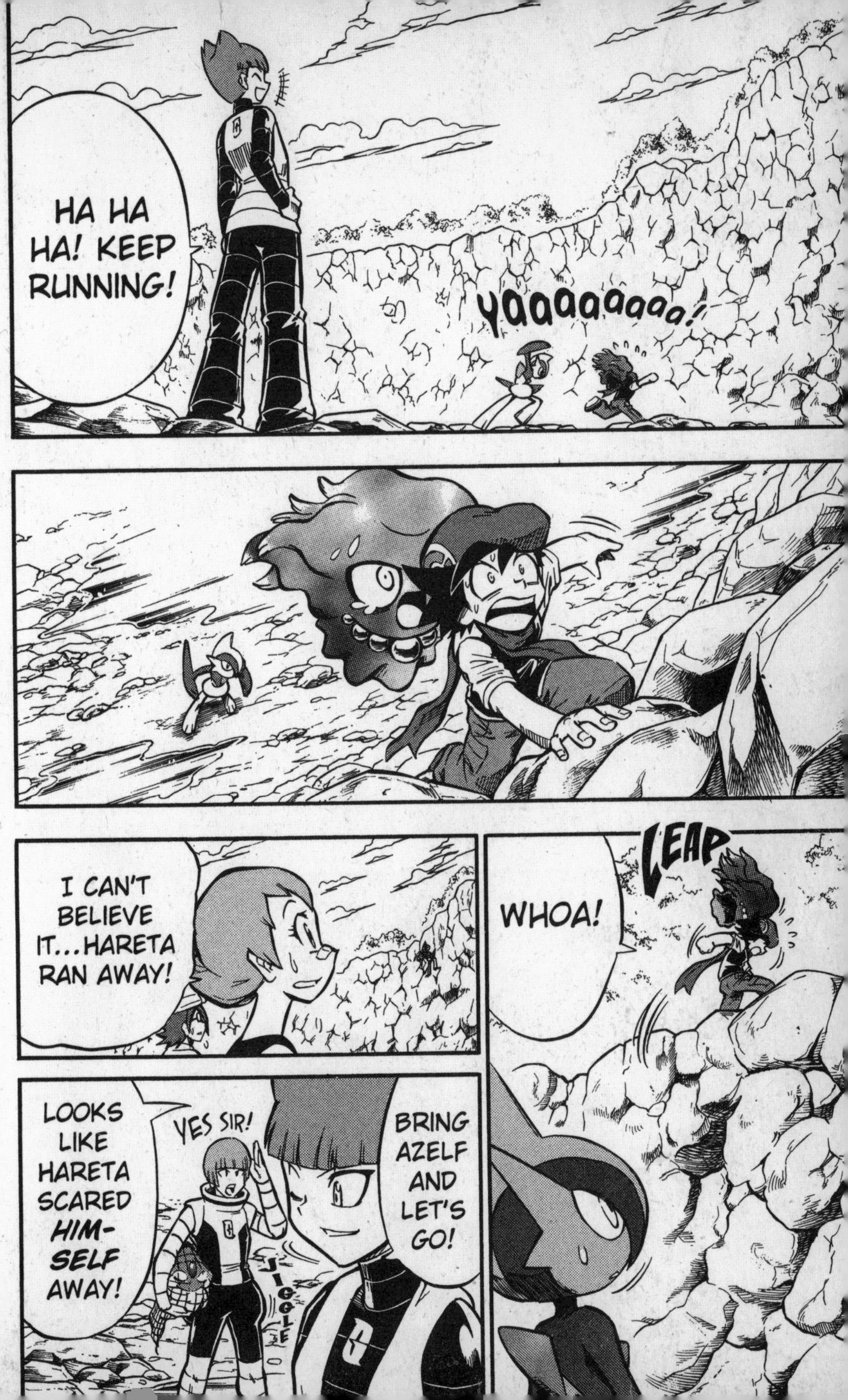
YAAAAAAAA!
HA HA HA! KEEP RUNNING!
LEAP
WHOA!
I CAN'T BELIEVE IT...HARETA RAN AWAY!
BRING AZELF AND LET'S GO!
YES SIR!
LOOKS LIKE HARETA SCARED *HIM-SELF* AWAY!
JIGGLE

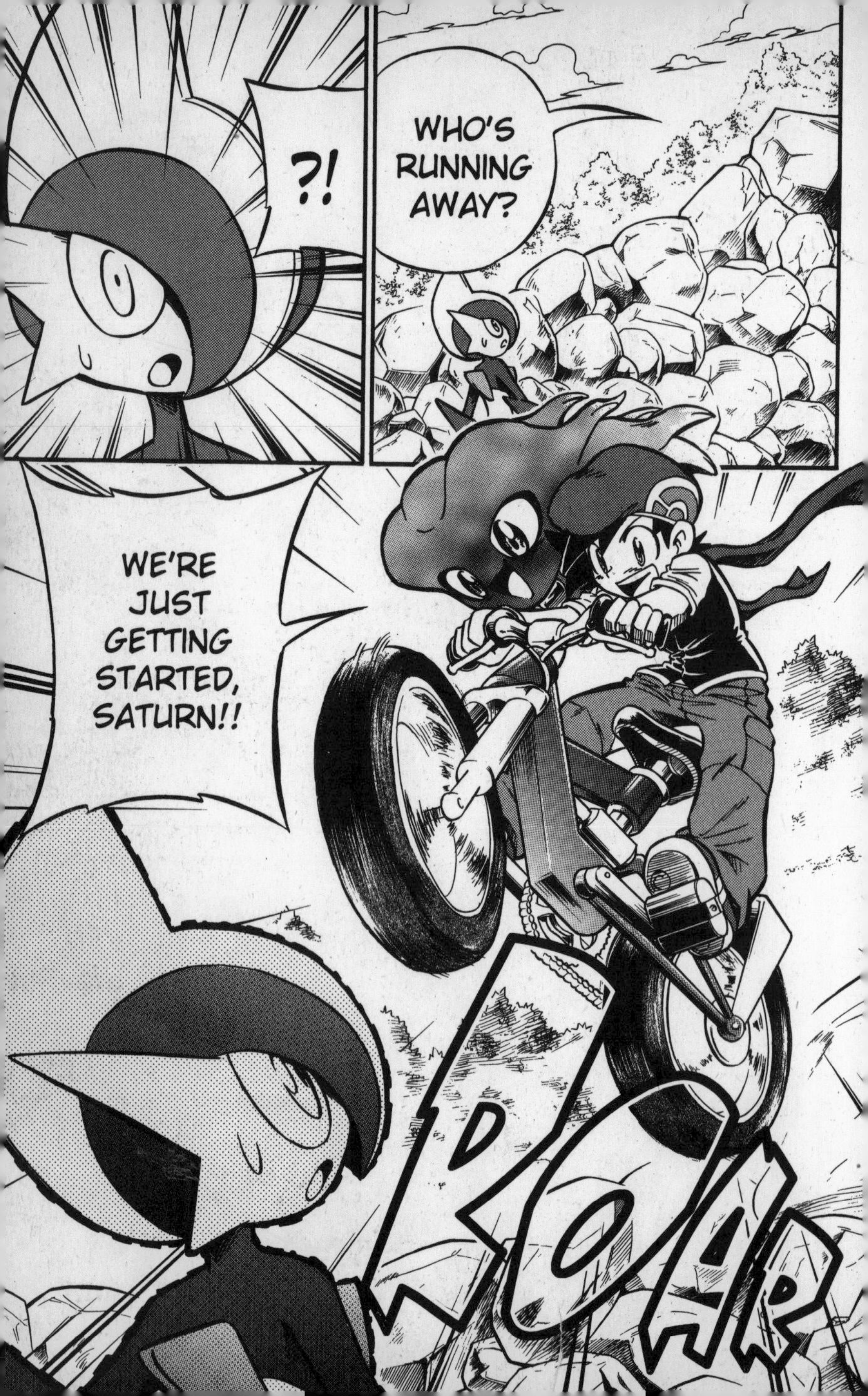
WHO'S RUNNING AWAY?
?!
WE'RE JUST GETTING STARTED, SATURN!!
DOOAR

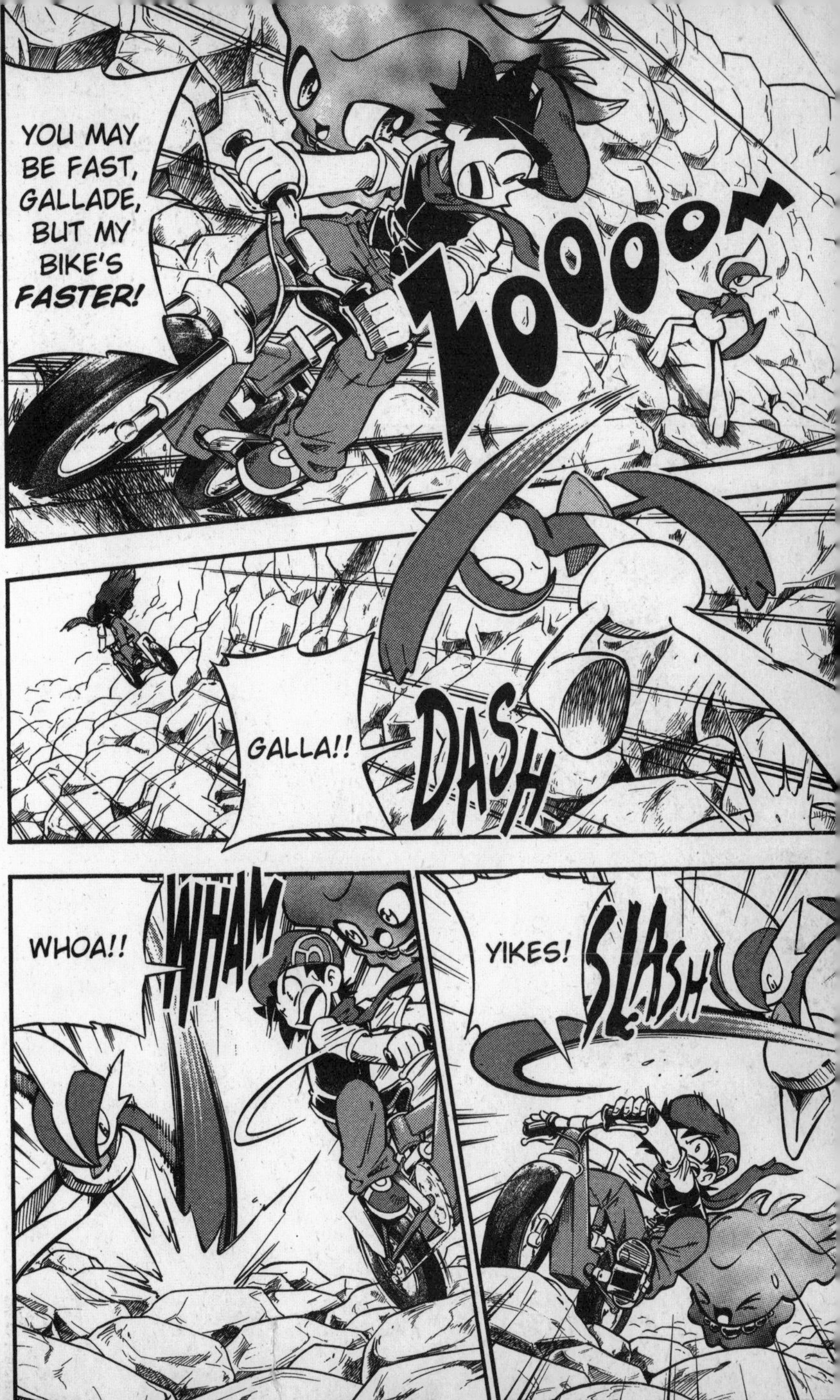
YOU MAY BE FAST, GALLADE, BUT MY BIKE'S FASTER!
ZOOOOOM
GALLA!!
DASH
YIKES!
SLASH
WHOA!!
WHAM

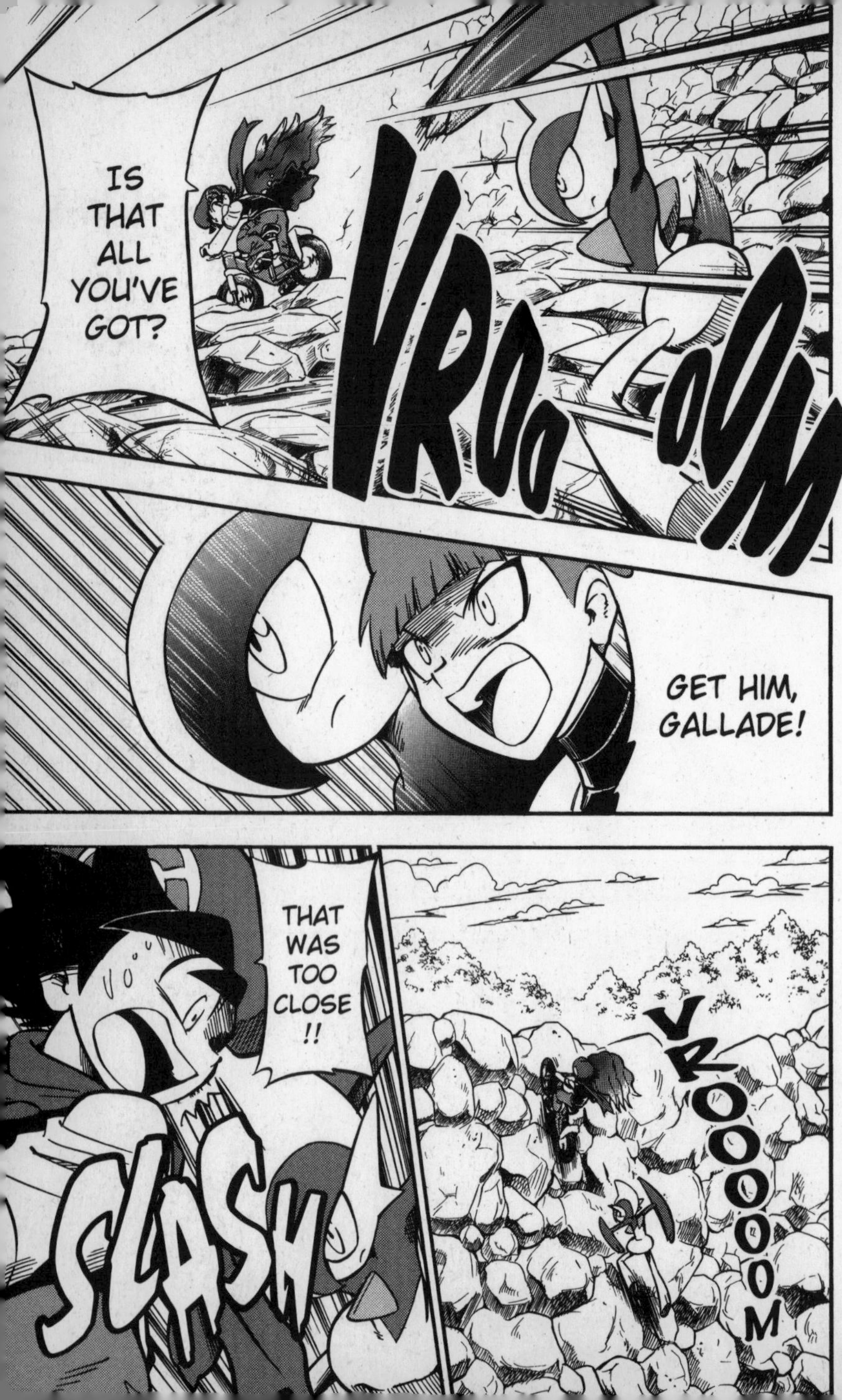
VROOOOOM
IS THAT ALL YOU'VE GOT?
GET HIM, GALLADE!
VROOOOOOM
THAT WAS TOO CLOSE!!
SLASH

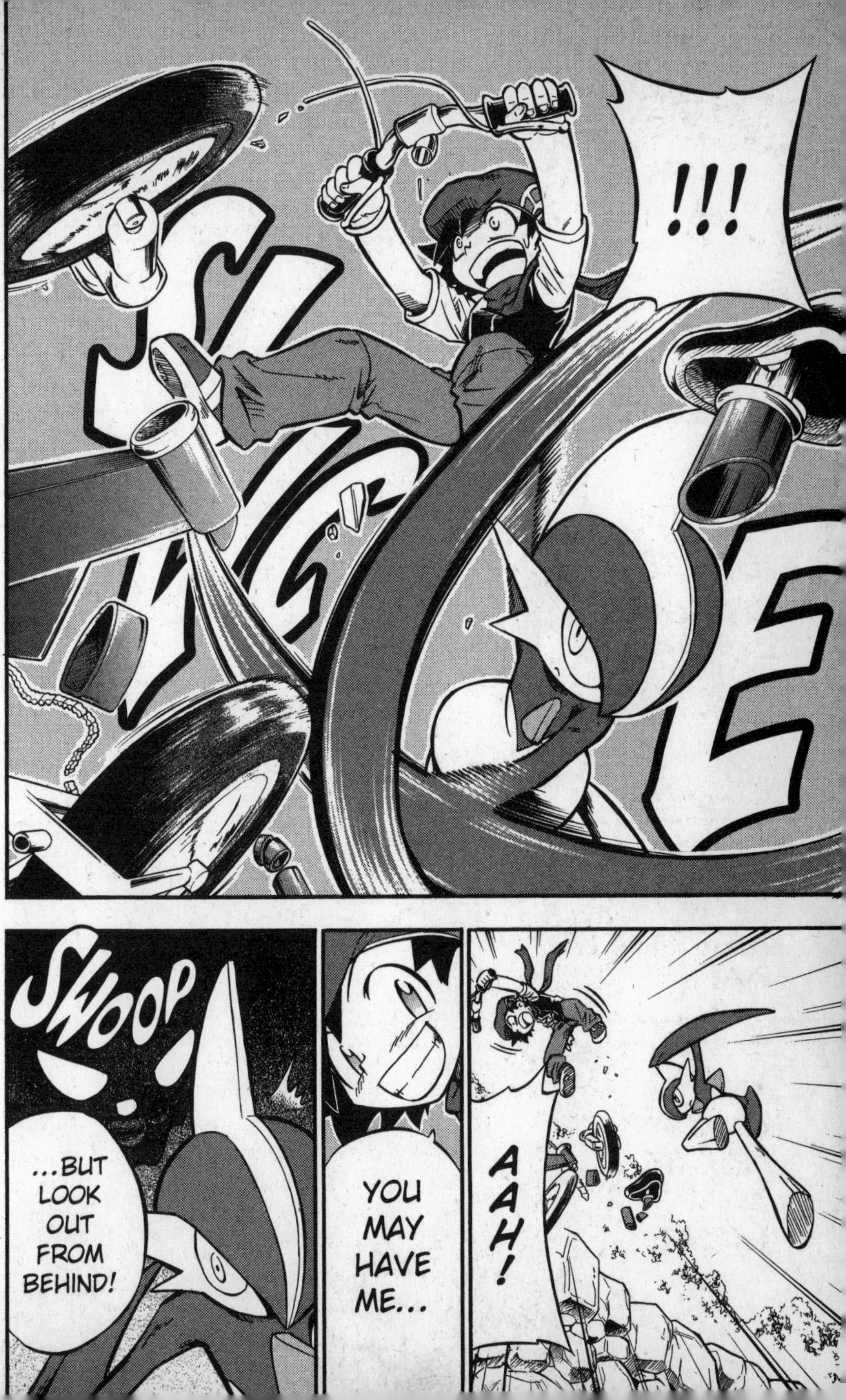
!!!
AAH!
YOU MAY HAVE ME...
SHOOP
...BUT LOOK OUT FROM BEHIND!

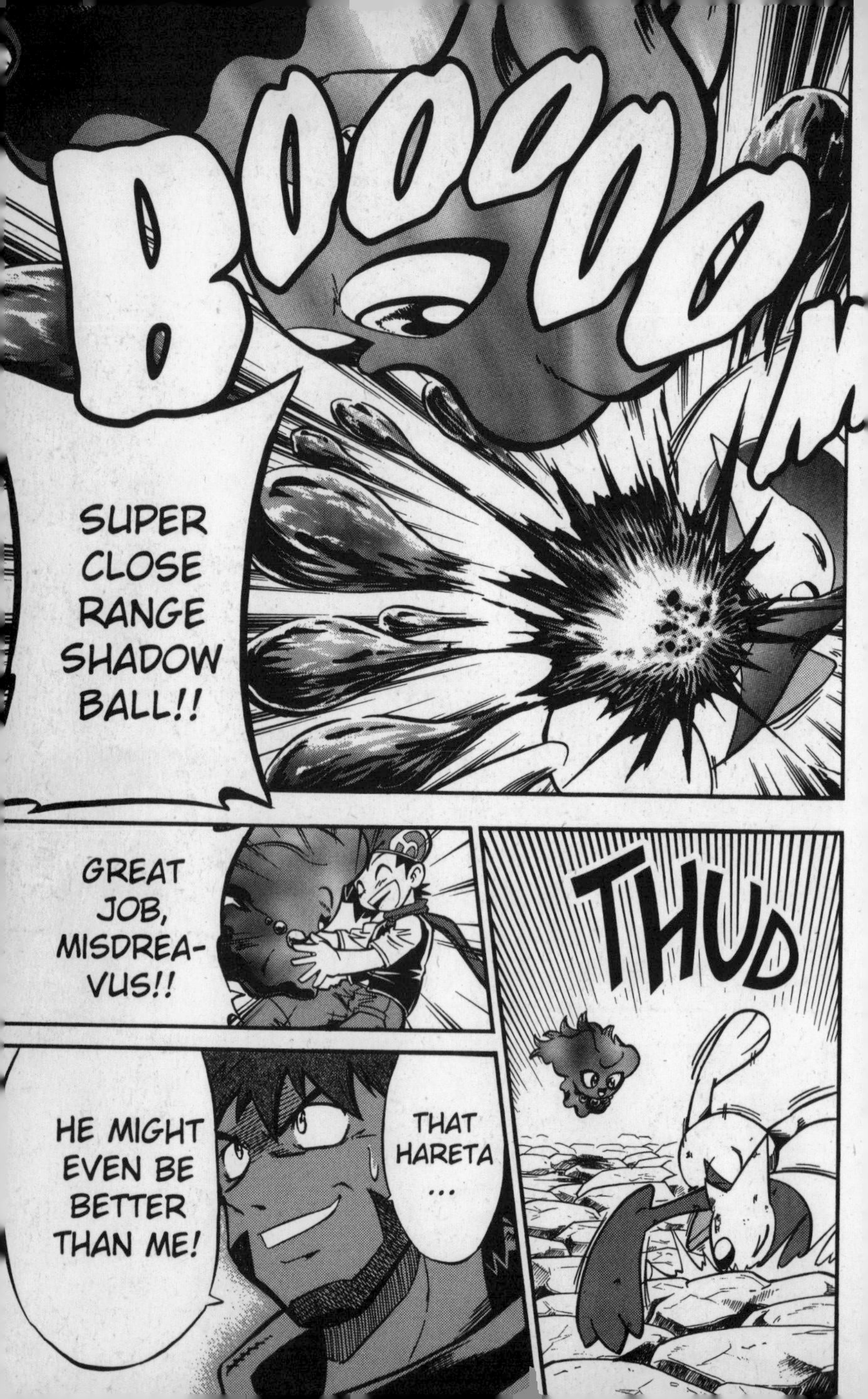
BOOOOOM
SUPER CLOSE RANGE SHADOW BALL!!
THUD
GREAT JOB, MISDREAVUS!!
THAT HARETA...
HE MIGHT EVEN BE BETTER THAN ME!

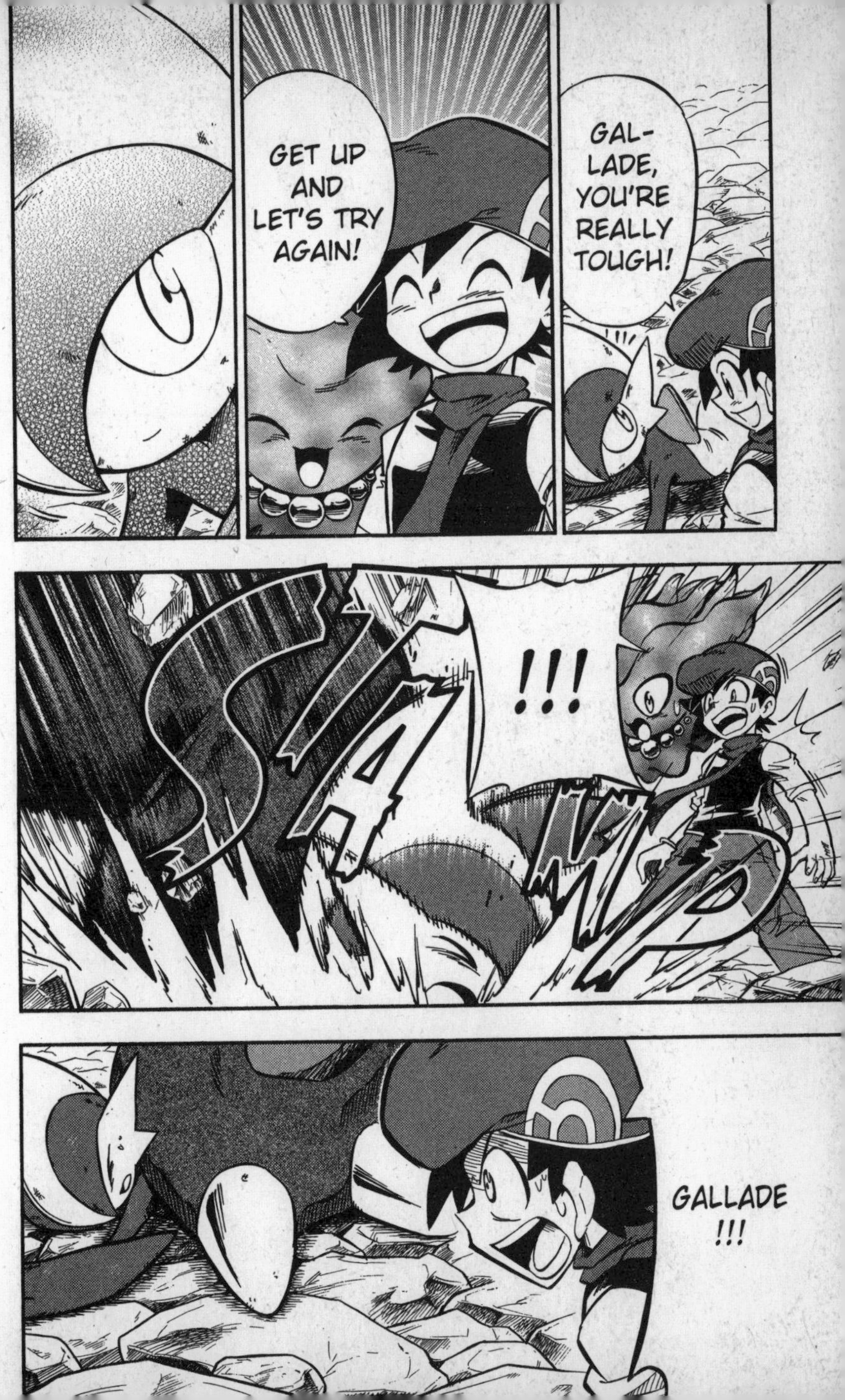
GAL-
LADE,
YOU'RE
REALLY
TOUGH!
GET UP
AND
LET'S TRY
AGAIN!
!!!
SLAM
GALLADE
!!!

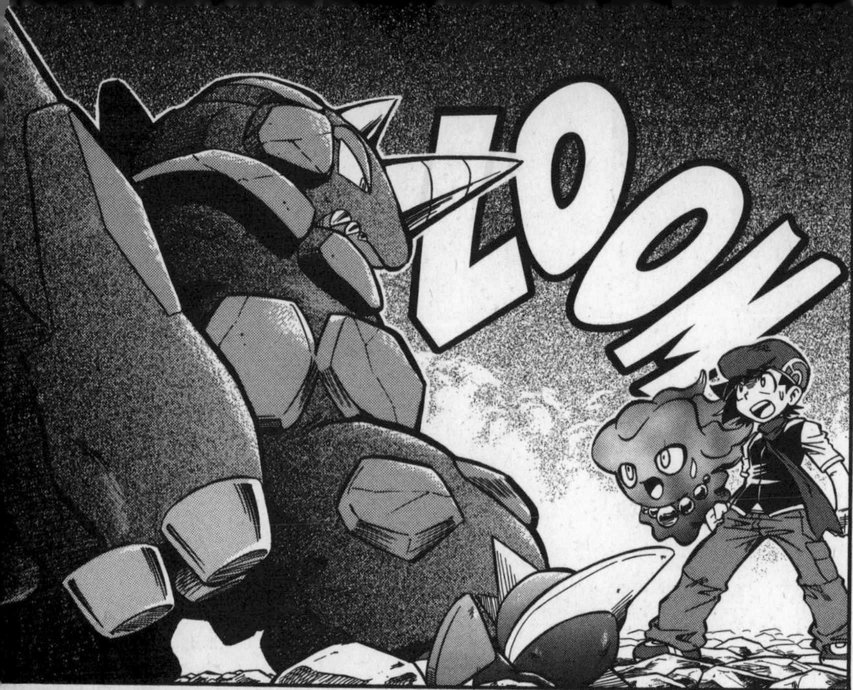
ZOOM

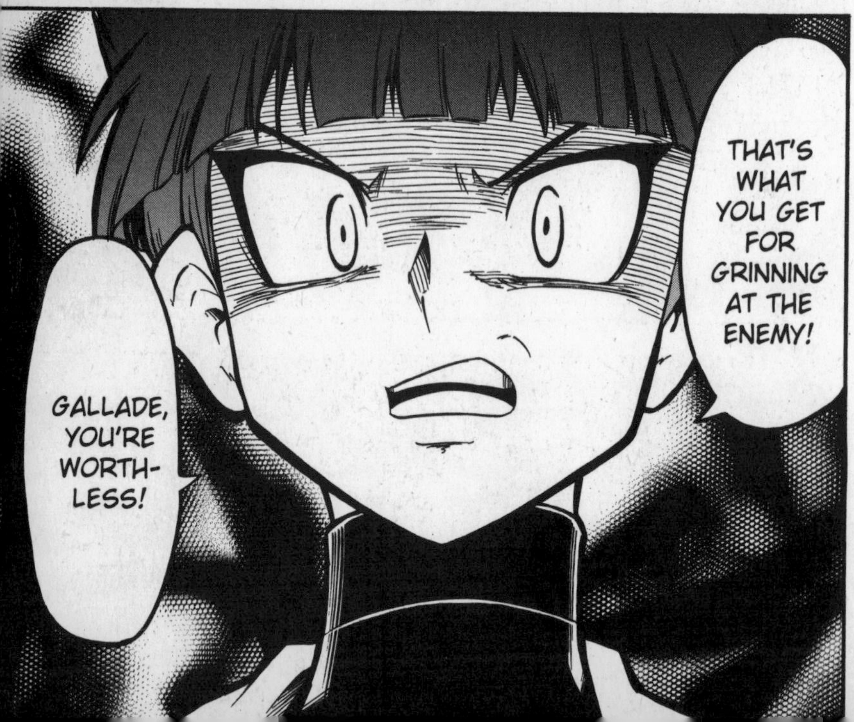
THAT'S WHAT YOU GET FOR GRINNING AT THE ENEMY!
GALLADE, YOU'RE WORTH-LESS!

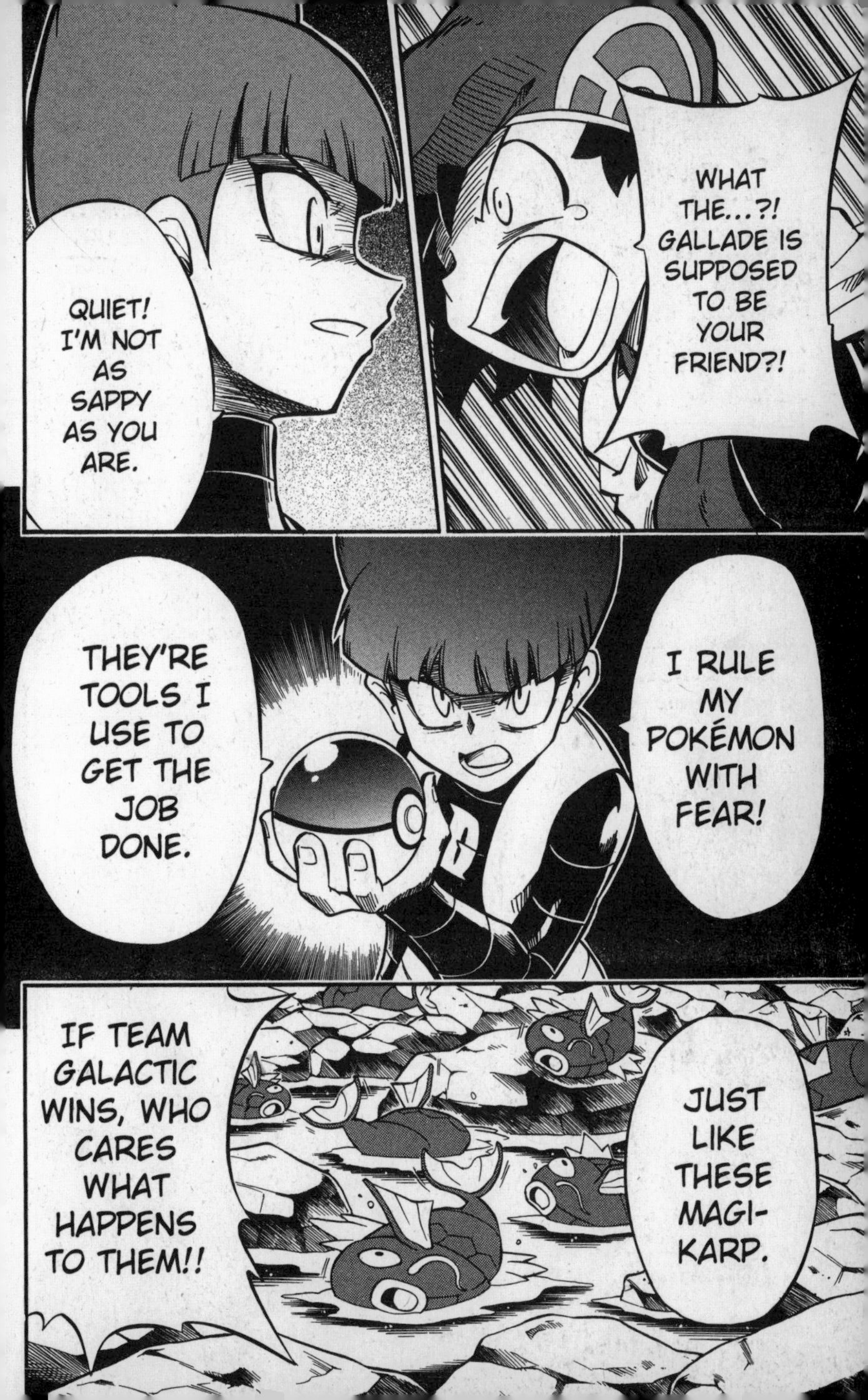
WHAT THE...?! GALLADE IS SUPPOSED TO BE YOUR FRIEND?!
QUIET! I'M NOT AS SAPPY AS YOU ARE.
I RULE MY POKÉMON WITH FEAR!
THEY'RE TOOLS I USE TO GET THE JOB DONE.
JUST LIKE THESE MAGI-KARP.
IF TEAM GALACTIC WINS, WHO CARES WHAT HAPPENS TO THEM!!

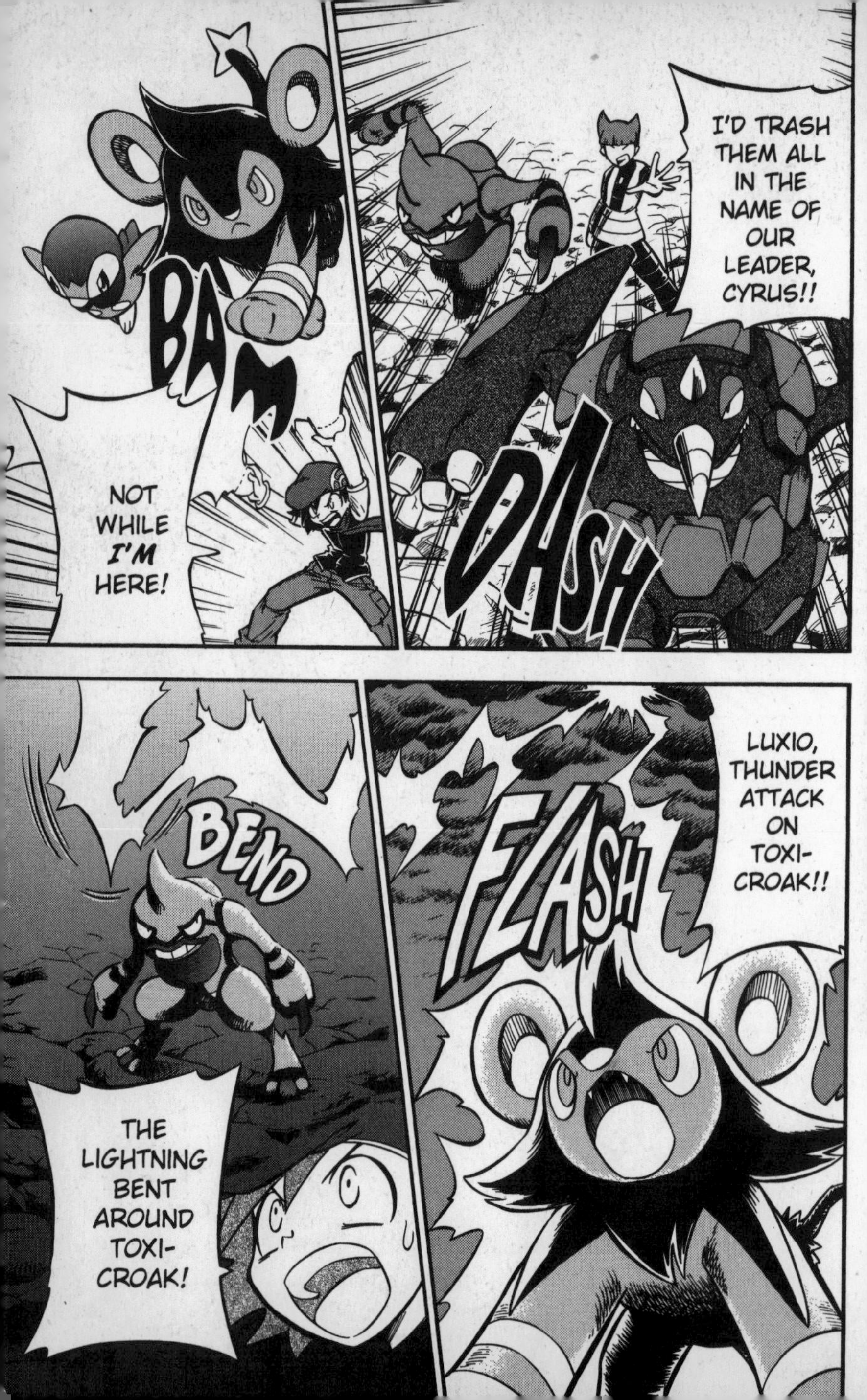
I'D TRASH THEM ALL IN THE NAME OF OUR LEADER, CYRUS!!
DASH
BAM
NOT WHILE I'M HERE!
LUXIO, THUNDER ATTACK ON TOXI-CROAK!!
FLASH
BEND
THE LIGHTNING BENT AROUND TOXI-CROAK!

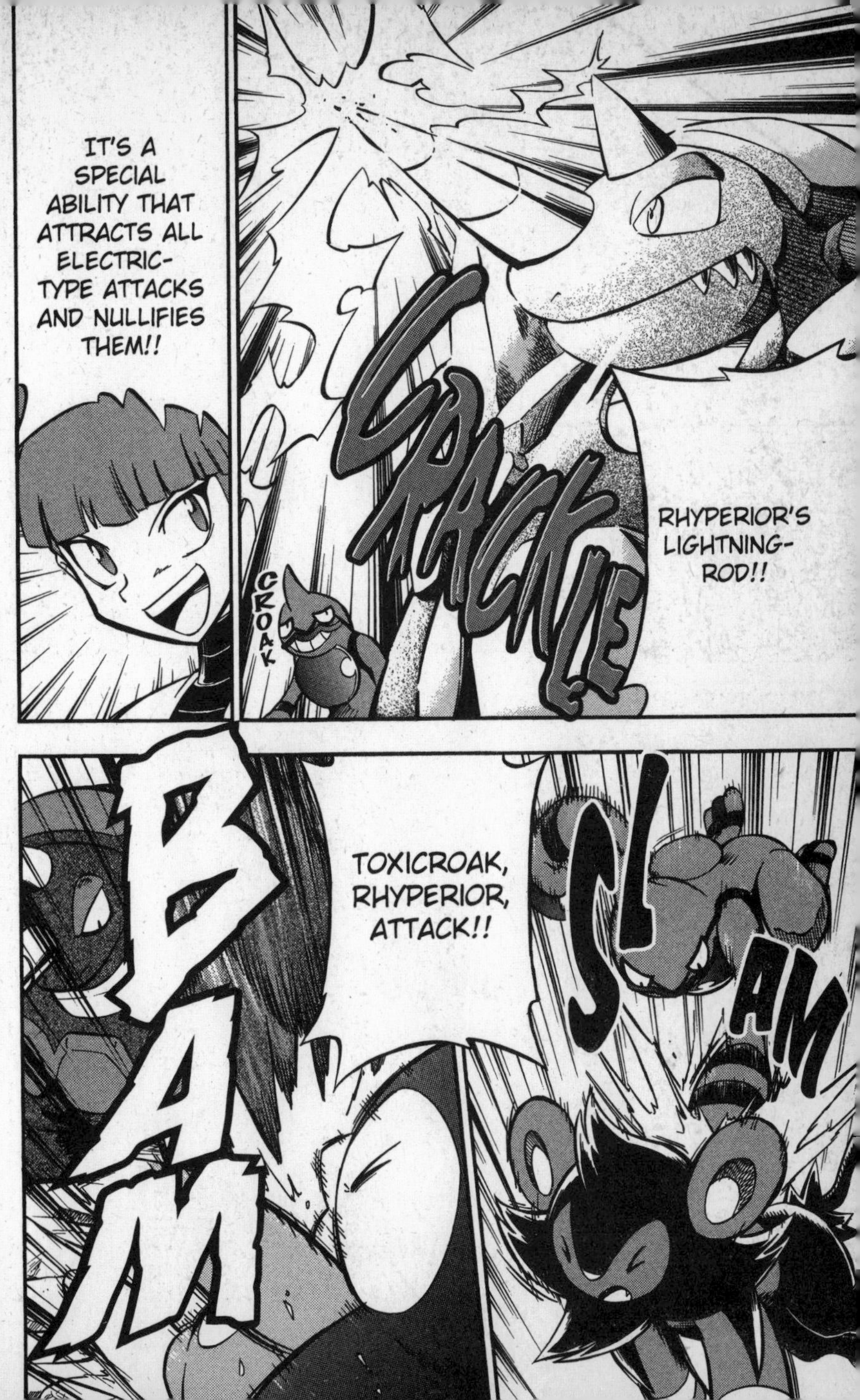
RHYPERIOR'S LIGHTNING-ROD!!
CRACKLE
CROAK
IT'S A SPECIAL ABILITY THAT ATTRACTS ALL ELECTRIC-TYPE ATTACKS AND NULLIFIES THEM!!
SLAM
TOXICROAK, RHYPERIOR, ATTACK!!
BAM

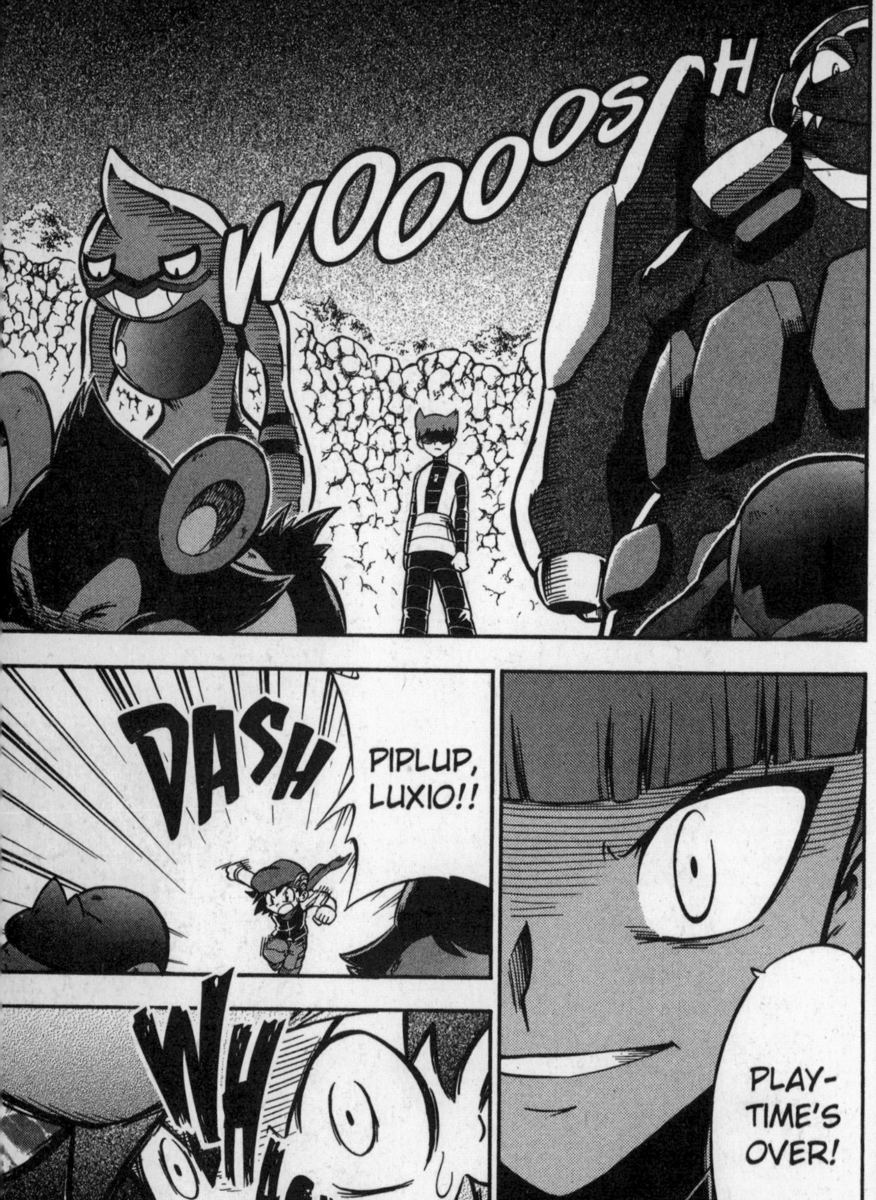
WOOOOOSH
PLAY-TIME'S OVER!
DASH
PIPLUP, LUXIO!!
WHACK

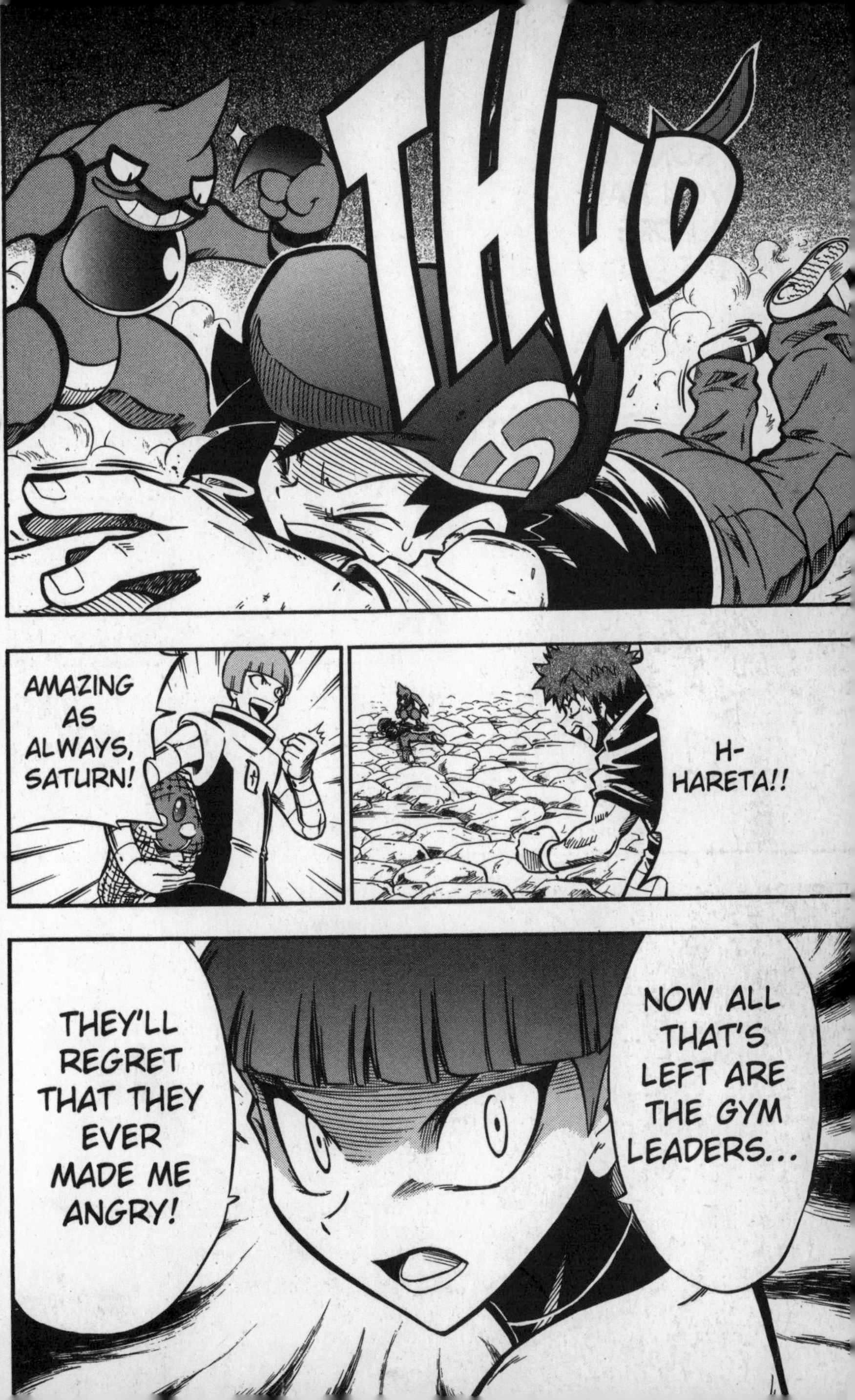
THUD
H-HARETA!!
AMAZING AS ALWAYS, SATURN!
NOW ALL THAT'S LEFT ARE THE GYM LEADERS...
THEY'LL REGRET THAT THEY EVER MADE ME ANGRY!

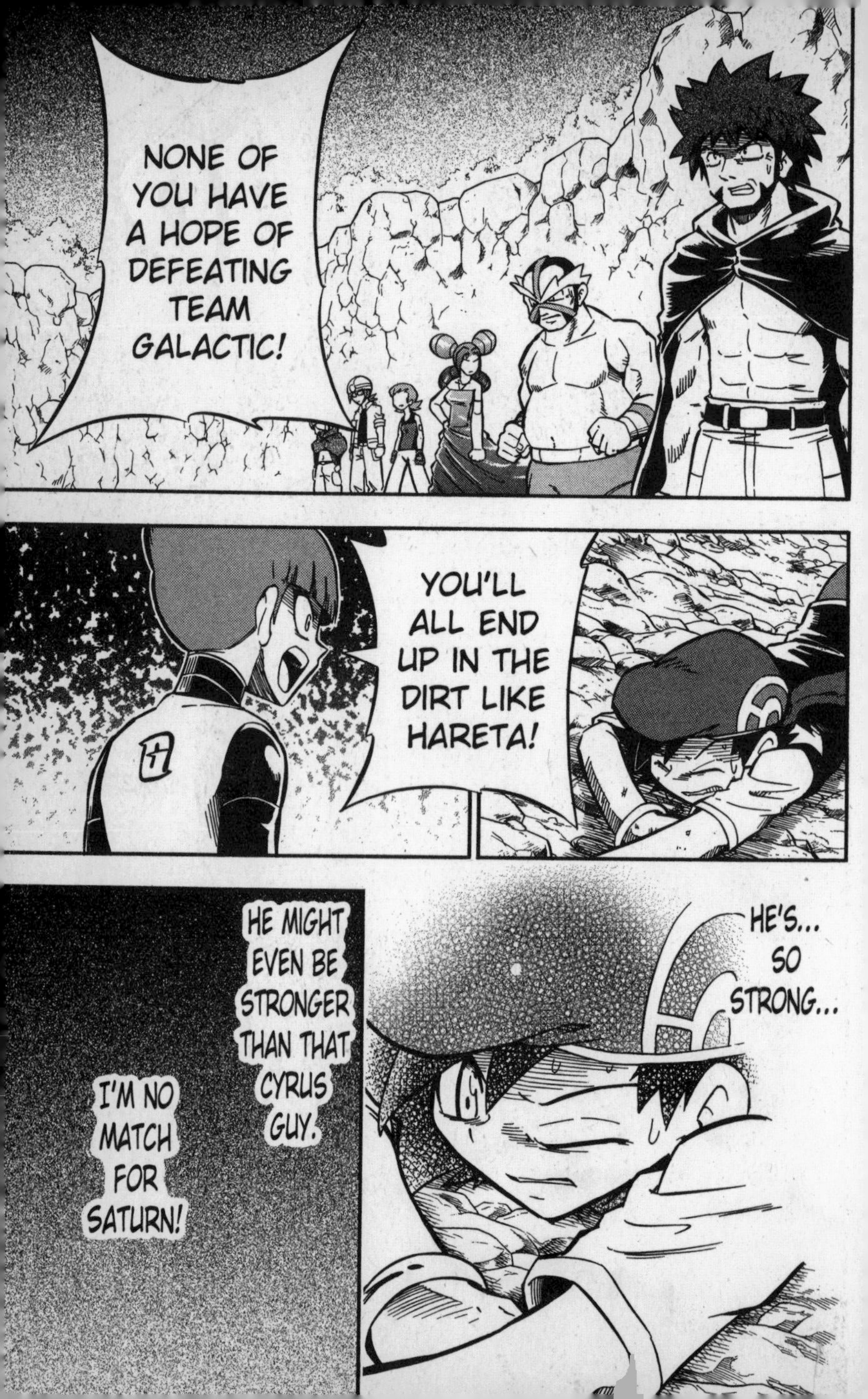
NONE OF YOU HAVE A HOPE OF DEFEATING TEAM GALACTIC!
YOU'LL ALL END UP IN THE DIRT LIKE HARETA!
HE'S... SO STRONG...
HE MIGHT EVEN BE STRONGER THAN THAT CYRUS GUY.
I'M NO MATCH FOR SATURN!

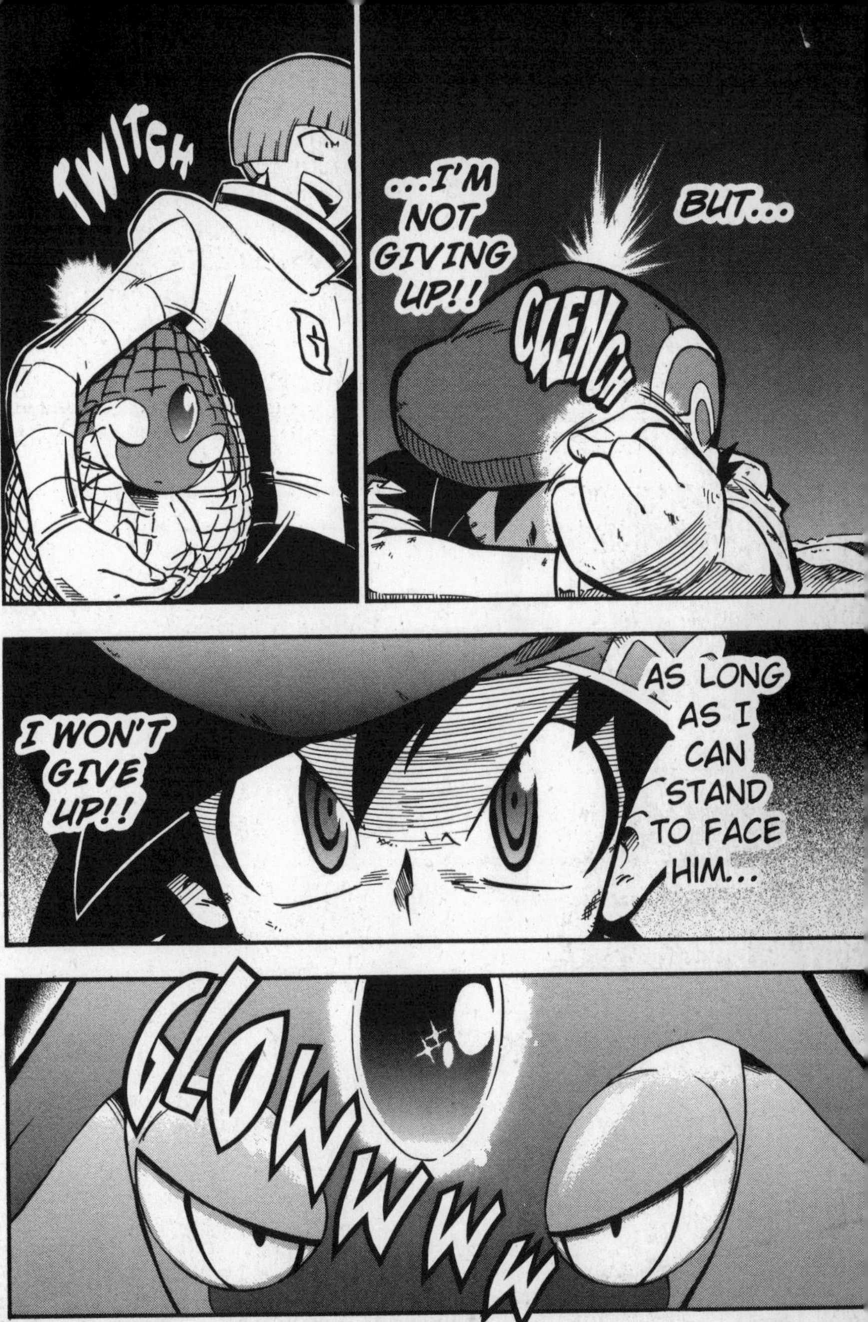
BUT...
...I'M NOT GIVING UP!!
CLENCH
TWITCH
AS LONG AS I CAN STAND TO FACE HIM...
I WON'T GIVE UP!!
GLOWWWWWWW

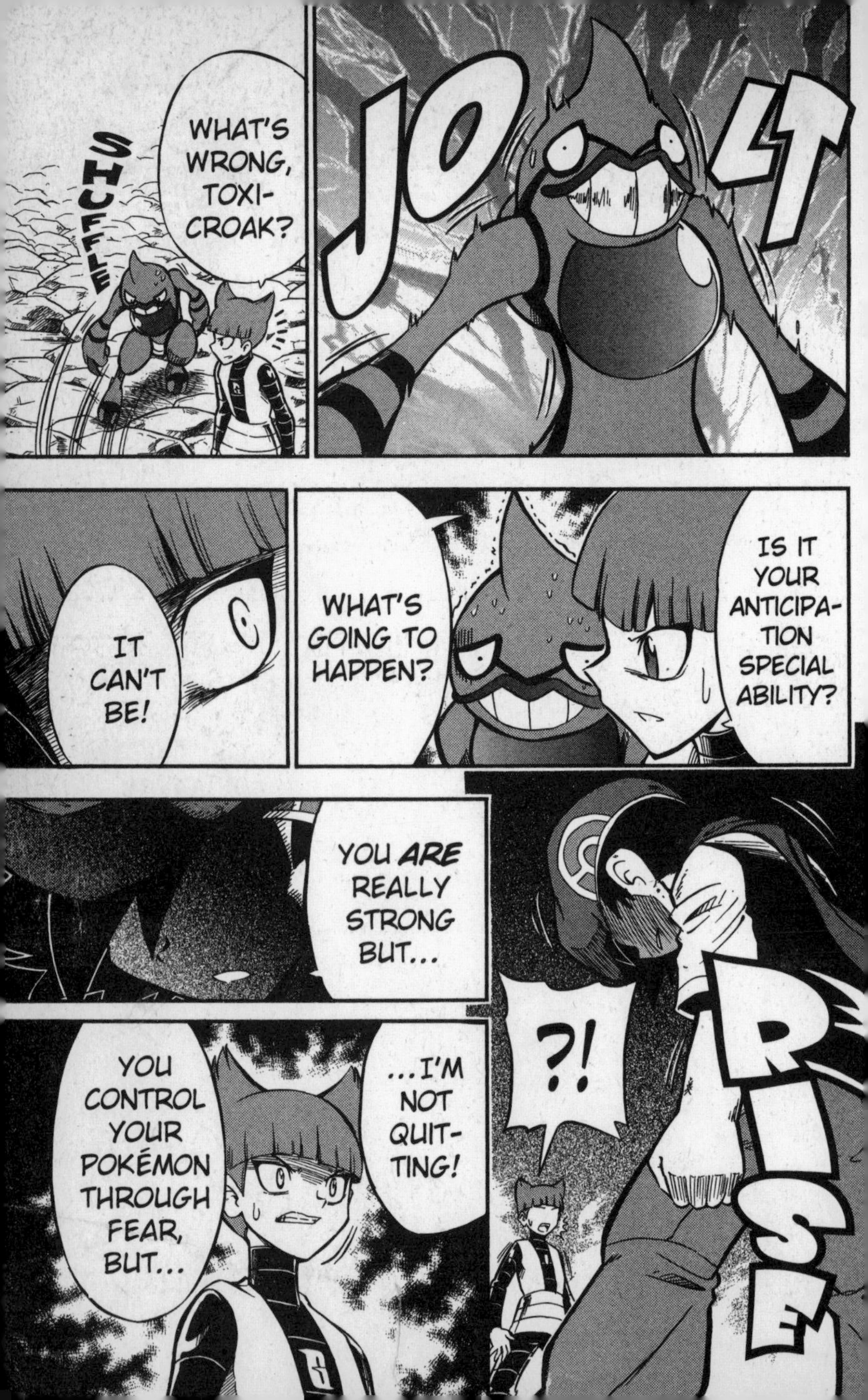
JOLT
WHAT'S WRONG, TOXI-CROAK?
SHUFFLE
IS IT YOUR ANTICIPA-TION SPECIAL ABILITY?
WHAT'S GOING TO HAPPEN?
IT CAN'T BE!
?!
RISE
YOU *ARE* REALLY STRONG BUT...
...I'M NOT QUIT-TING!
YOU CONTROL YOUR POKÉMON THROUGH FEAR, BUT...

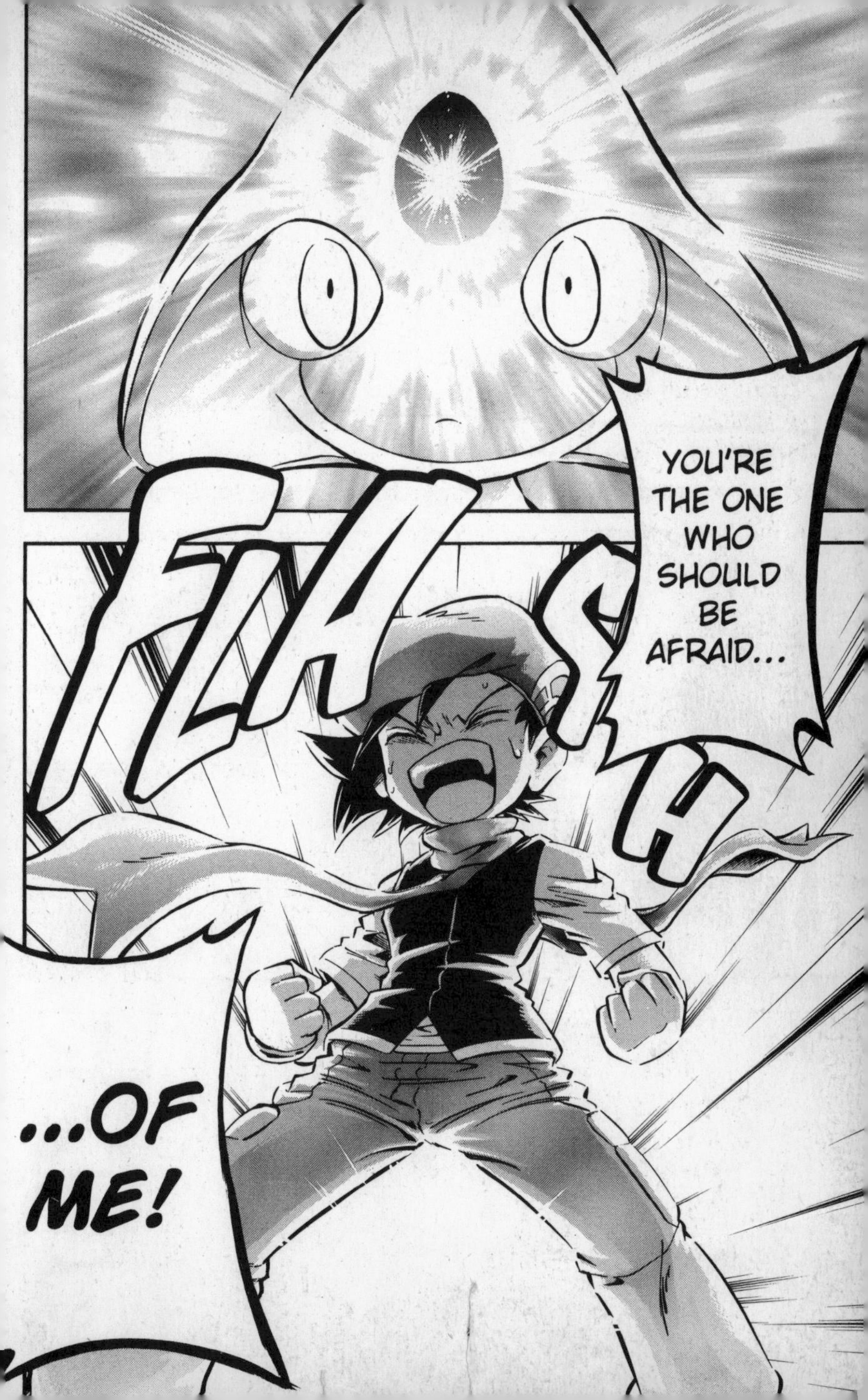
FLASH
YOU'RE THE ONE WHO SHOULD BE AFRAID...
...OF ME!

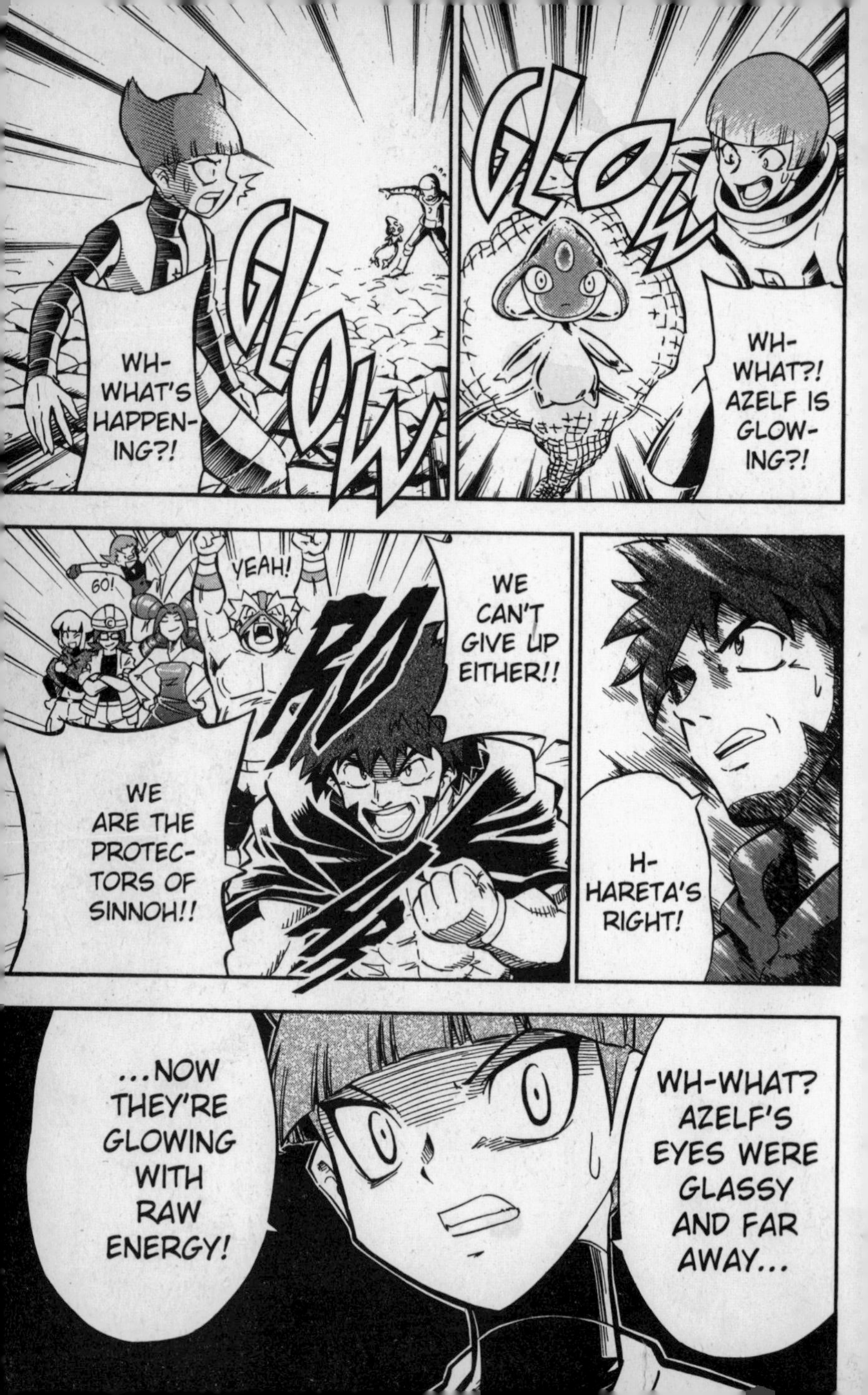
GLOW
WH- WHAT?! AZELF IS GLOW- ING?!
WH- WHAT'S HAPPEN- ING?!
GLOW
H- HARETA'S RIGHT!
WE CAN'T GIVE UP EITHER!!
YEAH!
GO!
WE ARE THE PROTEC- TORS OF SINNOH!!
WH-WHAT? AZELF'S EYES WERE GLASSY AND FAR AWAY...
...NOW THEY'RE GLOWING WITH RAW ENERGY!

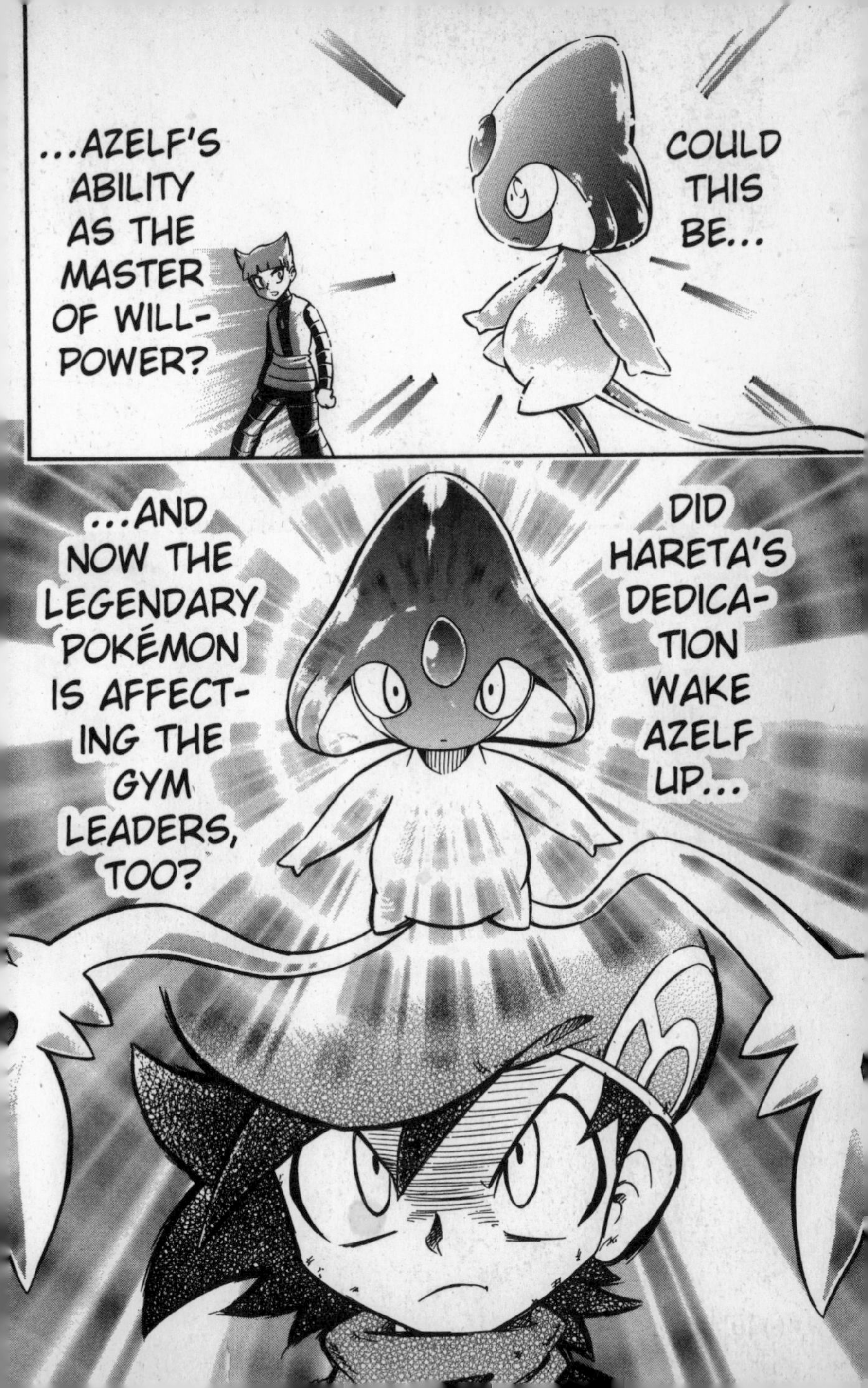
COULD THIS BE...
...AZELF'S ABILITY AS THE MASTER OF WILL-POWER?
DID HARETA'S DEDICATION WAKE AZELF UP...
...AND NOW THE LEGENDARY POKÉMON IS AFFECTING THE GYM LEADERS, TOO?

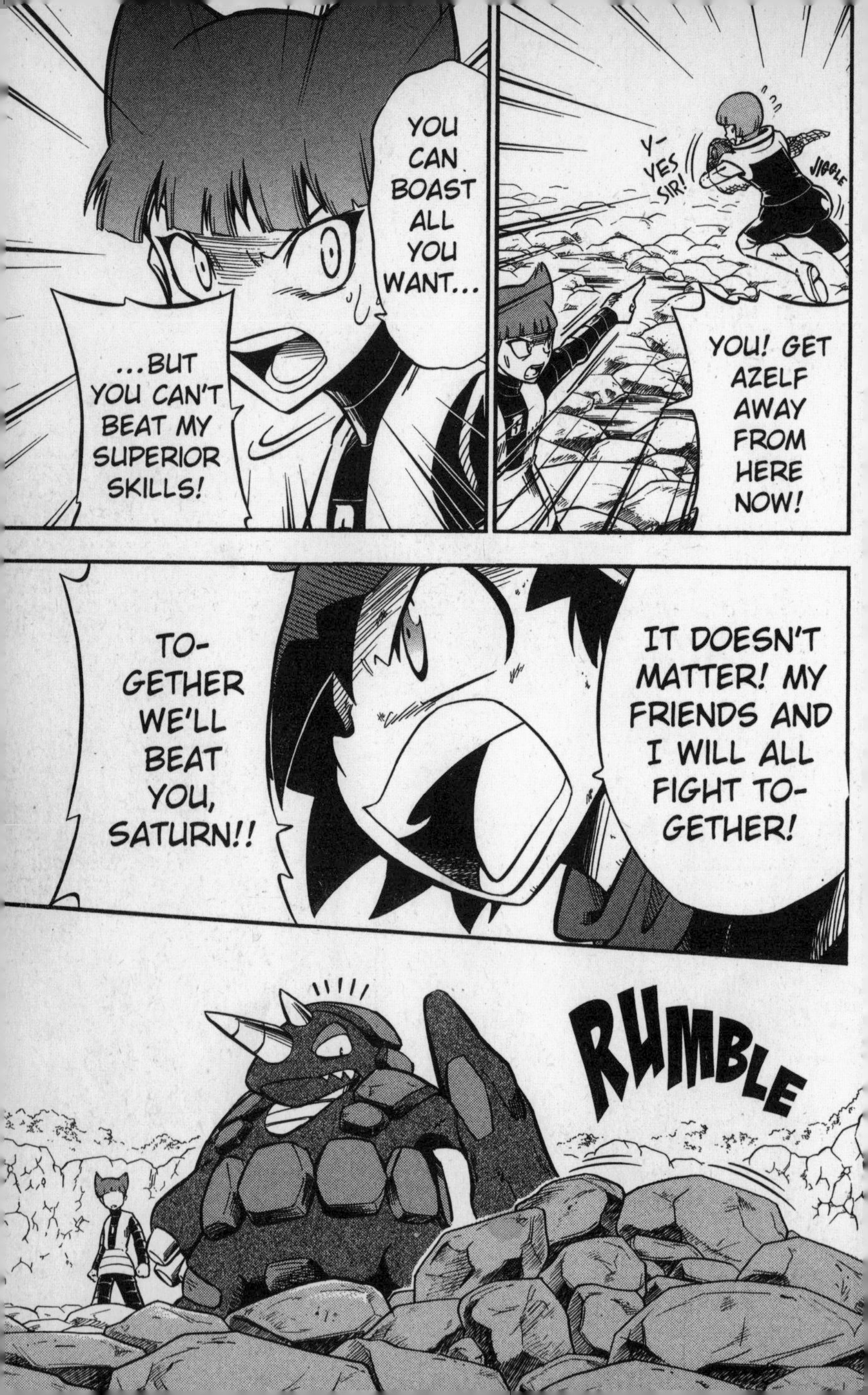
Y-YES SIR!
JIGGLE
YOU! GET AZELF AWAY FROM HERE NOW!
YOU CAN BOAST ALL YOU WANT...
...BUT YOU CAN'T BEAT MY SUPERIOR SKILLS!
IT DOESN'T MATTER! MY FRIENDS AND I WILL ALL FIGHT TO-GETHER!
TO-GETHER WE'LL BEAT YOU, SATURN!!
RUMBLE

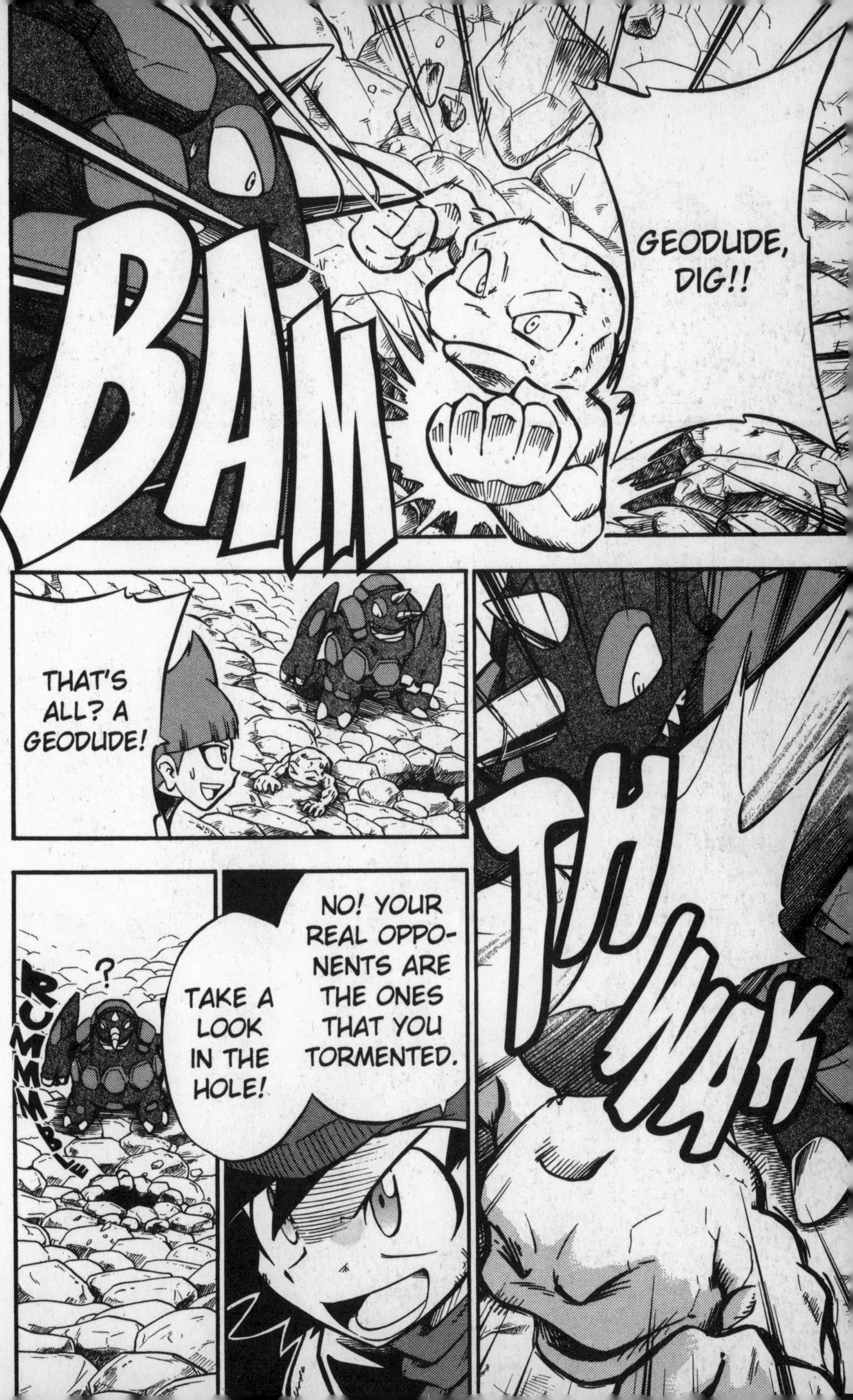
GEODUDE, DIG!!
BAM
THWAK
THAT'S ALL? A GEODUDE!
NO! YOUR REAL OPPONENTS ARE THE ONES THAT YOU TORMENTED.
TAKE A LOOK IN THE HOLE!
?
RUMMMBLE

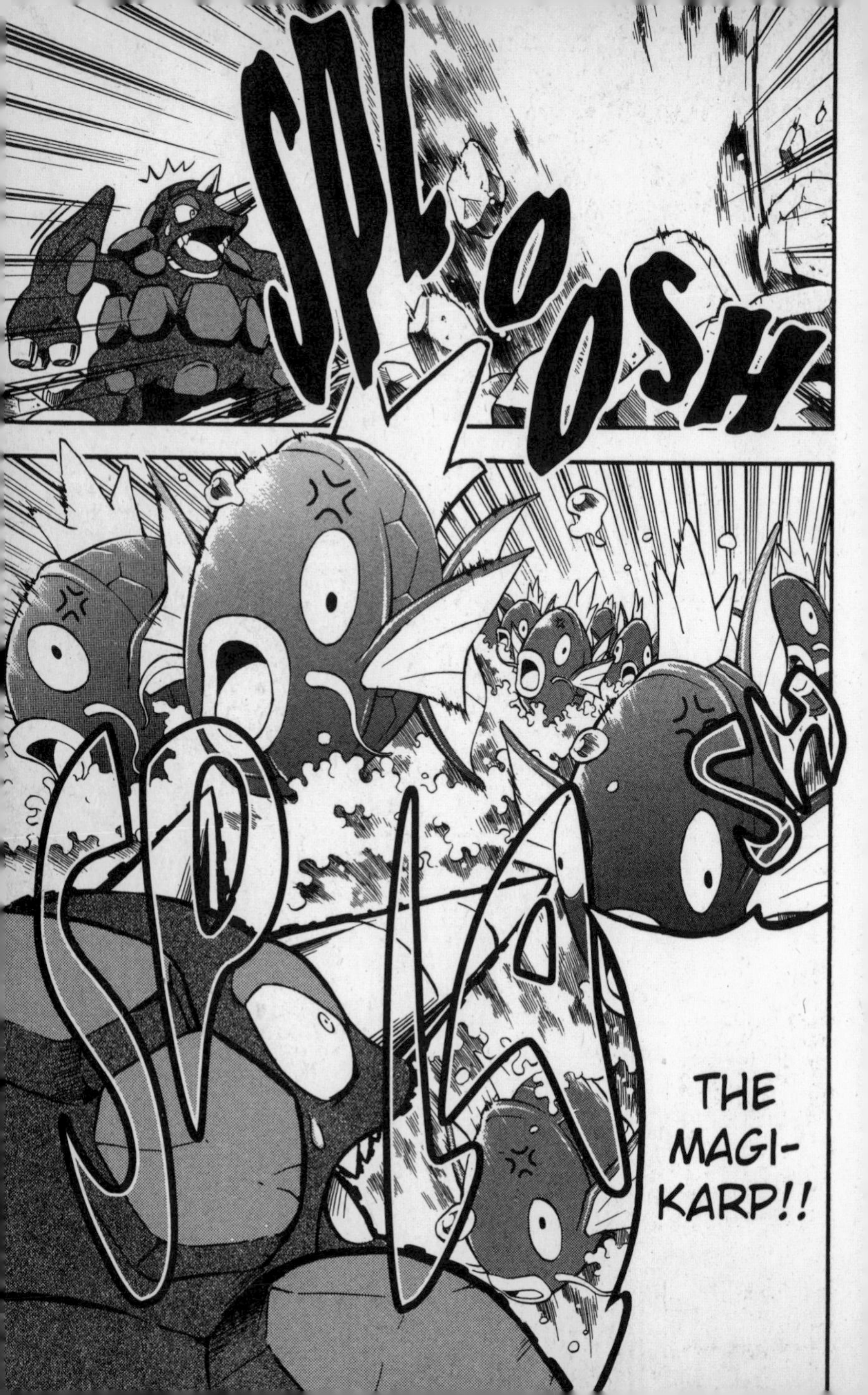
SPLOOSH
SPLASH
THE MAGI-KARP!!

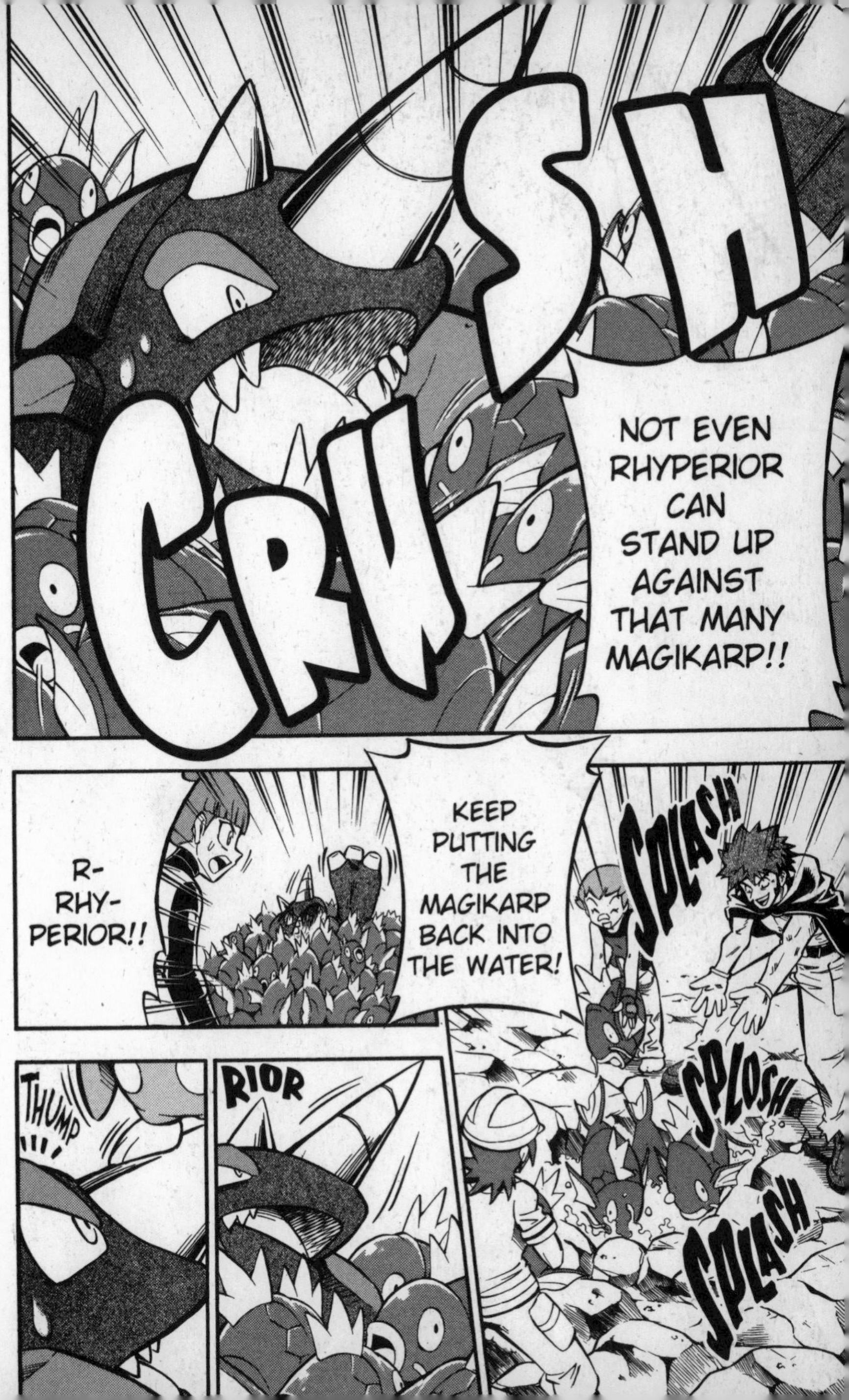
CRUSH
NOT EVEN RHYPERIOR CAN STAND UP AGAINST THAT MANY MAGIKARP!!
KEEP PUTTING THE MAGIKARP BACK INTO THE WATER!
SPLASH
SPLOSH
SPLASH
R-RHY-PERIOR!!
RIOR
THUMP

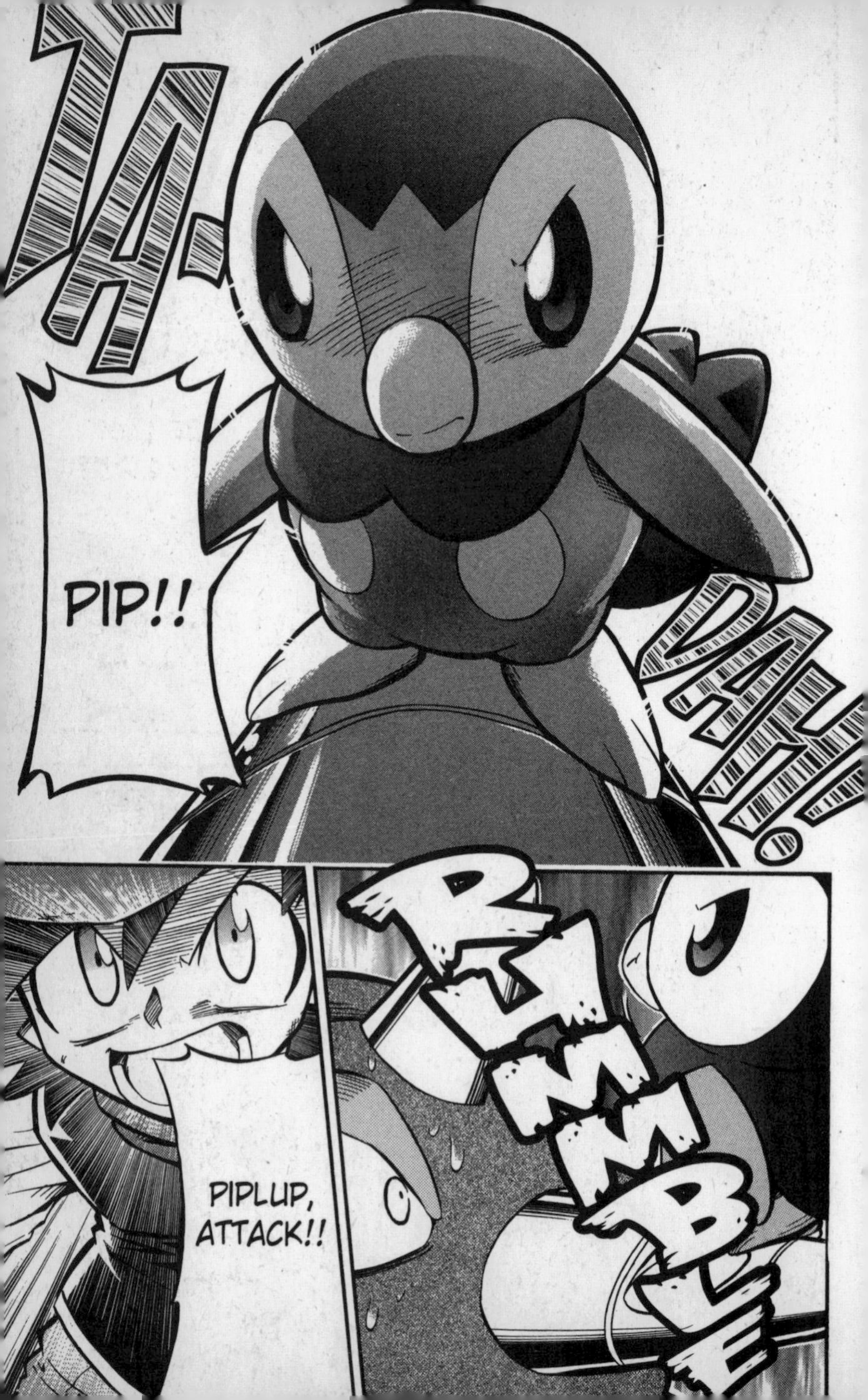
TA-
DAH!!
PIP!!
RMMBLE
PIPLUP, ATTACK!!

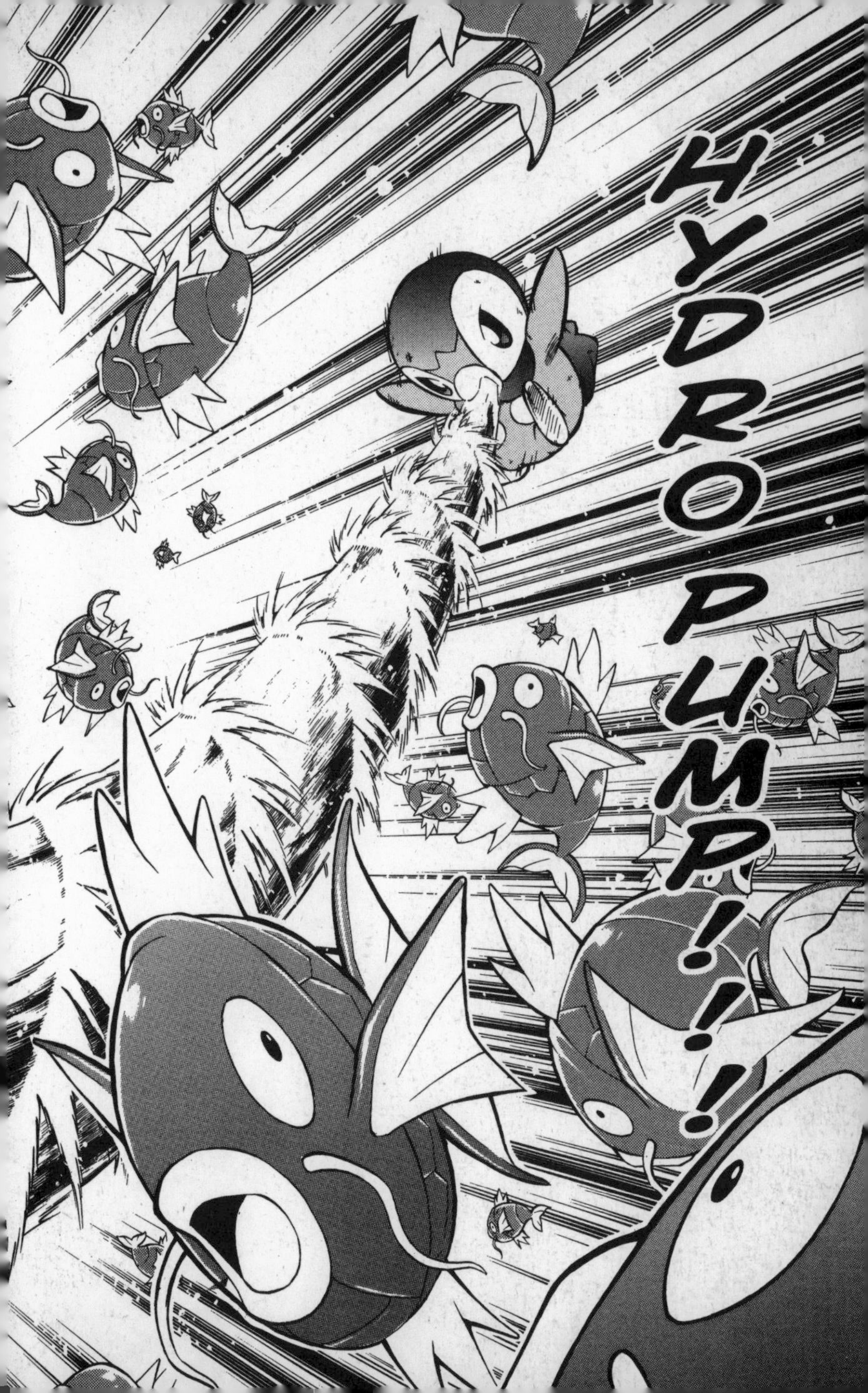
HYDRO PUMP!!!

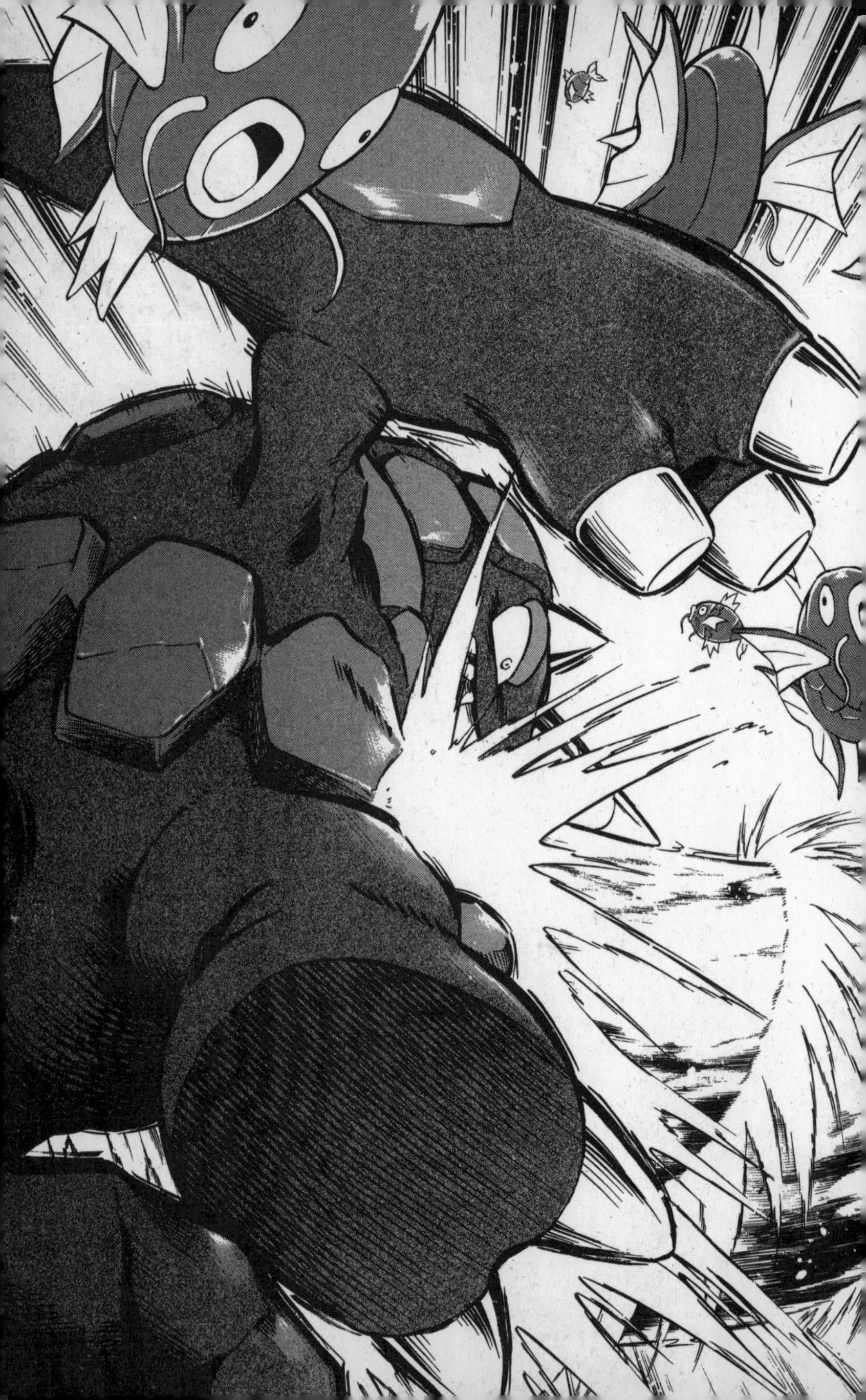

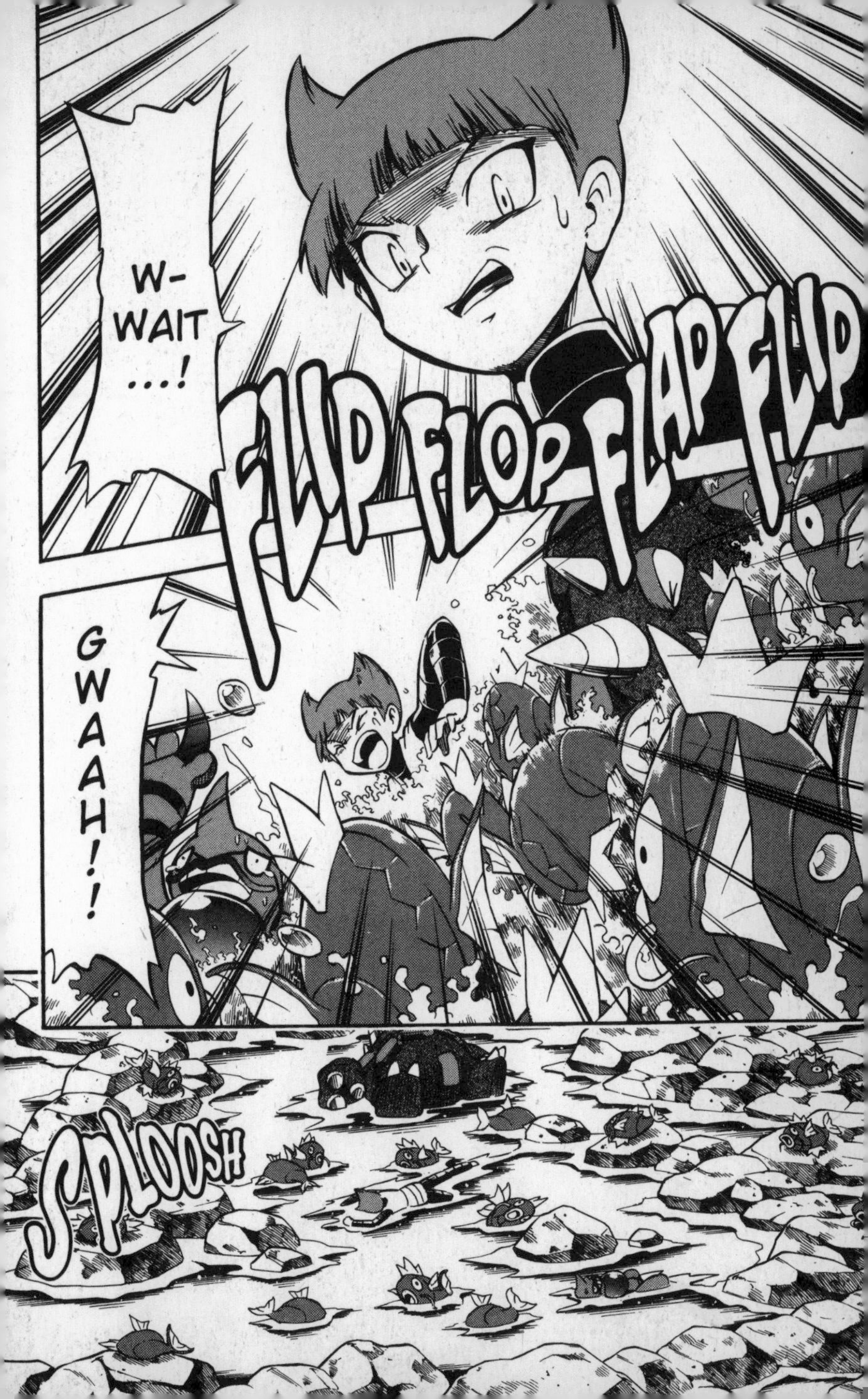
W-WAIT...!
FLIP FLOP FLAP FLIP
GWAAAH!!
SPLOOSH

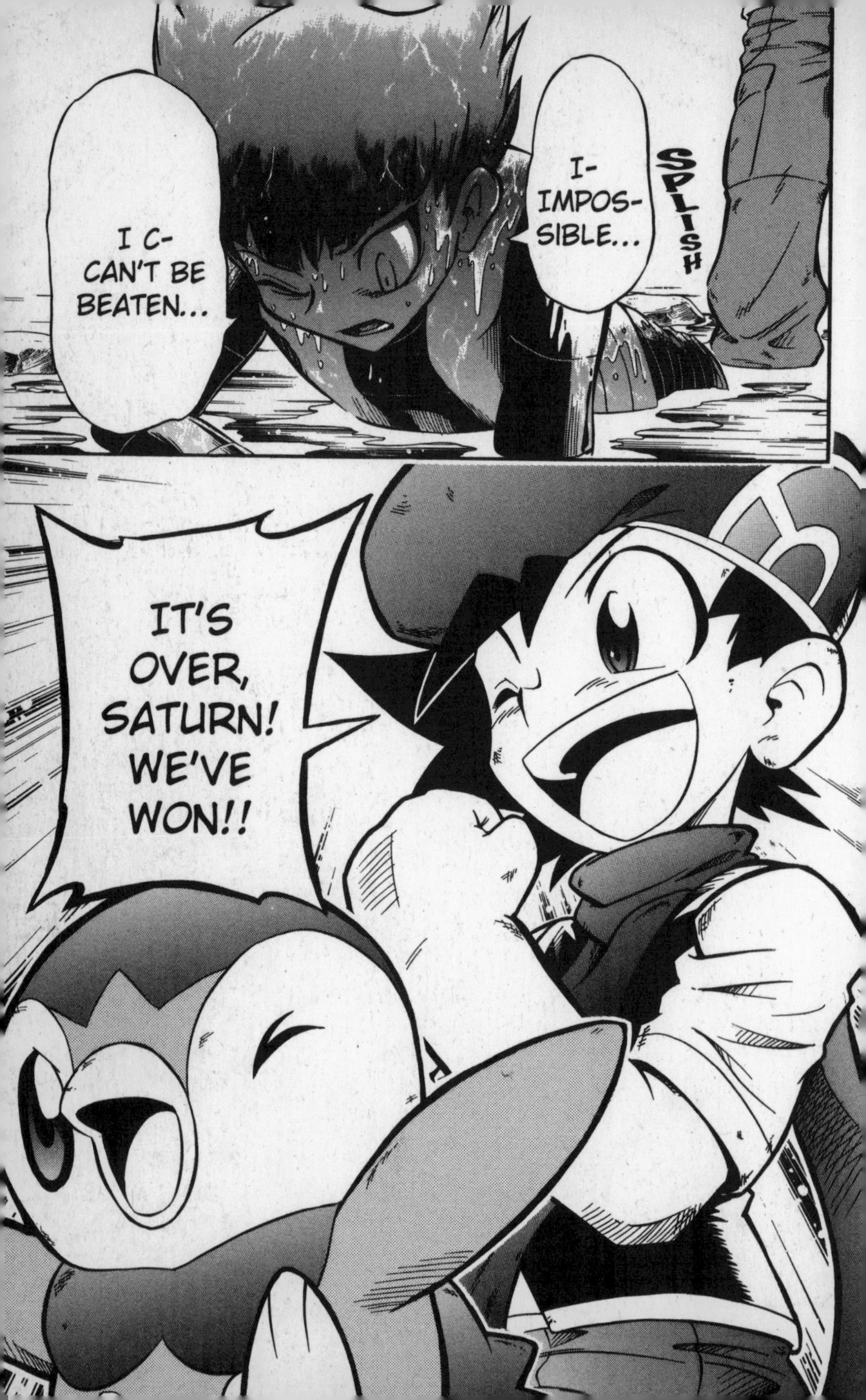
SPLISH
I- IMPOSSIBLE...
I C- CAN'T BE BEATEN...
IT'S OVER, SATURN! WE'VE WON!!

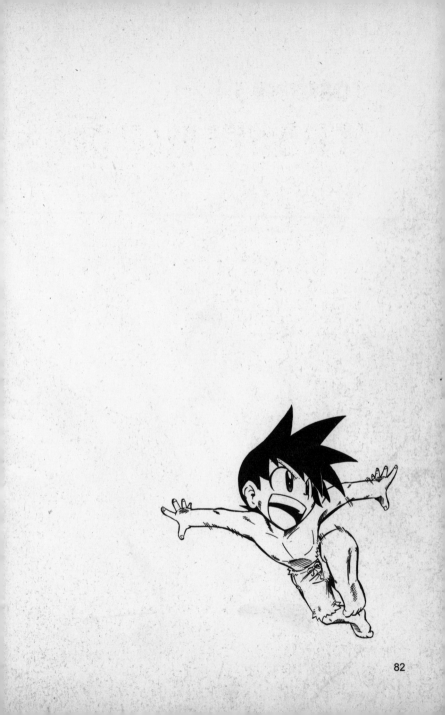

CHAPTER 3
THE BATTLE RAGES ON

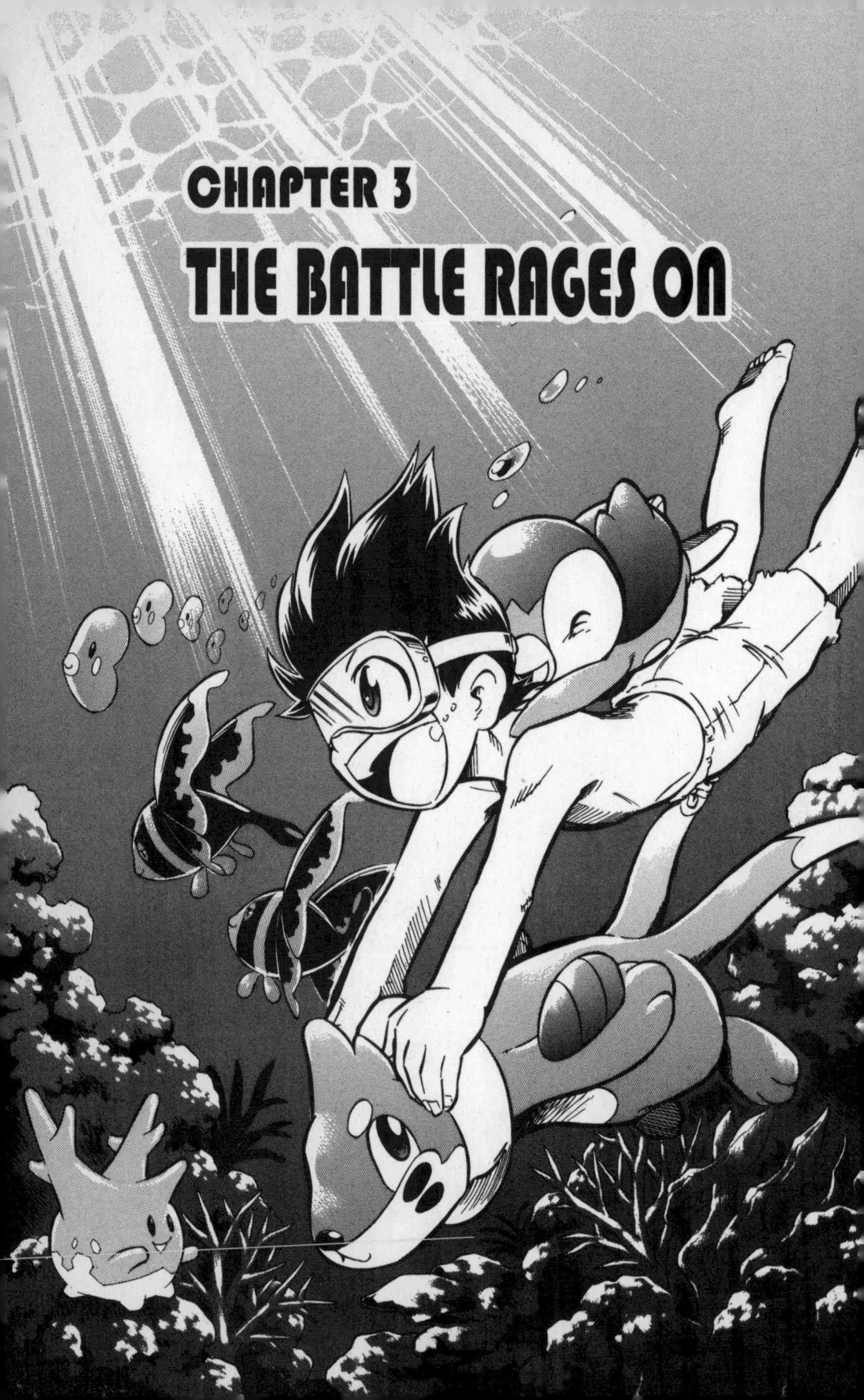

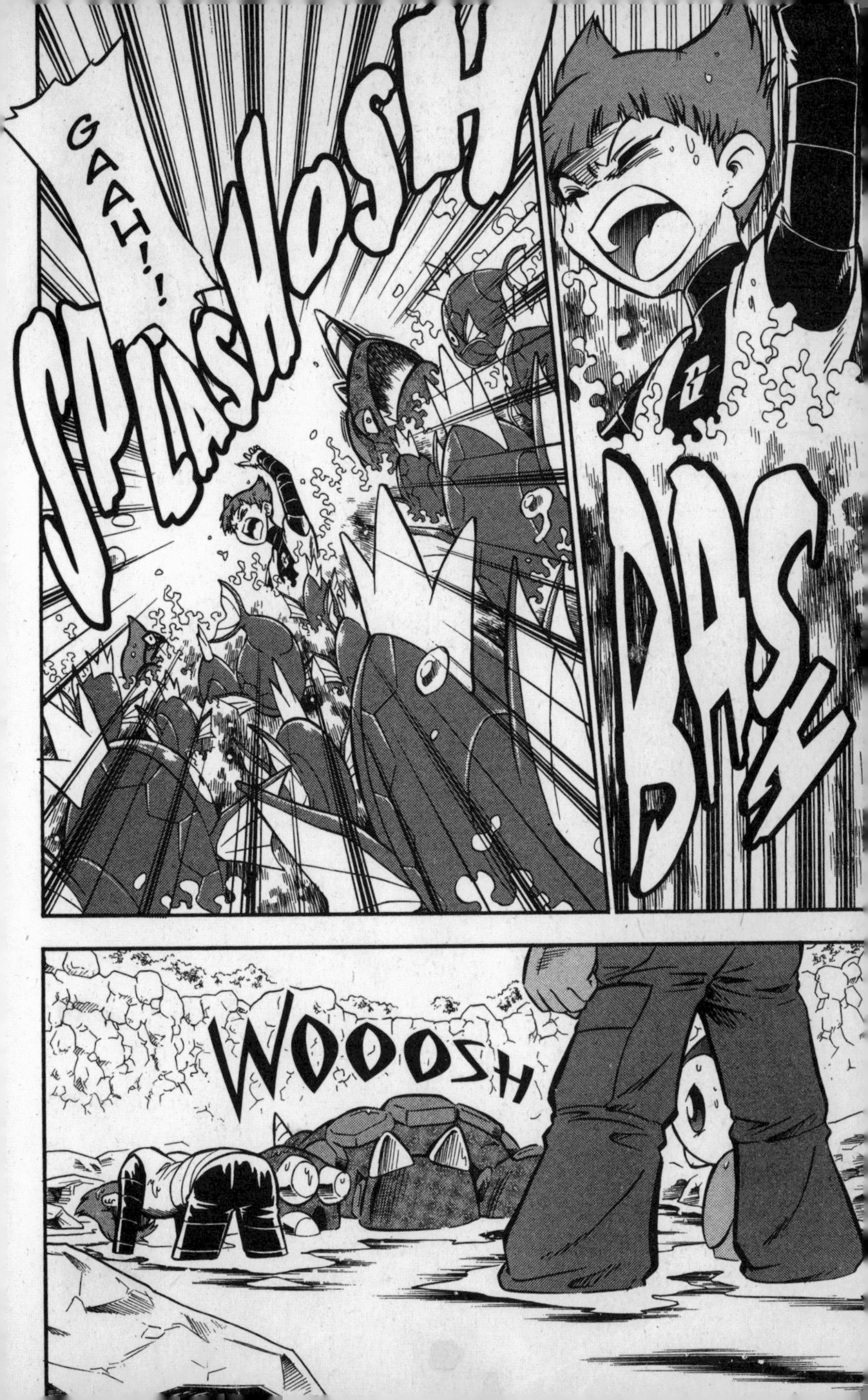
BASH
SPLASHOSH
GAAH!!!
WOOOSH

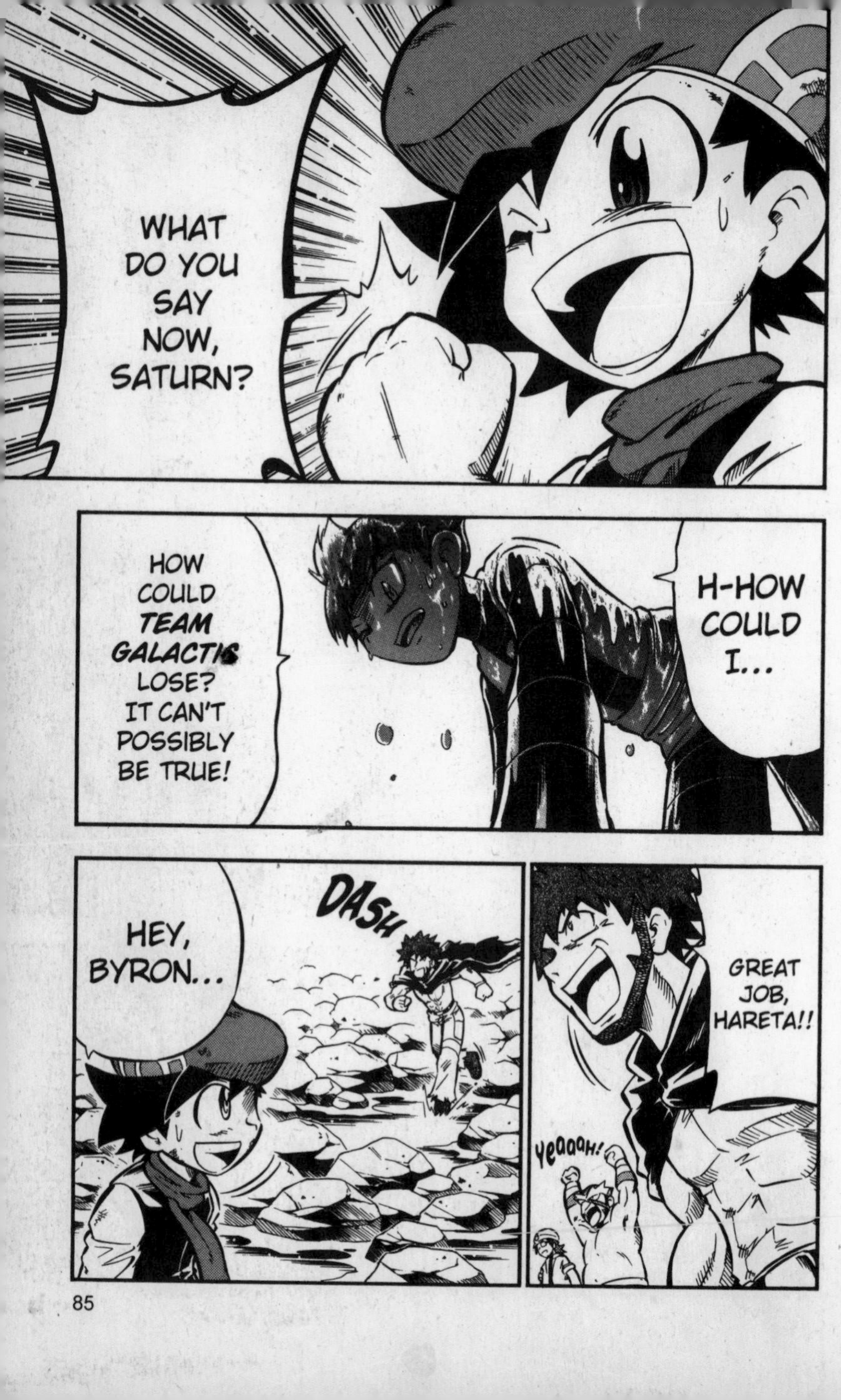
WHAT DO YOU SAY NOW, SATURN?
H-HOW COULD I...
HOW COULD TEAM GALACTIC LOSE? IT CAN'T POSSIBLY BE TRUE!
GREAT JOB, HARETA!!
YEAAAH!
DASH
HEY, BYRON...

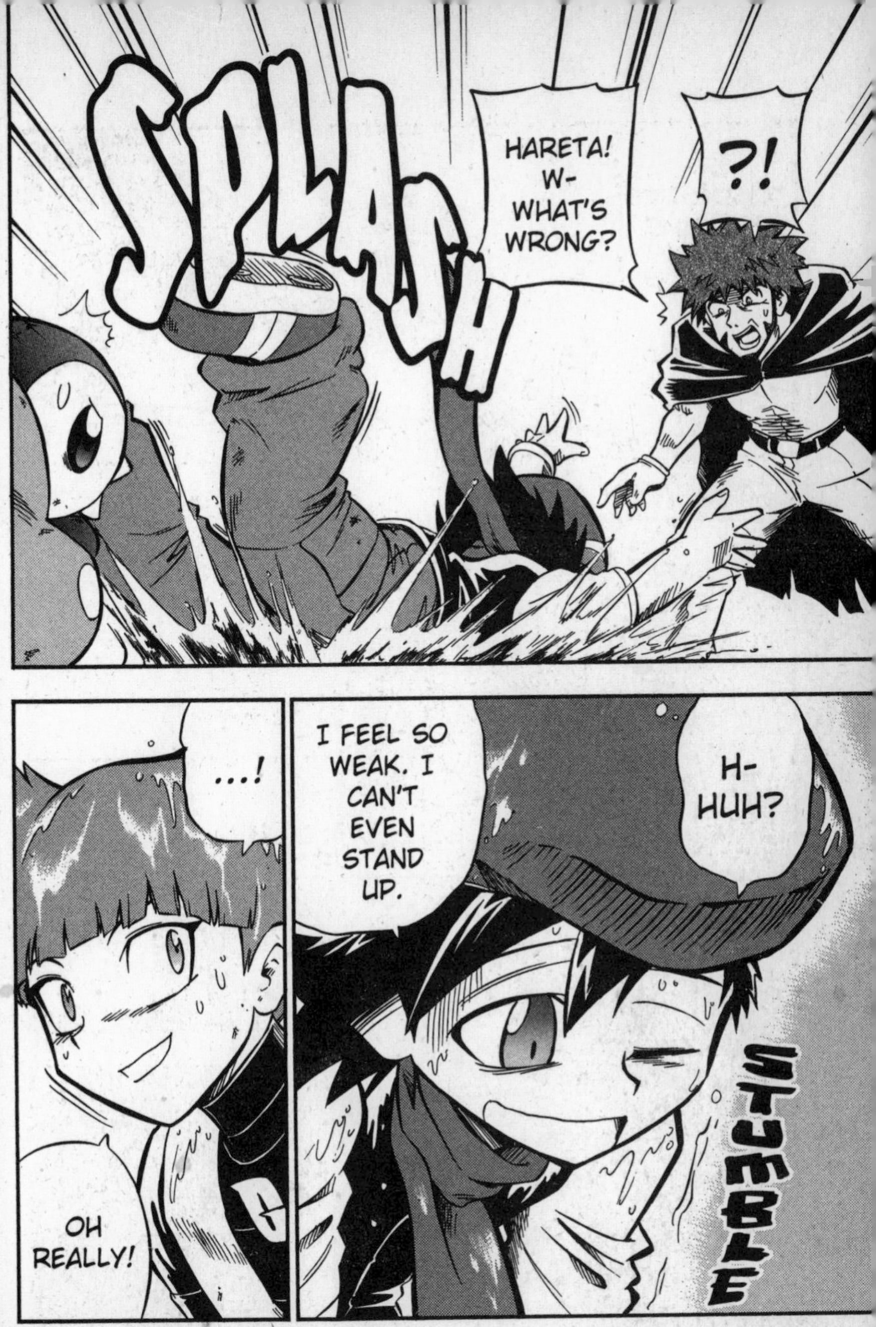
?!
HARETA! W-WHAT'S WRONG?
SPLASH
H-HUH?
I FEEL SO WEAK. I CAN'T EVEN STAND UP.
STUMBLE
...!
OH REALLY!

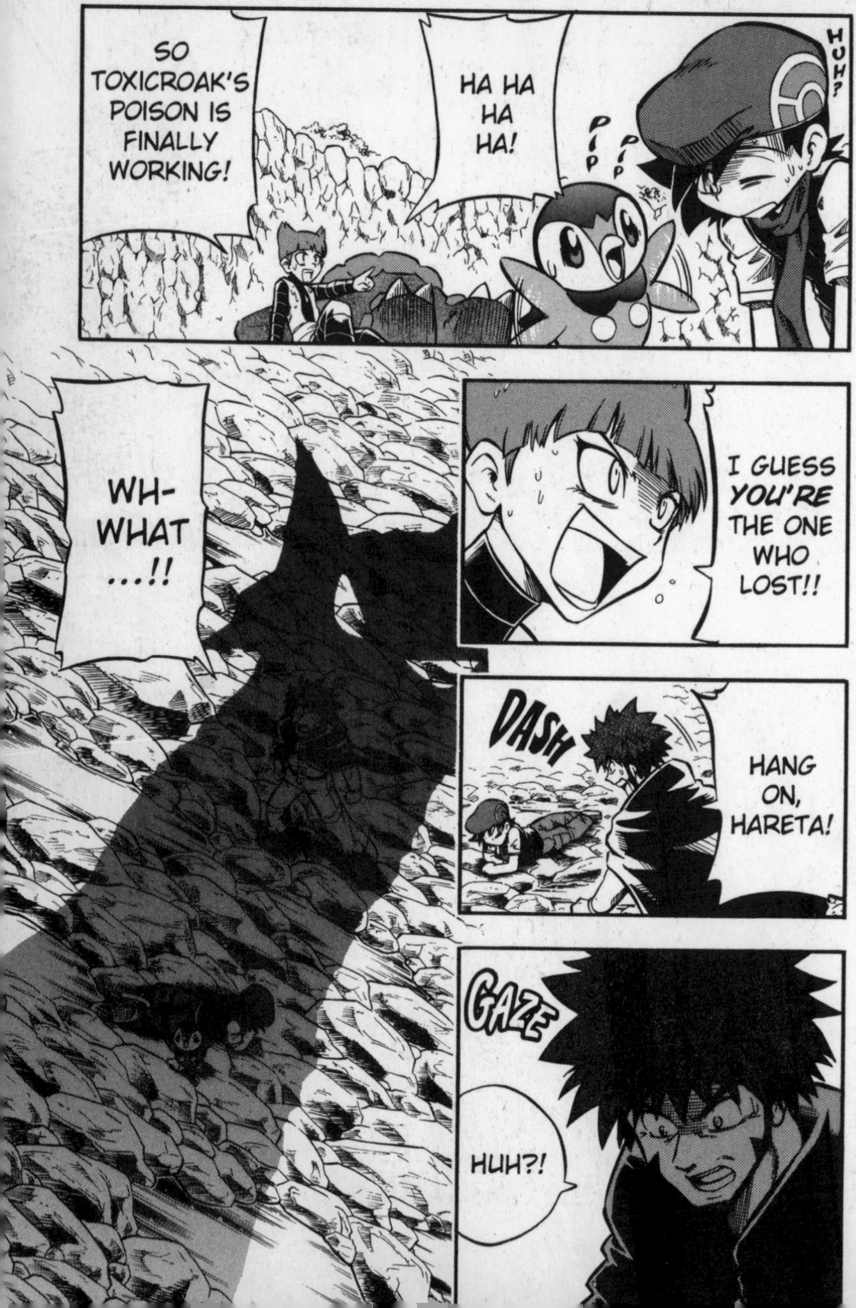
HUH?
PIP PIP
HA HA HA HA!
SO TOXICROAK'S POISON IS FINALLY WORKING!
I GUESS *YOU'RE* THE ONE WHO LOST!!
DASH
HANG ON, HARETA!
GAZE
HUH?!
WH-WHAT ...!!

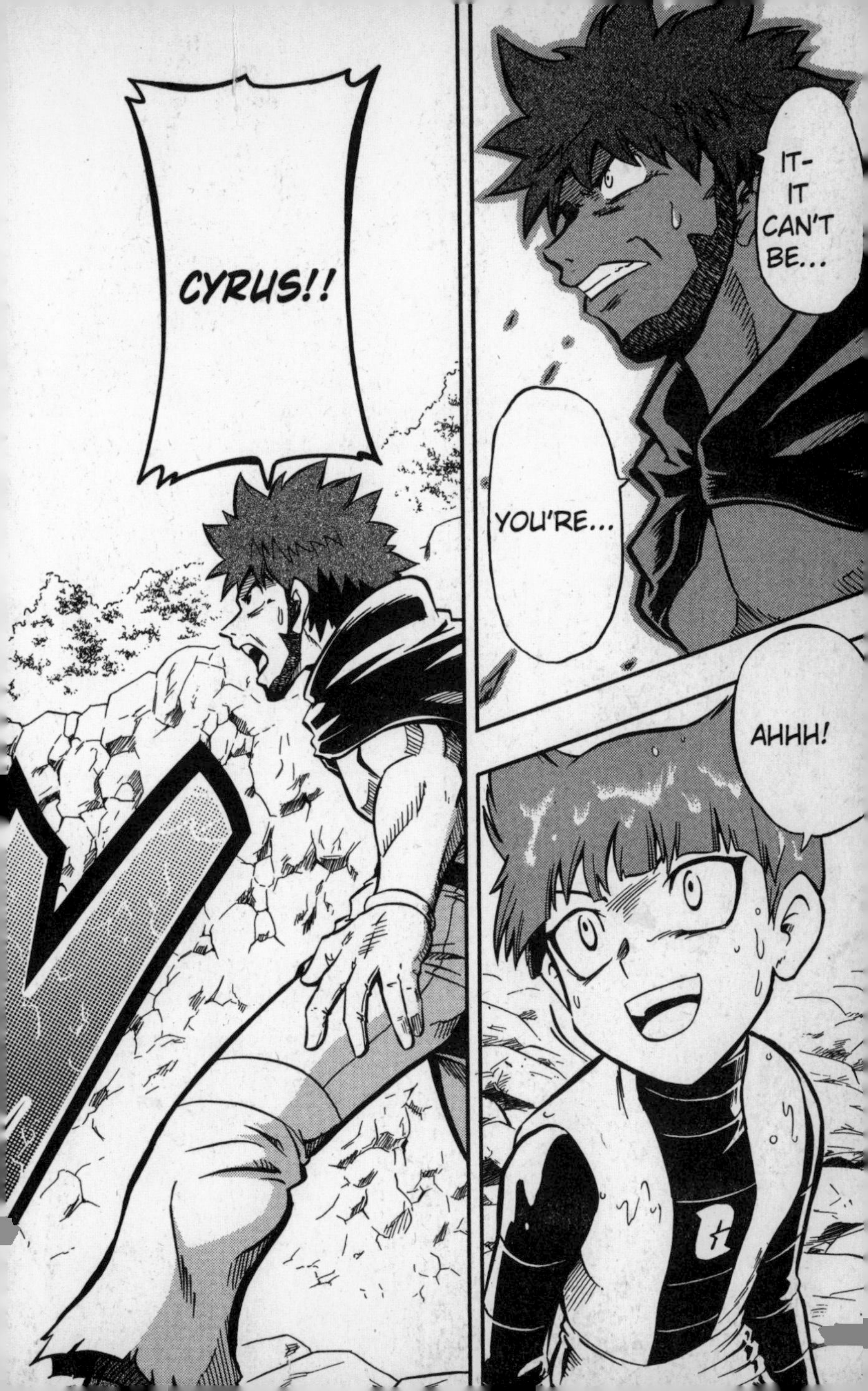
IT- IT CAN'T BE...
YOU'RE...
AHHH!
CYRUS!!

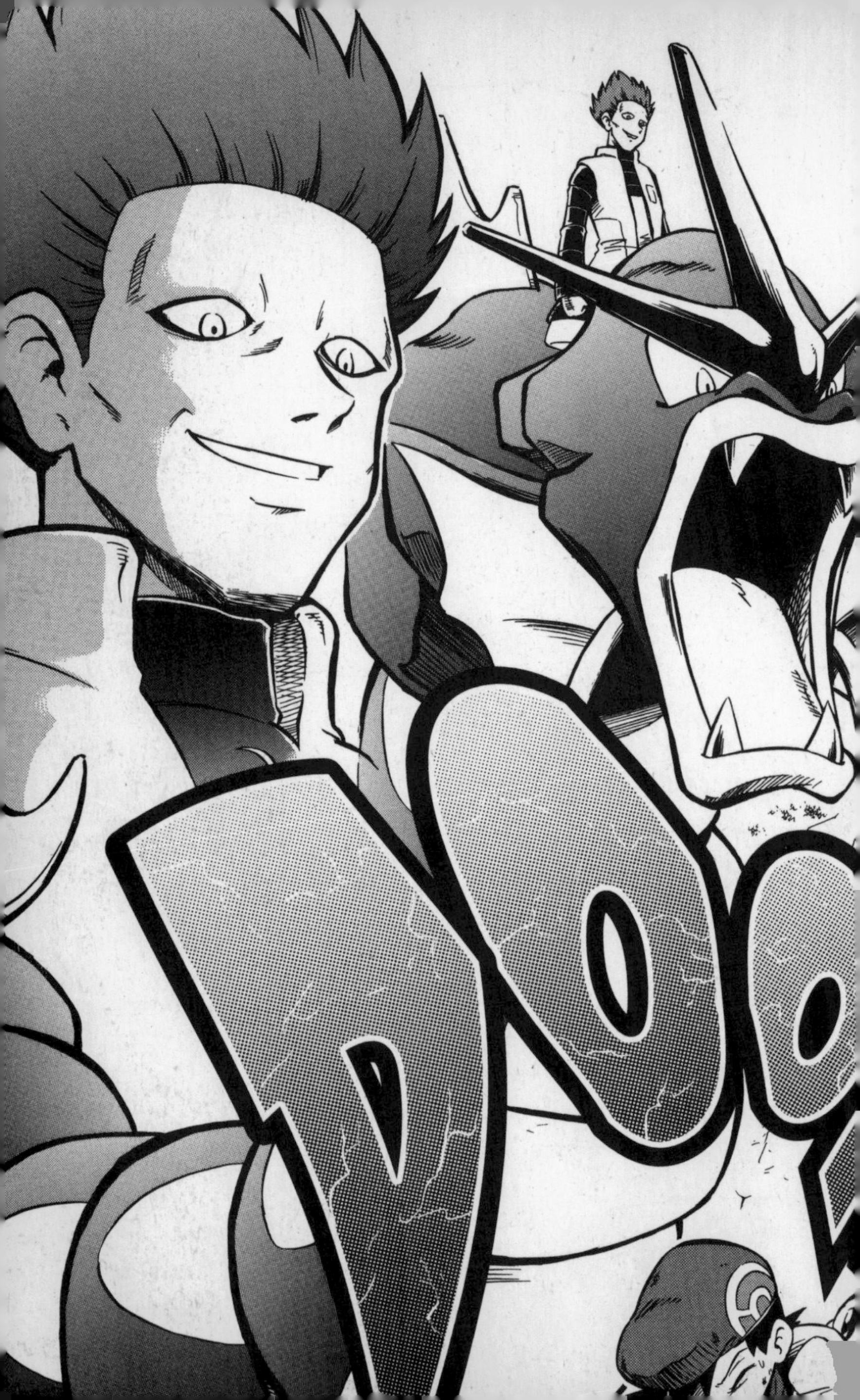

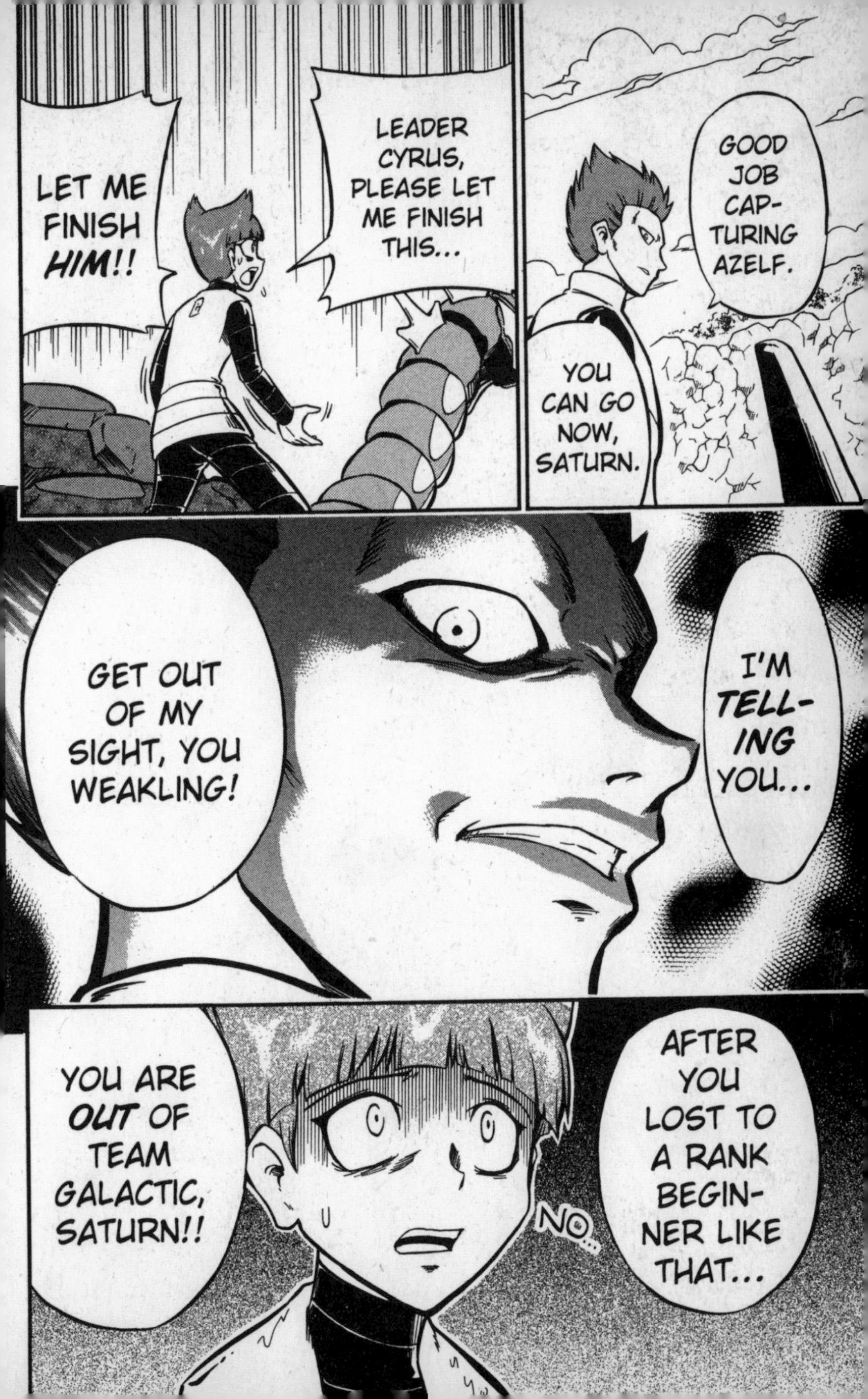
GOOD JOB CAP-TURING AZELF.
YOU CAN GO NOW, SATURN.
LEADER CYRUS, PLEASE LET ME FINISH THIS...
LET ME FINISH *HIM*!!
I'M *TELL-ING* YOU...
GET OUT OF MY SIGHT, YOU WEAKLING!
AFTER YOU LOST TO A RANK BEGIN-NER LIKE THAT...
NO...
YOU ARE *OUT* OF TEAM GALACTIC, SATURN!!

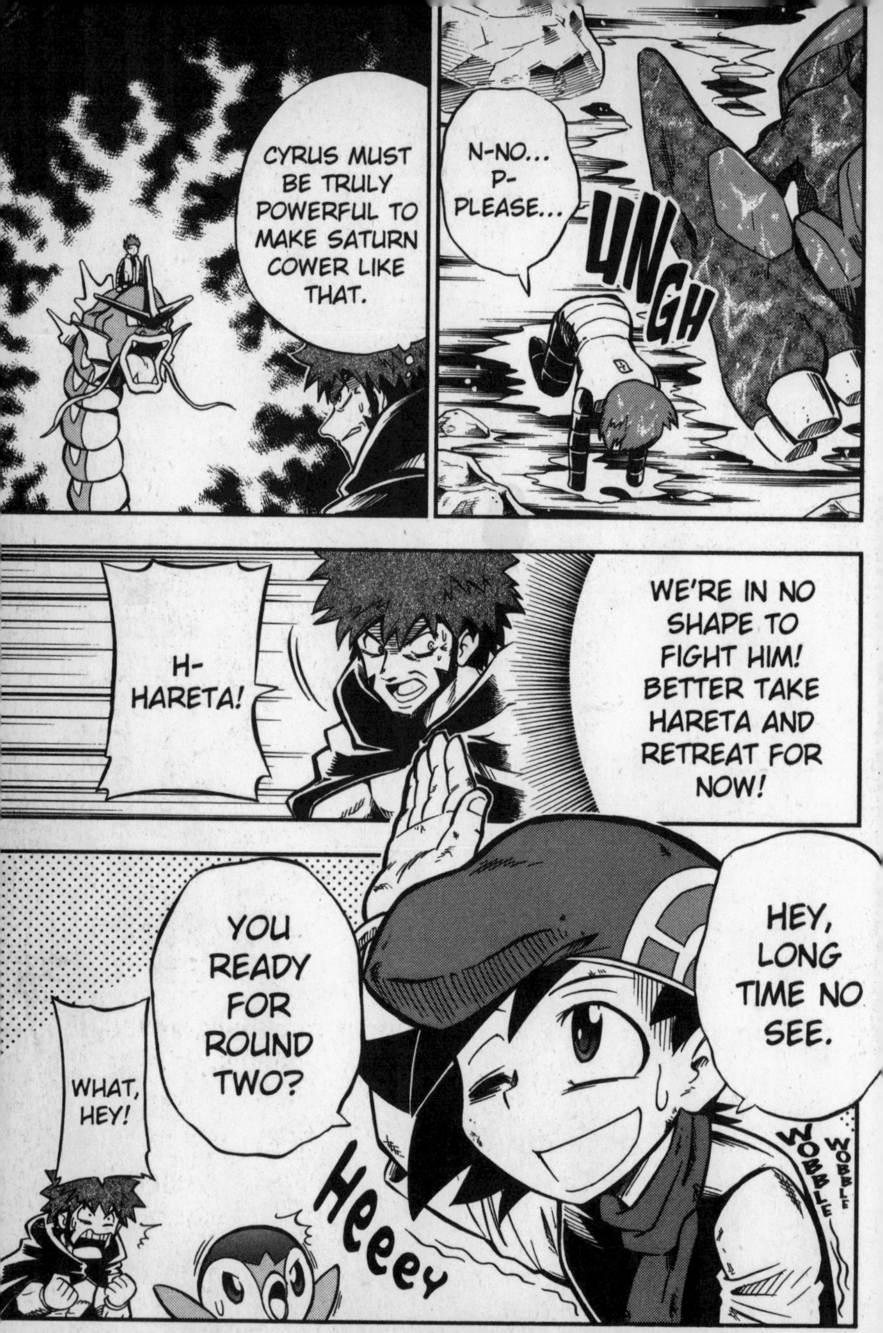
N-NO... P-PLEASE...
UNGH
CYRUS MUST BE TRULY POWERFUL TO MAKE SATURN COWER LIKE THAT.
WE'RE IN NO SHAPE TO FIGHT HIM! BETTER TAKE HARETA AND RETREAT FOR NOW!
H-HARETA!
HEY, LONG TIME NO SEE.
WOBBLE WOBBLE
YOU READY FOR ROUND TWO?
WHAT, HEY!
Heeeey

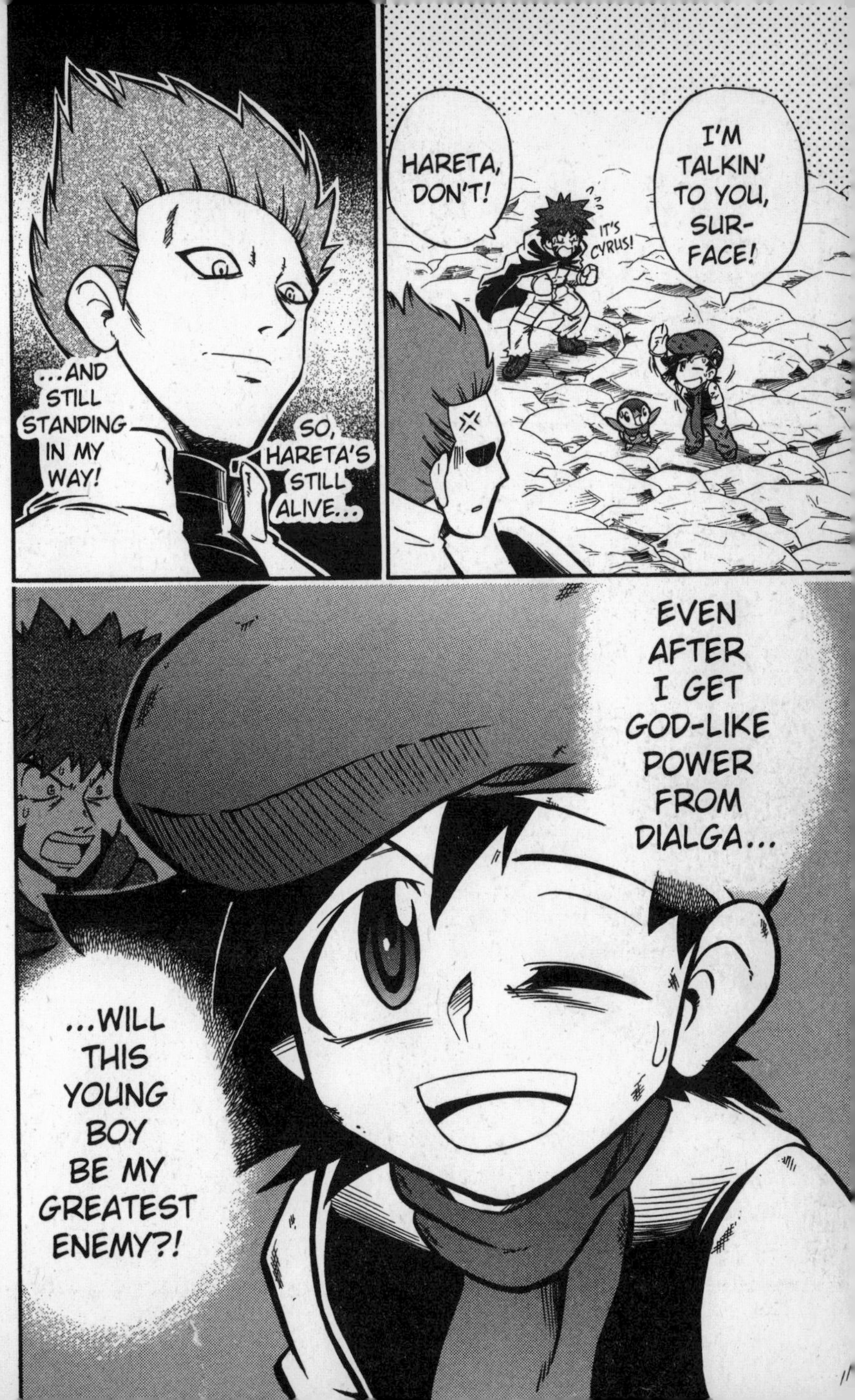
I'M TALKIN' TO YOU, SUR-FACE!
HARETA, DON'T!
IT'S CYRUS!
SO, HARETA'S STILL ALIVE...
...AND STILL STANDING IN MY WAY!
EVEN AFTER I GET GOD-LIKE POWER FROM DIALGA...
...WILL THIS YOUNG BOY BE MY GREATEST ENEMY?!

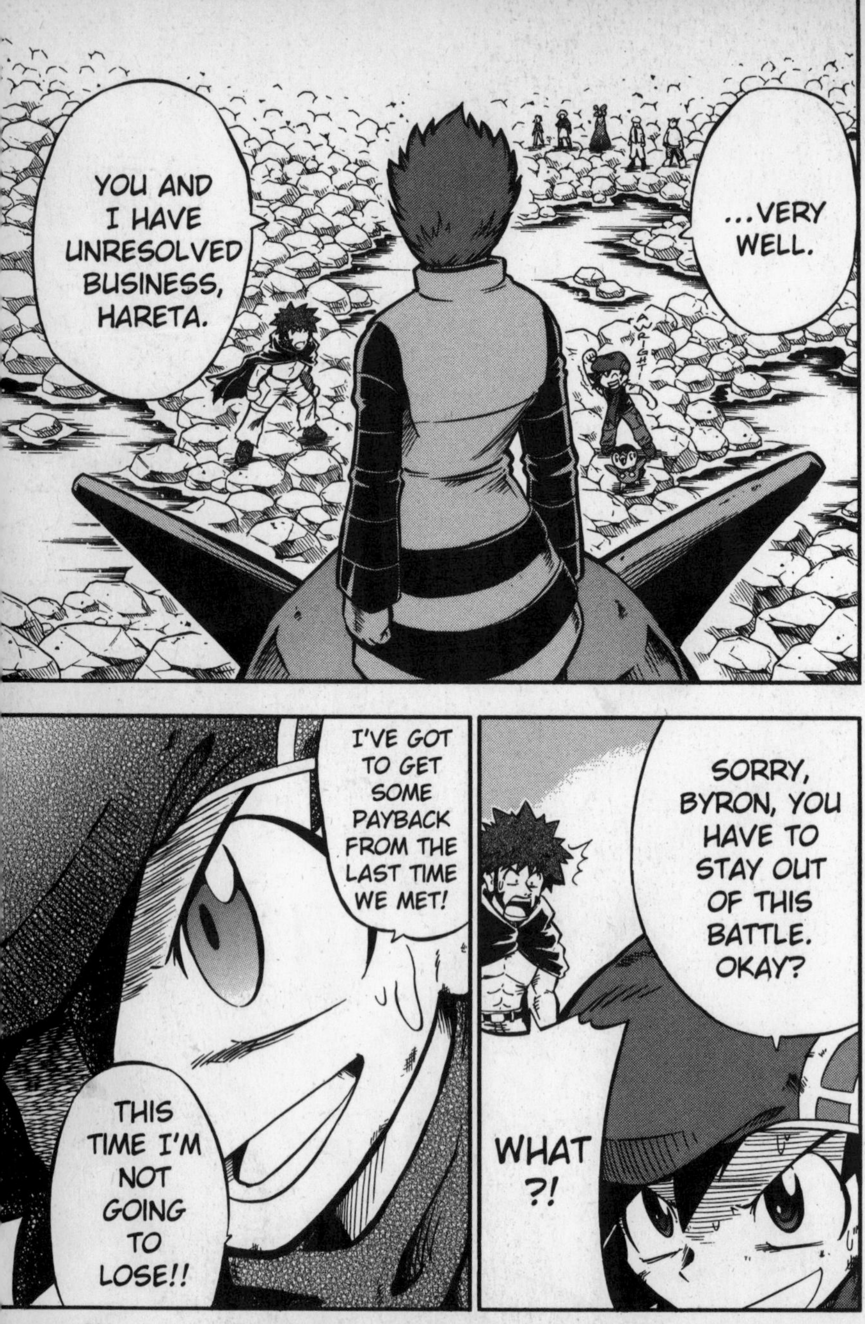
YOU AND I HAVE UNRESOLVED BUSINESS, HARETA.
...VERY WELL.
AWRIGHT!
SORRY, BYRON, YOU HAVE TO STAY OUT OF THIS BATTLE. OKAY?
WHAT ?!
I'VE GOT TO GET SOME PAYBACK FROM THE LAST TIME WE MET!
THIS TIME I'M NOT GOING TO LOSE!!

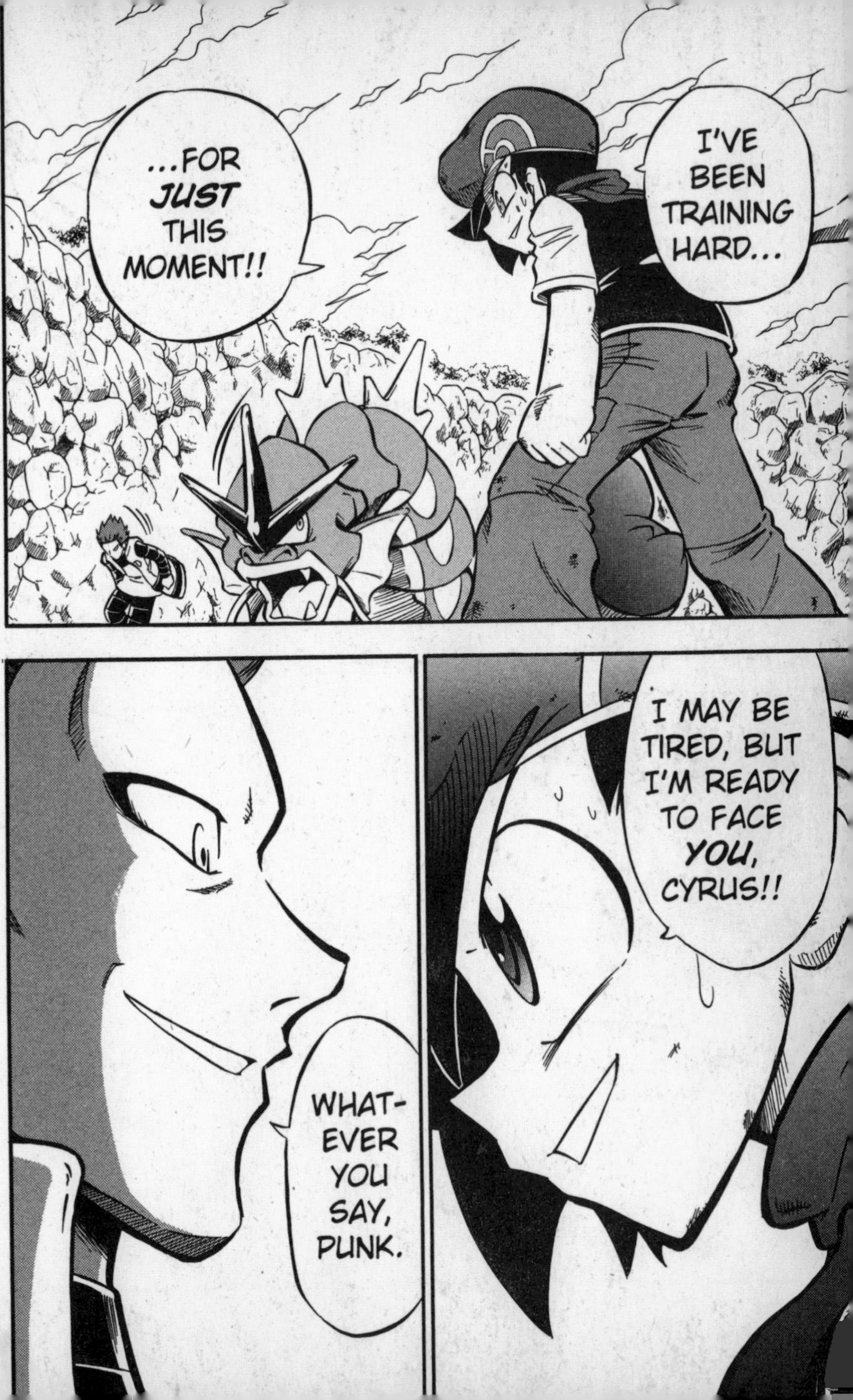
I'VE BEEN TRAINING HARD...
...FOR JUST THIS MOMENT!!
I MAY BE TIRED, BUT I'M READY TO FACE YOU, CYRUS!!
WHAT-EVER YOU SAY, PUNK.

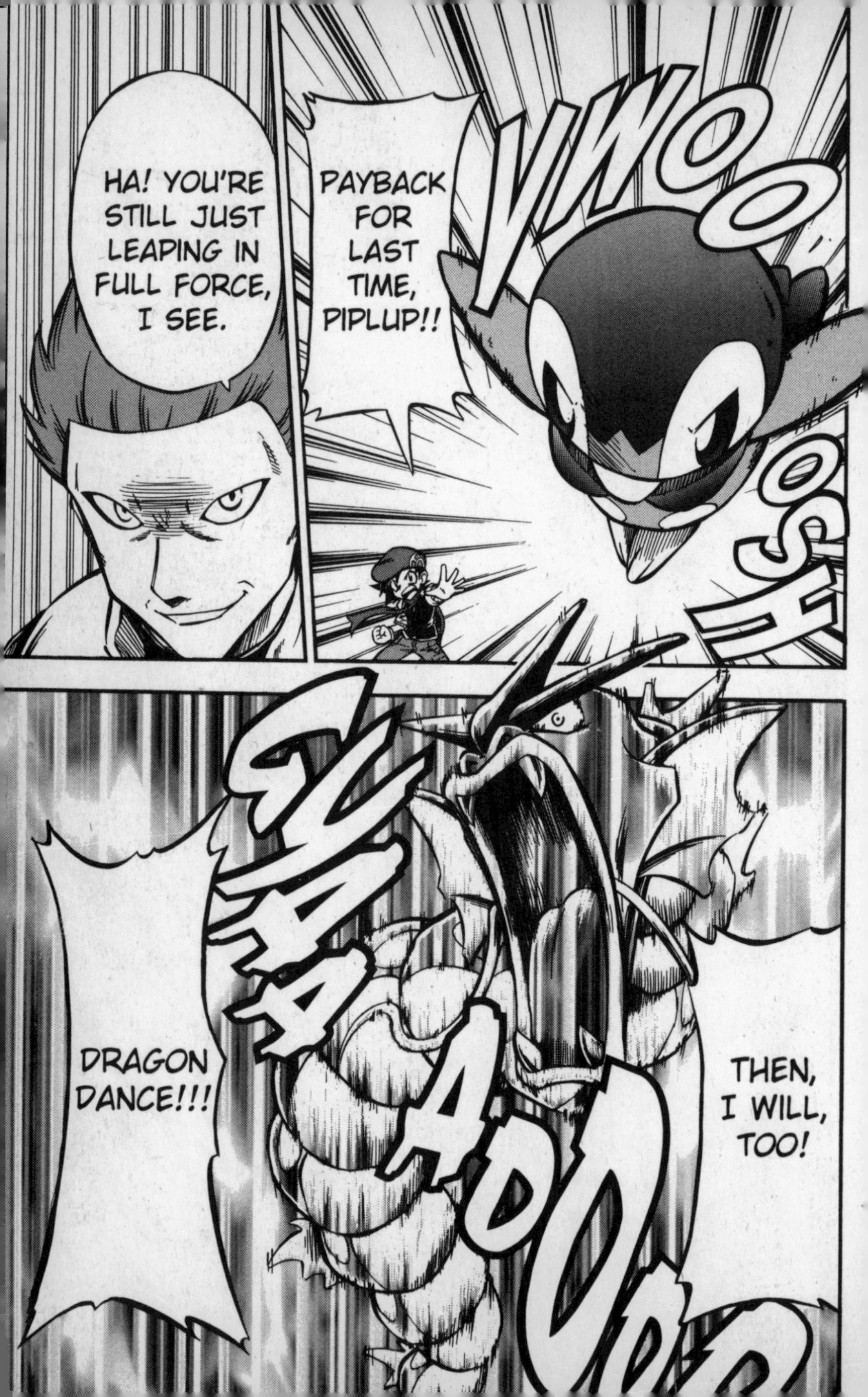
PAYBACK FOR LAST TIME, PIPLUP!!
VWOOOOSH
HA! YOU'RE STILL JUST LEAPING IN FULL FORCE, I SEE.
THEN, I WILL, TOO!
DRAGON DANCE!!!

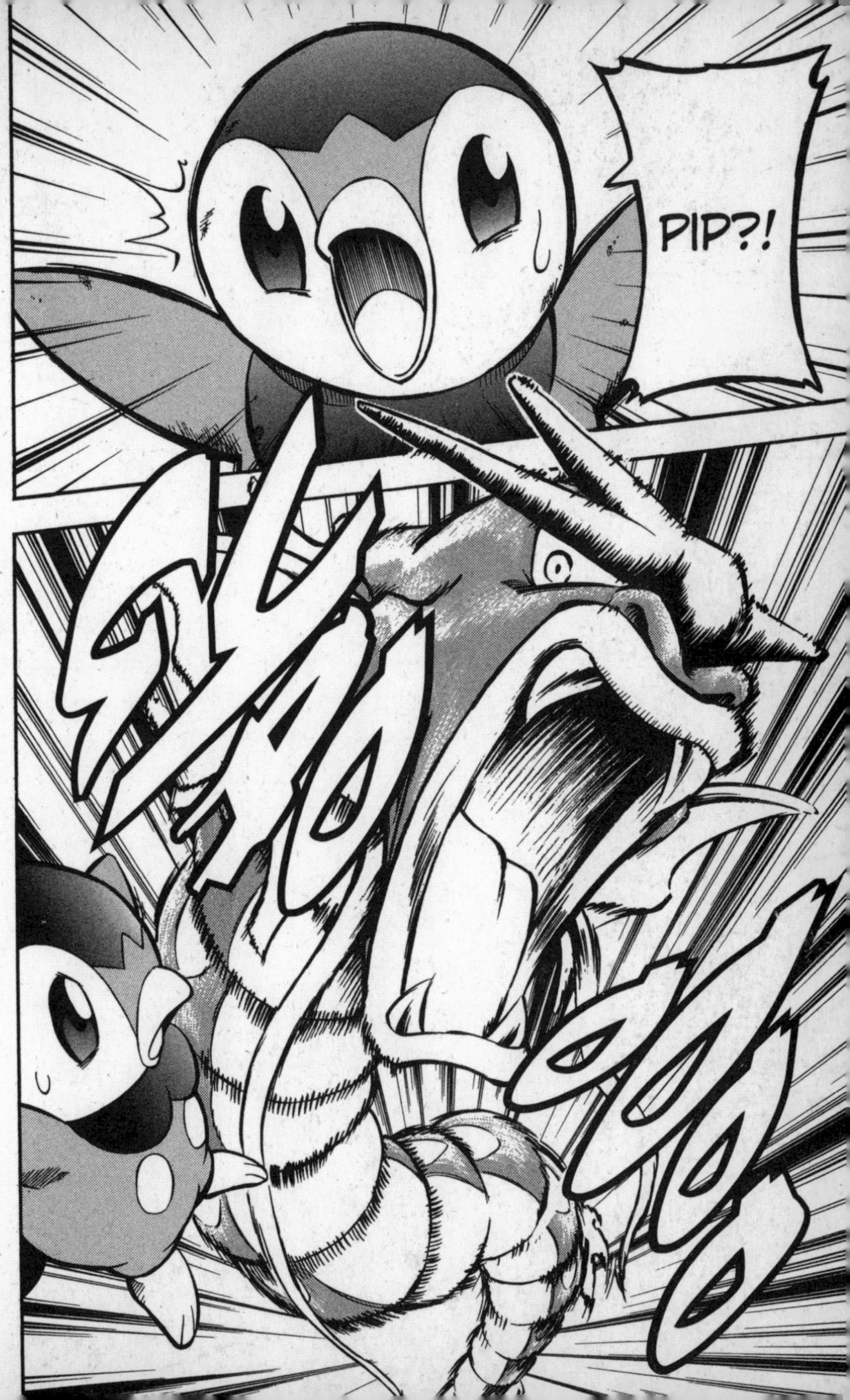
PIP?!

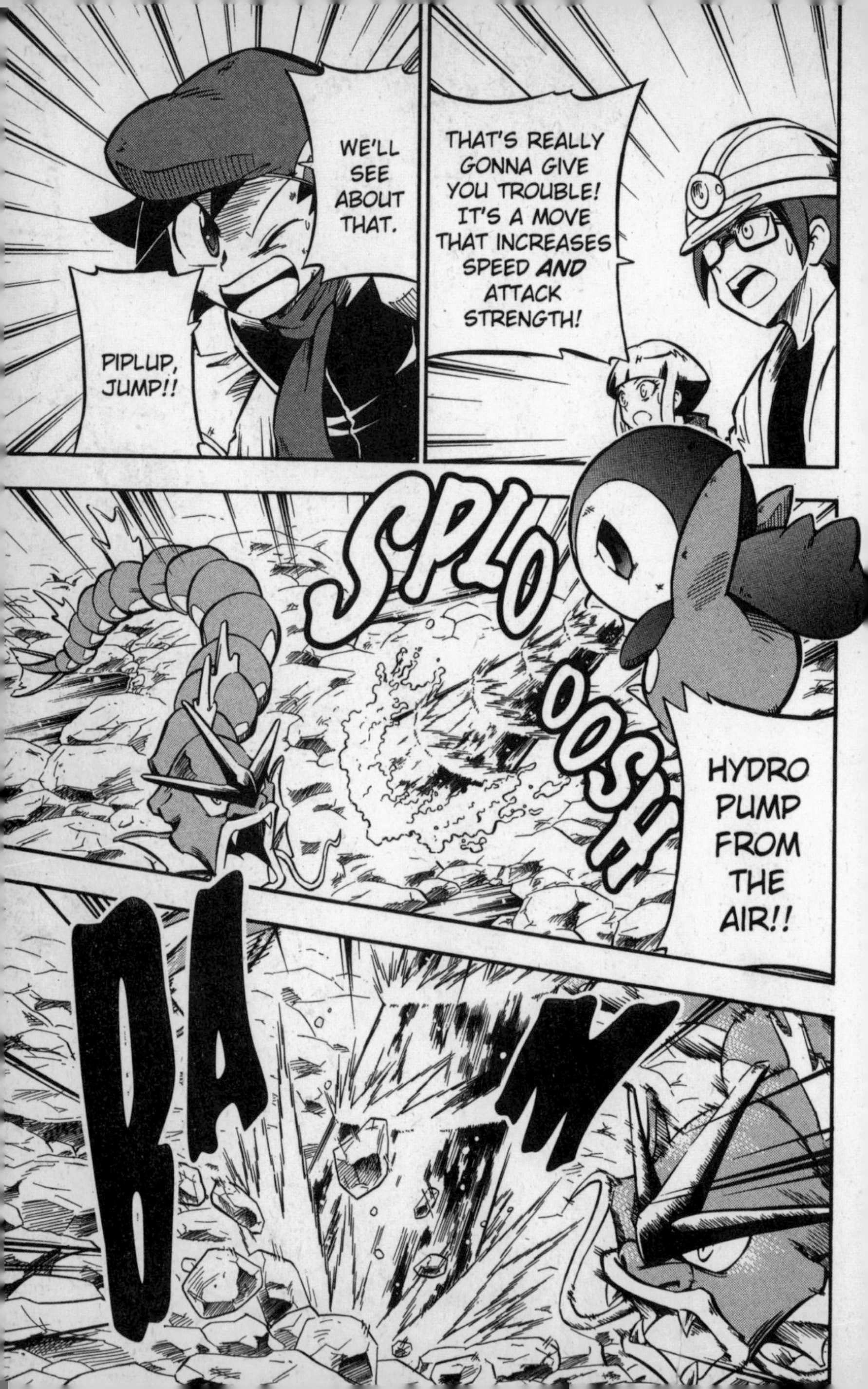
THAT'S REALLY GONNA GIVE YOU TROUBLE! IT'S A MOVE THAT INCREASES SPEED *AND* ATTACK STRENGTH!
WE'LL SEE ABOUT THAT.
PIPLUP, JUMP!!
SPLOOOSH
HYDRO PUMP FROM THE AIR!!
BAM

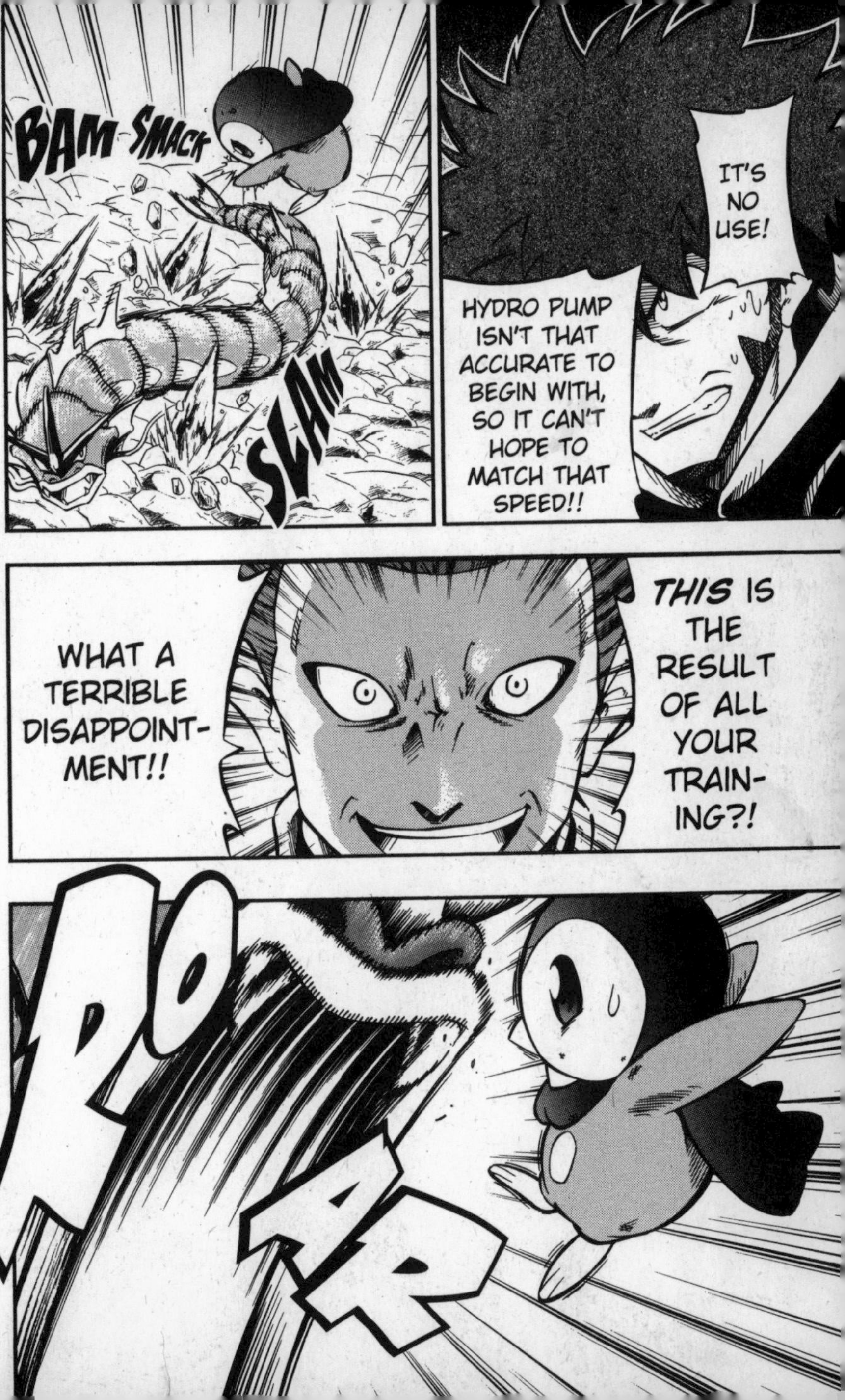
IT'S NO USE!
HYDRO PUMP ISN'T THAT ACCURATE TO BEGIN WITH, SO IT CAN'T HOPE TO MATCH THAT SPEED!!
BAM
SMACK
SLAM
THIS IS THE RESULT OF ALL YOUR TRAIN-ING?!
WHAT A TERRIBLE DISAPPOINT-MENT!!

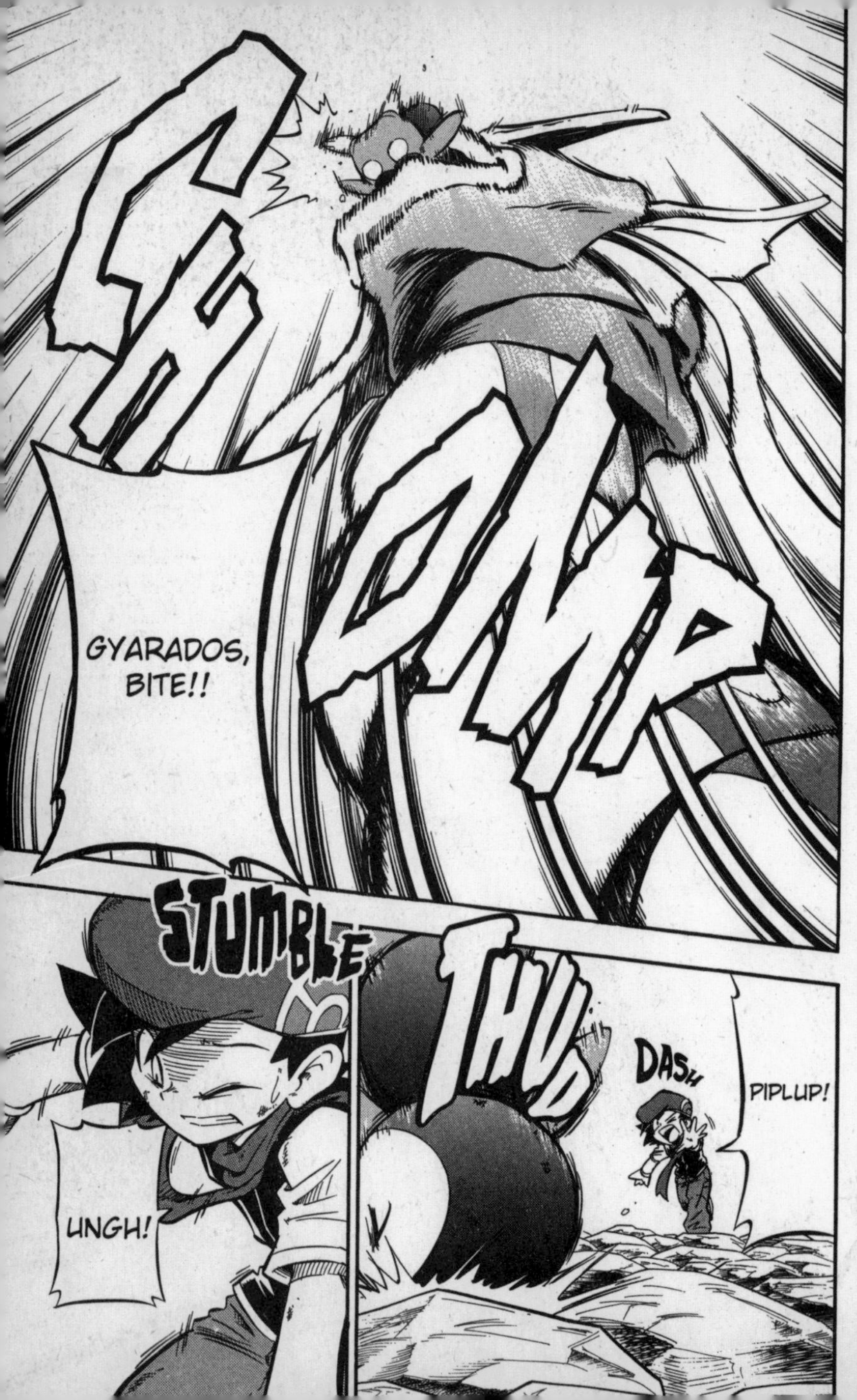
GYARADOS, BITE!!
PIPLUP!
DASH
THUD
STUMBLE
UNGH!

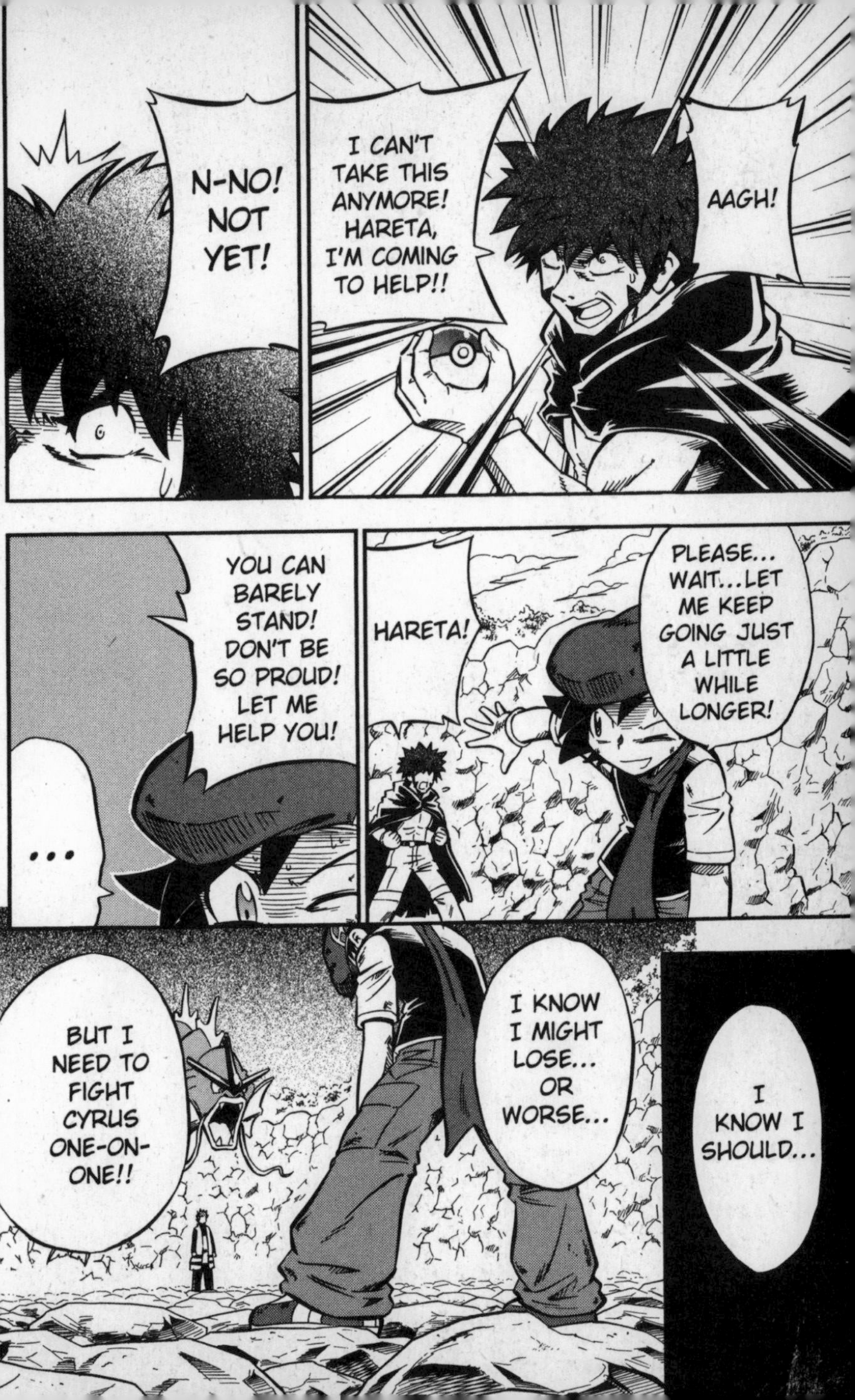
AAGH!
I CAN'T TAKE THIS ANYMORE! HARETA, I'M COMING TO HELP!!
N-NO! NOT YET!
PLEASE... WAIT...LET ME KEEP GOING JUST A LITTLE WHILE LONGER!
HARETA!
YOU CAN BARELY STAND! DON'T BE SO PROUD! LET ME HELP YOU!
...
I KNOW I SHOULD...
I KNOW I MIGHT LOSE... OR WORSE...
BUT I NEED TO FIGHT CYRUS ONE-ON-ONE!!

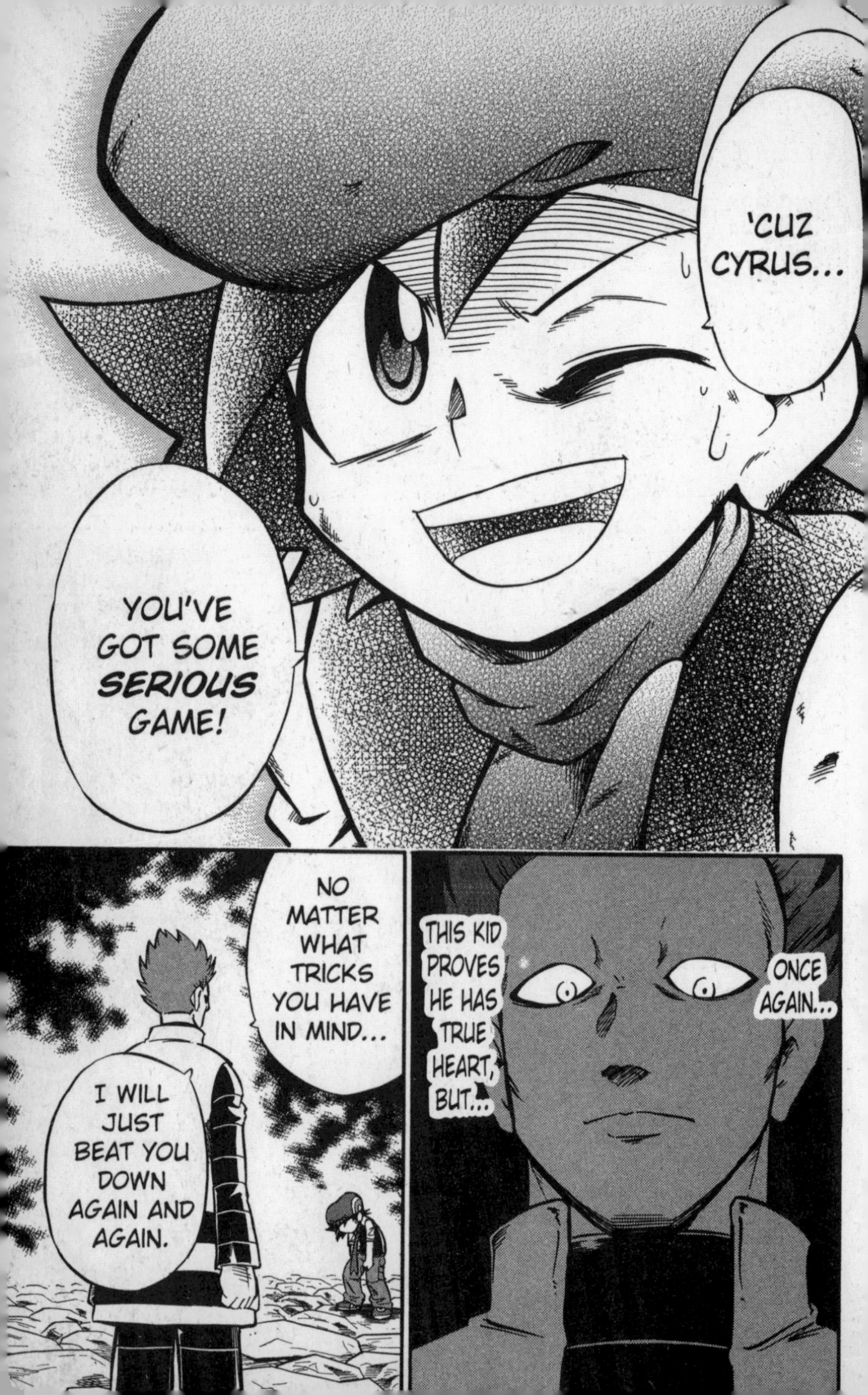
'CUZ CYRUS...
YOU'VE GOT SOME *SERIOUS* GAME!
ONCE AGAIN...
THIS KID PROVES HE HAS TRUE HEART, BUT...
NO MATTER WHAT TRICKS YOU HAVE IN MIND...
I WILL JUST BEAT YOU DOWN AGAIN AND AGAIN.

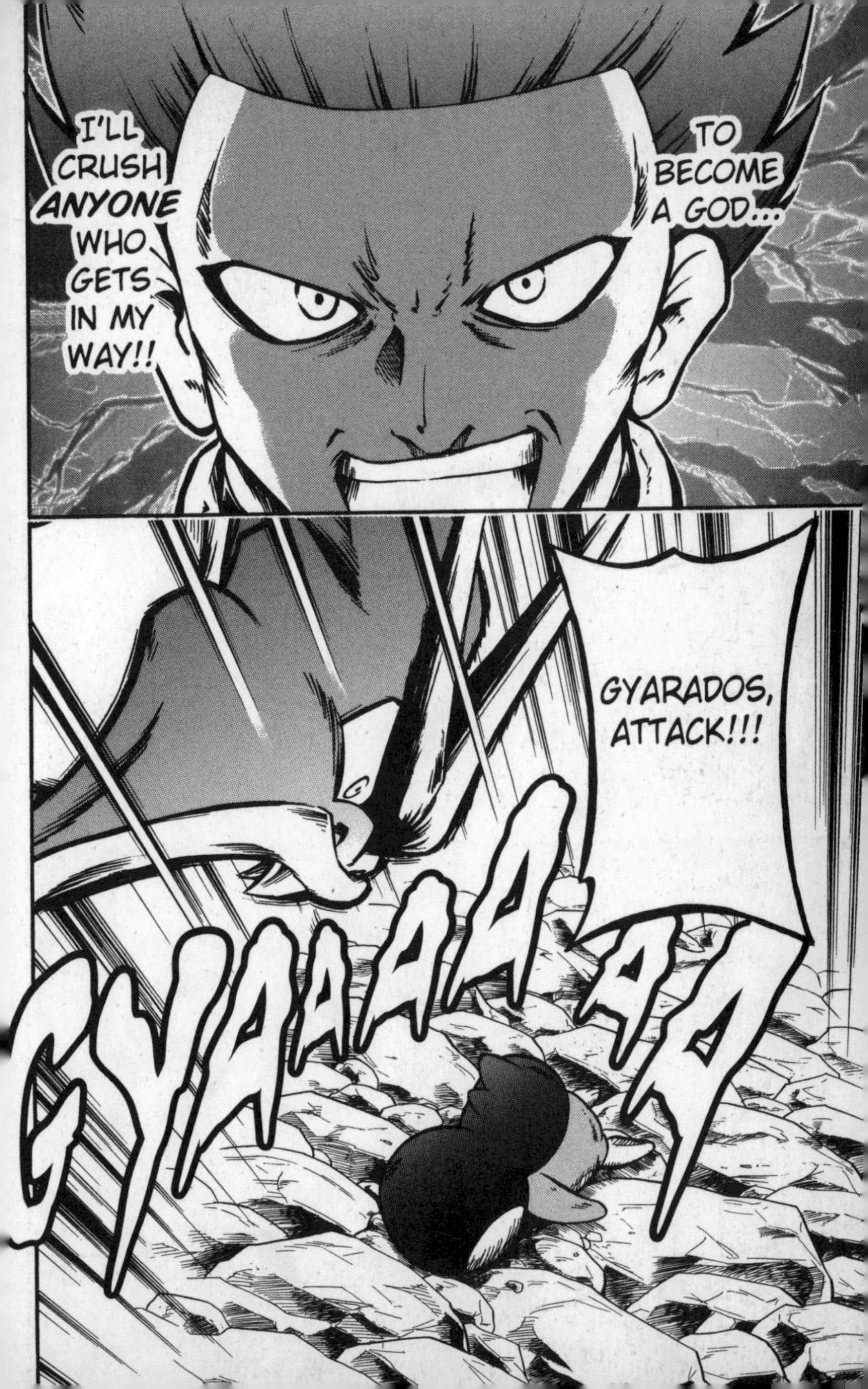
TO BECOME A GOD...
I'LL CRUSH *ANYONE* WHO GETS IN MY WAY!!
GYARADOS, ATTACK!!!
GYAAAAAA

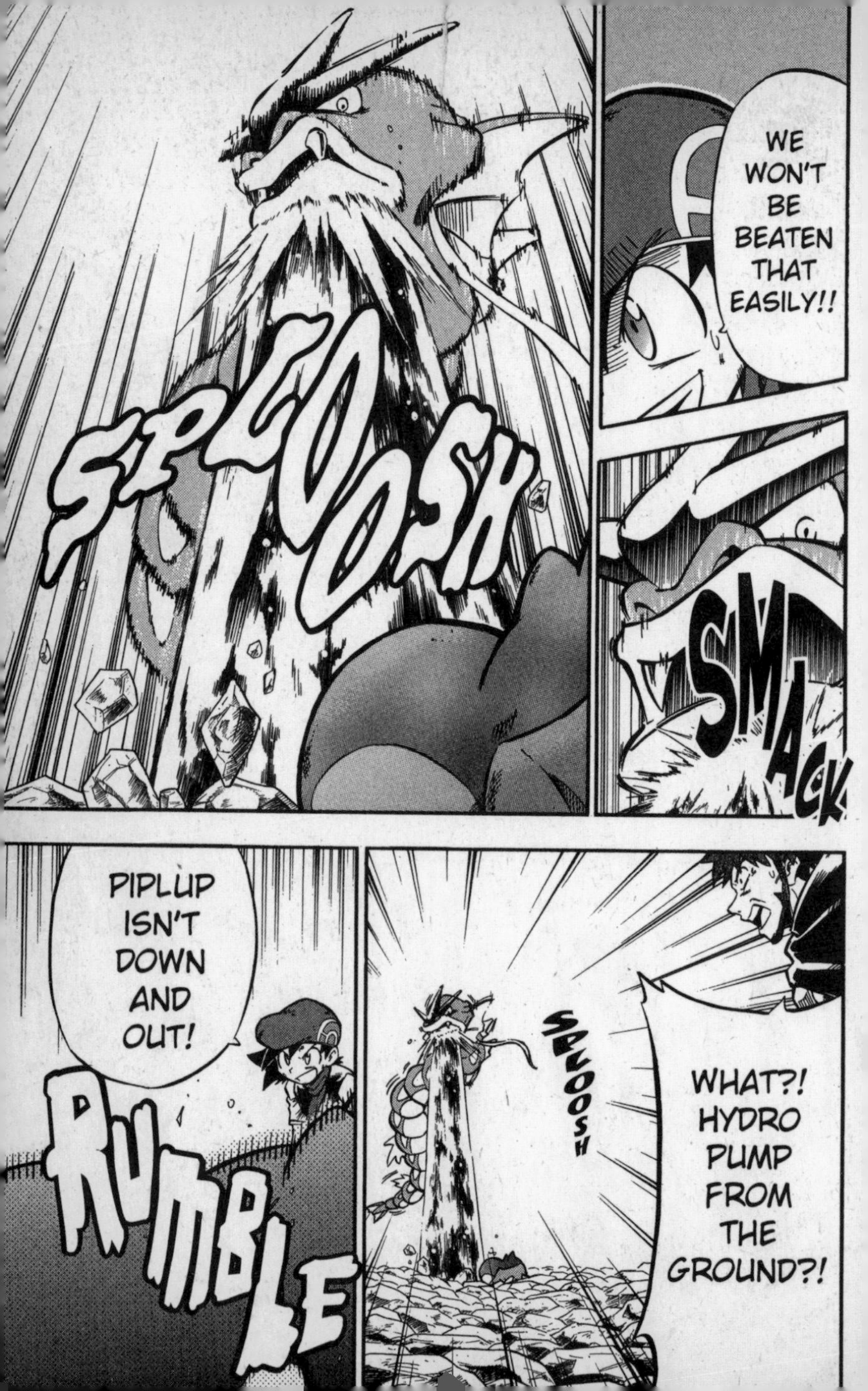
WE WON'T BE BEATEN THAT EASILY!!
SMACK
SPLOOSH
WHAT?! HYDRO PUMP FROM THE GROUND?!
SPLOOSH
PIPLUP ISN'T DOWN AND OUT!
RUMBLE

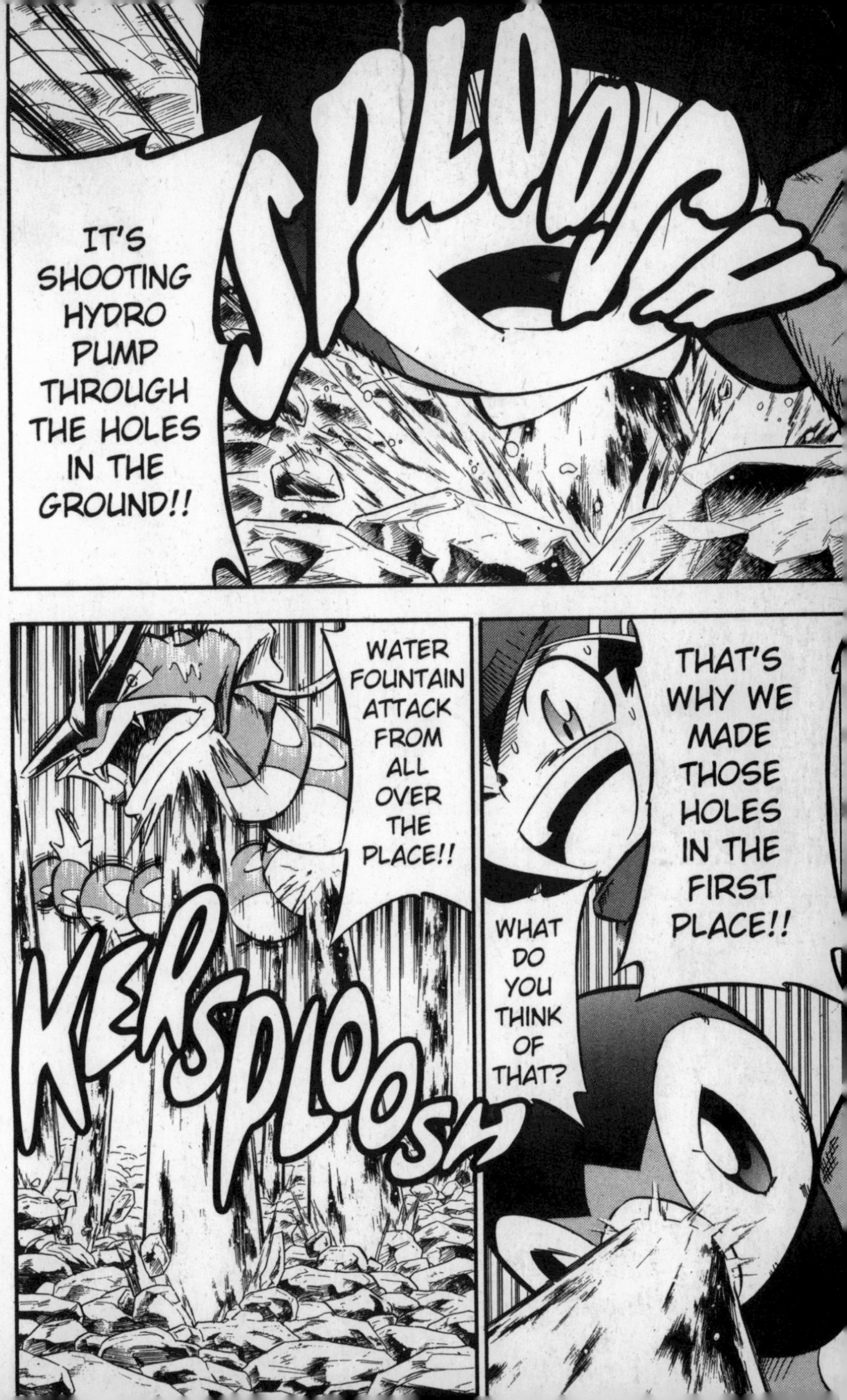
SPLOOSH
IT'S SHOOTING HYDRO PUMP THROUGH THE HOLES IN THE GROUND!!
THAT'S WHY WE MADE THOSE HOLES IN THE FIRST PLACE!!
WHAT DO YOU THINK OF THAT?
WATER FOUNTAIN ATTACK FROM ALL OVER THE PLACE!!
KERSPLOOSH

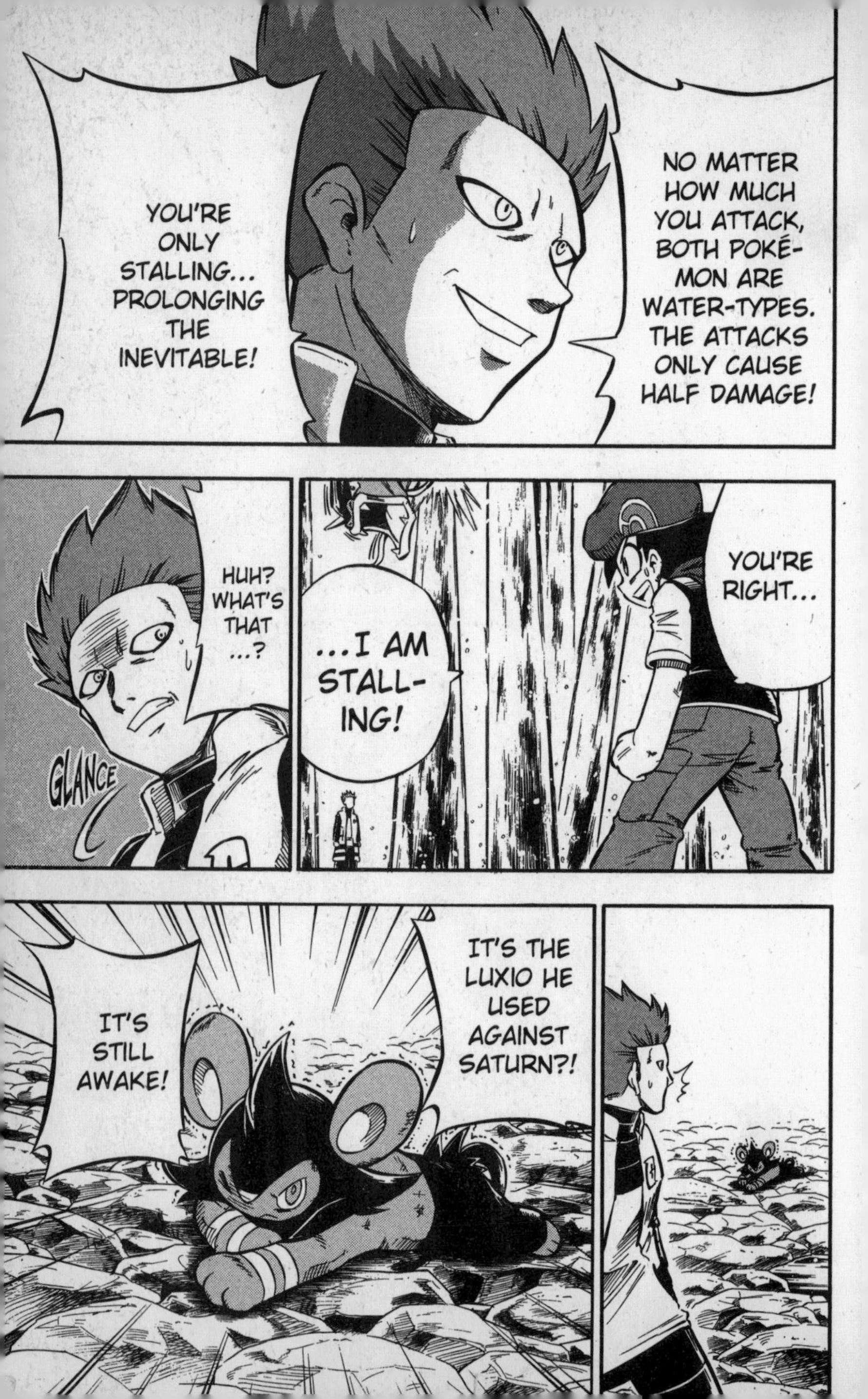
NO MATTER HOW MUCH YOU ATTACK, BOTH POKÉ-MON ARE WATER-TYPES. THE ATTACKS ONLY CAUSE HALF DAMAGE!
YOU'RE ONLY STALLING... PROLONGING THE INEVITABLE!
YOU'RE RIGHT...
...I AM STALL-ING!
HUH? WHAT'S THAT ...?
GLANCE
IT'S THE LUXIO HE USED AGAINST SATURN?!
IT'S STILL AWAKE!

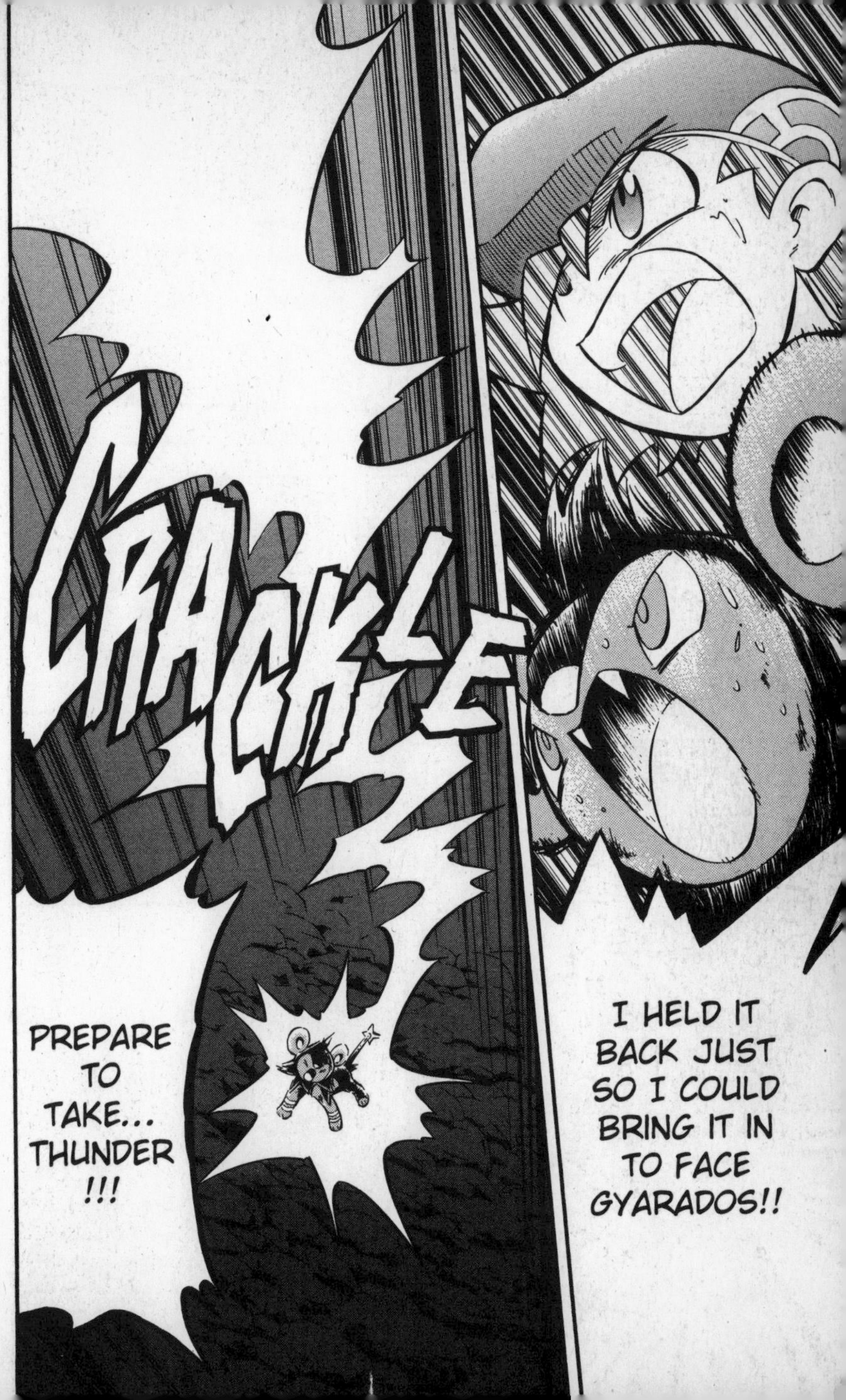
I HELD IT BACK JUST SO I COULD BRING IT IN TO FACE GYARADOS!!
CRACKLE
PREPARE TO TAKE... THUNDER!!!

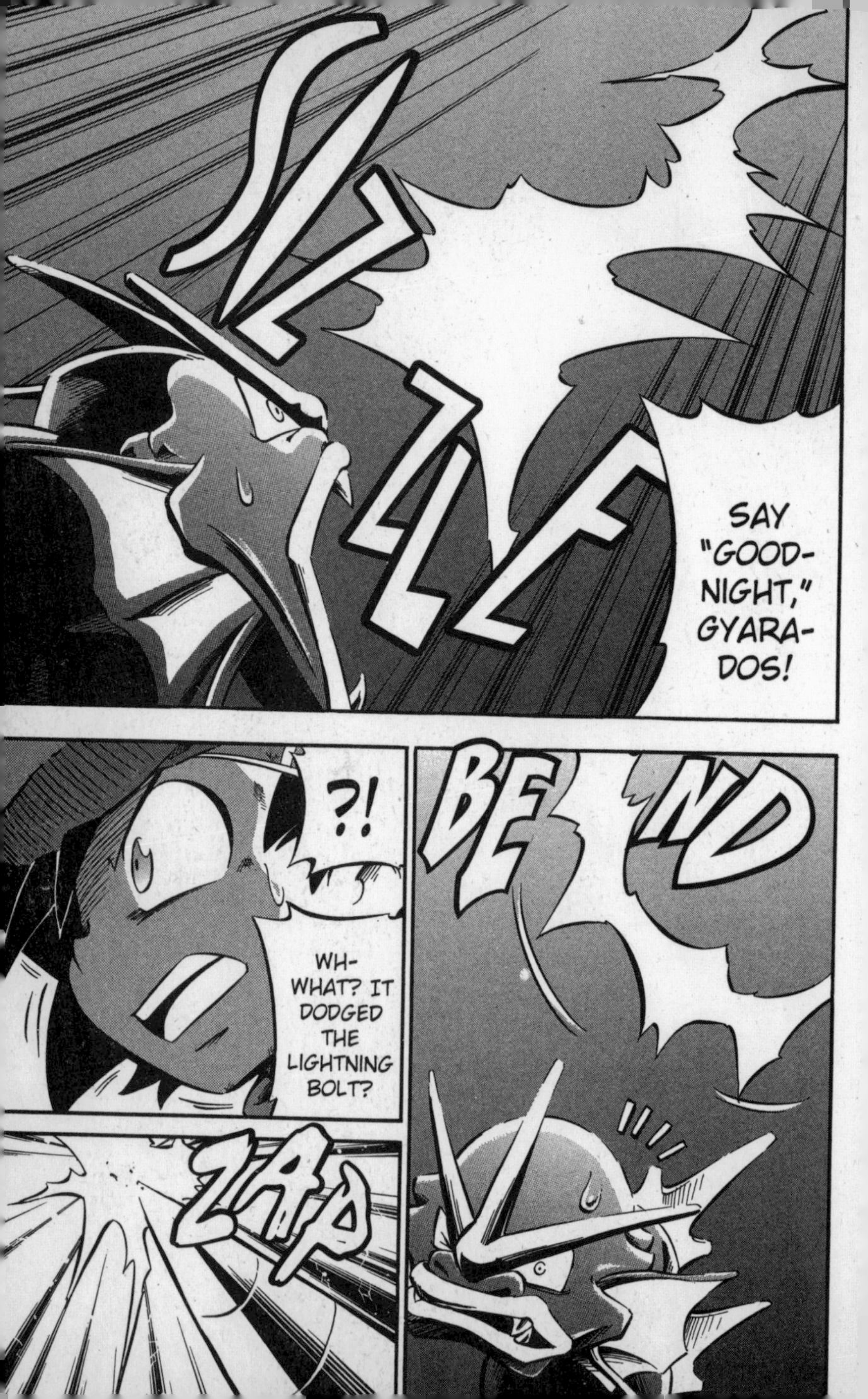
SAY "GOOD-NIGHT," GYARADOS!
BEND
?!
WH-WHAT? IT DODGED THE LIGHTNING BOLT?
ZAP

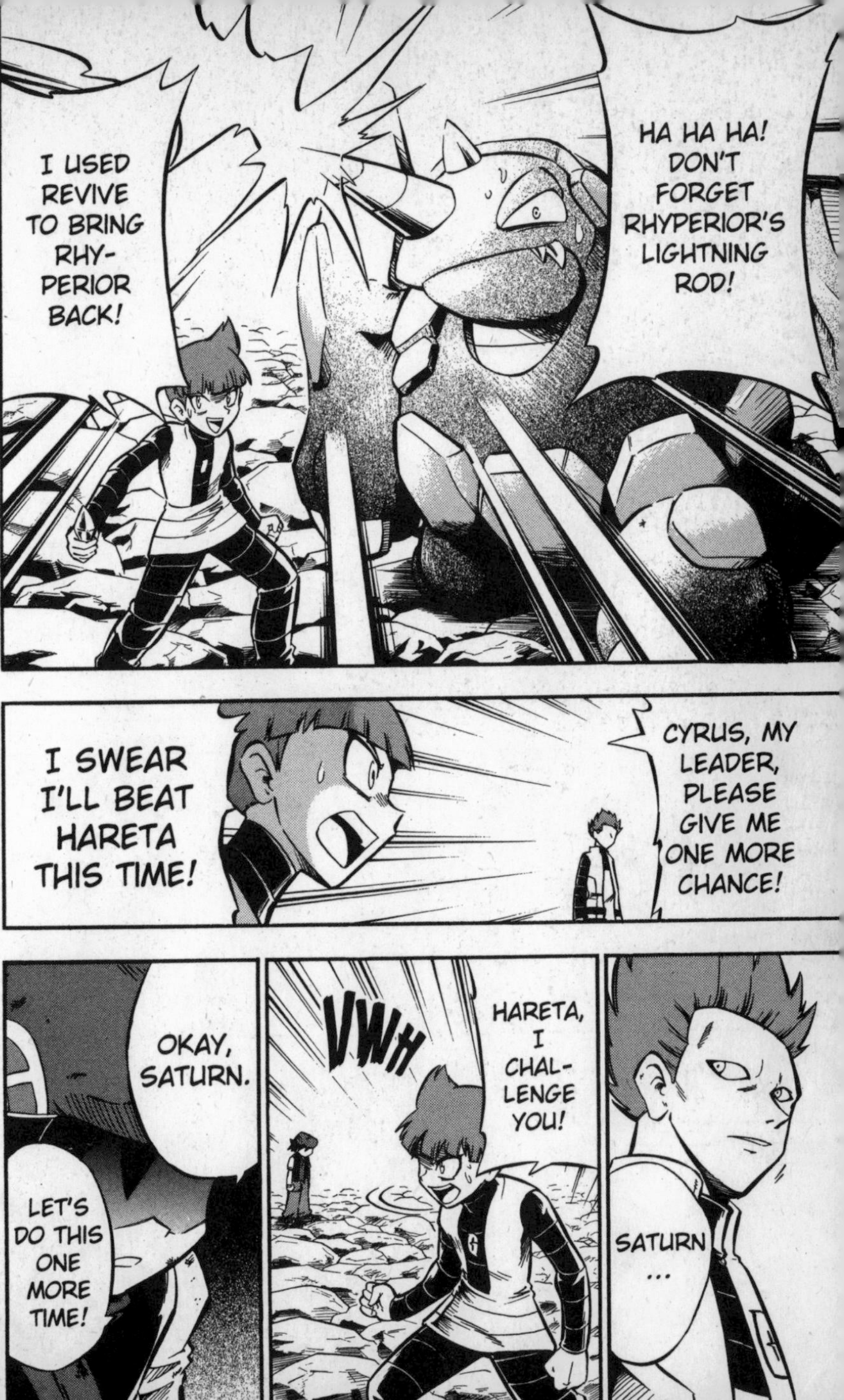
HA HA HA! DON'T FORGET RHYPERIOR'S LIGHTNING ROD!
I USED REVIVE TO BRING RHY-PERIOR BACK!
CYRUS, MY LEADER, PLEASE GIVE ME ONE MORE CHANCE!
I SWEAR I'LL BEAT HARETA THIS TIME!
SATURN ...
VWH
HARETA, I CHAL-LENGE YOU!
OKAY, SATURN.
LET'S DO THIS ONE MORE TIME!

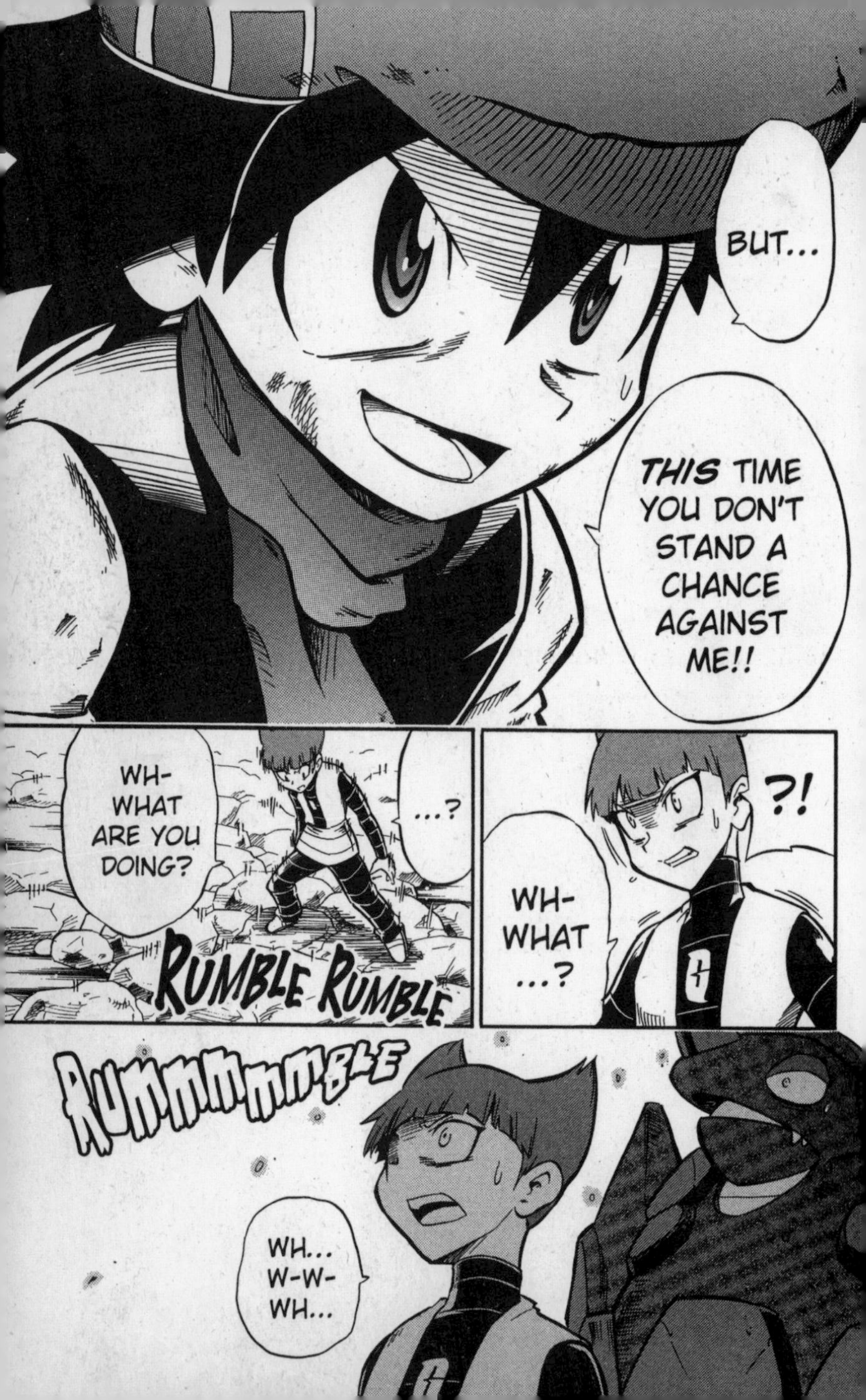
BUT...
THIS TIME YOU DON'T STAND A CHANCE AGAINST ME!!
?!
WH-WHAT...?
...?
WH-WHAT ARE YOU DOING?
RUMBLE RUMBLE
RUMMMMMMBLE
WH... W-W-WH...

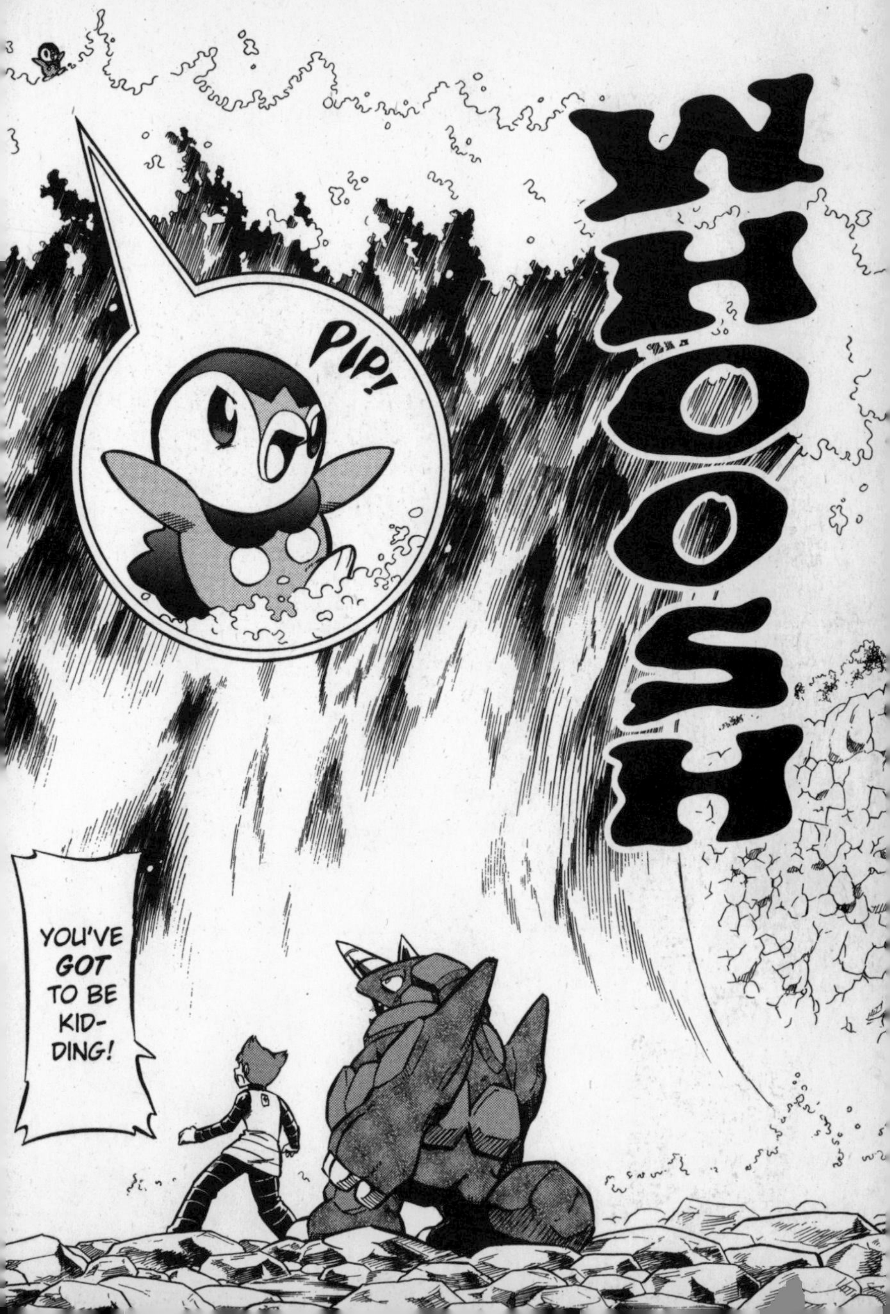
WHOOSH
PIP!
YOU'VE *GOT* TO BE KID-DING!

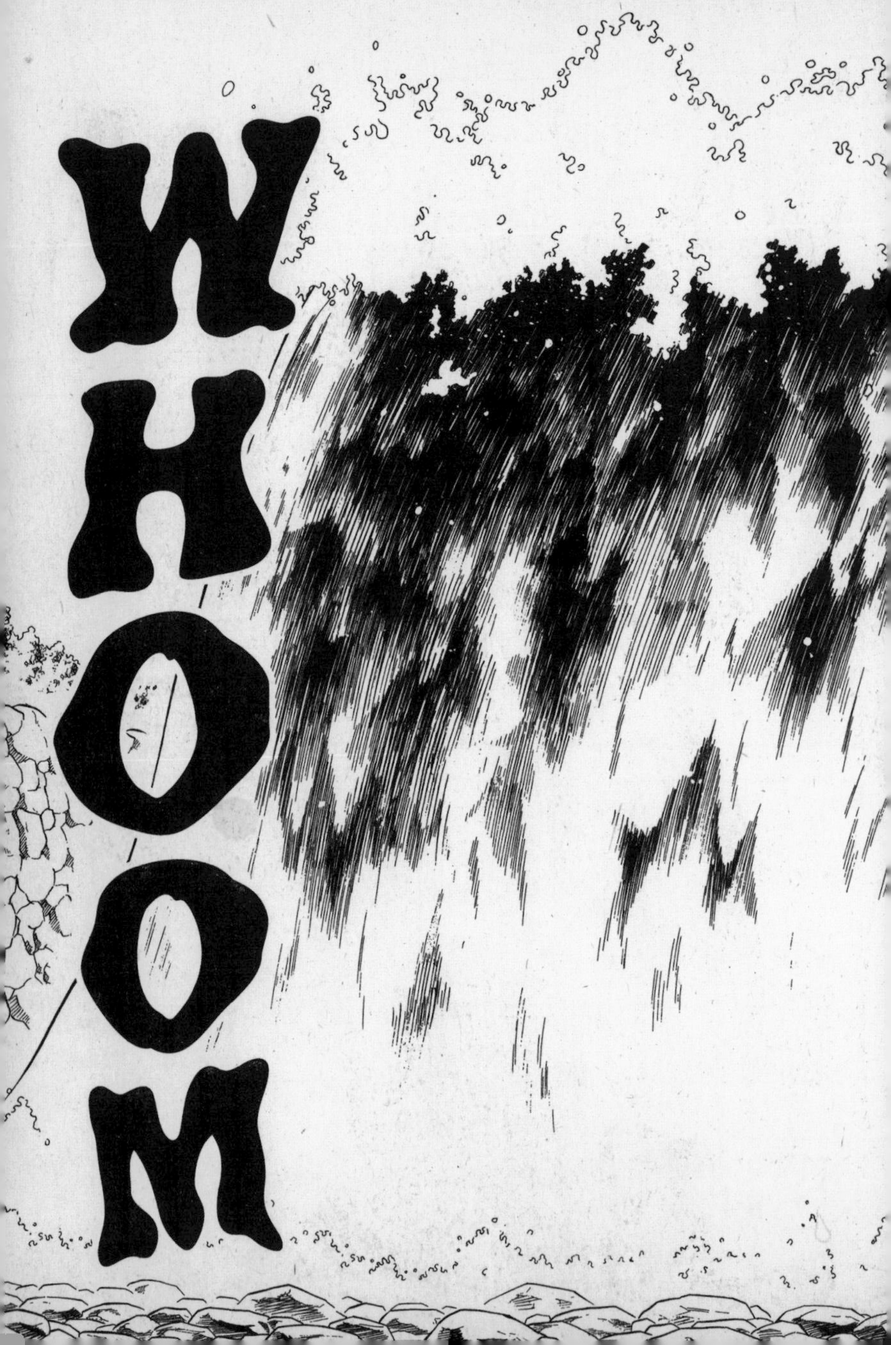
WHOOM

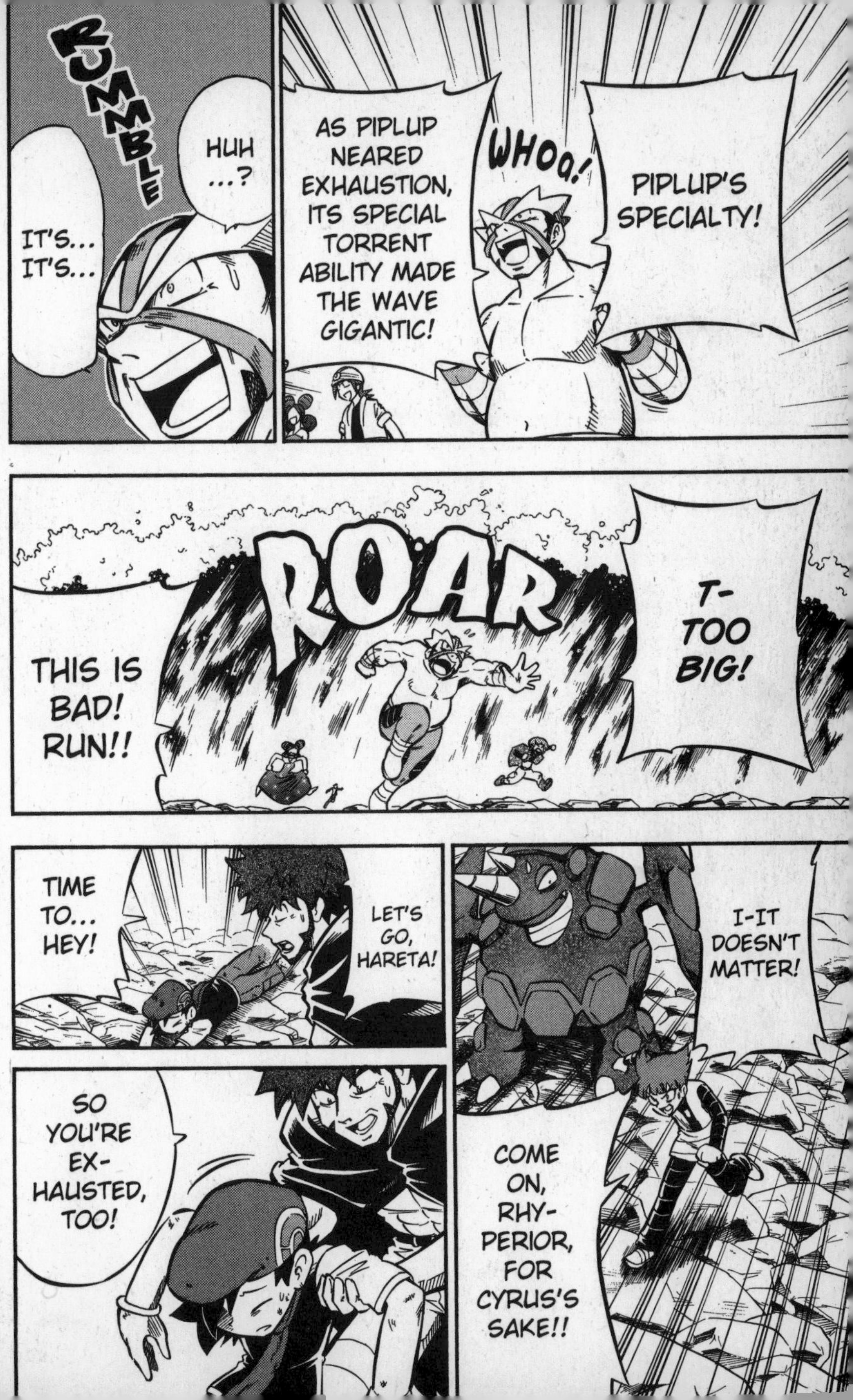
PIPLUP'S SPECIALTY!
WHOa!
AS PIPLUP NEARED EXHAUSTION, ITS SPECIAL TORRENT ABILITY MADE THE WAVE GIGANTIC!
RUMBLE
HUH ...?
IT'S... IT'S...
T-TOO BIG!
ROAR
THIS IS BAD! RUN!!
I-IT DOESN'T MATTER!
COME ON, RHY-PERIOR, FOR CYRUS'S SAKE!!
LET'S GO, HARETA!
TIME TO... HEY!
SO YOU'RE EX-HAUSTED, TOO!

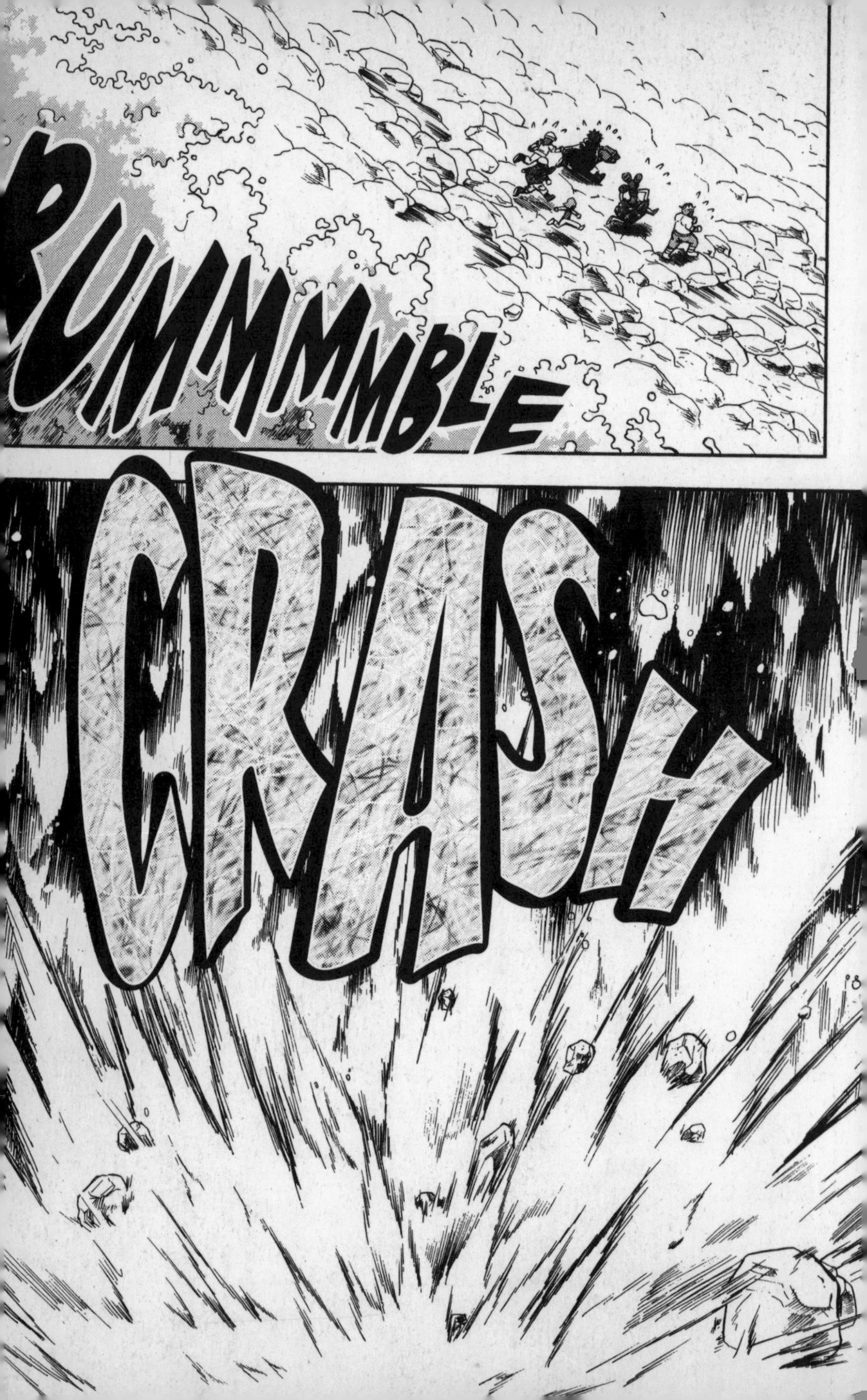
RUMMMMBLE
CRASH

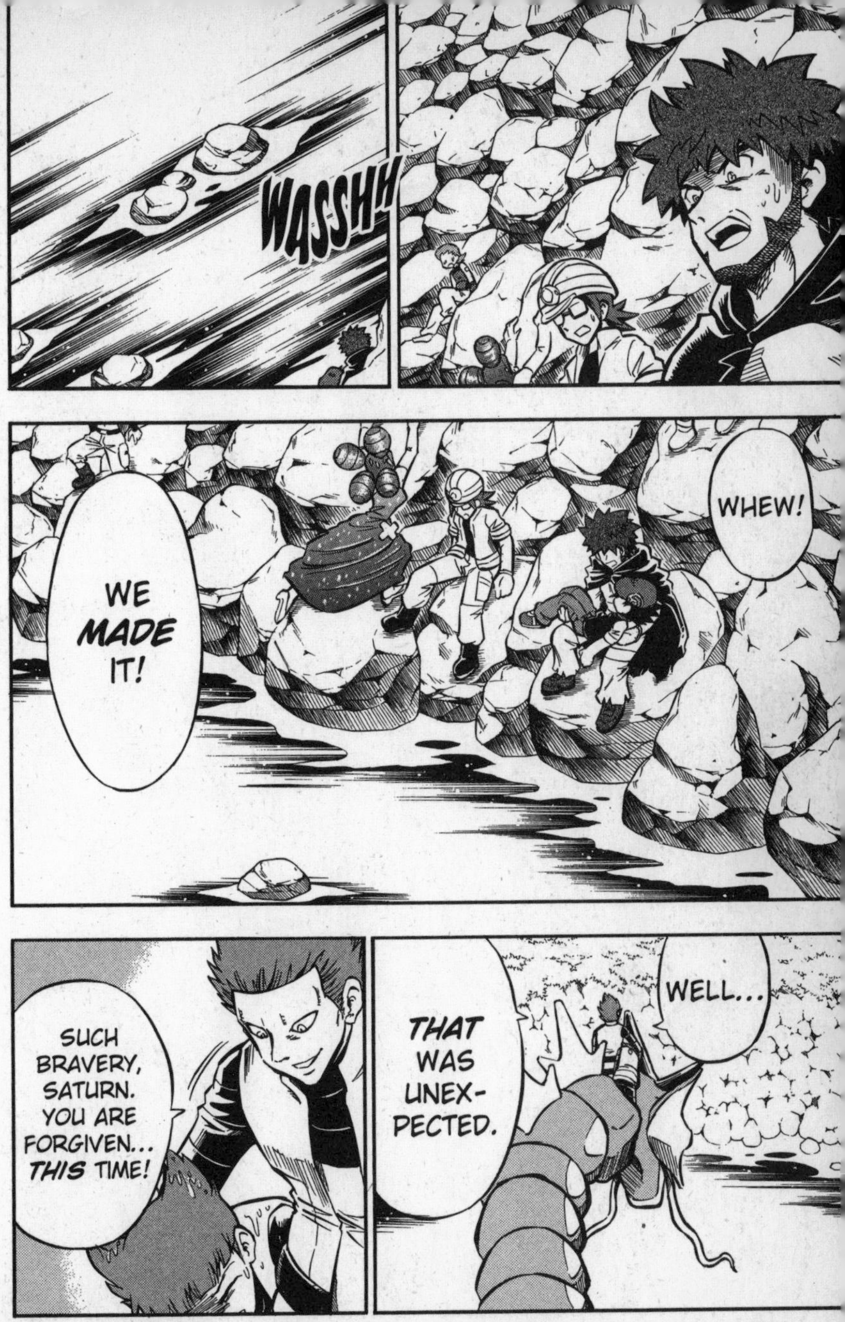
WASSHH
WHEW!
WE *MADE* IT!
WELL...
THAT WAS UNEX-PECTED.
SUCH BRAVERY, SATURN. YOU ARE FORGIVEN... *THIS* TIME!

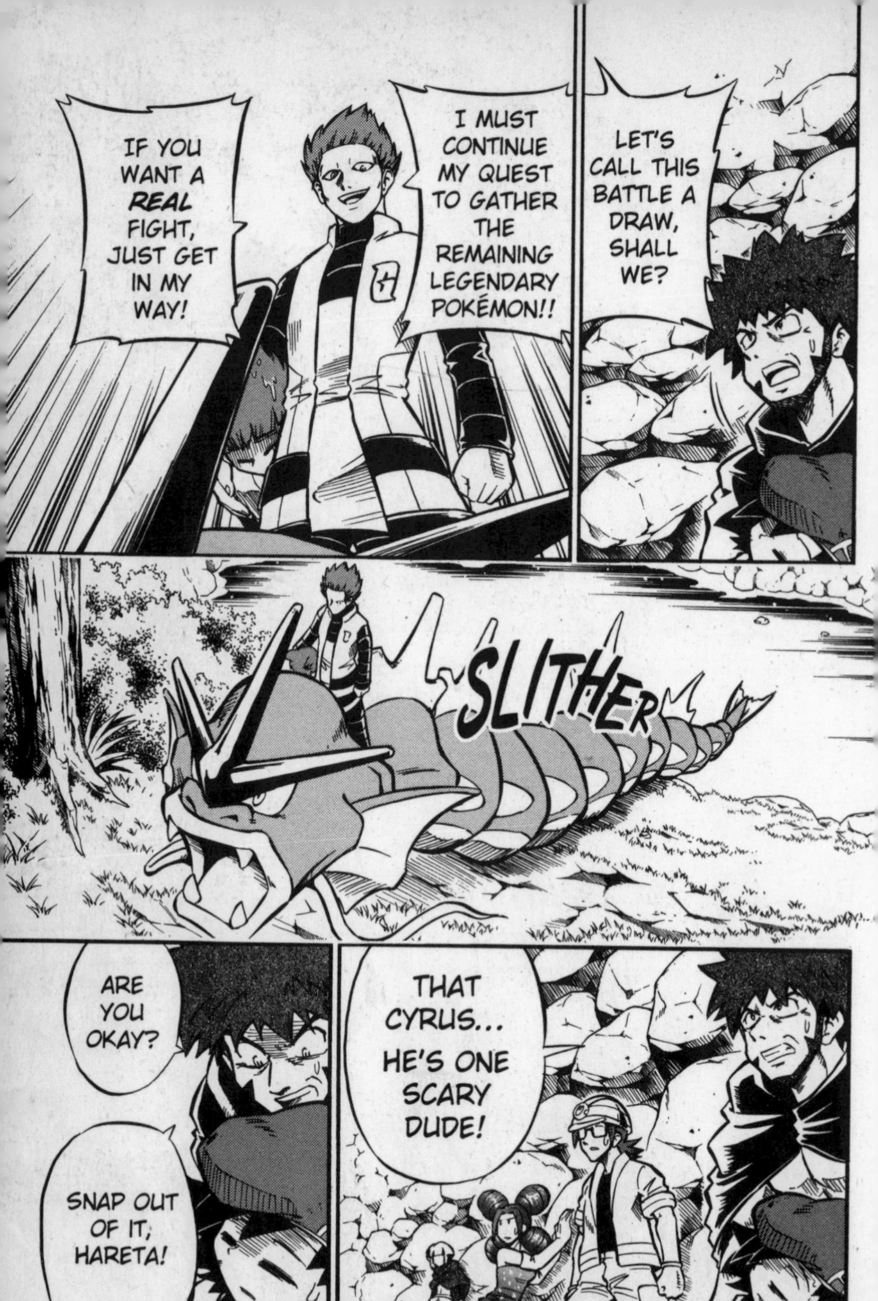
LET'S CALL THIS BATTLE A DRAW, SHALL WE?
I MUST CONTINUE MY QUEST TO GATHER THE REMAINING LEGENDARY POKÉMON!!
IF YOU WANT A *REAL* FIGHT, JUST GET IN MY WAY!
SLITHER
THAT CYRUS... HE'S ONE SCARY DUDE!
ARE YOU OKAY?
SNAP OUT OF IT, HARETA!

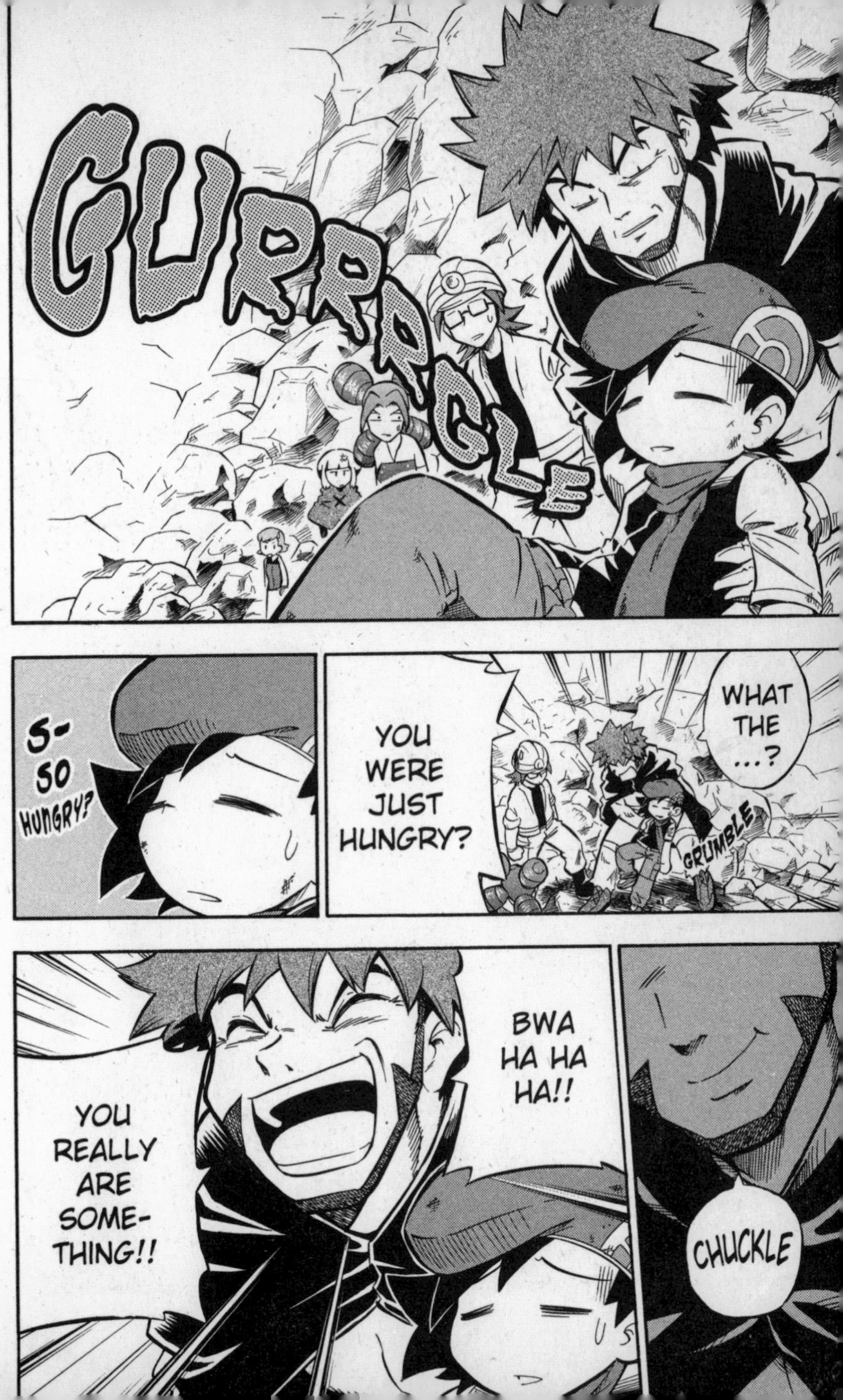
GURRRGLE
WHAT THE ...?
GRUMBLE
YOU WERE JUST HUNGRY?
S-SO HUNGRY?
CHUCKLE
BWA HA HA HA!!
YOU REALLY ARE SOME-THING!!

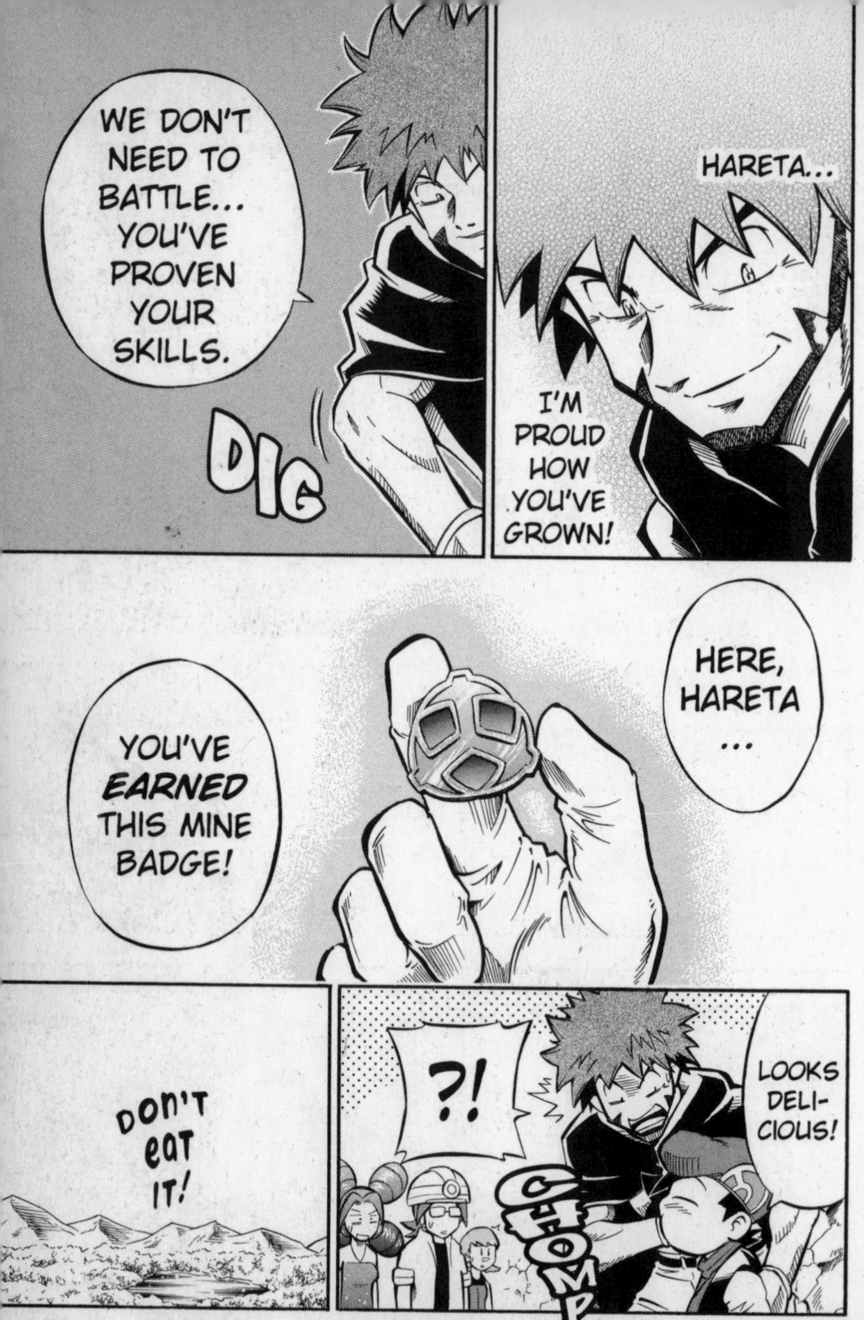
HARETA...
I'M PROUD HOW YOU'VE GROWN!
WE DON'T NEED TO BATTLE... YOU'VE PROVEN YOUR SKILLS.
DIG
HERE, HARETA ...
YOU'VE EARNED THIS MINE BADGE!
LOOKS DELI-CIOUS!
?!
CHOMP
don't eat it!

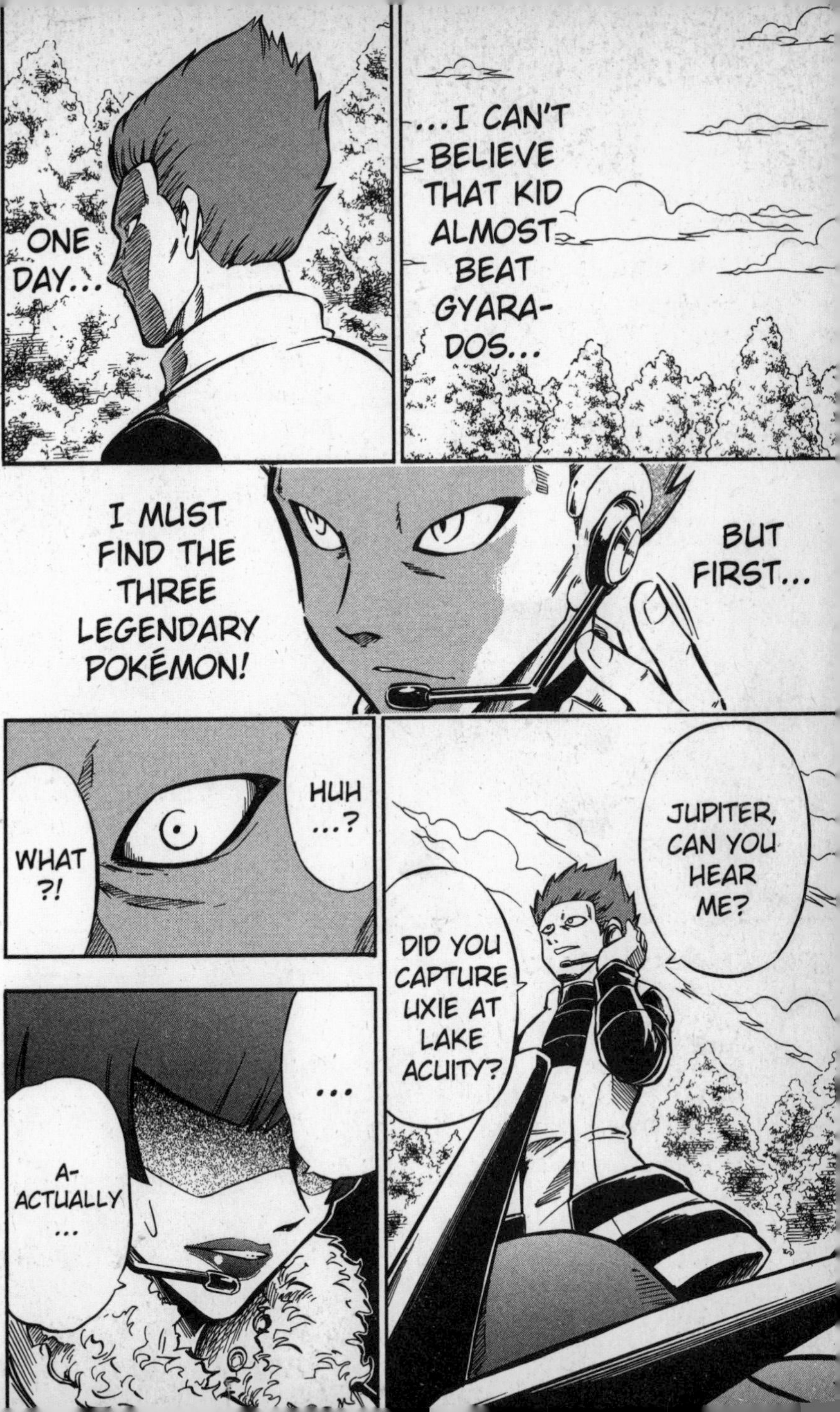
...I CAN'T BELIEVE THAT KID ALMOST BEAT GYARADOS...
ONE DAY...
I MUST FIND THE THREE LEGENDARY POKÉMON!
BUT FIRST...
JUPITER, CAN YOU HEAR ME?
DID YOU CAPTURE UXIE AT LAKE ACUITY?
HUH ...?
WHAT ?!
...
A-ACTUALLY ...

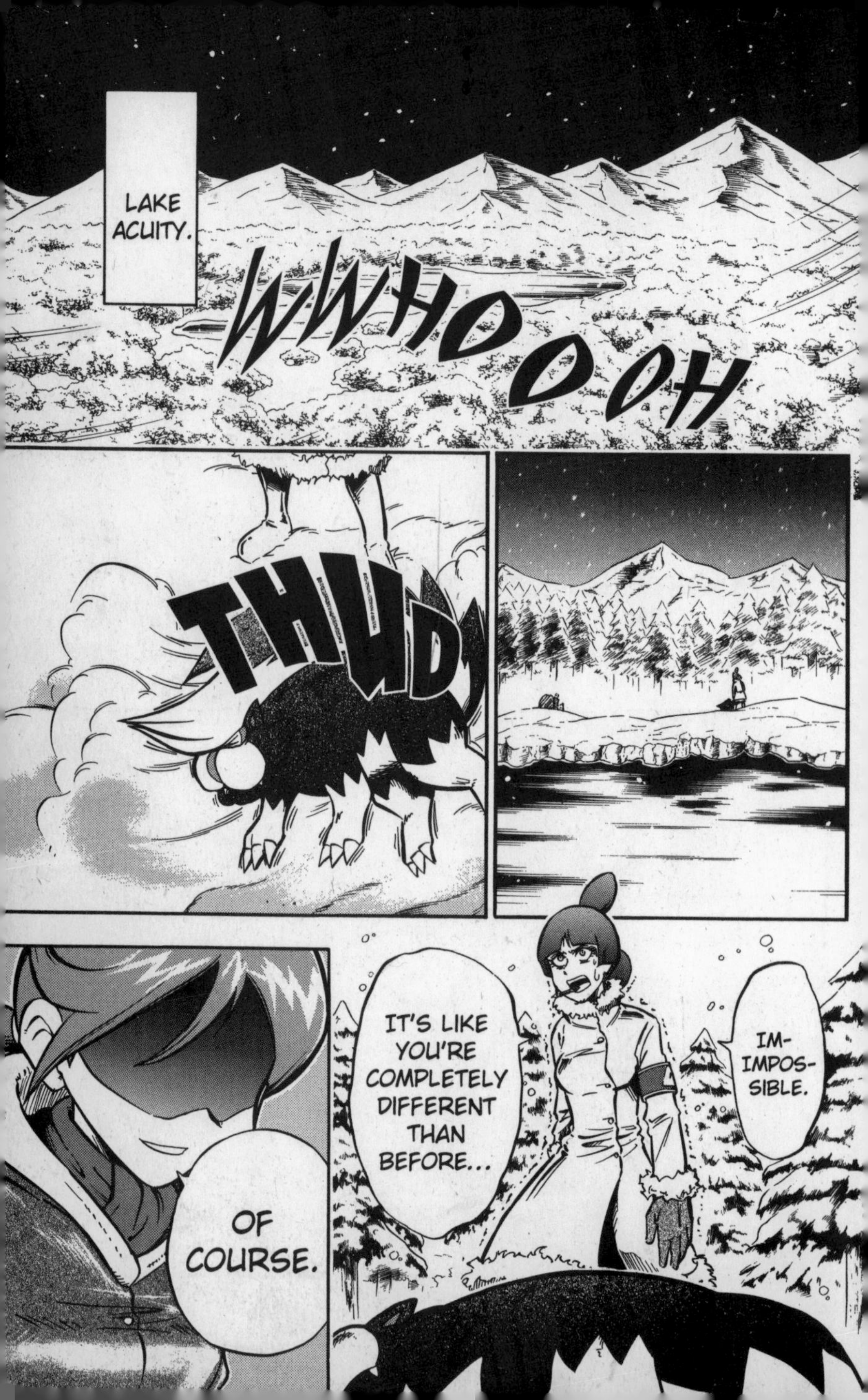
LAKE ACUITY.
WWHOOOH
THUD
IM-IMPOSSIBLE.
IT'S LIKE YOU'RE COMPLETELY DIFFERENT THAN BEFORE...
OF COURSE.

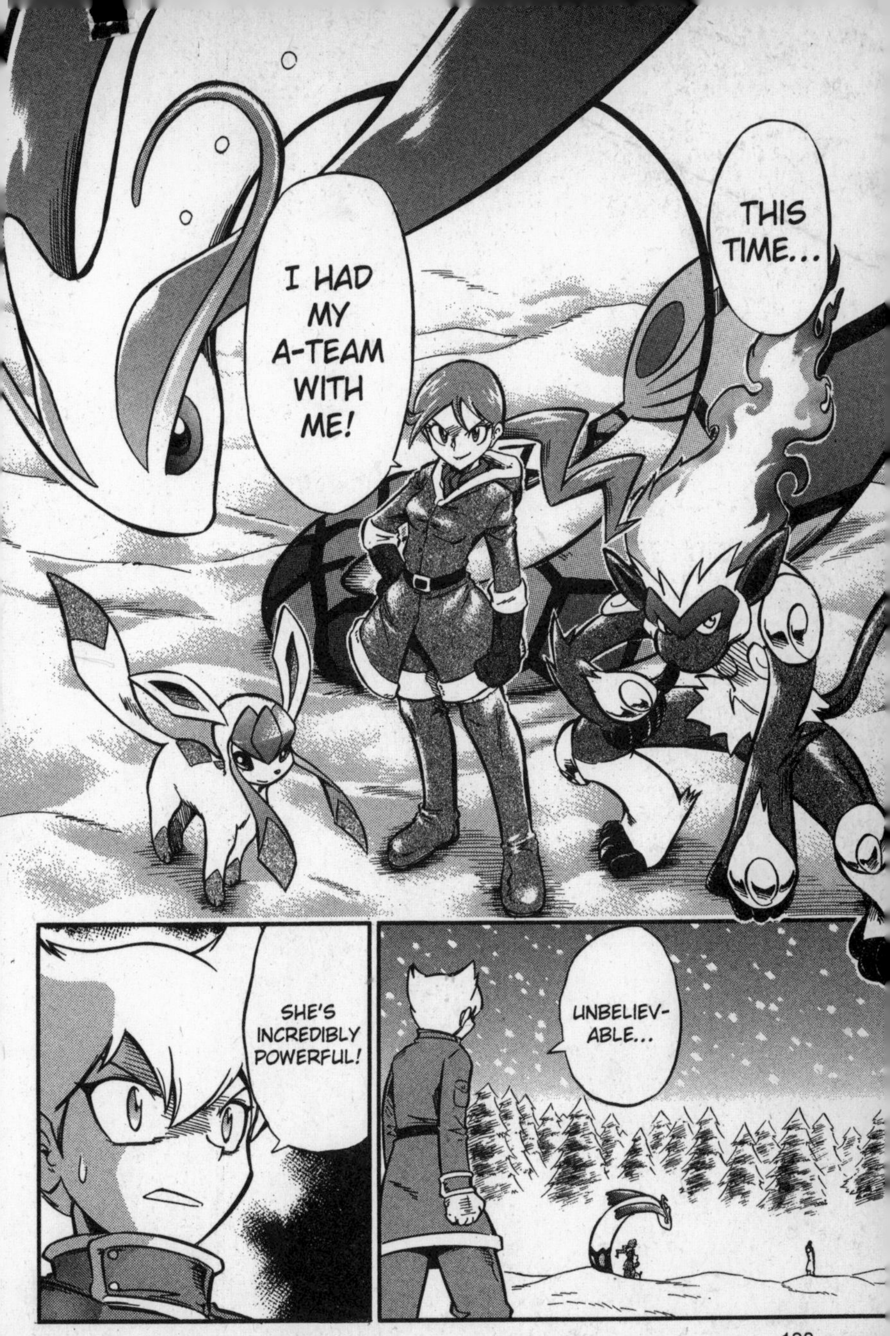
THIS TIME...
I HAD MY A-TEAM WITH ME!
UNBELIEV-ABLE...
SHE'S INCREDIBLY POWERFUL!

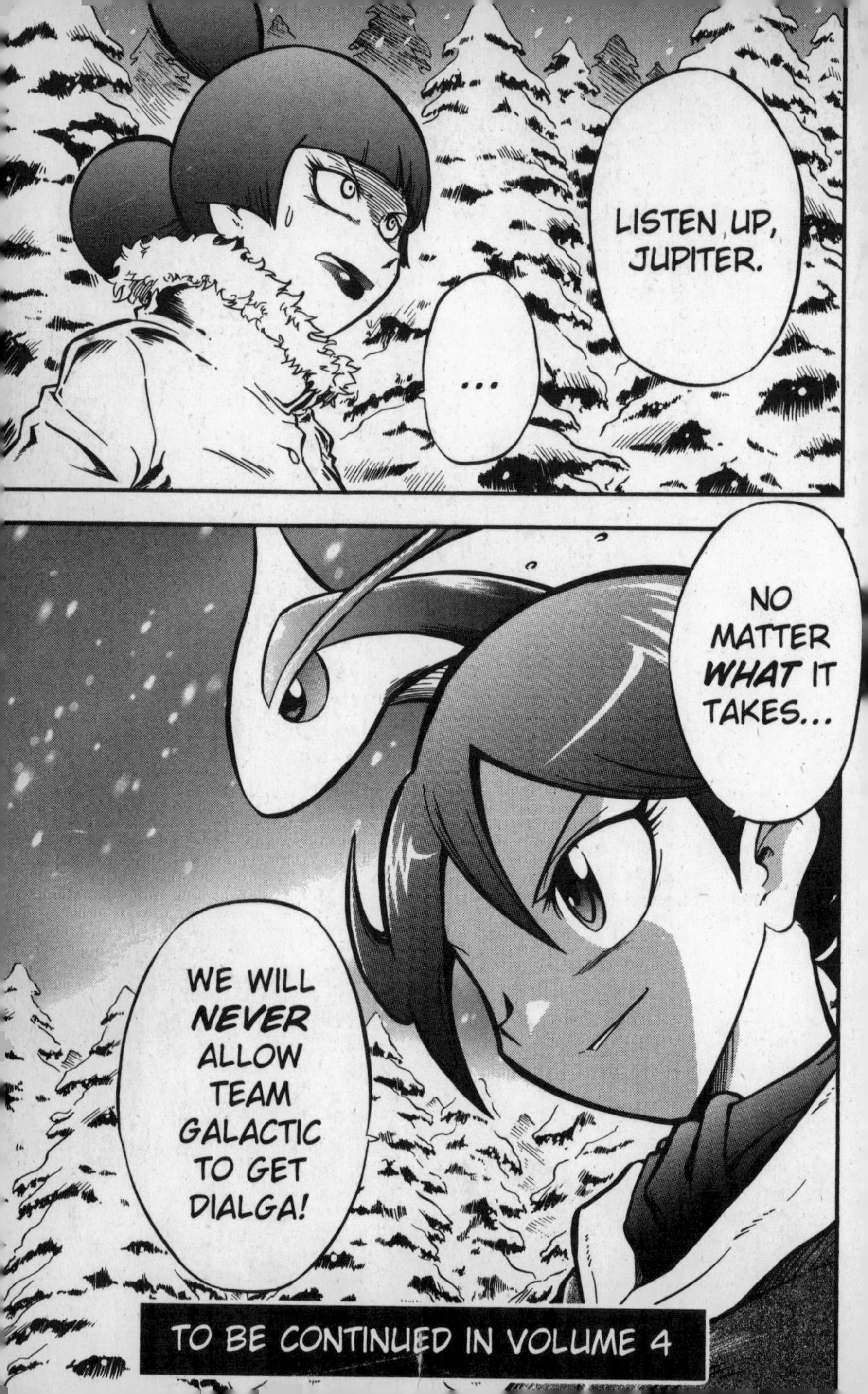
LISTEN UP, JUPITER.
...
NO MATTER **WHAT** IT TAKES...
WE WILL **NEVER** ALLOW TEAM GALACTIC TO GET DIALGA!
TO BE CONTINUED IN VOLUME 4

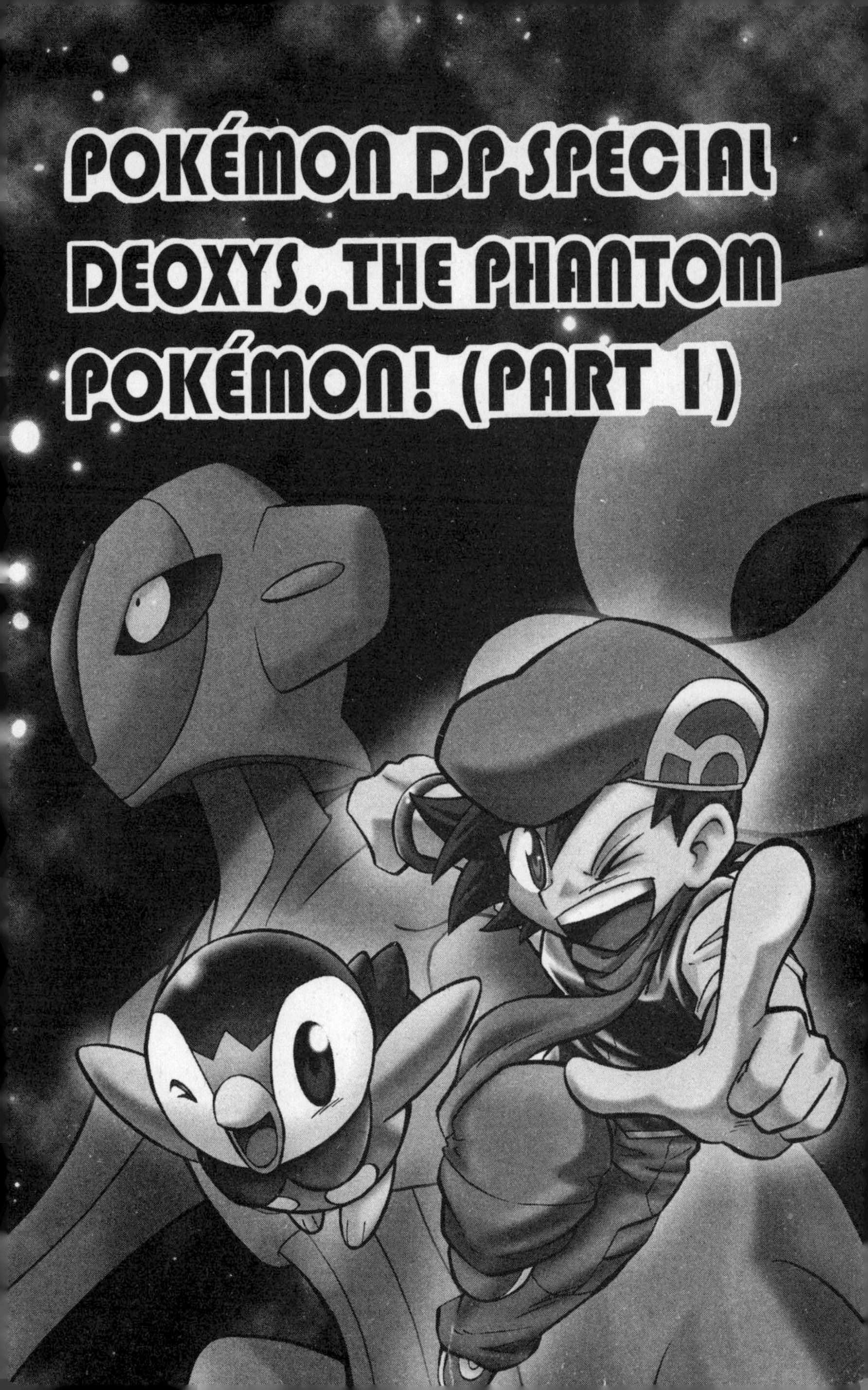
POKÉMON DP SPECIAL
DEOXYS, THE PHANTOM
POKÉMON! (PART 1)

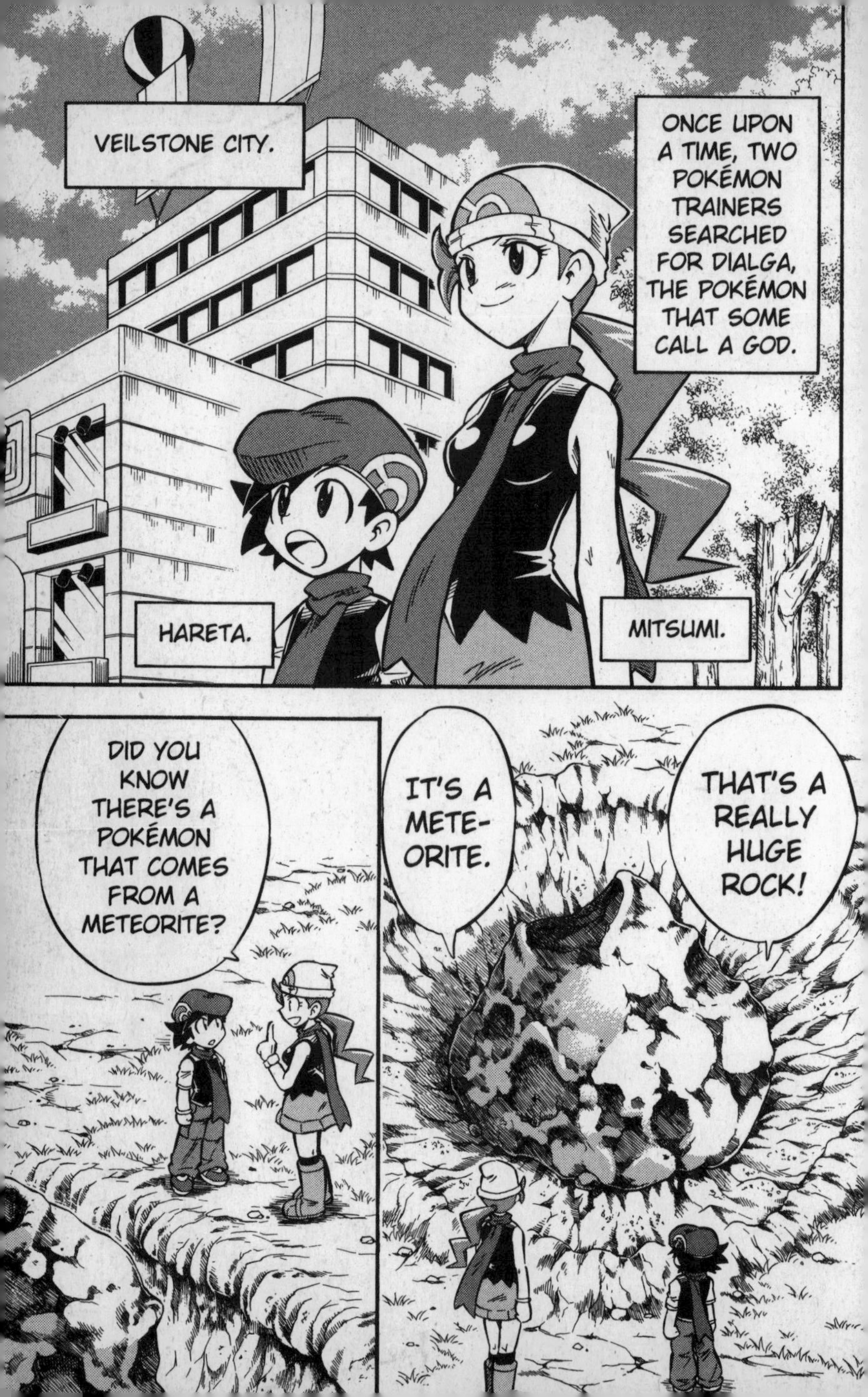
ONCE UPON A TIME, TWO POKéMON TRAINERS SEARCHED FOR DIALGA, THE POKéMON THAT SOME CALL A GOD.
VEILSTONE CITY.
MITSUMI.
HARETA.
THAT'S A REALLY HUGE ROCK!
IT'S A METE-ORITE.
DID YOU KNOW THERE'S A POKéMON THAT COMES FROM A METEORITE?

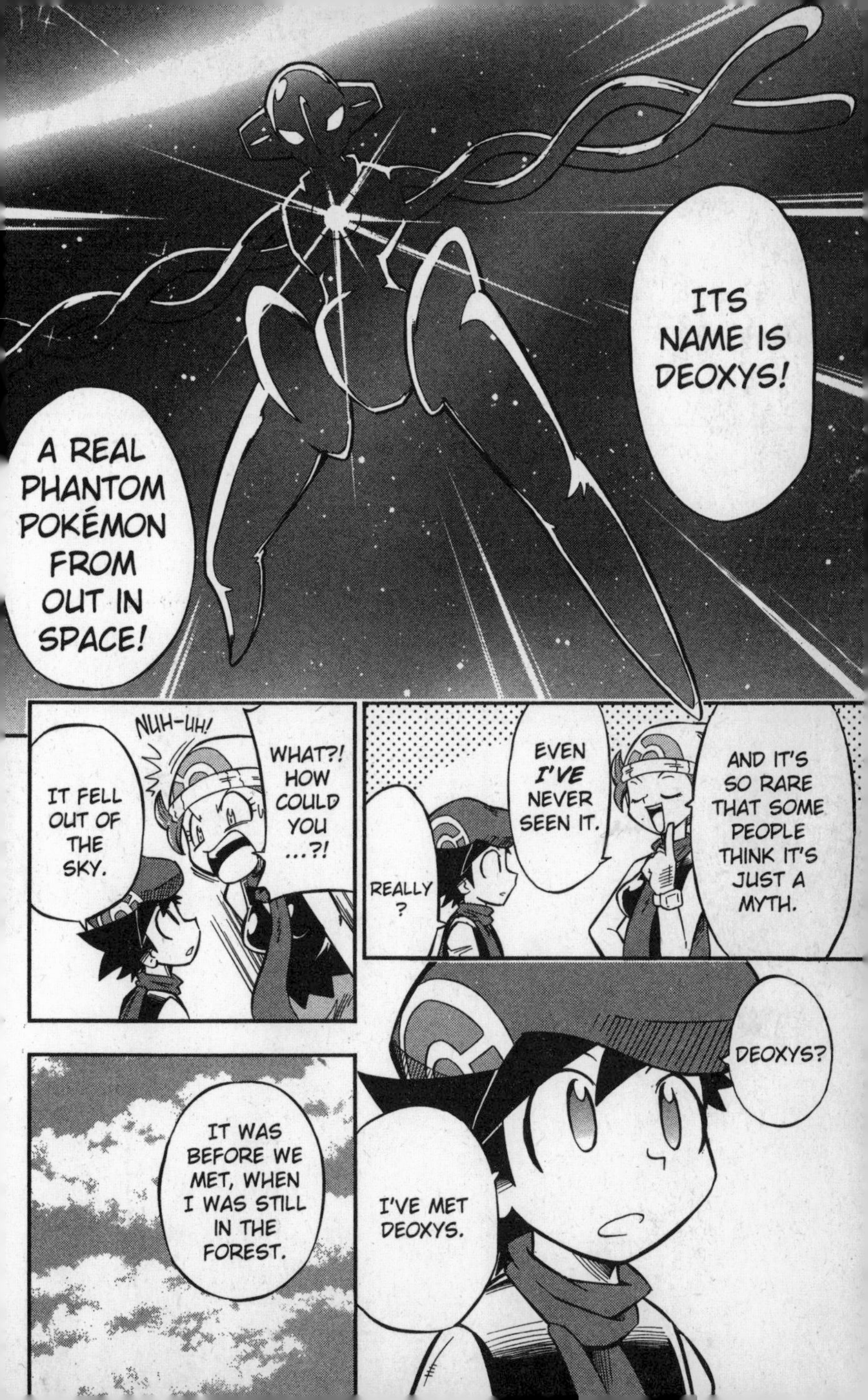
ITS NAME IS DEOXYS!
A REAL PHANTOM POKÉMON FROM OUT IN SPACE!
AND IT'S SO RARE THAT SOME PEOPLE THINK IT'S JUST A MYTH.
EVEN I'VE NEVER SEEN IT.
REALLY?
WHAT?! HOW COULD YOU ...?!
NUH-UH!
IT FELL OUT OF THE SKY.
DEOXYS?
I'VE MET DEOXYS.
IT WAS BEFORE WE MET, WHEN I WAS STILL IN THE FOREST.

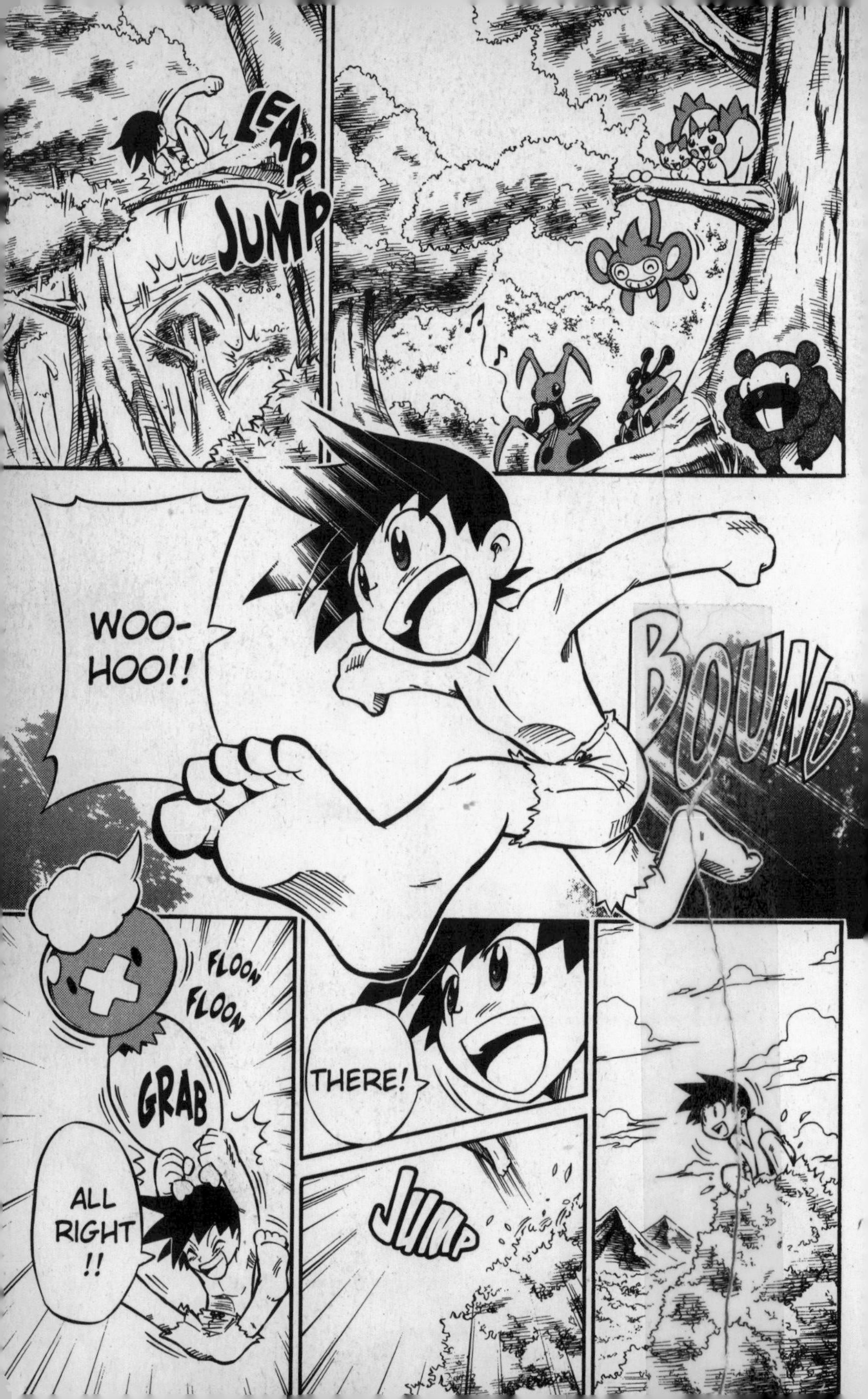
LEAP
JUMP
WOO-HOO!!
BOUND
THERE!
JUMP
FLOON
FLOON
GRAB
ALL RIGHT!!

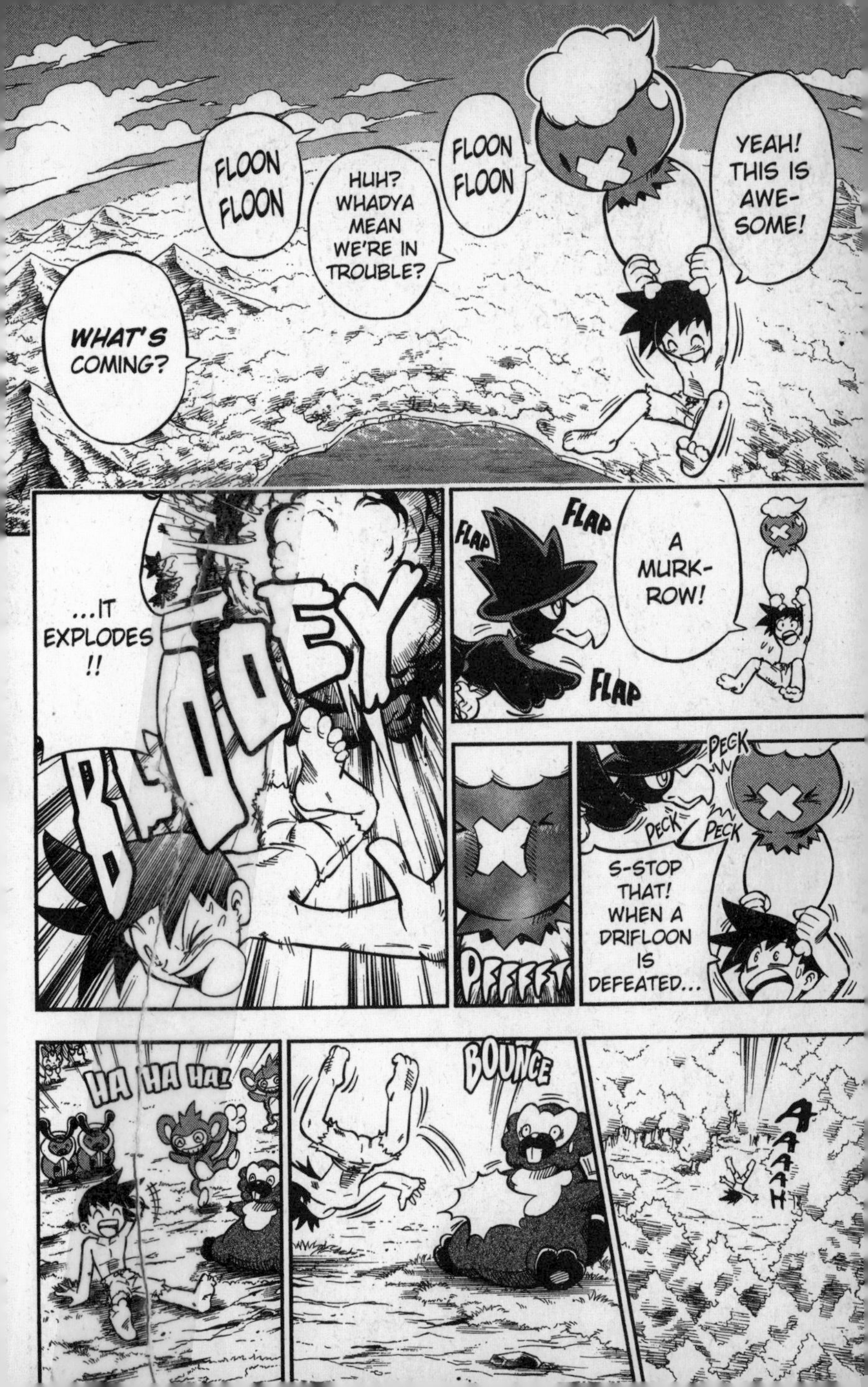
YEAH! THIS IS AWE-SOME!
FLOON FLOON
HUH? WHADYA MEAN WE'RE IN TROUBLE?
FLOON FLOON
WHAT'S COMING?
FLAP
FLAP
A MURK-ROW!
FLAP
PECK
PECK
PECK
S-STOP THAT! WHEN A DRIFLOON IS DEFEATED...
PFFFFT
...IT EXPLODES!!
BLOOEY
AAAAH!
BOUNCE
HA HA HA!

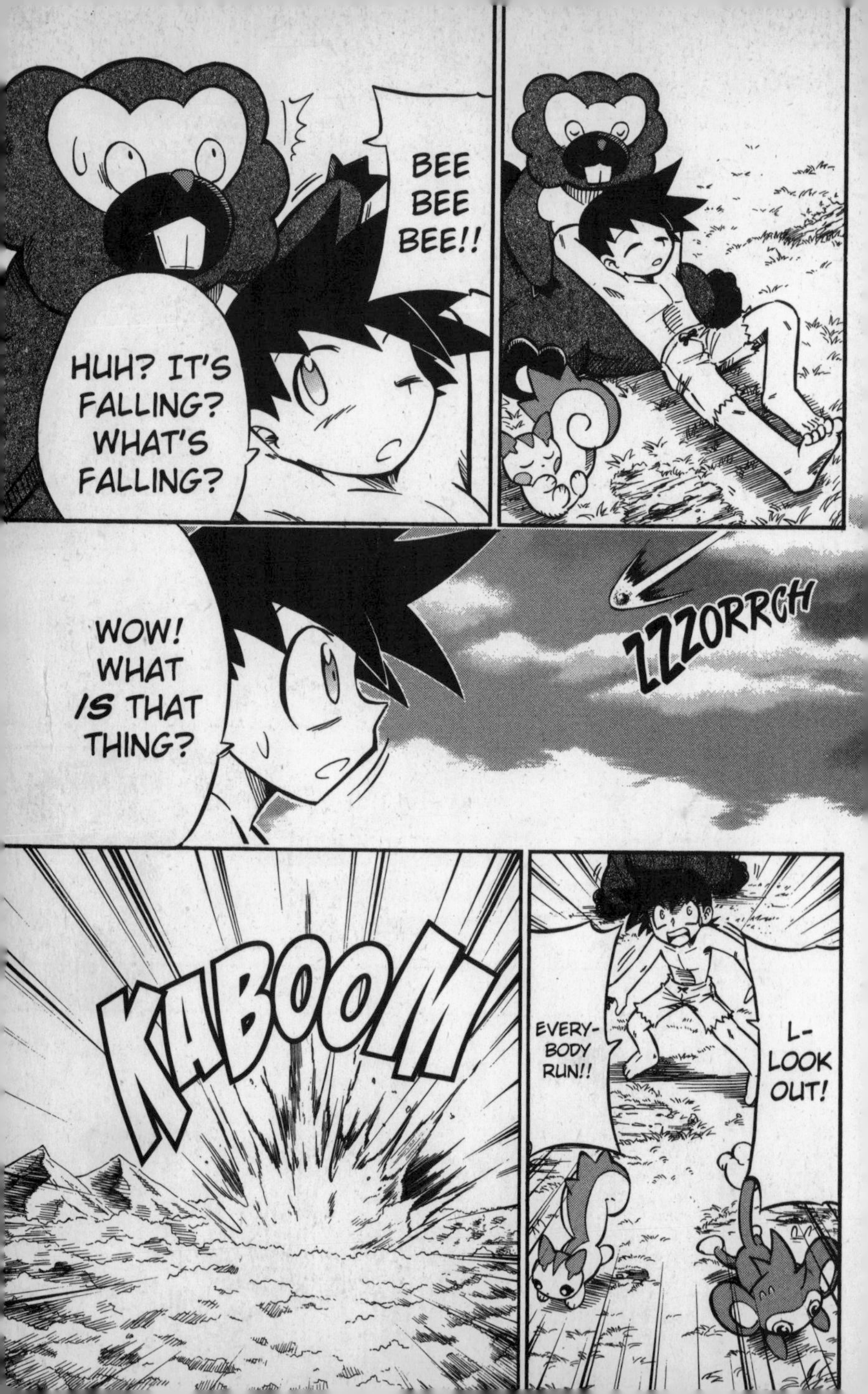
BEE BEE BEE!!
HUH? IT'S FALLING? WHAT'S FALLING?
ZZZORRCH
WOW! WHAT *IS* THAT THING?
L- LOOK OUT!
EVERY-BODY RUN!!
KABOOM

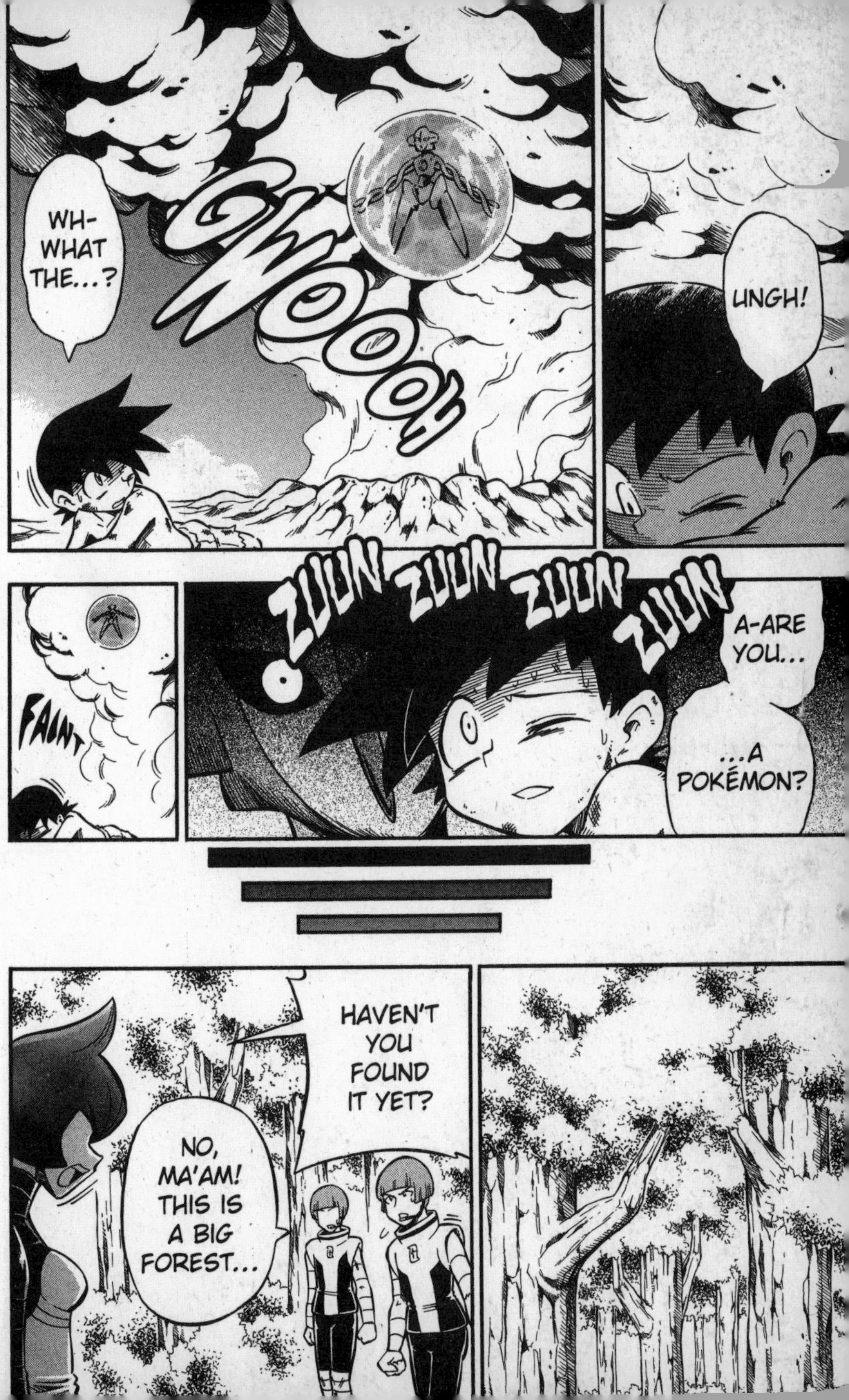
UNGH!
WH- WHAT THE...?
GWOOOOH
ZUUN ZUUN ZUUN ZUUN
A-ARE YOU...
...A POKÉMON?
FAINT
HAVEN'T YOU FOUND IT YET?
NO, MA'AM! THIS IS A BIG FOREST...

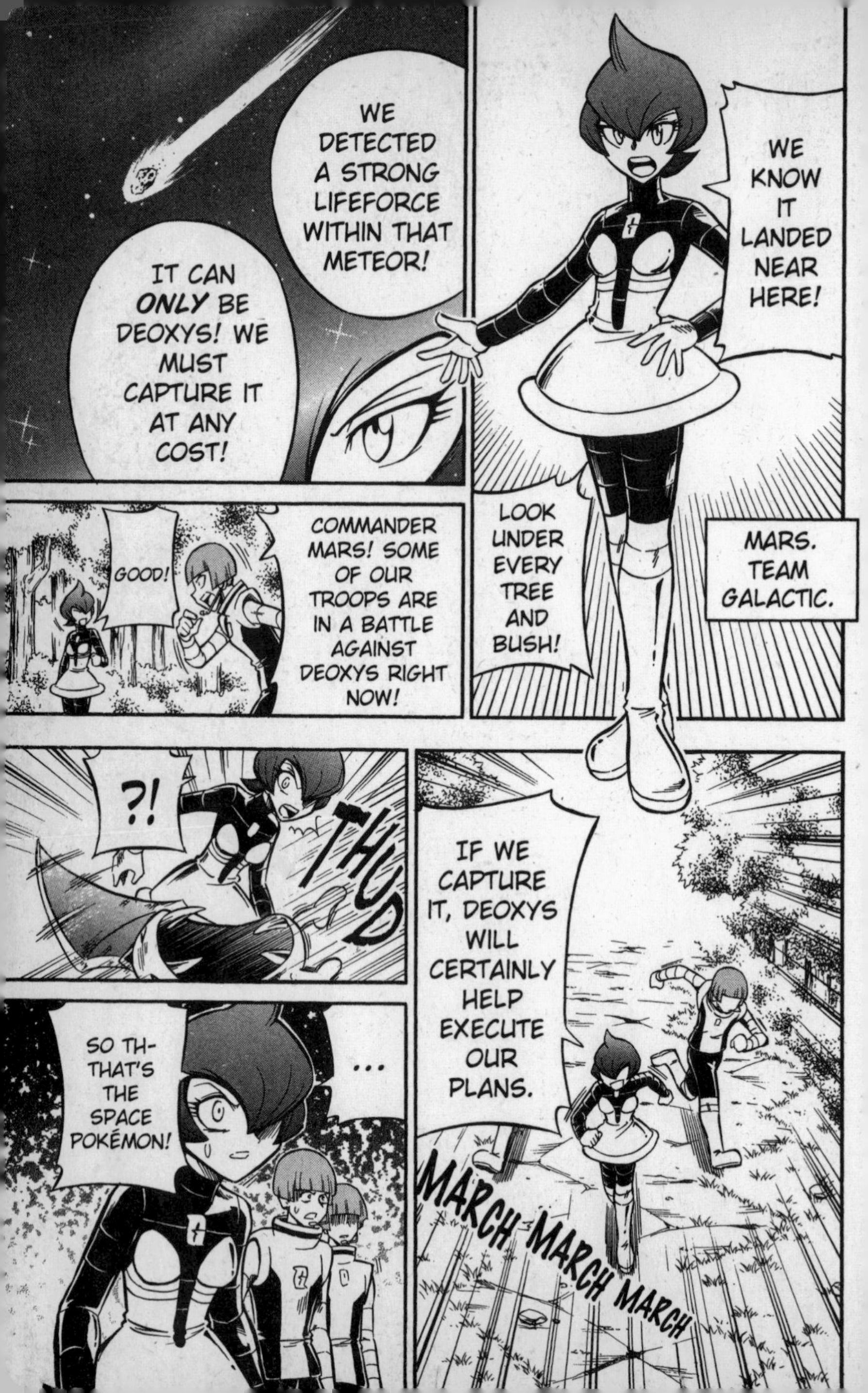
WE KNOW IT LANDED NEAR HERE!
MARS. TEAM GALACTIC.
LOOK UNDER EVERY TREE AND BUSH!
WE DETECTED A STRONG LIFEFORCE WITHIN THAT METEOR!
IT CAN *ONLY* BE DEOXYS! WE MUST CAPTURE IT AT ANY COST!
COMMANDER MARS! SOME OF OUR TROOPS ARE IN A BATTLE AGAINST DEOXYS RIGHT NOW!
GOOD!
IF WE CAPTURE IT, DEOXYS WILL CERTAINLY HELP EXECUTE OUR PLANS.
MARCH MARCH MARCH MARCH
?!
THUD
...
SO TH-THAT'S THE SPACE POKÉMON!

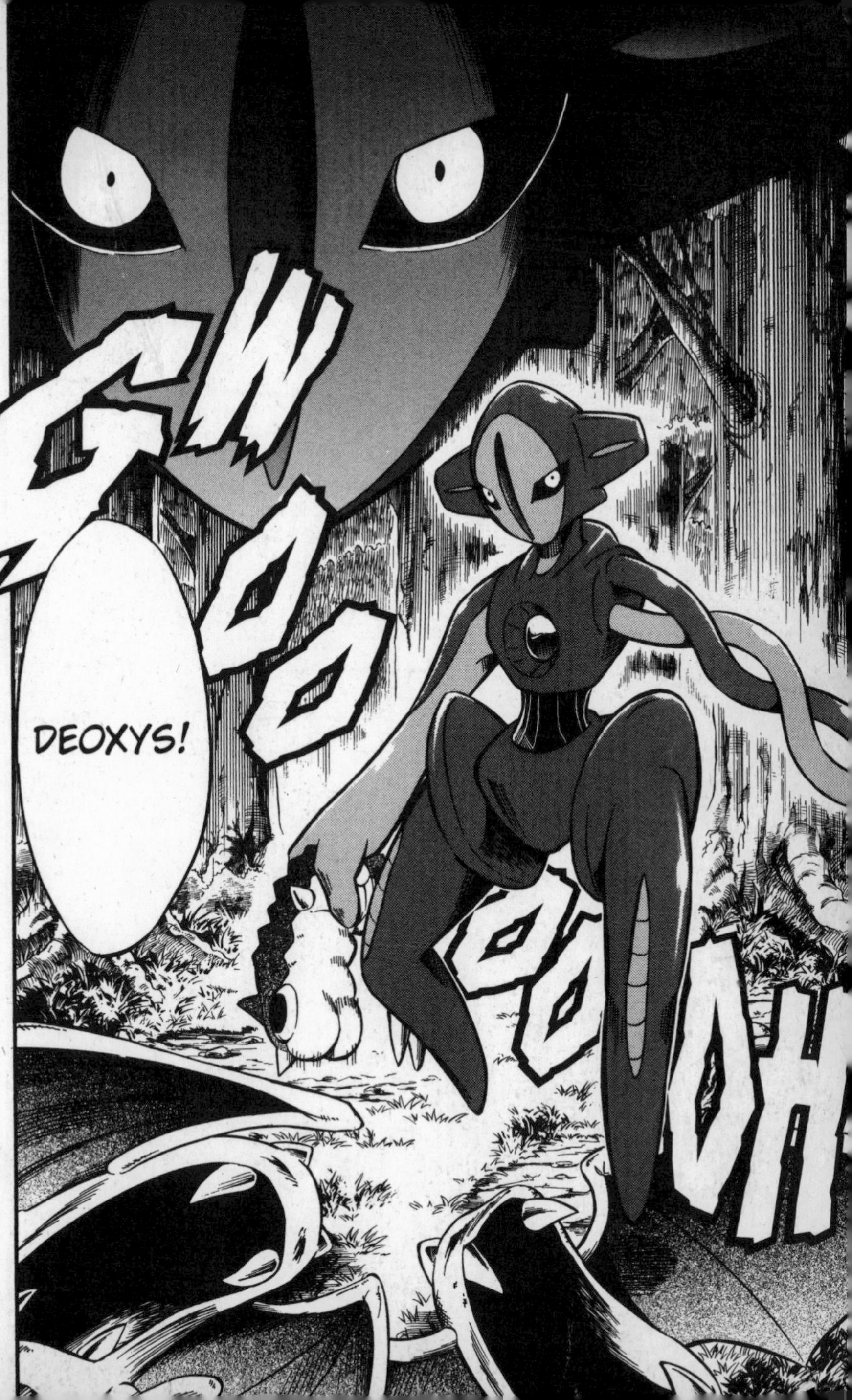
DEOXYS!

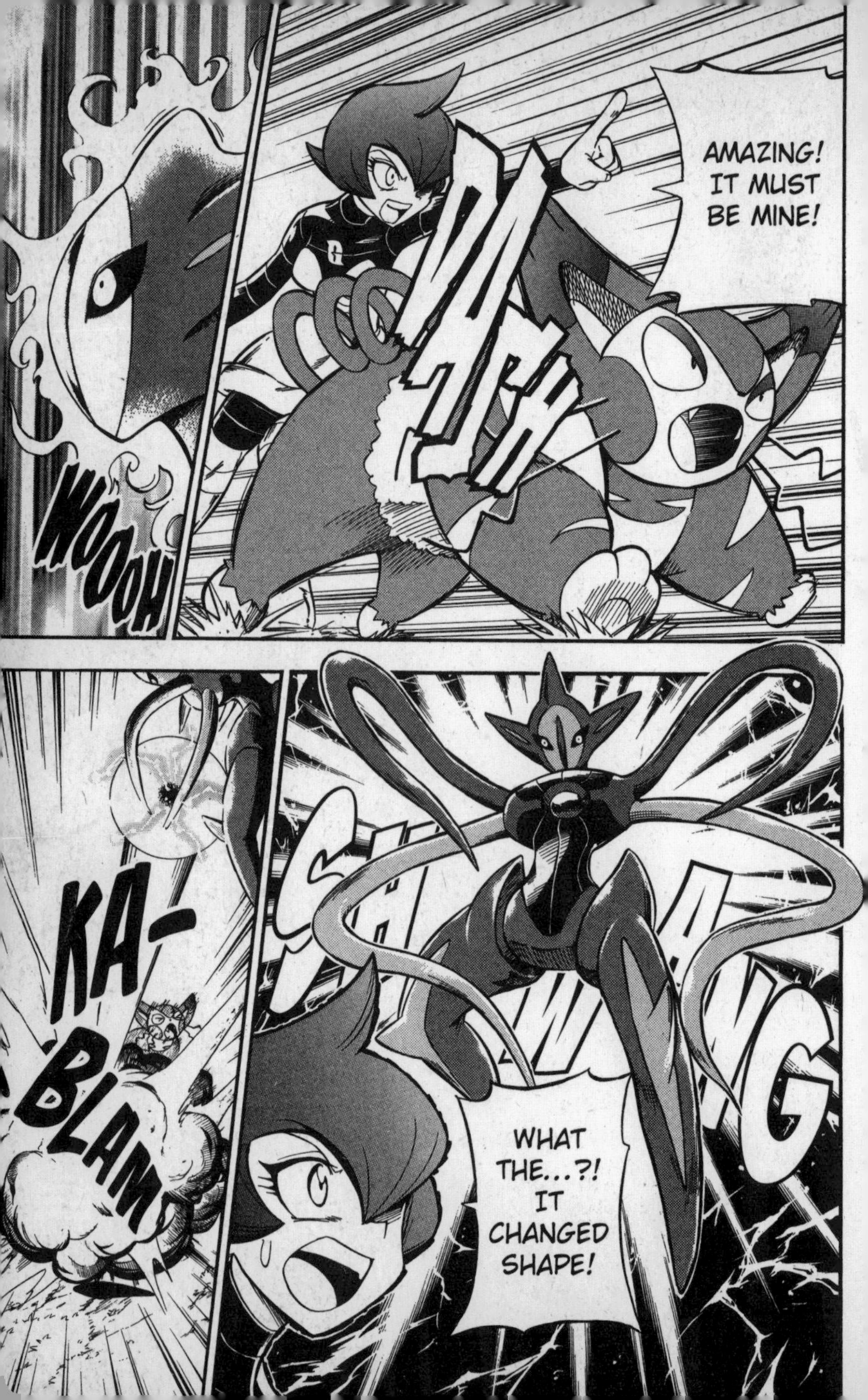
AMAZING! IT MUST BE MINE!
WOOOOH
WHAT THE...?! IT CHANGED SHAPE!
KA-BLAM

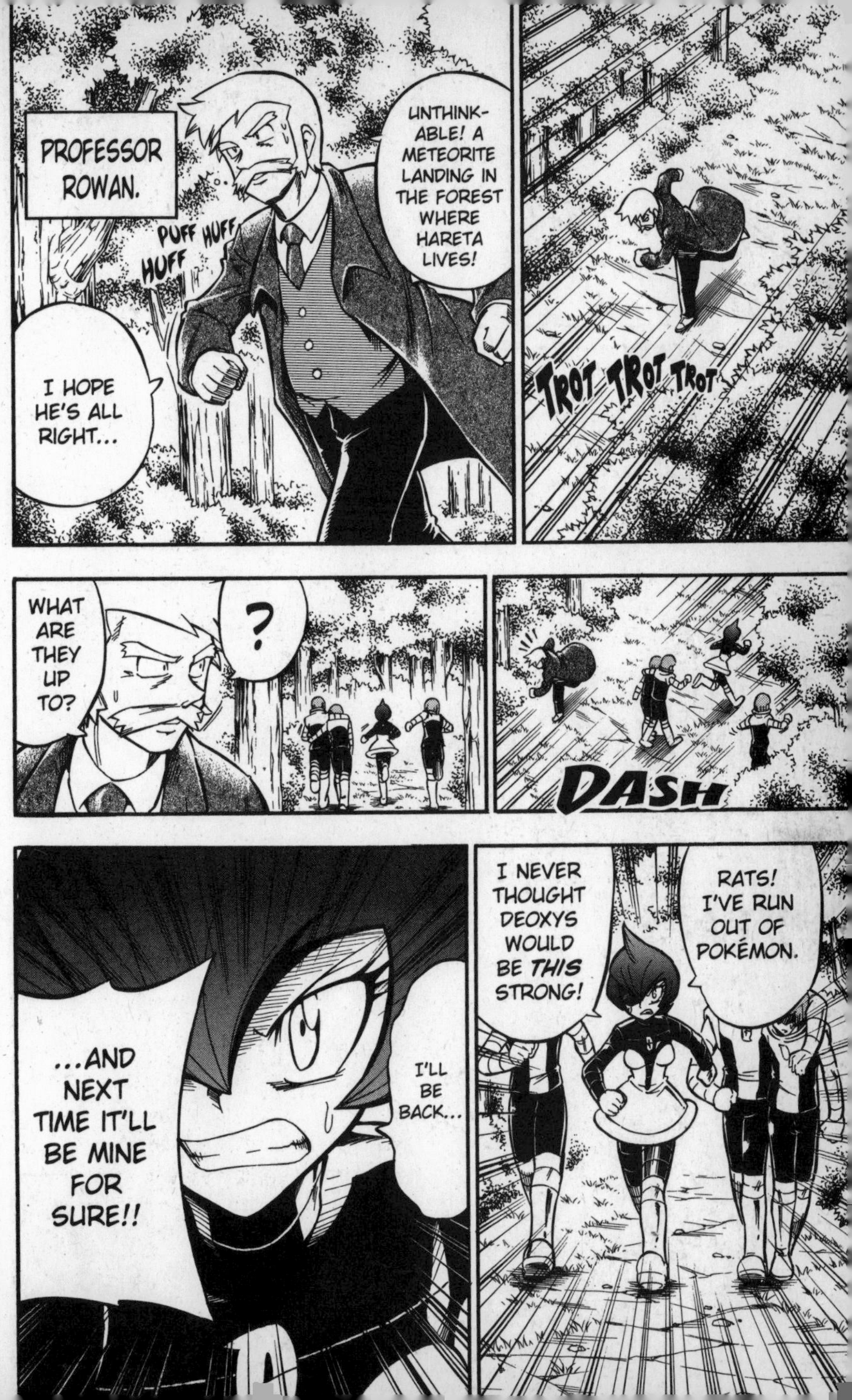
TROT TROT TROT
PROFESSOR ROWAN.
UNTHINKABLE! A METEORITE LANDING IN THE FOREST WHERE HARETA LIVES!
PUFF HUFF HUFF
I HOPE HE'S ALL RIGHT...
DASH
?
WHAT ARE THEY UP TO?
RATS! I'VE RUN OUT OF POKÉMON.
I NEVER THOUGHT DEOXYS WOULD BE *THIS* STRONG!
I'LL BE BACK...
...AND NEXT TIME IT'LL BE MINE FOR SURE!!

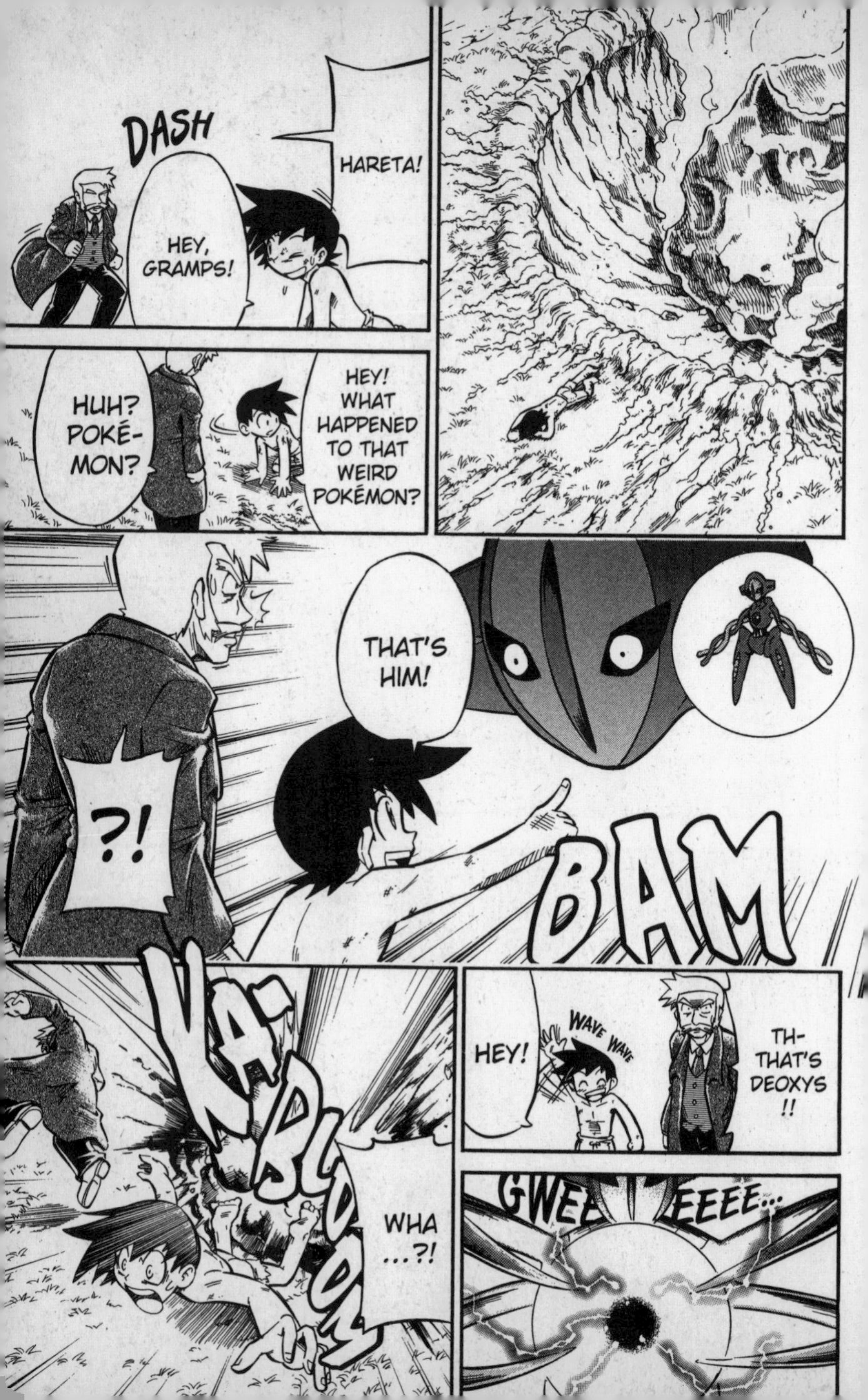
HARETA!
DASH
HEY, GRAMPS!
HEY! WHAT HAPPENED TO THAT WEIRD POKÉMON?
HUH? POKÉ-MON?
THAT'S HIM!
BAM
?!
HEY!
WAVE WAVE
TH-THAT'S DEOXYS !!
GWEE EEEE...
KA BLOOM
WHA ...?!

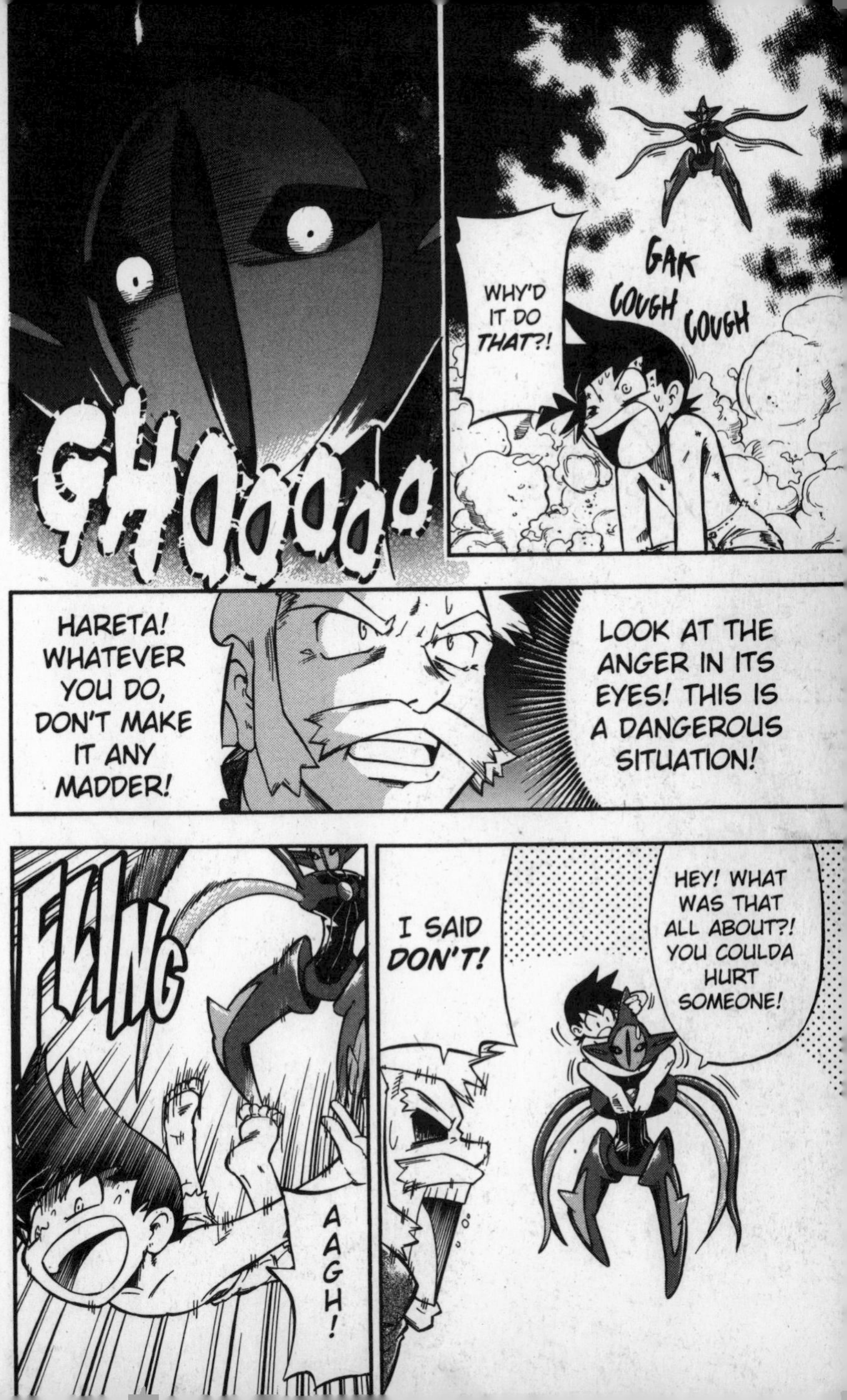
GAK
COUGH
COUGH
WHY'D IT DO *THAT?!*
GHOOOOOO
LOOK AT THE ANGER IN ITS EYES! THIS IS A DANGEROUS SITUATION!
HARETA! WHATEVER YOU DO, DON'T MAKE IT ANY MADDER!
HEY! WHAT WAS THAT ALL ABOUT?! YOU COULDA HURT SOMEONE!
I SAID ***DON'T!***
FLING
AAGH!

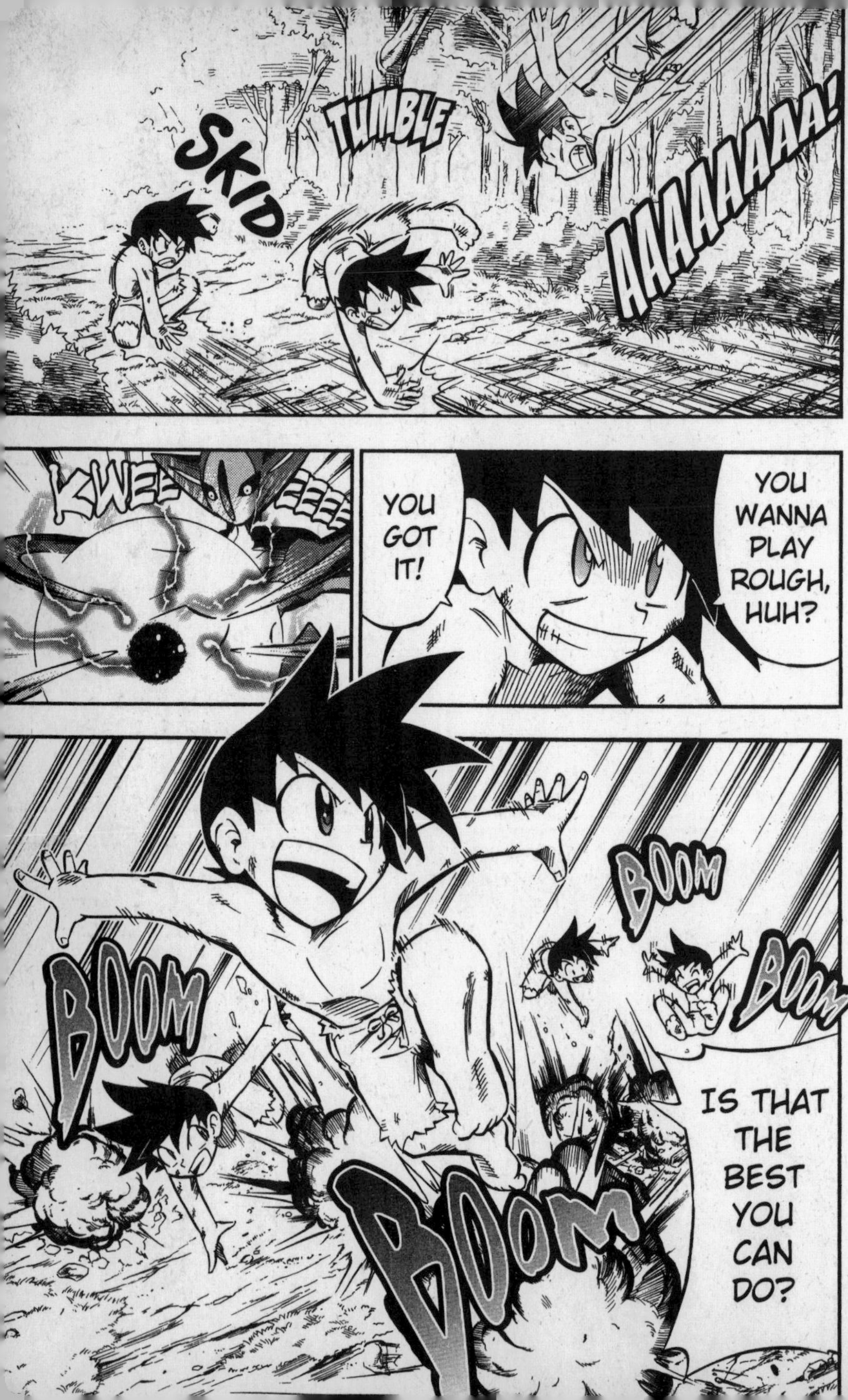
AAAAAAAA!
TUMBLE
SKID
YOU WANNA PLAY ROUGH, HUH?
YOU GOT IT!
KWEEEEEE
BOOM
BOOM
IS THAT THE BEST YOU CAN DO?
BOOM
BOOM

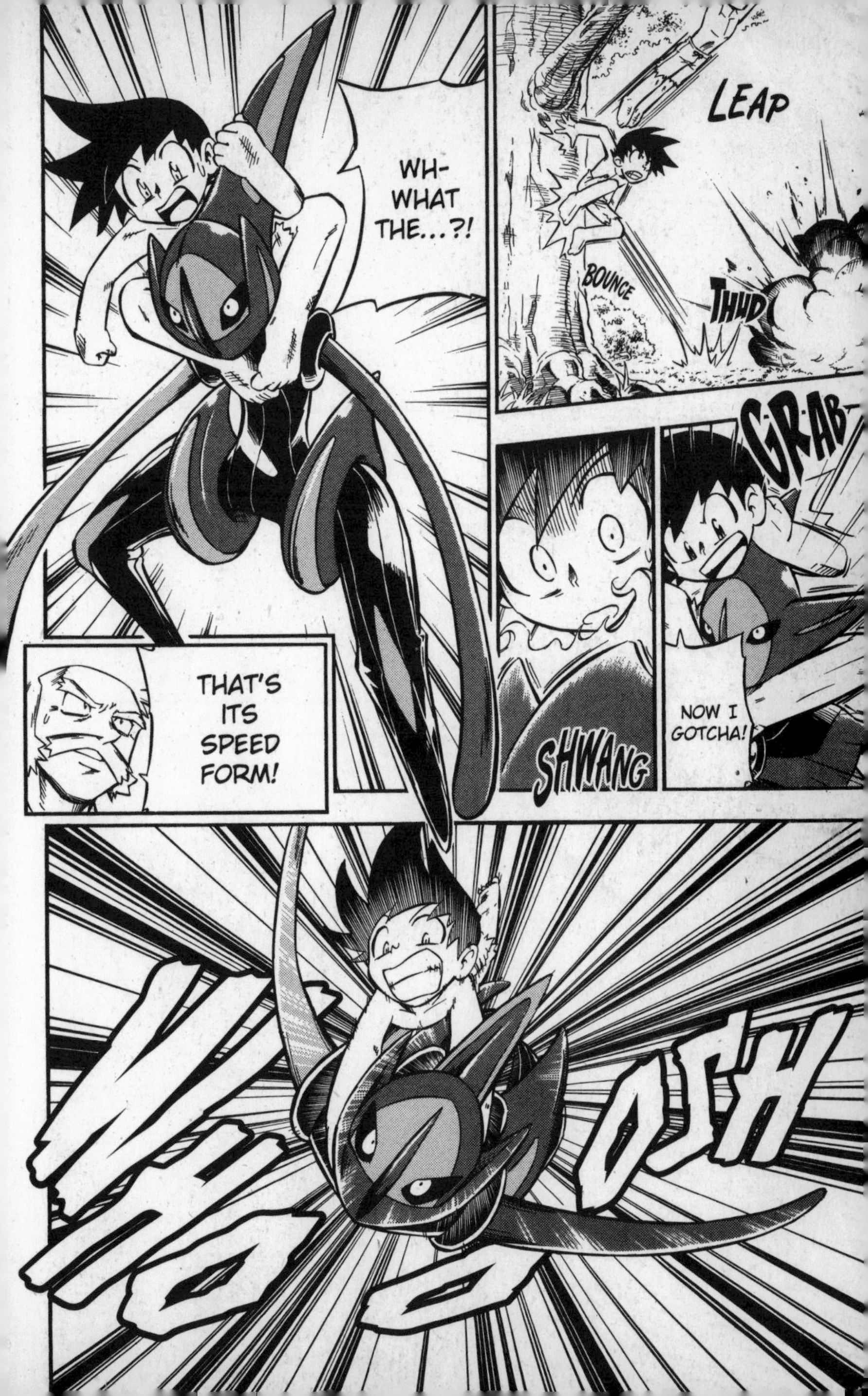
LEAP
BOUNCE
THUD
GRAB
NOW I GOTCHA!
SHWANG
WH-WHAT THE...?!
THAT'S ITS SPEED FORM!
WHOOSH

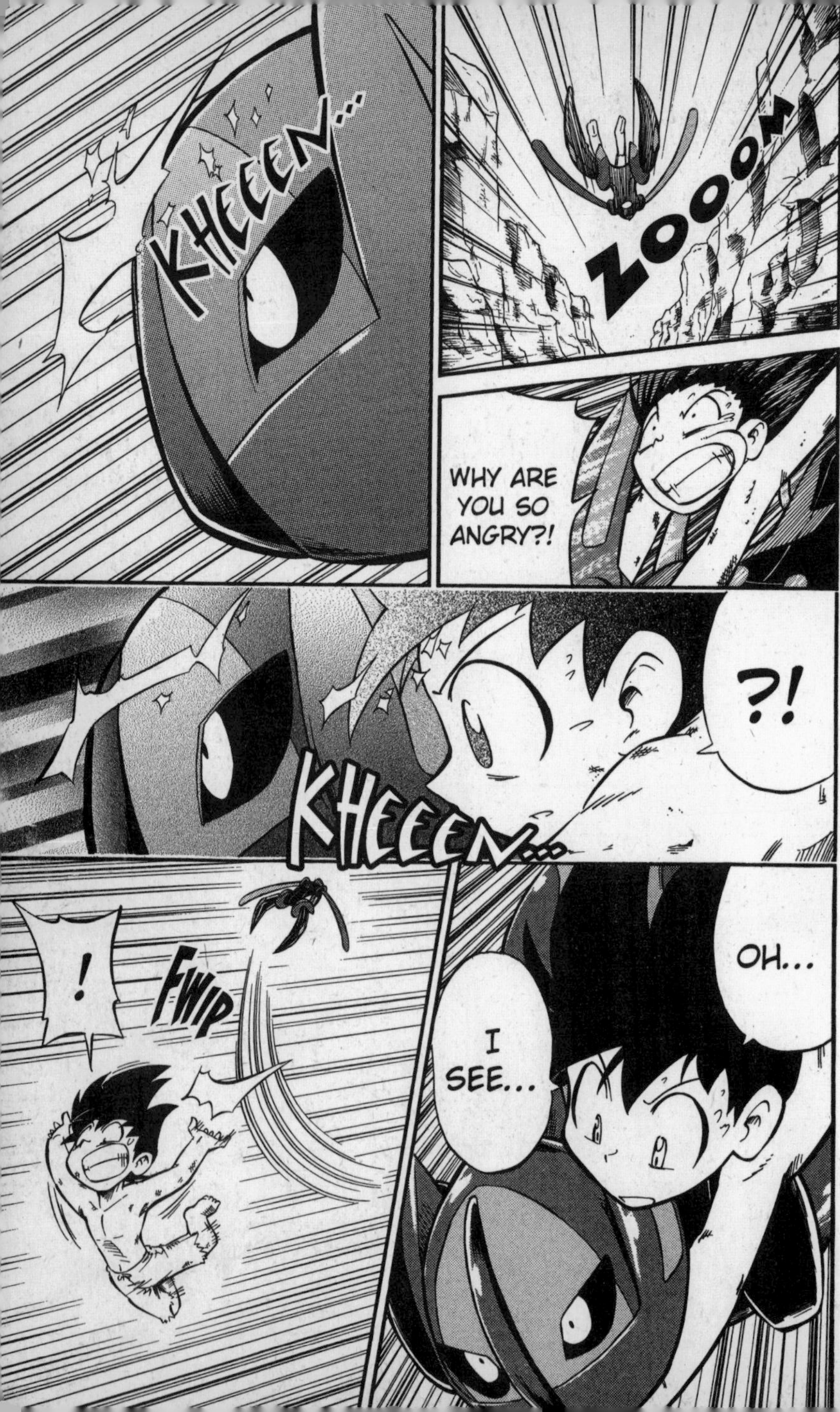
ZOOOM
WHY ARE YOU SO ANGRY?!
KHEEEN...
?!
KHEEEN...
OH...
I SEE...
!
FWIP

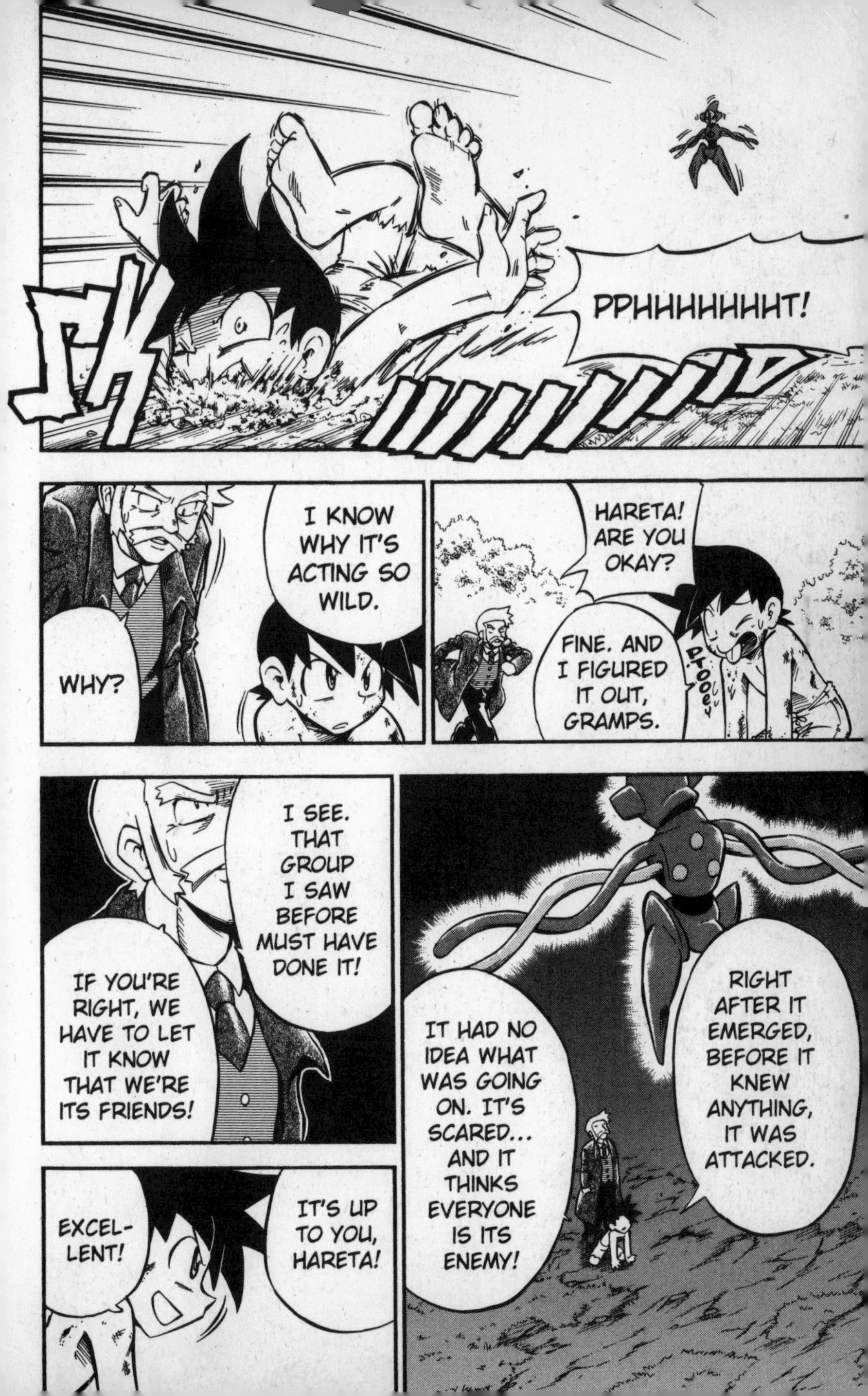
PPHHHHHHHT!
HARETA! ARE YOU OKAY?
FINE. AND I FIGURED IT OUT, GRAMPS.
PTOOEY
I KNOW WHY IT'S ACTING SO WILD.
WHY?
RIGHT AFTER IT EMERGED, BEFORE IT KNEW ANYTHING, IT WAS ATTACKED.
IT HAD NO IDEA WHAT WAS GOING ON. IT'S SCARED... AND IT THINKS EVERYONE IS ITS ENEMY!
I SEE. THAT GROUP I SAW BEFORE MUST HAVE DONE IT!
IF YOU'RE RIGHT, WE HAVE TO LET IT KNOW THAT WE'RE ITS FRIENDS!
IT'S UP TO YOU, HARETA!
EXCEL-LENT!

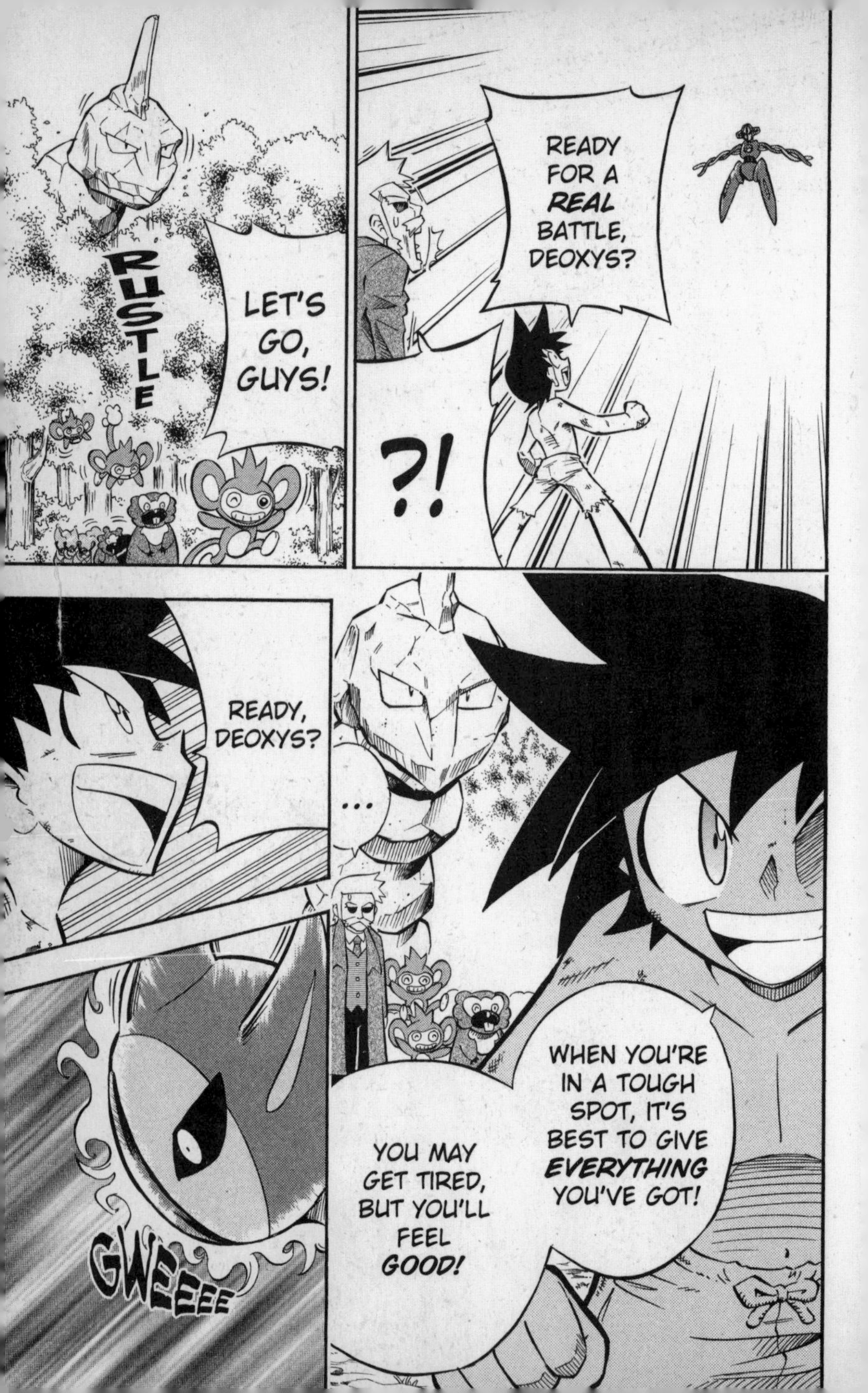
READY FOR A REAL BATTLE, DEOXYS?
?!
RUSTLE
LET'S GO, GUYS!
...
WHEN YOU'RE IN A TOUGH SPOT, IT'S BEST TO GIVE EVERYTHING YOU'VE GOT!
YOU MAY GET TIRED, BUT YOU'LL FEEL GOOD!
READY, DEOXYS?
GWEEEEE

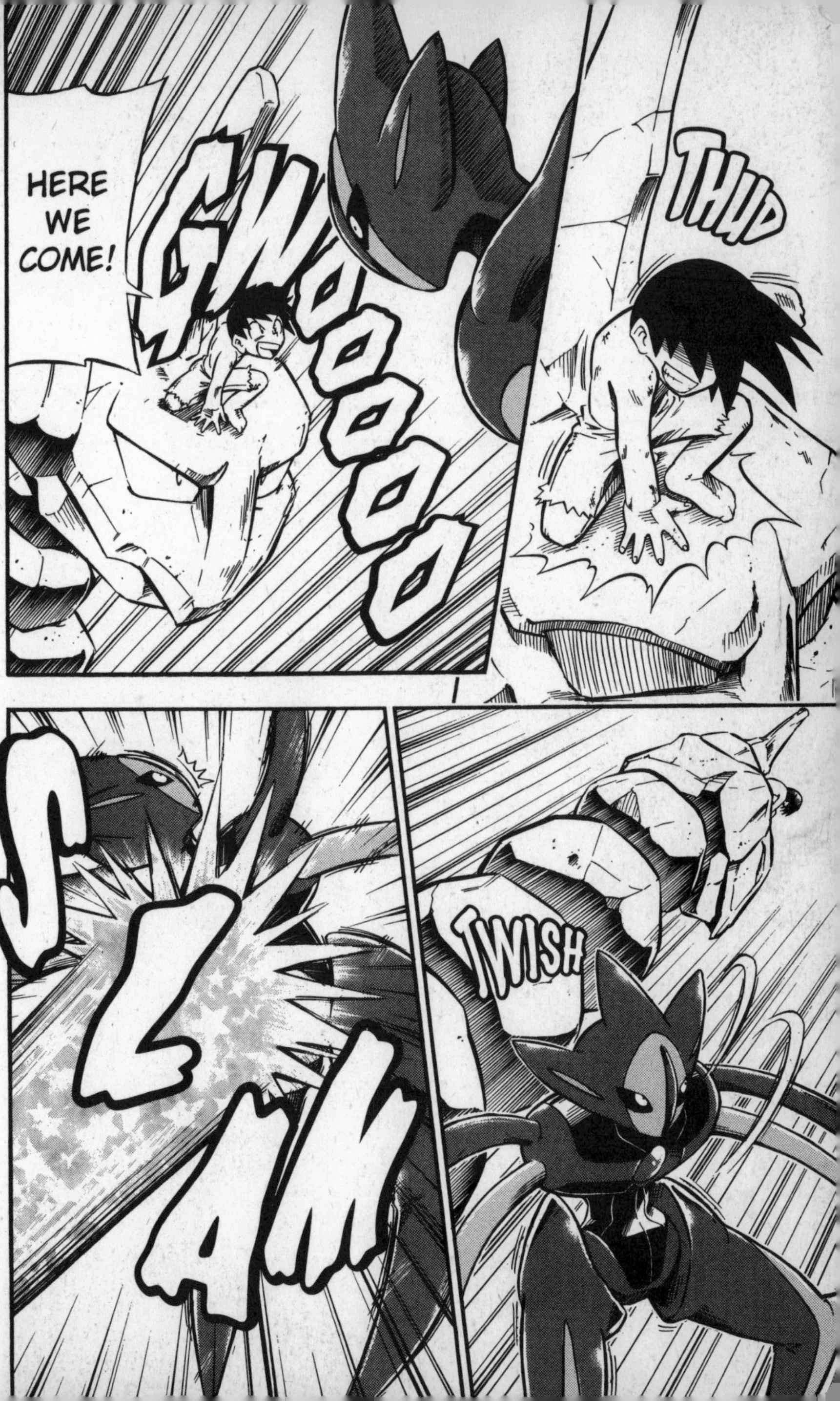
THUD
HERE WE COME!
GWOOOOOO
TWISH
SLAM

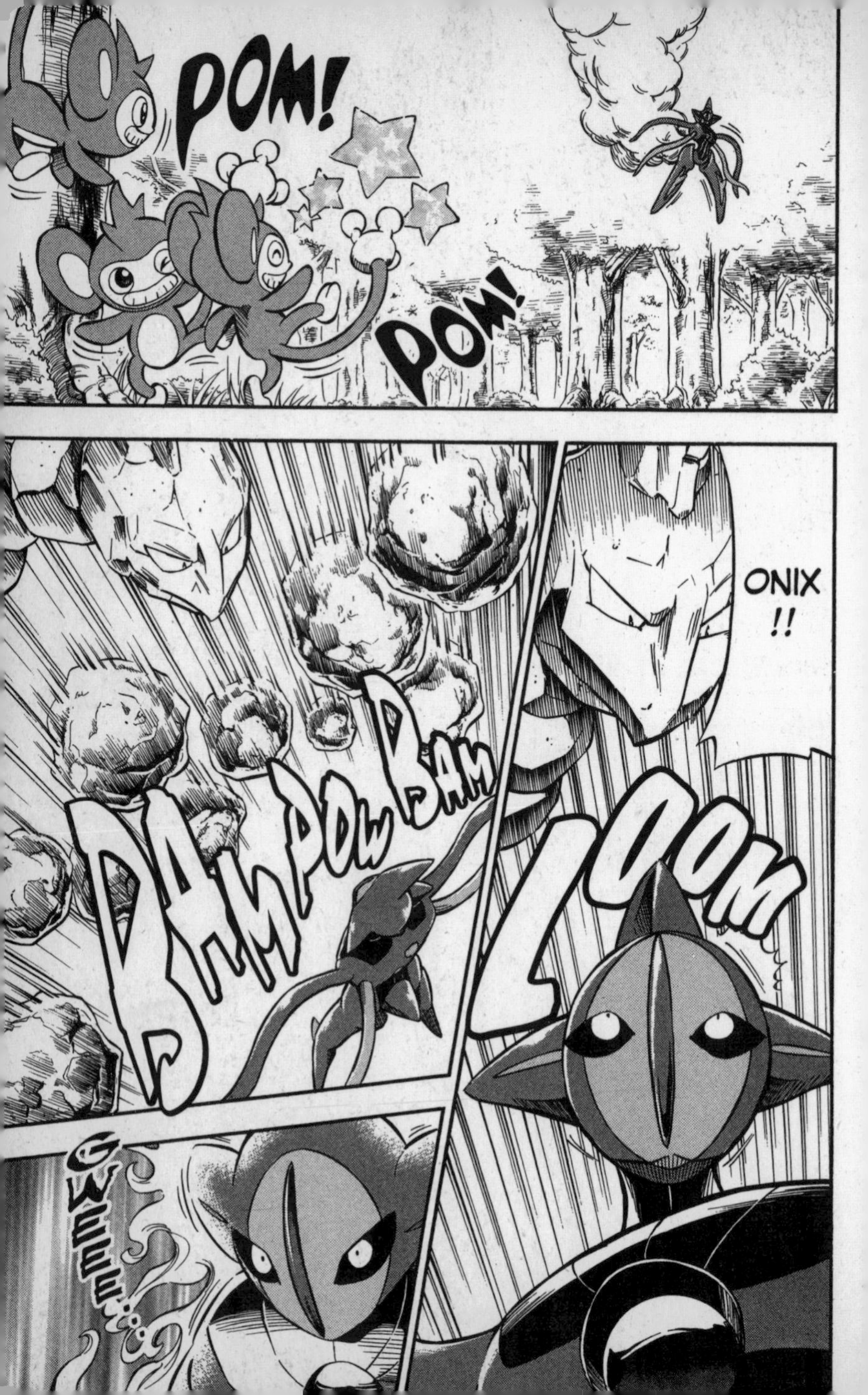
POM!
POM!
ONIX!!
VOOM
BAM POW BAM
GWEEEE...

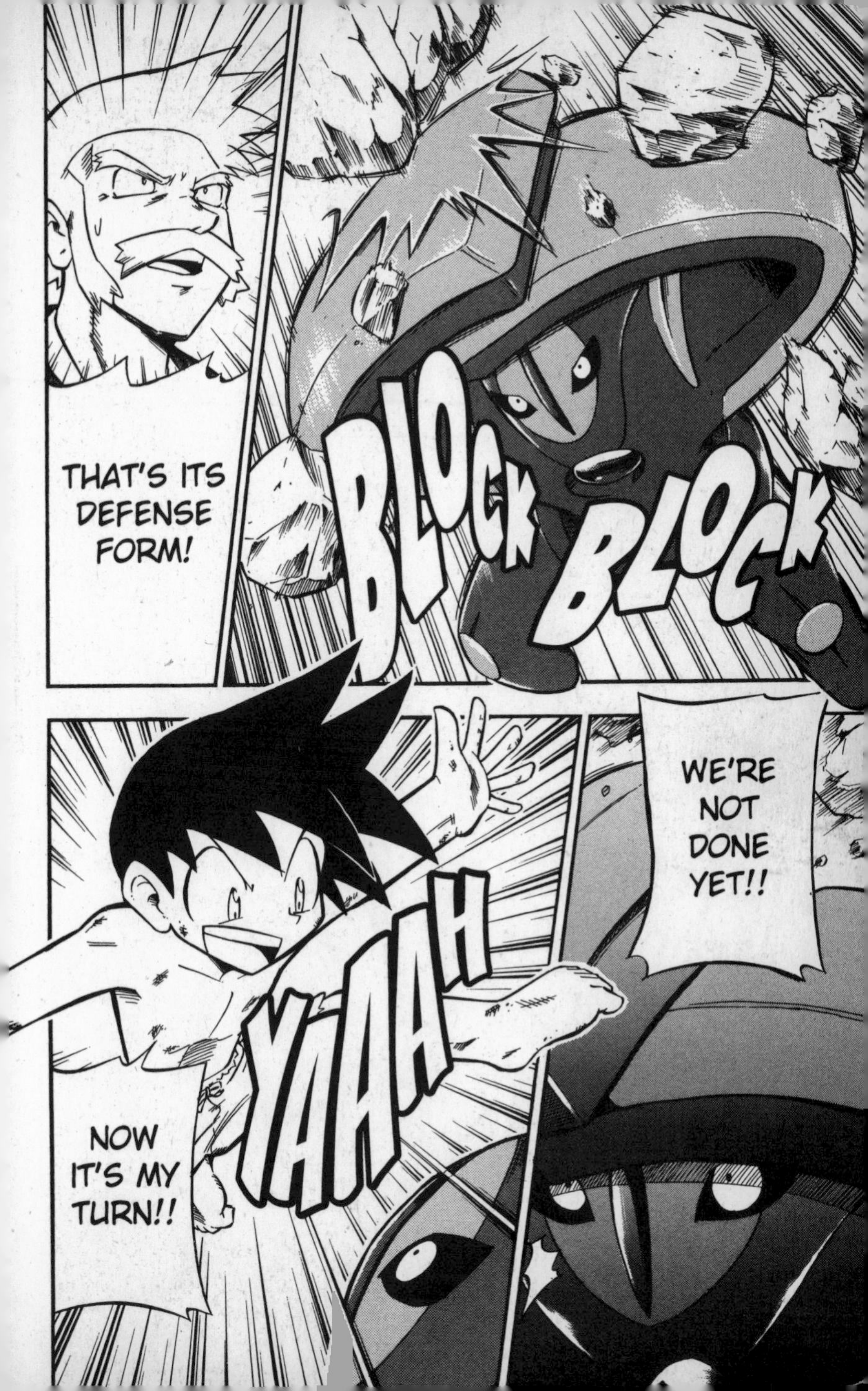
BLOCK
BLOCK
THAT'S ITS DEFENSE FORM!
WE'RE NOT DONE YET!!
YAAAH
NOW IT'S MY TURN!!

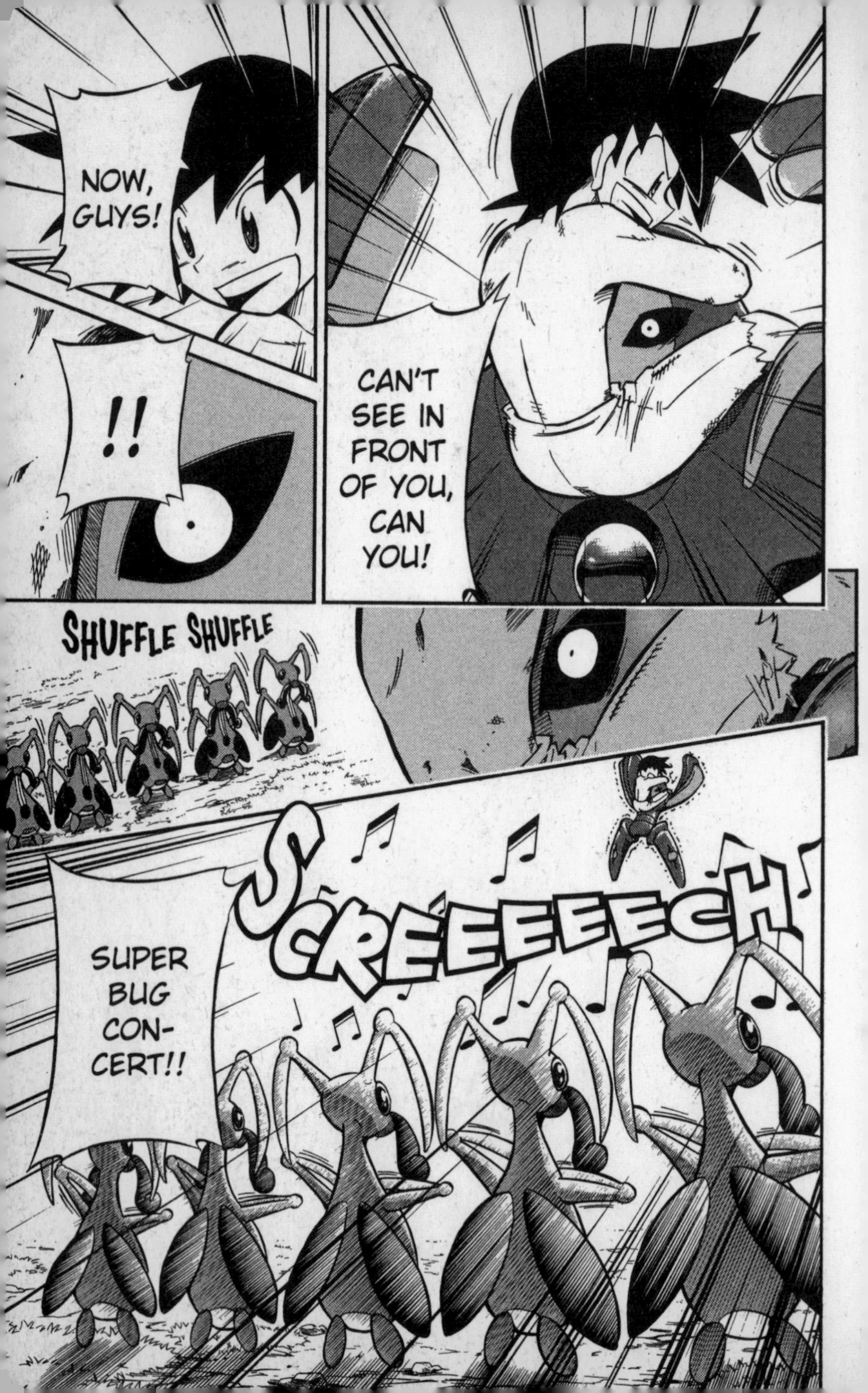
CAN'T SEE IN FRONT OF YOU, CAN YOU!
NOW, GUYS!
!!
SHUFFLE SHUFFLE
SCREEEEECH
SUPER BUG CON-CERT!!

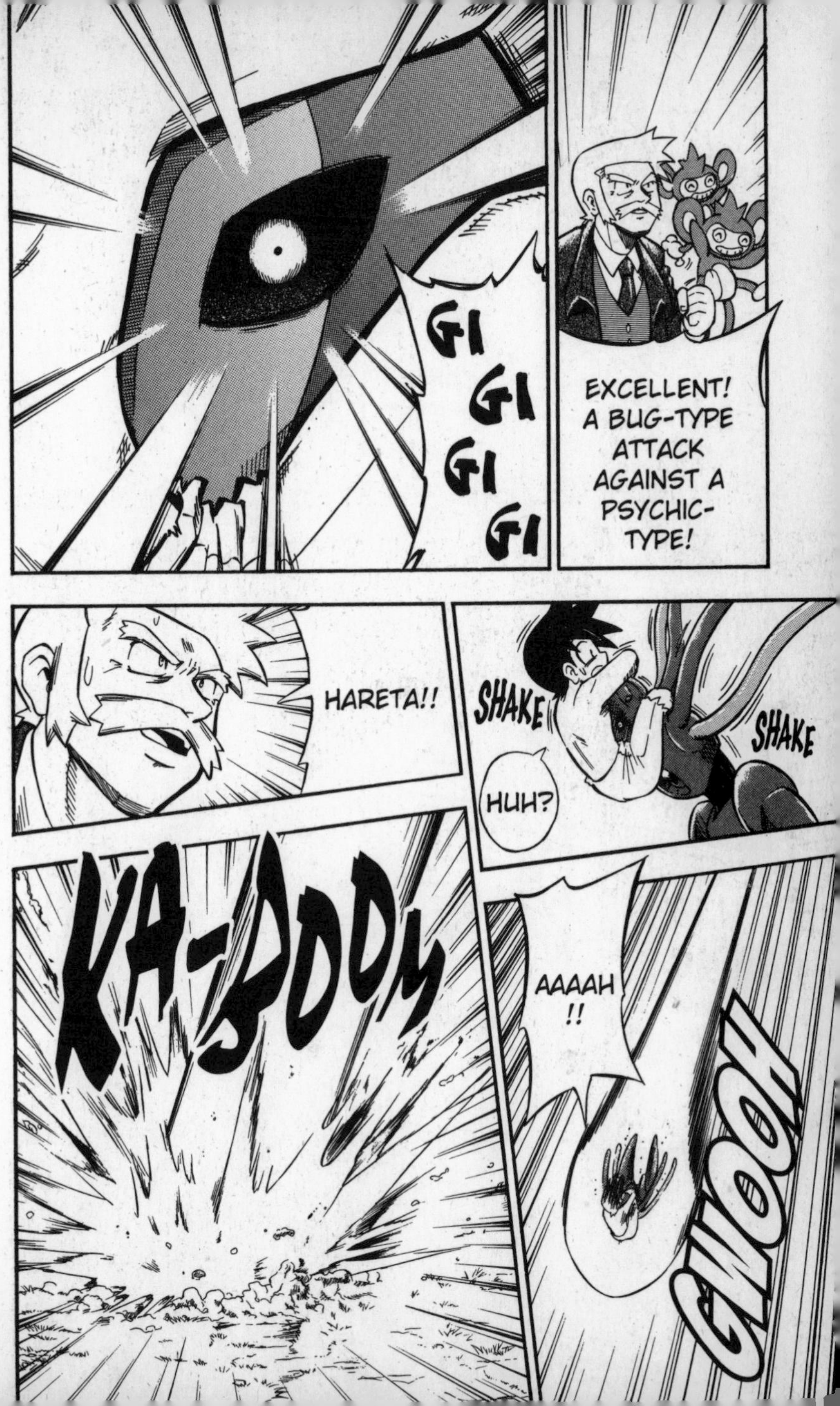
EXCELLENT! A BUG-TYPE ATTACK AGAINST A PSYCHIC-TYPE!
GI GI GI GI
SHAKE
SHAKE
HUH?
HARETA!!
AAAAH!!
GWOOH
KA-BOOM

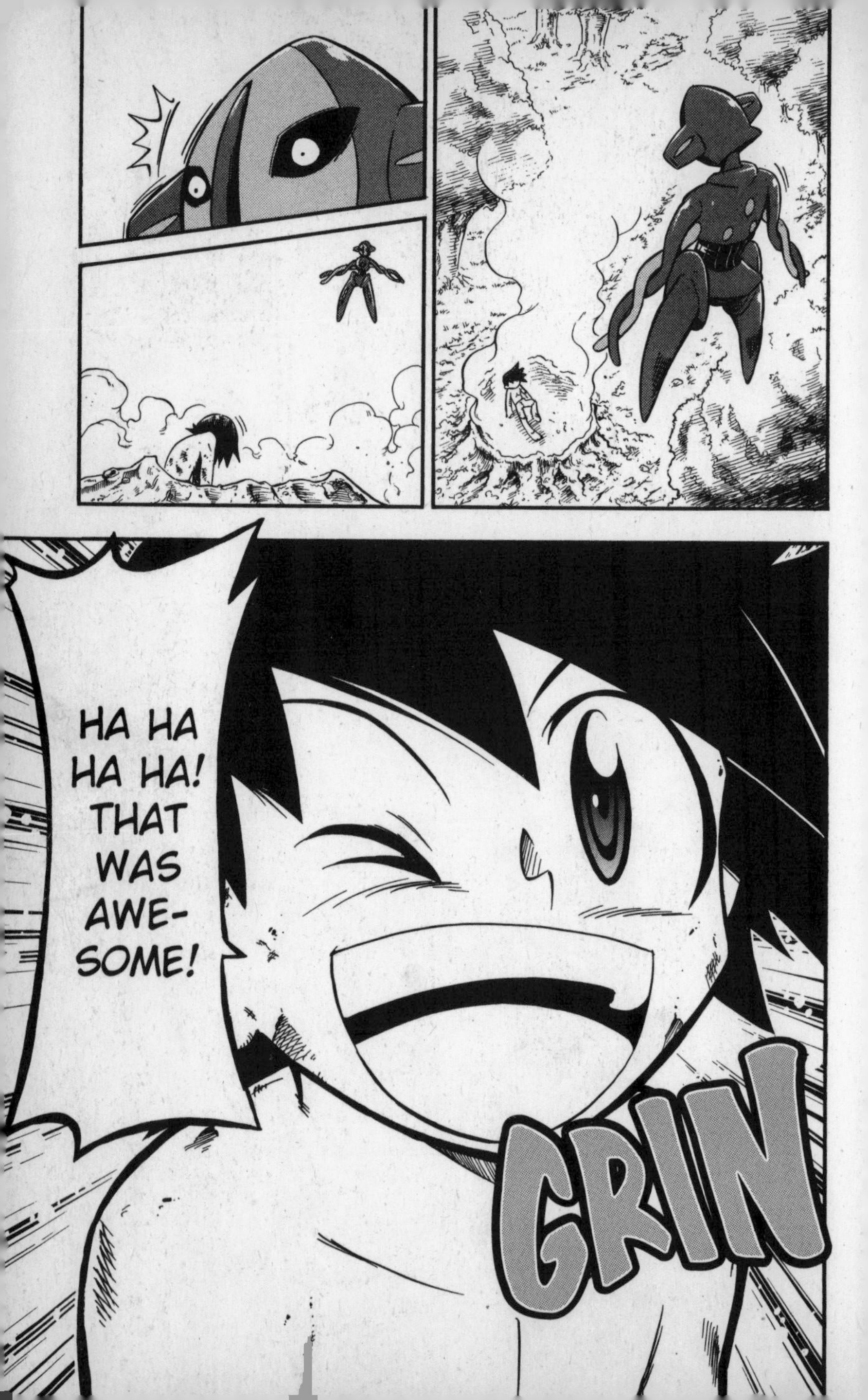
HA HA HA HA! THAT WAS AWE-SOME!
GRIN

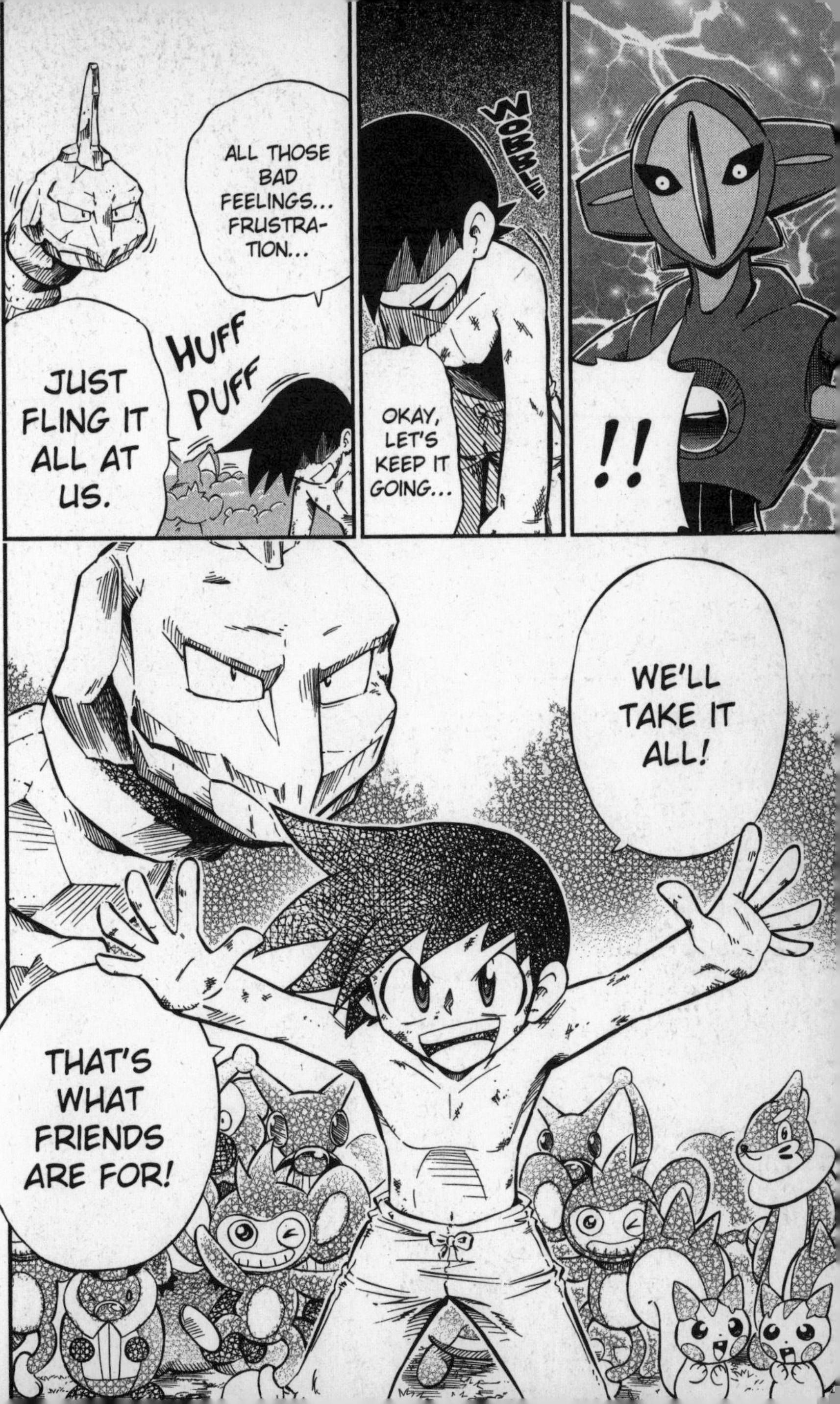
!!
WOBBLE
OKAY, LET'S KEEP IT GOING...
ALL THOSE BAD FEELINGS... FRUSTRATION...
HUFF PUFF
JUST FLING IT ALL AT US.
WE'LL TAKE IT ALL!
THAT'S WHAT FRIENDS ARE FOR!

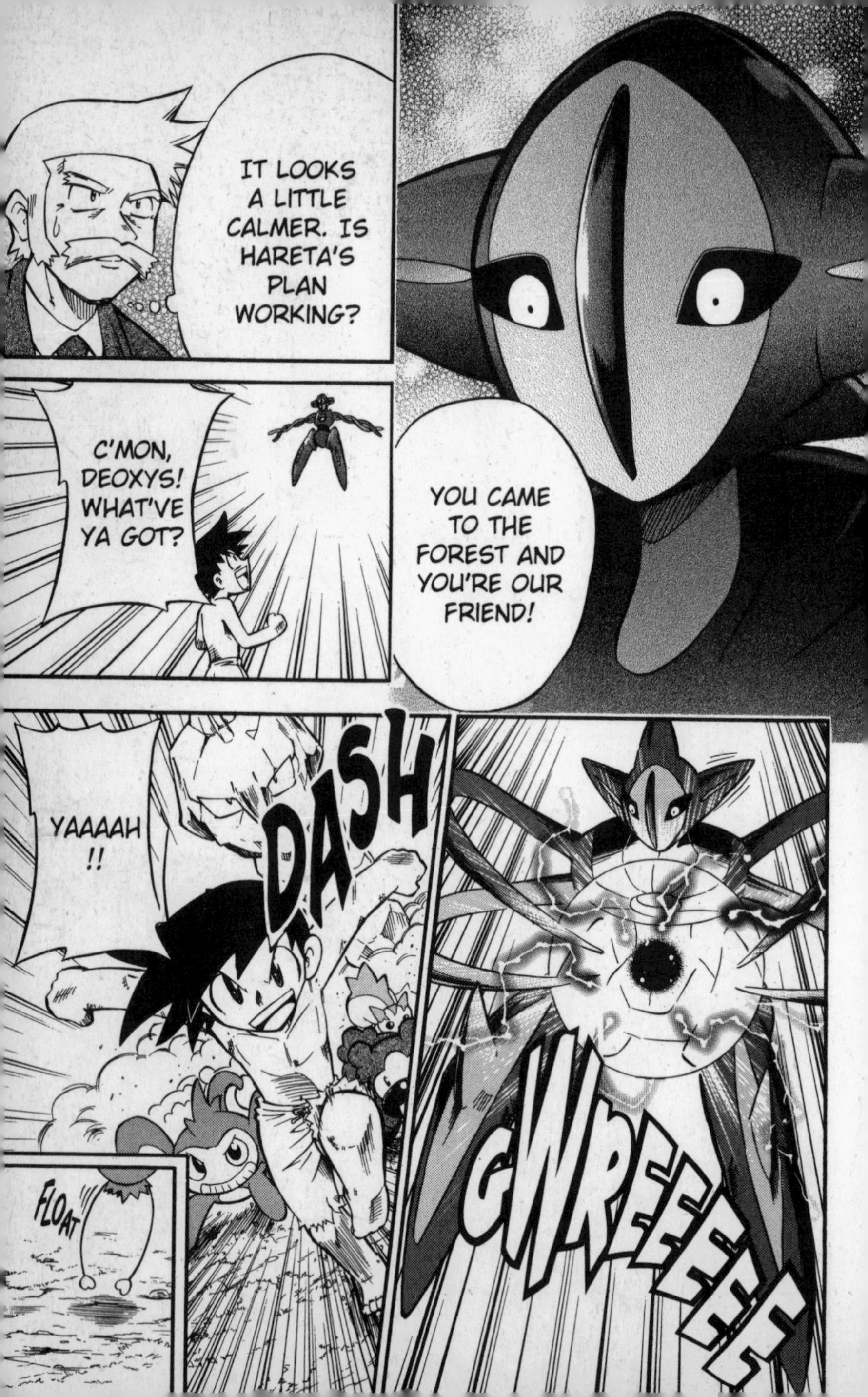
YOU CAME TO THE FOREST AND YOU'RE OUR FRIEND!
IT LOOKS A LITTLE CALMER. IS HARETA'S PLAN WORKING?
C'MON, DEOXYS! WHAT'VE YA GOT?
GWREEEEE
DASH
YAAAAH !!
FLOAT

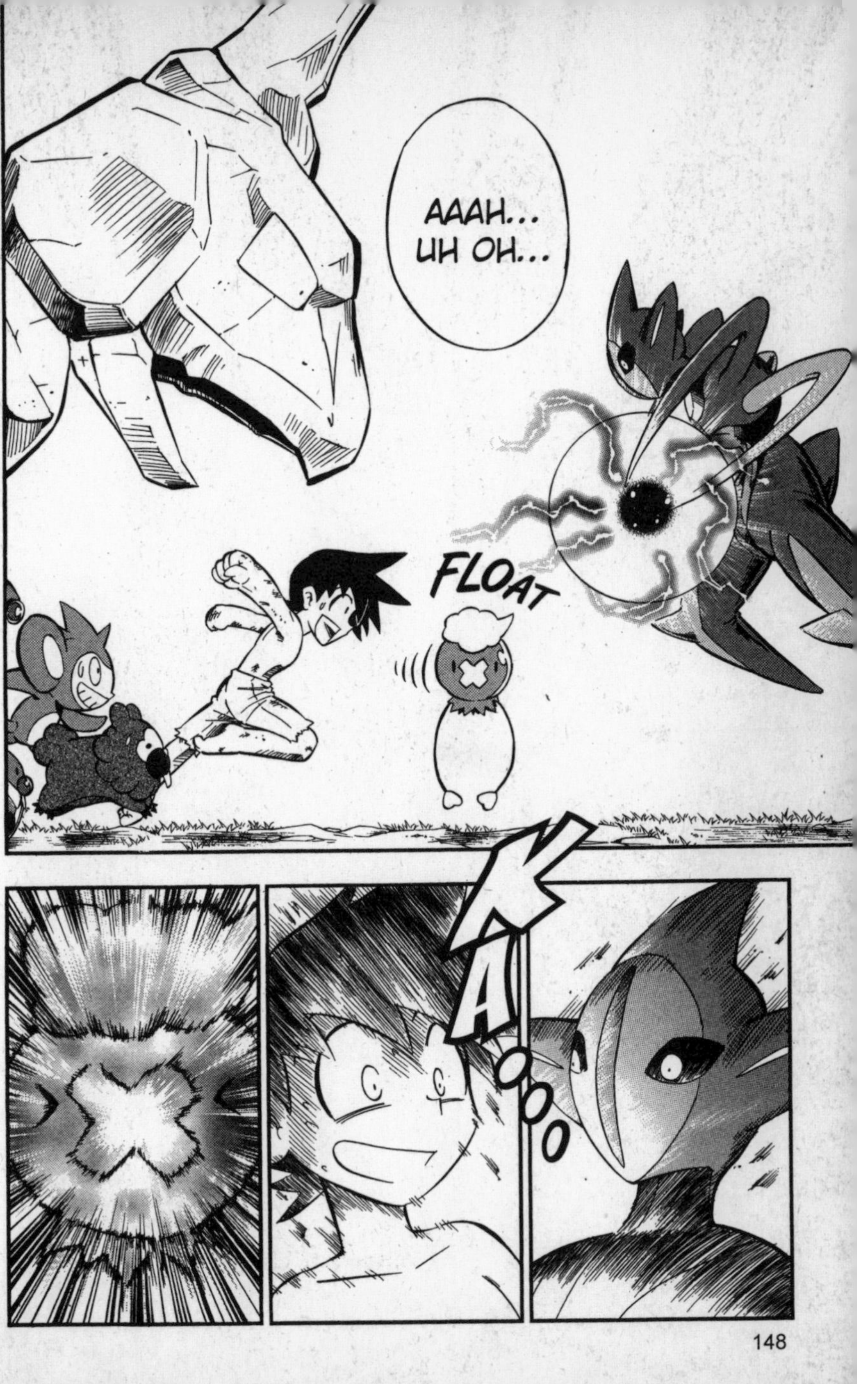
AAAH... UH OH...
FLOAT
KAOOOO

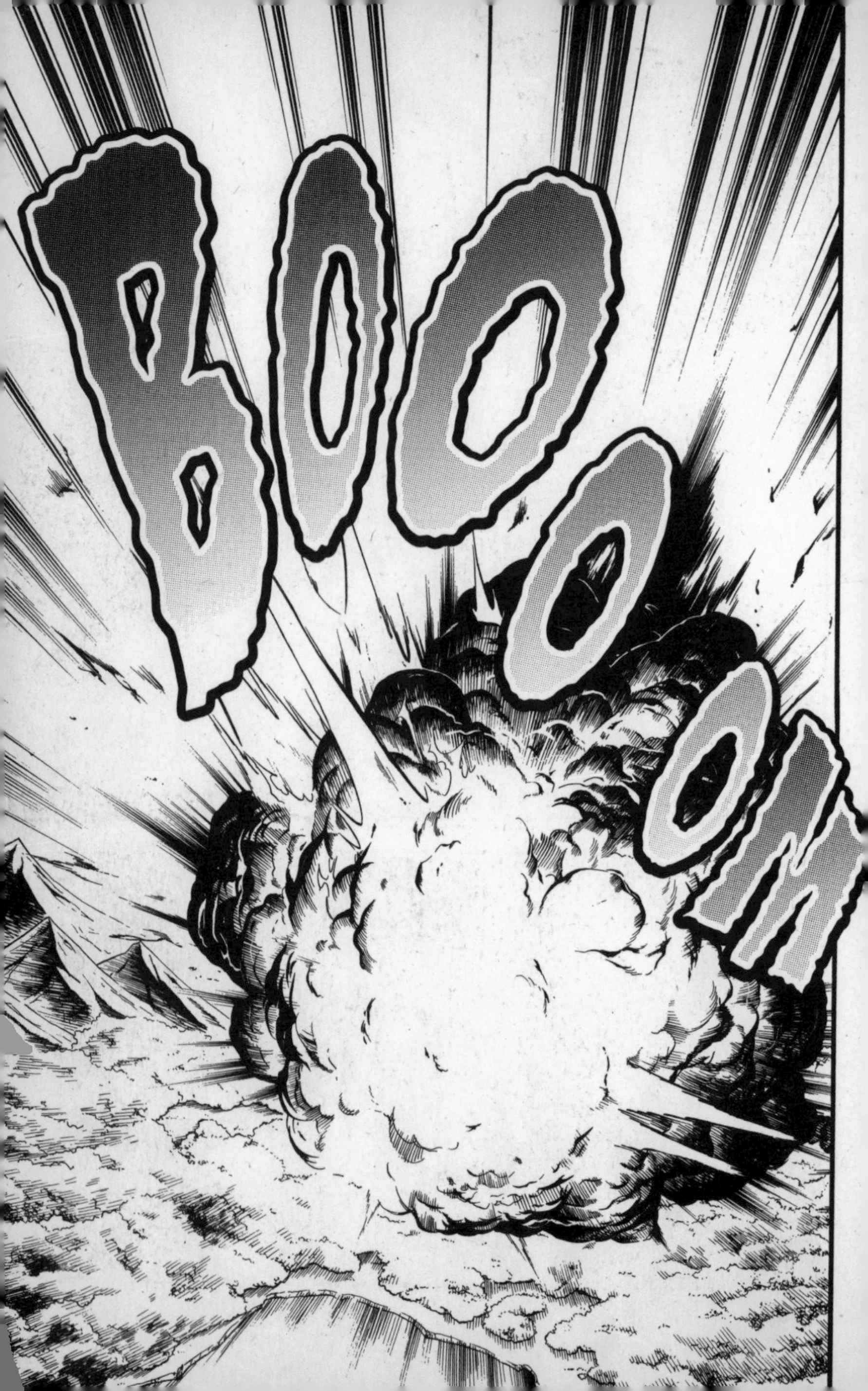
BOOOOOM

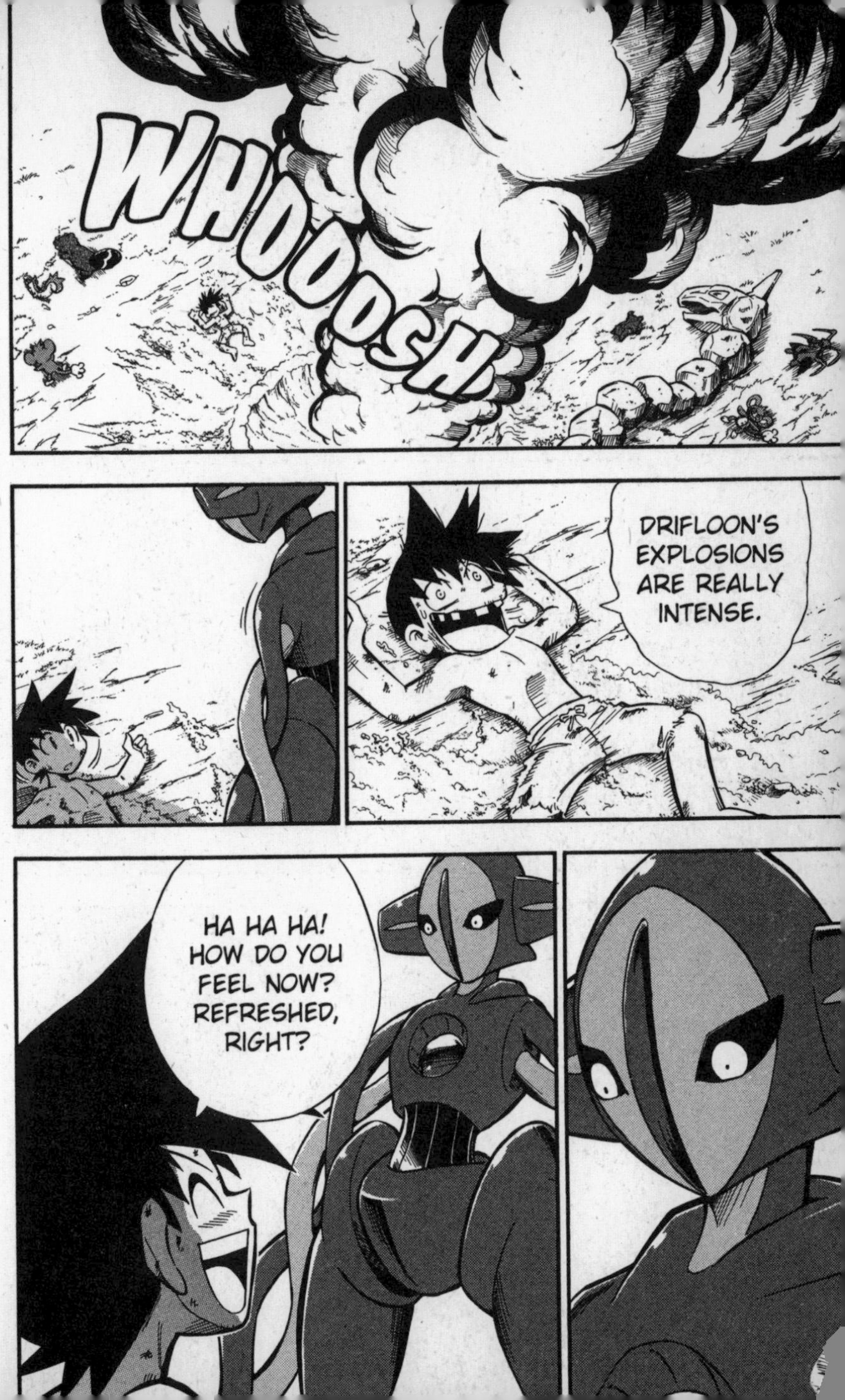
WHOOOSH
DRIFLOON'S EXPLOSIONS ARE REALLY INTENSE.
HA HA HA! HOW DO YOU FEEL NOW? REFRESHED, RIGHT?

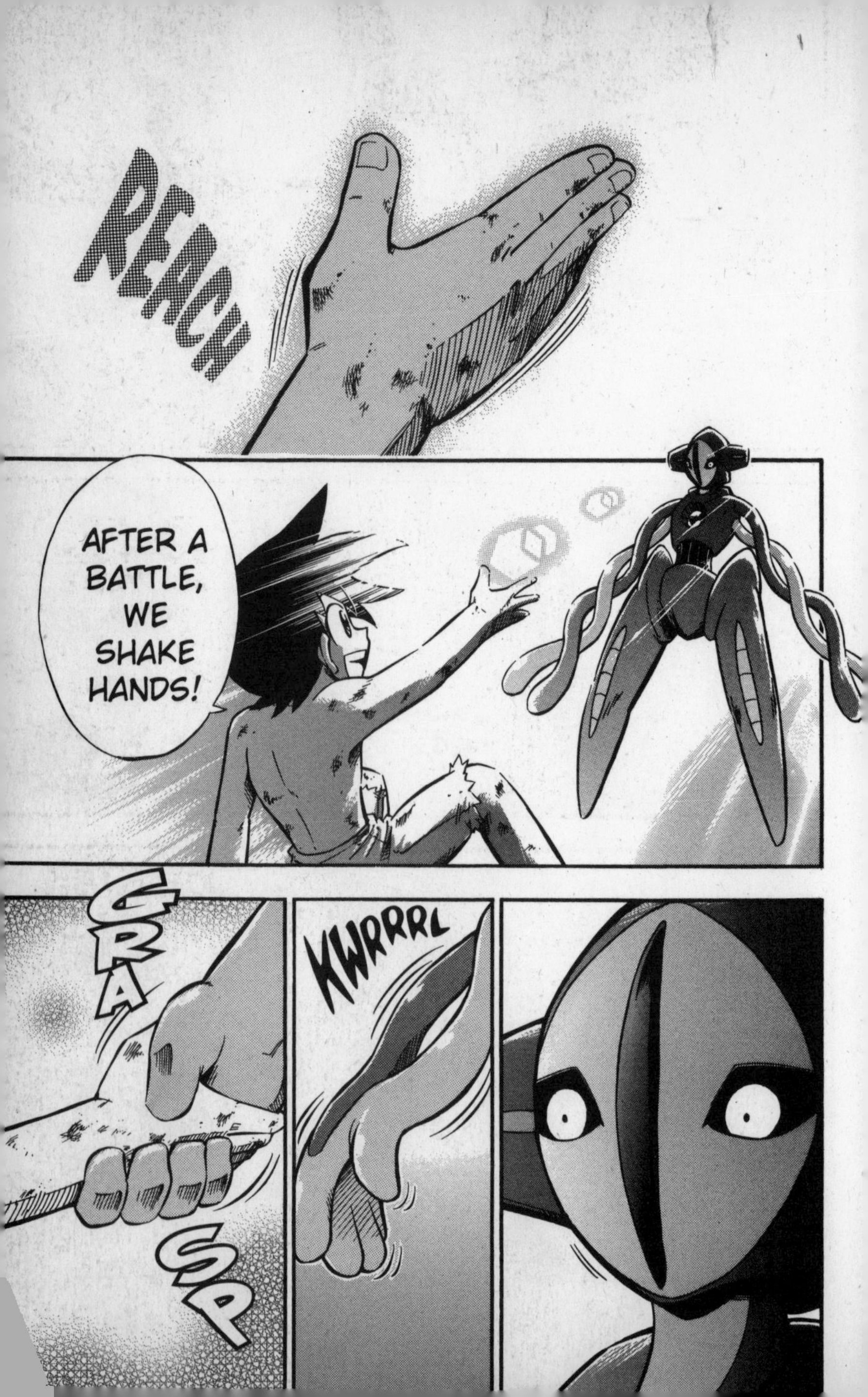
REACH
AFTER A BATTLE, WE SHAKE HANDS!
KWRRRL
GRA SP

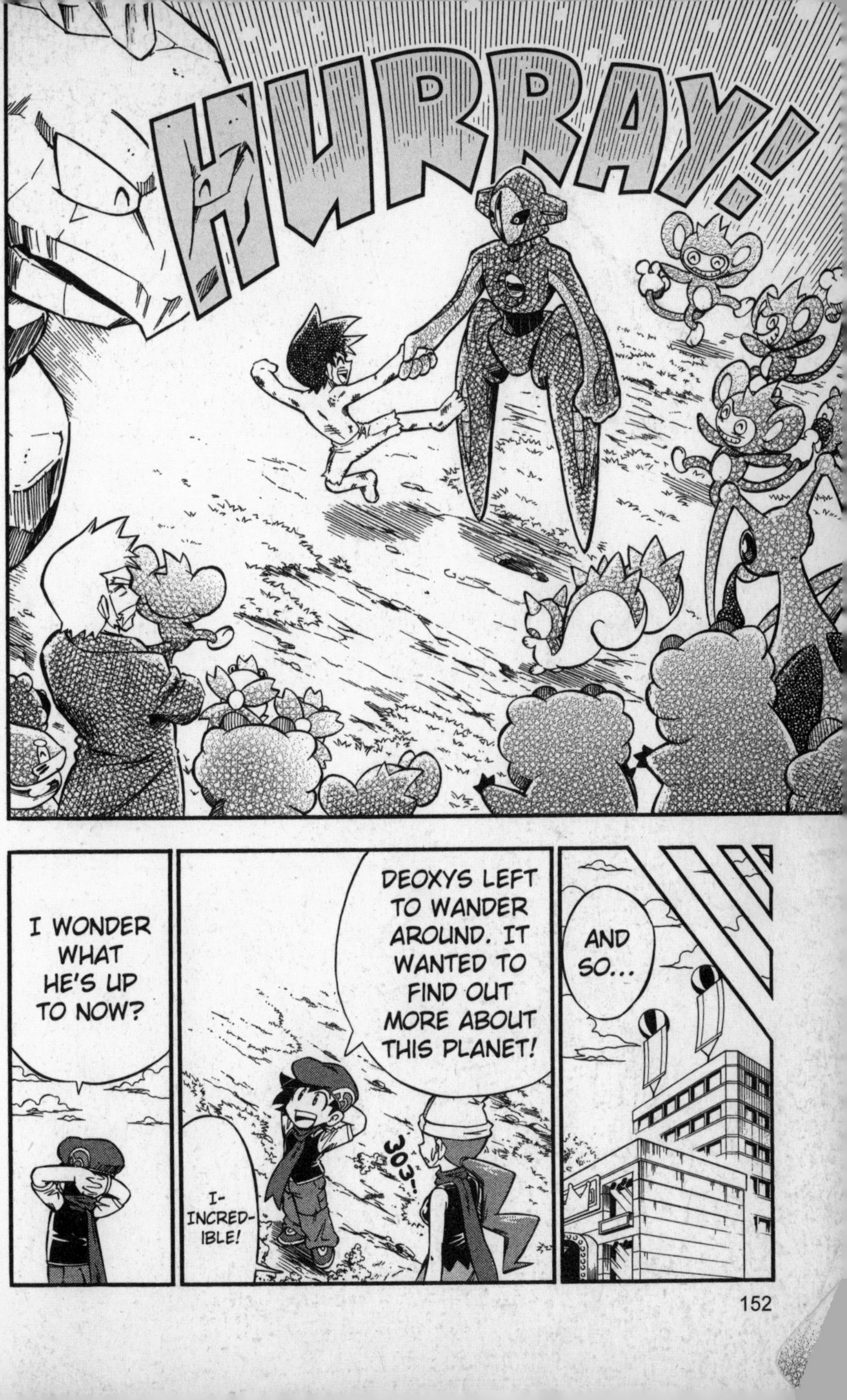
HURRAY!
AND SO...
DEOXYS LEFT TO WANDER AROUND. IT WANTED TO FIND OUT MORE ABOUT THIS PLANET!
I- INCREDIBLE!
I WONDER WHAT HE'S UP TO NOW?

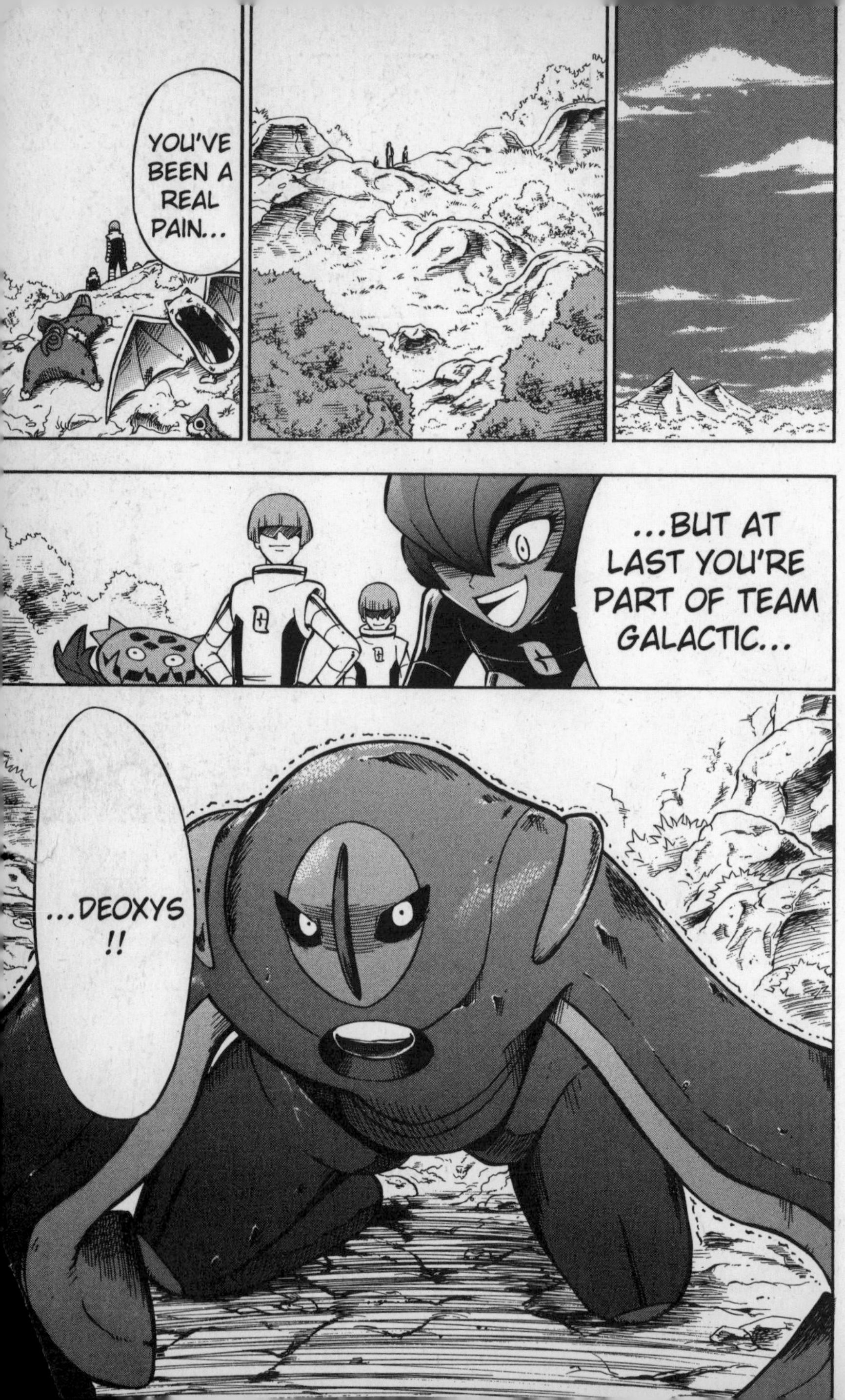
YOU'VE BEEN A REAL PAIN...
...BUT AT LAST YOU'RE PART OF TEAM GALACTIC...
...DEOXYS !!

DEOXYS, THE PHANTOM POKÉMON! (PART 2)

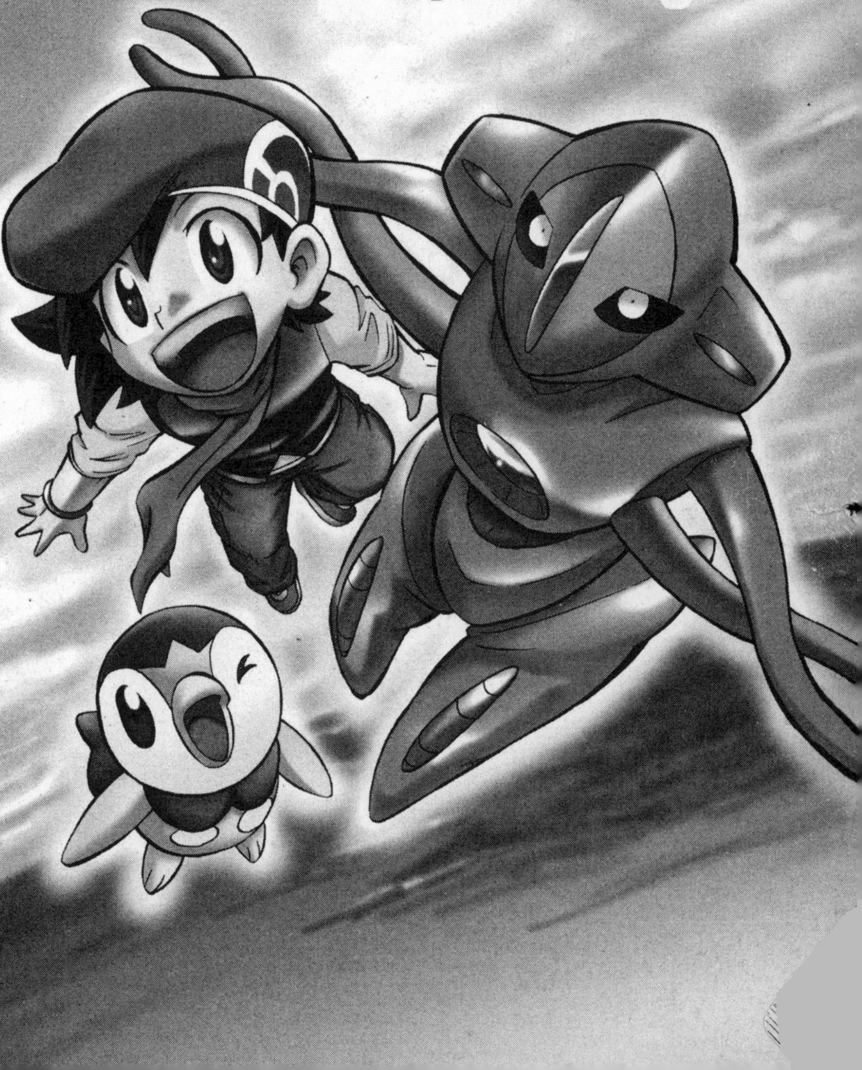

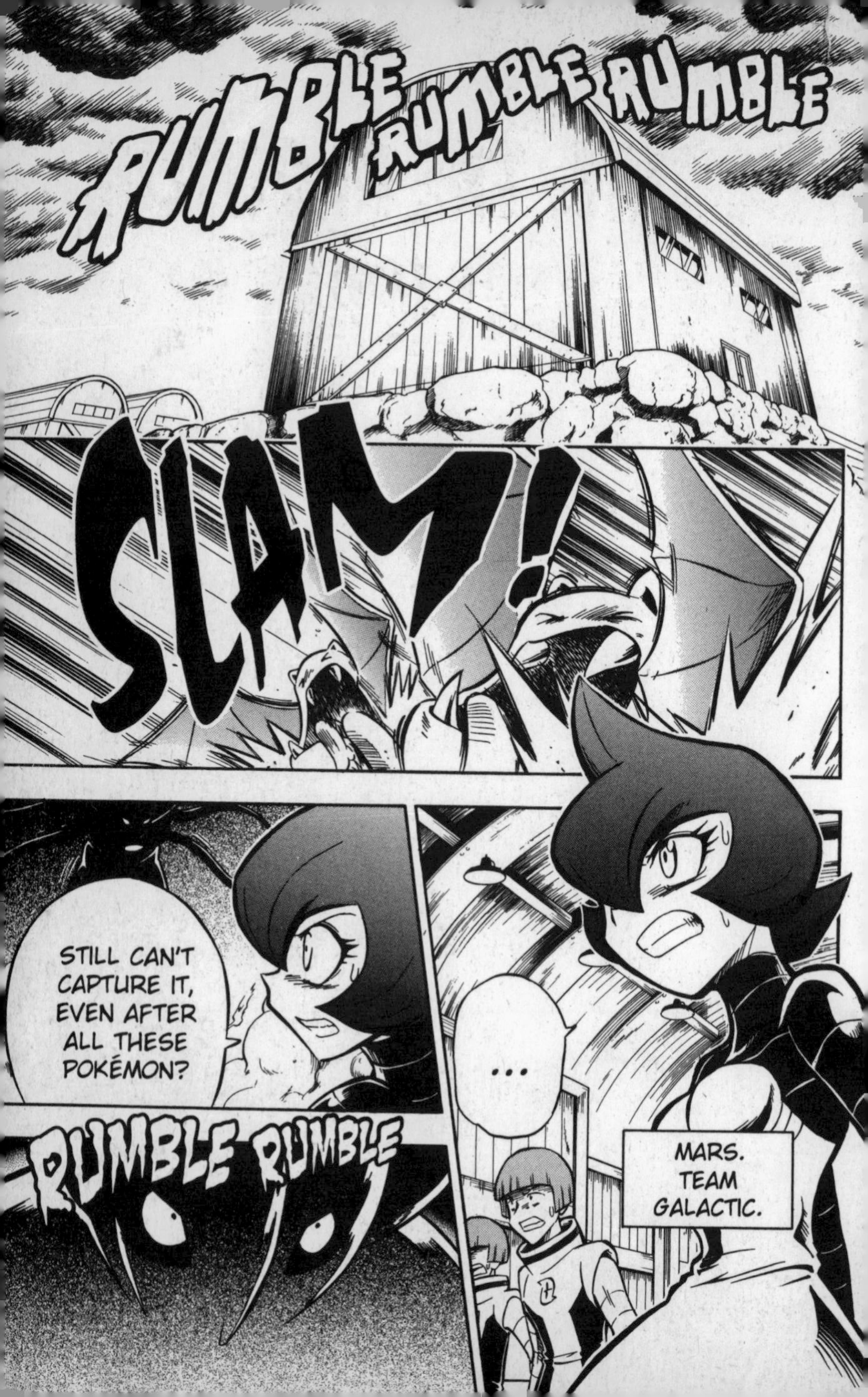
RUMBLE RUMBLE RUMBLE
SLAM!
...
MARS. TEAM GALACTIC.
STILL CAN'T CAPTURE IT, EVEN AFTER ALL THESE POKÉMON?
RUMBLE RUMBLE

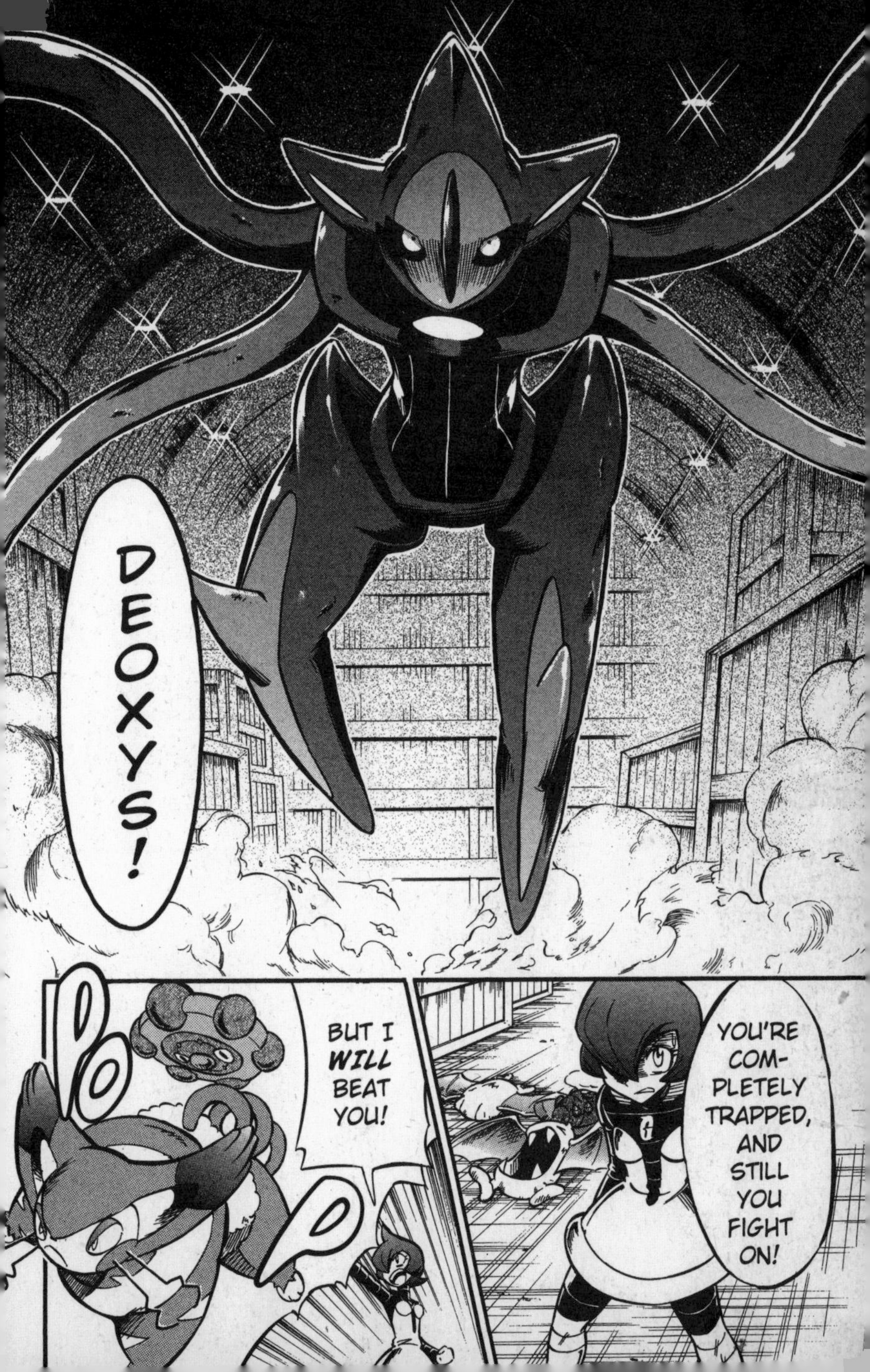
DEOXYS!
YOU'RE COMPLETELY TRAPPED, AND STILL YOU FIGHT ON!
BUT I *WILL* BEAT YOU!

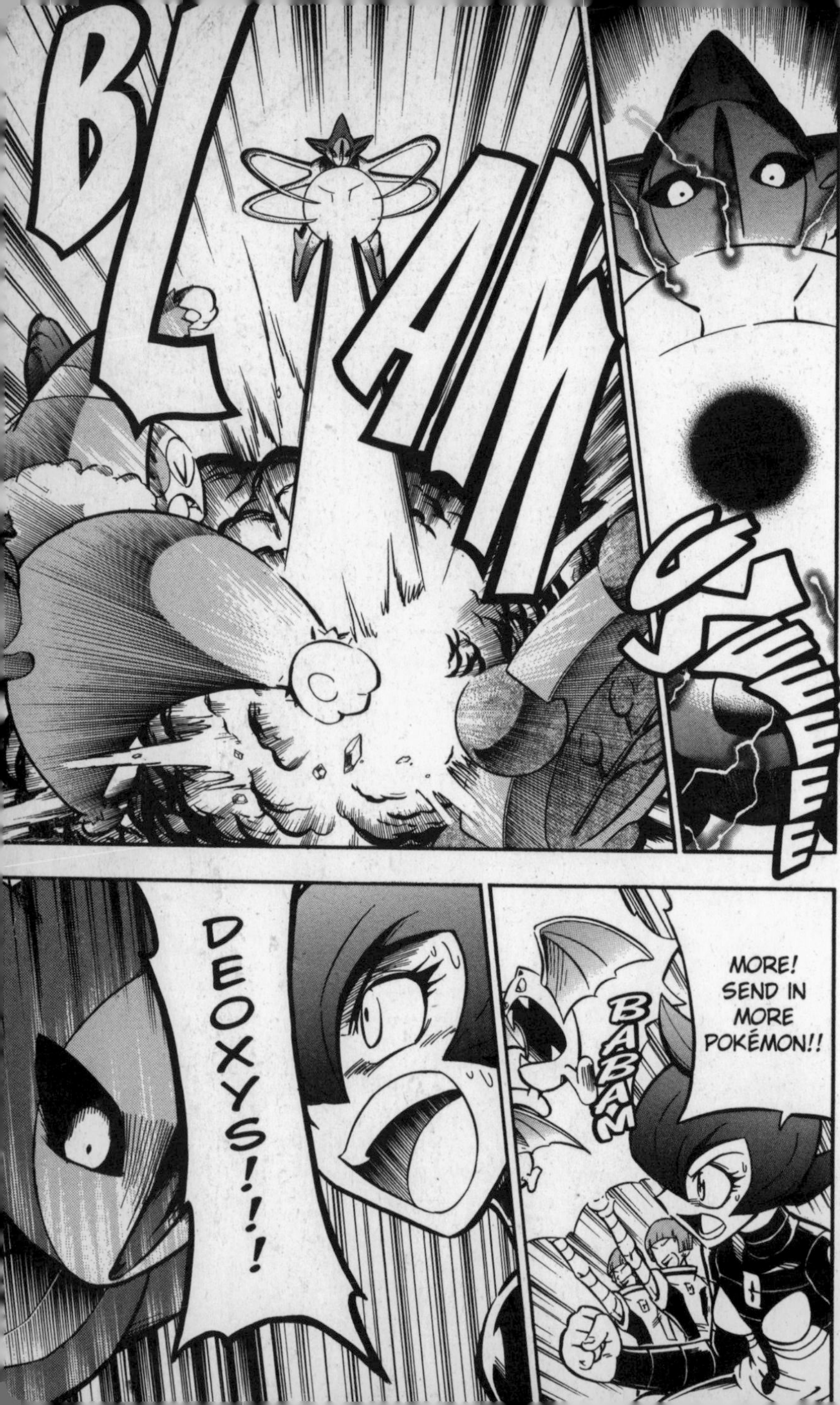
GYEEEEE
BLAM
MORE! SEND IN MORE POKÉMON!!
BABAM
DEOXYS!!!

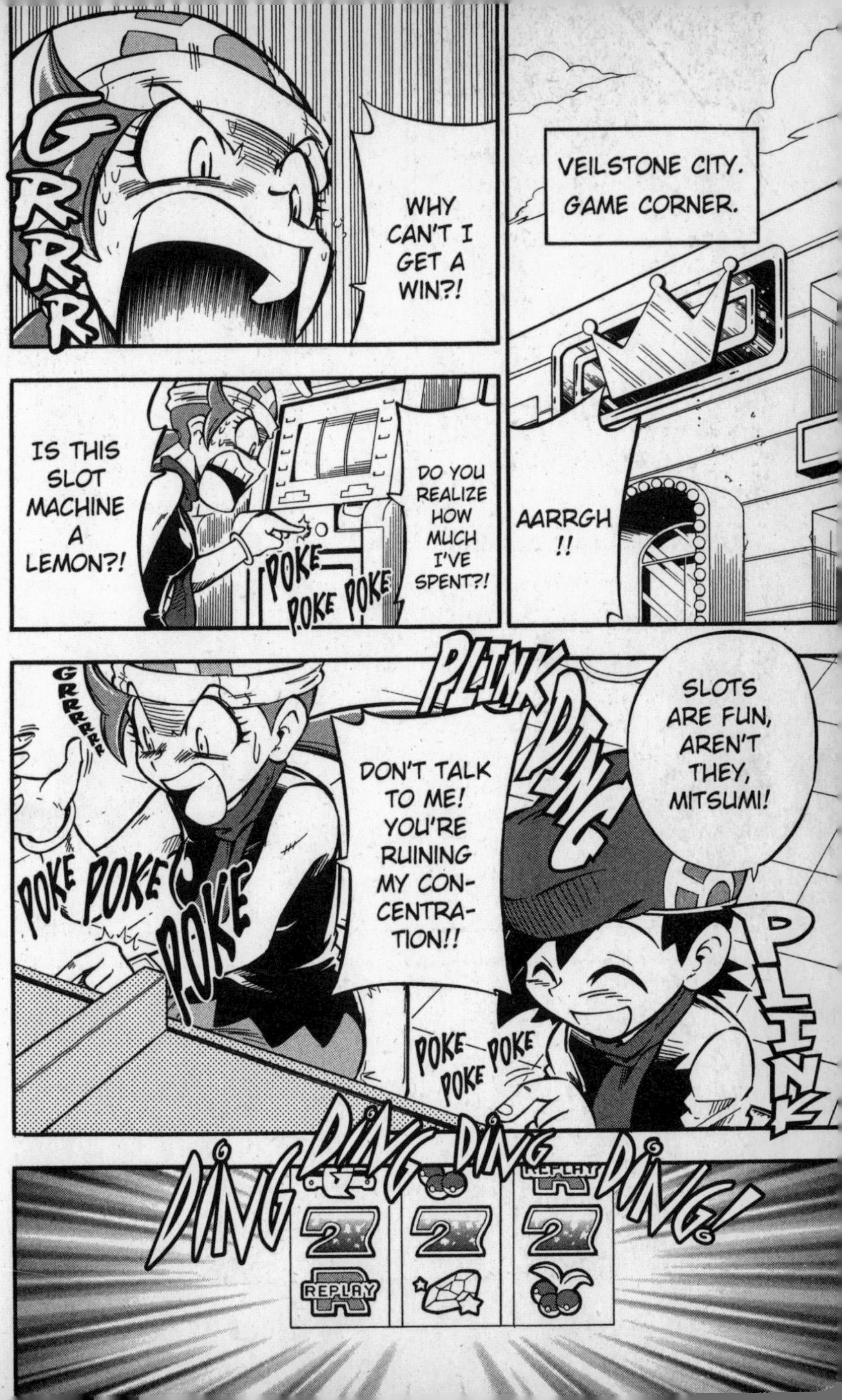
VEILSTONE CITY.
GAME CORNER.
AARRGH!!
GRRRR
WHY CAN'T I GET A WIN?!
DO YOU REALIZE HOW MUCH I'VE SPENT?!
IS THIS SLOT MACHINE A LEMON?!
POKE POKE POKE
PLINK
DING
SLOTS ARE FUN, AREN'T THEY, MITSUMI!
PLINK
DON'T TALK TO ME! YOU'RE RUINING MY CON-CENTRA-TION!!
GRRRRRR
POKE POKE POKE
POKE POKE POKE
DING DING DING DING!
REPLAY
REPLAY

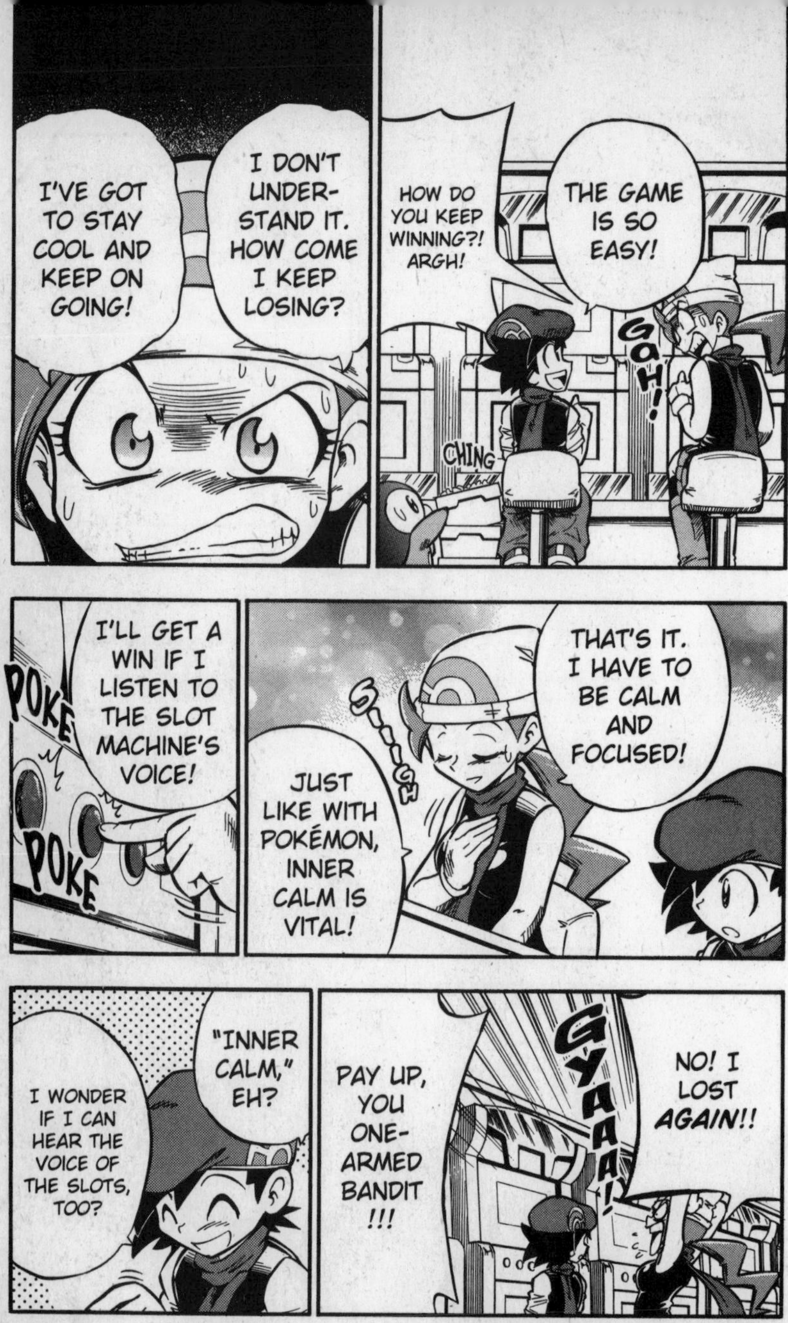
THE GAME IS SO EASY!
HOW DO YOU KEEP WINNING?! ARGH!
GAH!
CHING
I DON'T UNDER-STAND IT. HOW COME I KEEP LOSING?
I'VE GOT TO STAY COOL AND KEEP ON GOING!
THAT'S IT. I HAVE TO BE CALM AND FOCUSED!
SIGH
JUST LIKE WITH POKÉMON, INNER CALM IS VITAL!
I'LL GET A WIN IF I LISTEN TO THE SLOT MACHINE'S VOICE!
POKE
POKE
NO! I LOST AGAIN!!
GYAAA!
PAY UP, YOU ONE-ARMED BANDIT!!!
"INNER CALM," EH?
I WONDER IF I CAN HEAR THE VOICE OF THE SLOTS, TOO?

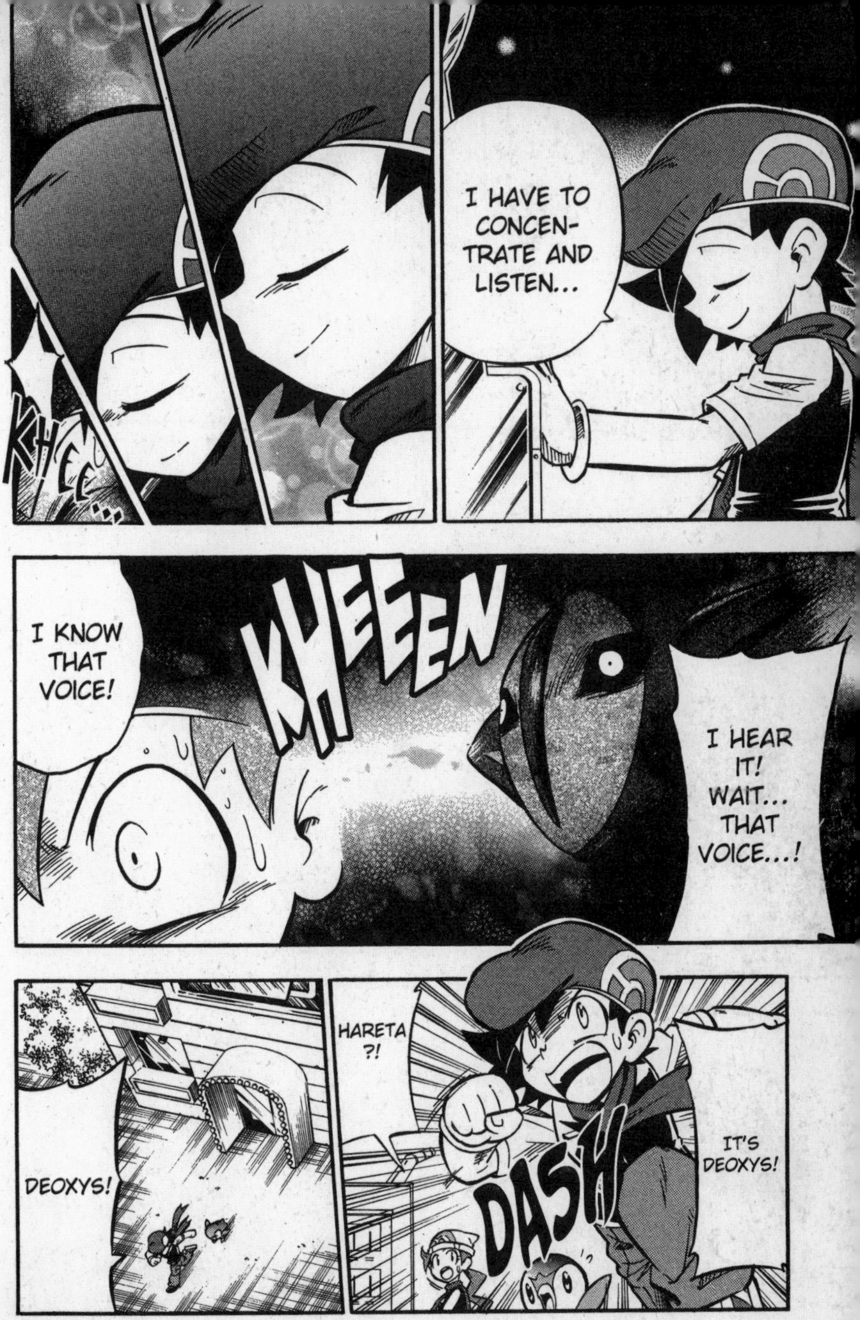
I HAVE TO CONCEN-TRATE AND LISTEN...
KHEE...
I HEAR IT! WAIT... THAT VOICE...!
KHEEEN
I KNOW THAT VOICE!
IT'S DEOXYS!
DASH
HARETA ?!
DEOXYS!

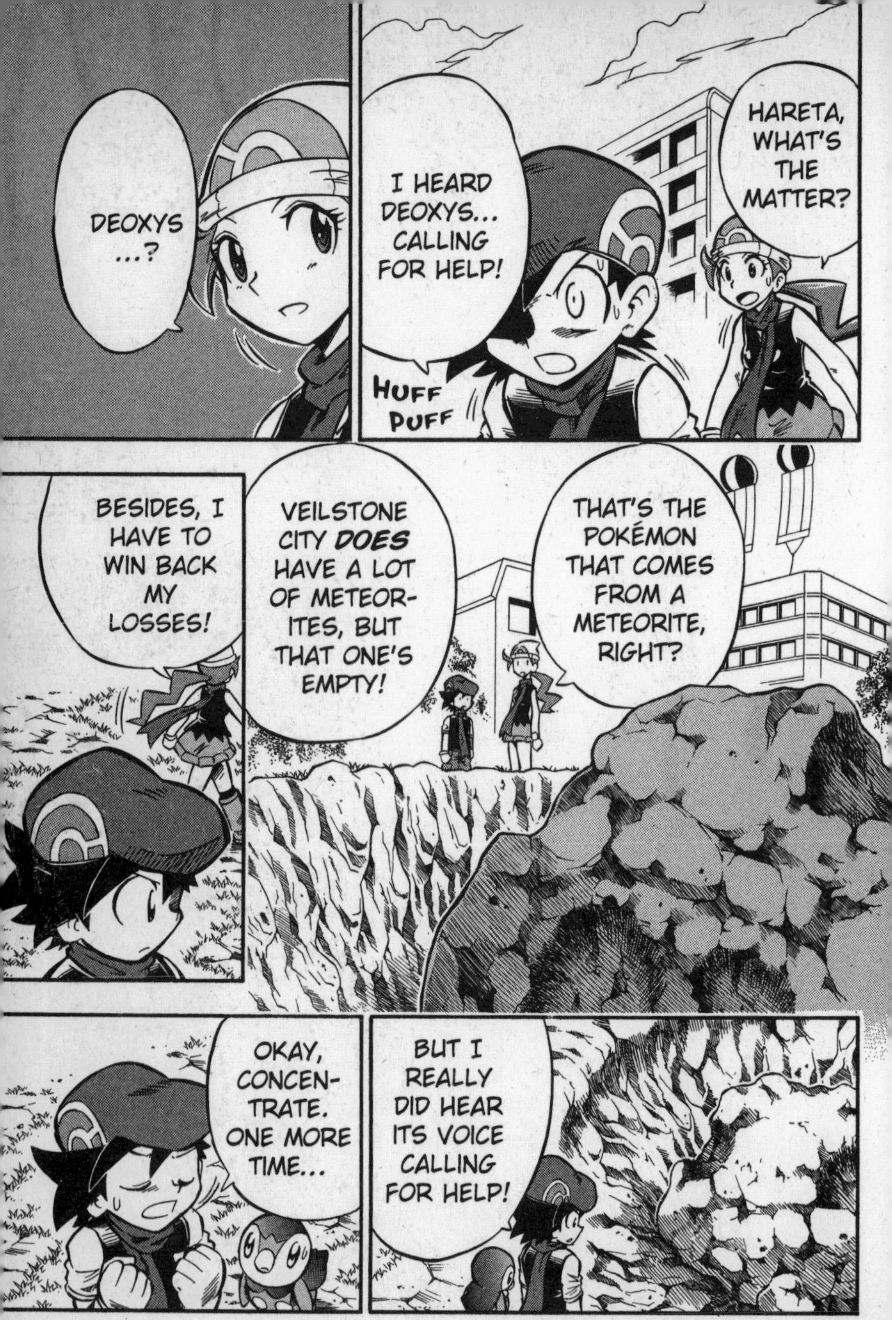
HARETA, WHAT'S THE MATTER?
I HEARD DEOXYS... CALLING FOR HELP!
HUFF PUFF
DEOXYS ...?
THAT'S THE POKÉMON THAT COMES FROM A METEORITE, RIGHT?
VEILSTONE CITY ***DOES*** HAVE A LOT OF METEOR-ITES, BUT THAT ONE'S EMPTY!
BESIDES, I HAVE TO WIN BACK MY LOSSES!
BUT I REALLY DID HEAR ITS VOICE CALLING FOR HELP!
OKAY, CONCEN-TRATE. ONE MORE TIME...

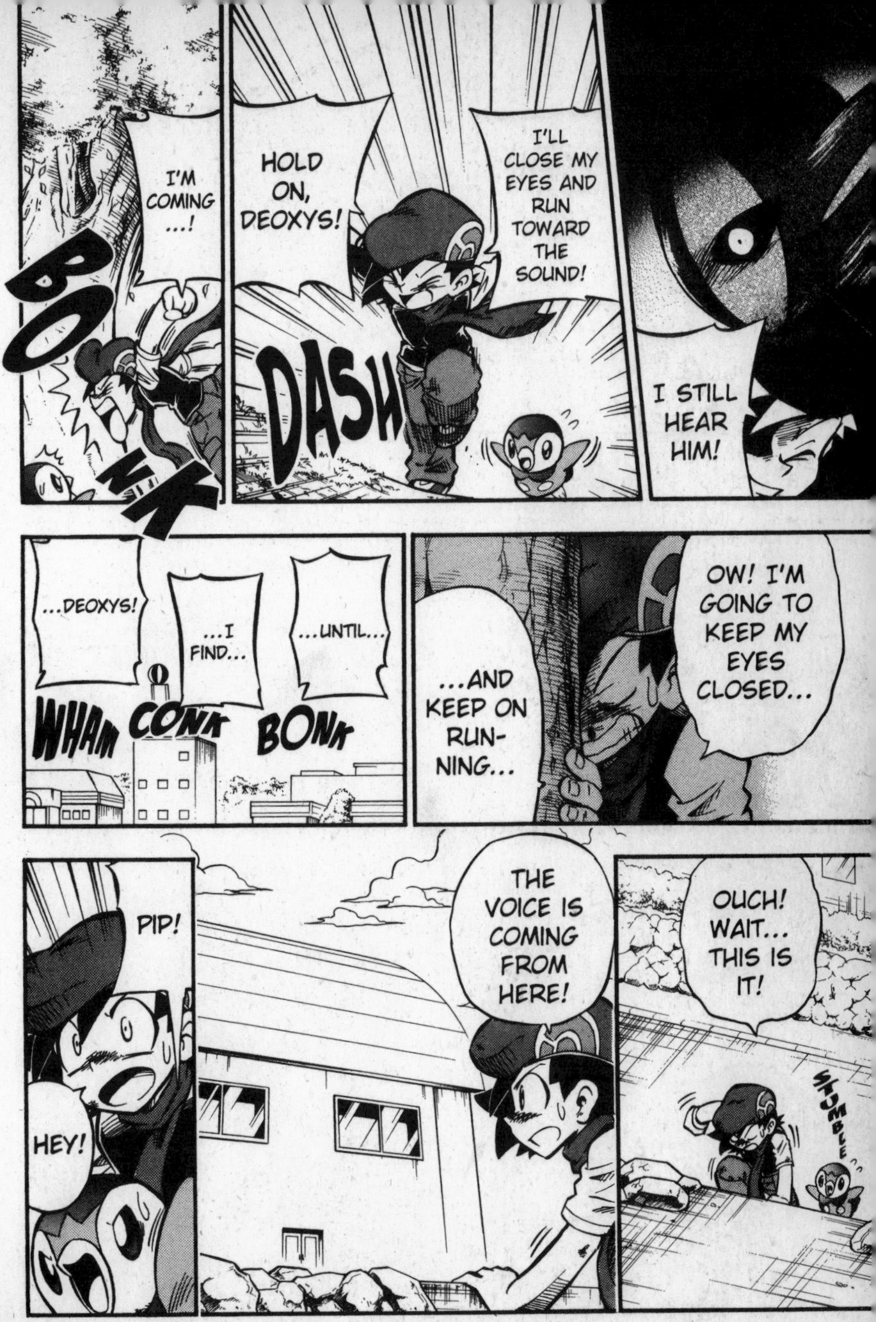
I STILL HEAR HIM!
I'LL CLOSE MY EYES AND RUN TOWARD THE SOUND!
HOLD ON, DEOXYS!
DASH
I'M COMING ...!
BONK
OW! I'M GOING TO KEEP MY EYES CLOSED...
...AND KEEP ON RUN-NING...
...UNTIL...
...I FIND...
...DEOXYS!
WHAM
CONK
BONK
OUCH! WAIT... THIS IS IT!
STUMBLE
THE VOICE IS COMING FROM HERE!
PIP!
HEY!

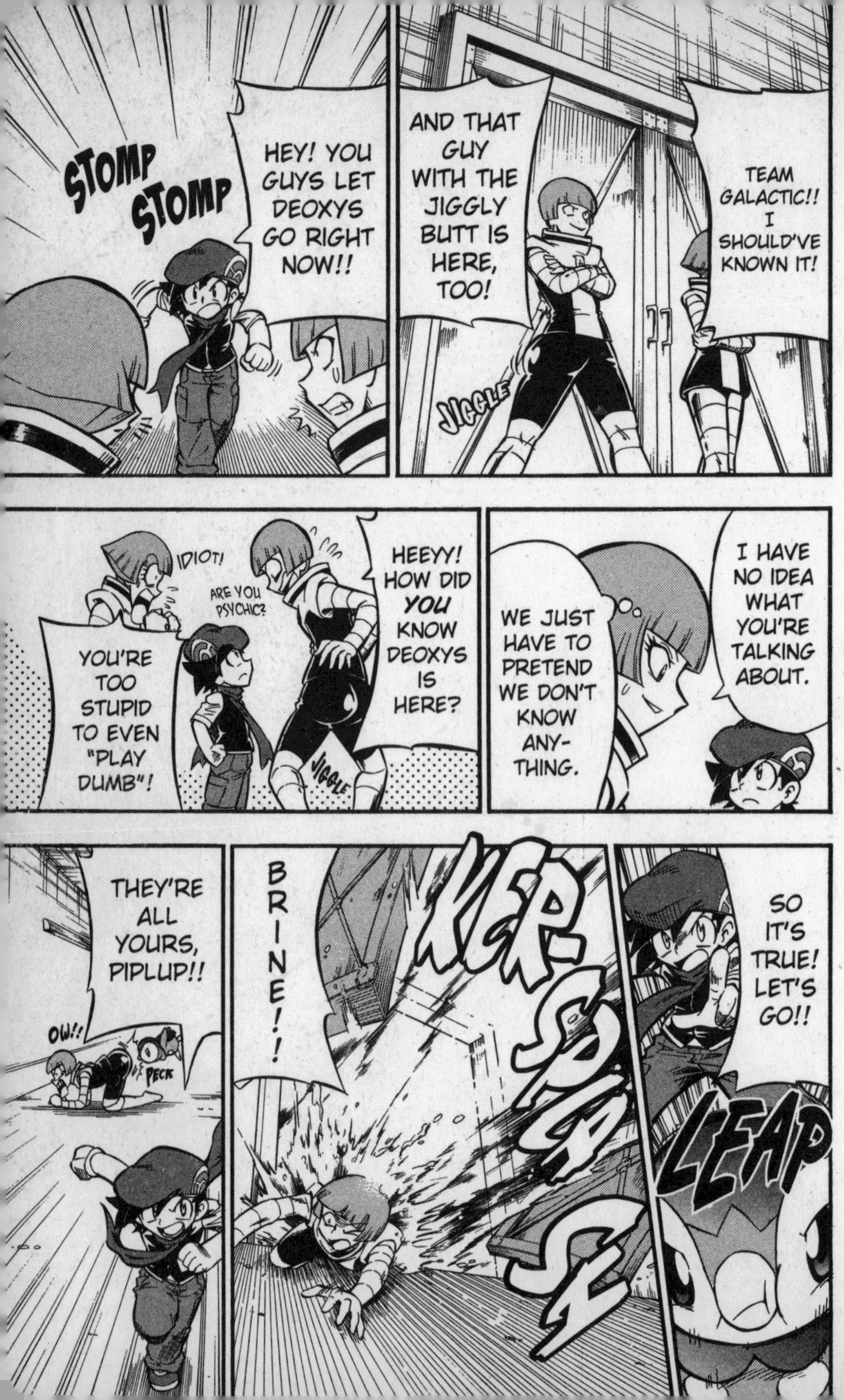
TEAM GALACTIC!! I SHOULD'VE KNOWN IT!
AND THAT GUY WITH THE JIGGLY BUTT IS HERE, TOO!
JIGGLE
HEY! YOU GUYS LET DEOXYS GO RIGHT NOW!!
STOMP
STOMP
I HAVE NO IDEA WHAT YOU'RE TALKING ABOUT.
WE JUST HAVE TO PRETEND WE DON'T KNOW ANYTHING.
HEEYY! HOW DID YOU KNOW DEOXYS IS HERE?
JIGGLE
ARE YOU PSYCHIC?
IDIOT!
YOU'RE TOO STUPID TO EVEN "PLAY DUMB"!
SO IT'S TRUE! LET'S GO!!
LEAP
BRINE!!
KER-SPLASH
THEY'RE ALL YOURS, PIPLUP!!
OW!!
PECK

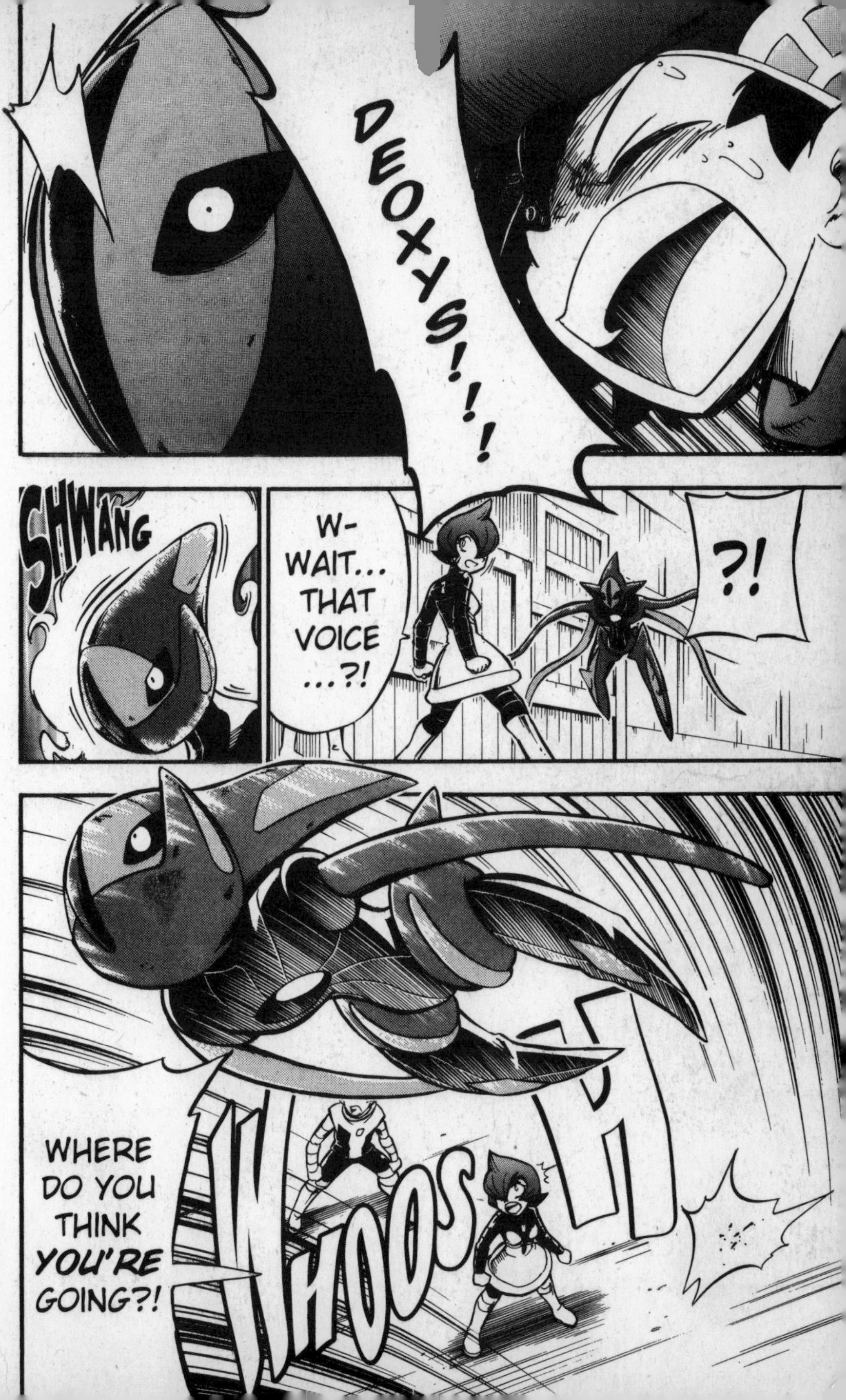
DEOXYS!!!
?!
W-WAIT... THAT VOICE...?!
SHWANG
WHOOSH
WHERE DO YOU THINK *YOU'RE* GOING?!

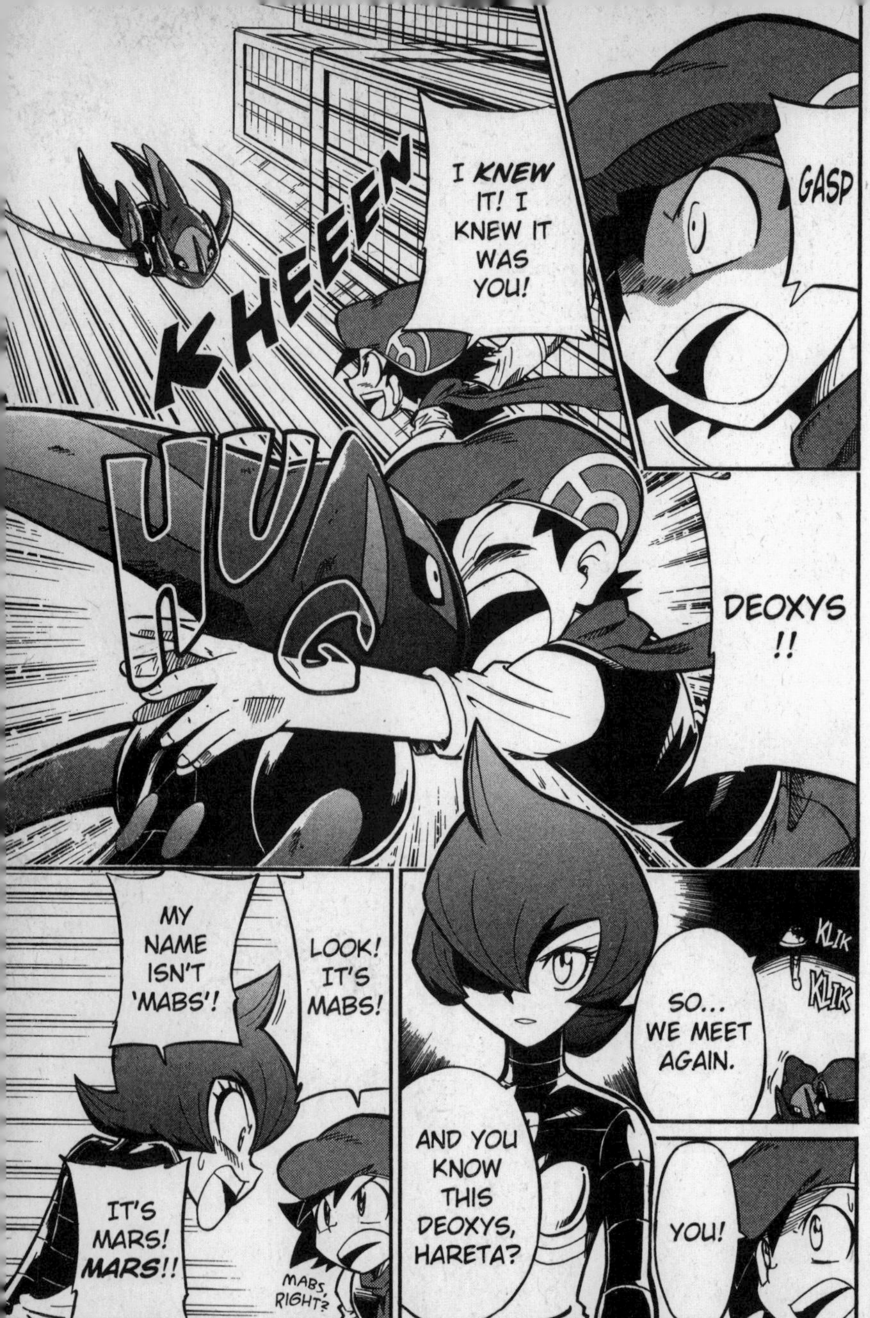
GASP
I KNEW IT! I KNEW IT WAS YOU!
KHEEEN
HUG
DEOXYS !!
KLIK
KLIK
SO... WE MEET AGAIN.
YOU!
AND YOU KNOW THIS DEOXYS, HARETA?
LOOK! IT'S MABS!
MY NAME ISN'T 'MABS'!
MABS, RIGHT?
IT'S MARS! MARS!!

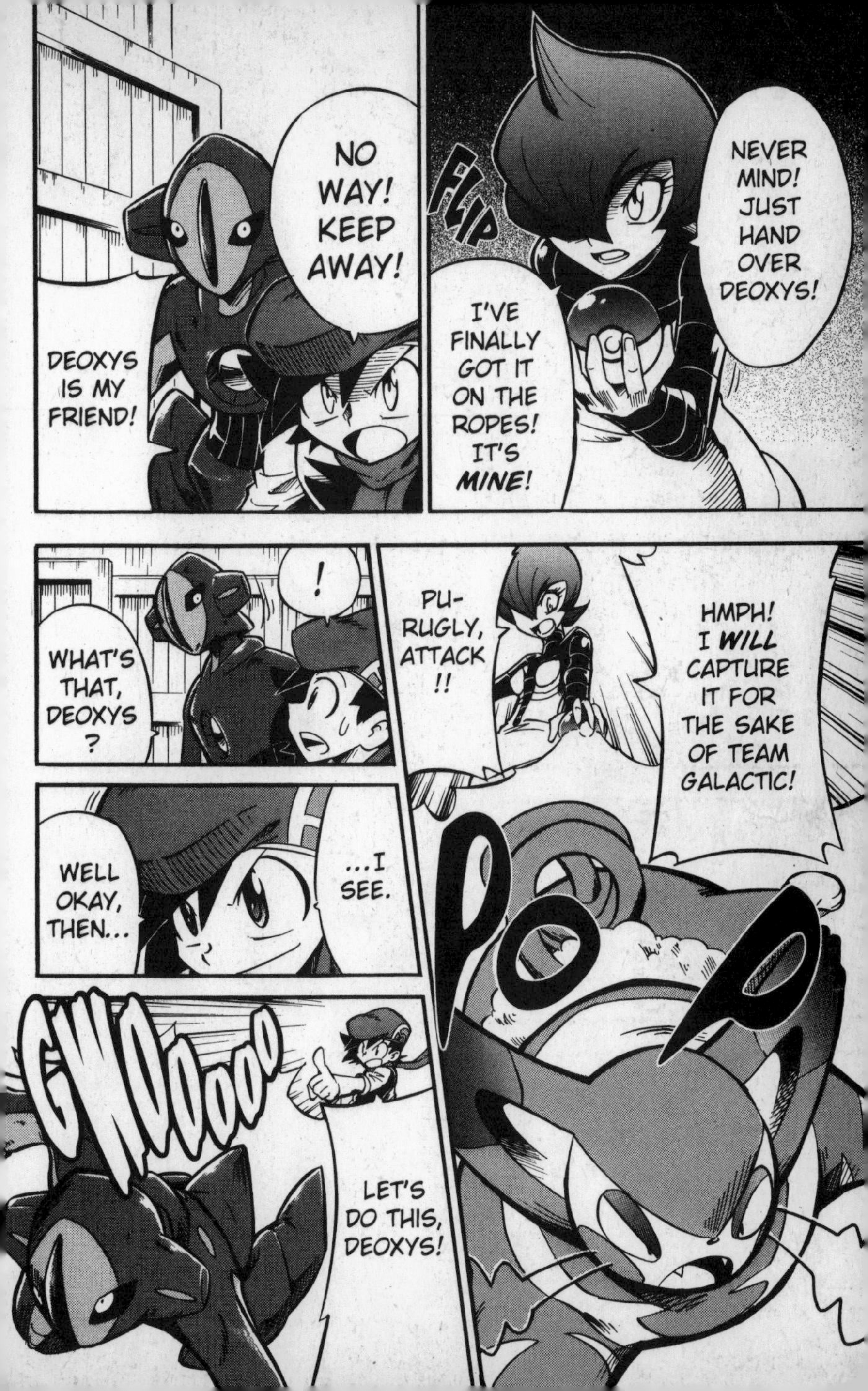
NEVER MIND! JUST HAND OVER DEOXYS!
FLIP
I'VE FINALLY GOT IT ON THE ROPES! IT'S MINE!
NO WAY! KEEP AWAY!
DEOXYS IS MY FRIEND!
HMPH! I WILL CAPTURE IT FOR THE SAKE OF TEAM GALACTIC!
PU-RUGLY, ATTACK!!
POP
!
WHAT'S THAT, DEOXYS?
...I SEE.
WELL OKAY, THEN...
GWOOooo
LET'S DO THIS, DEOXYS!

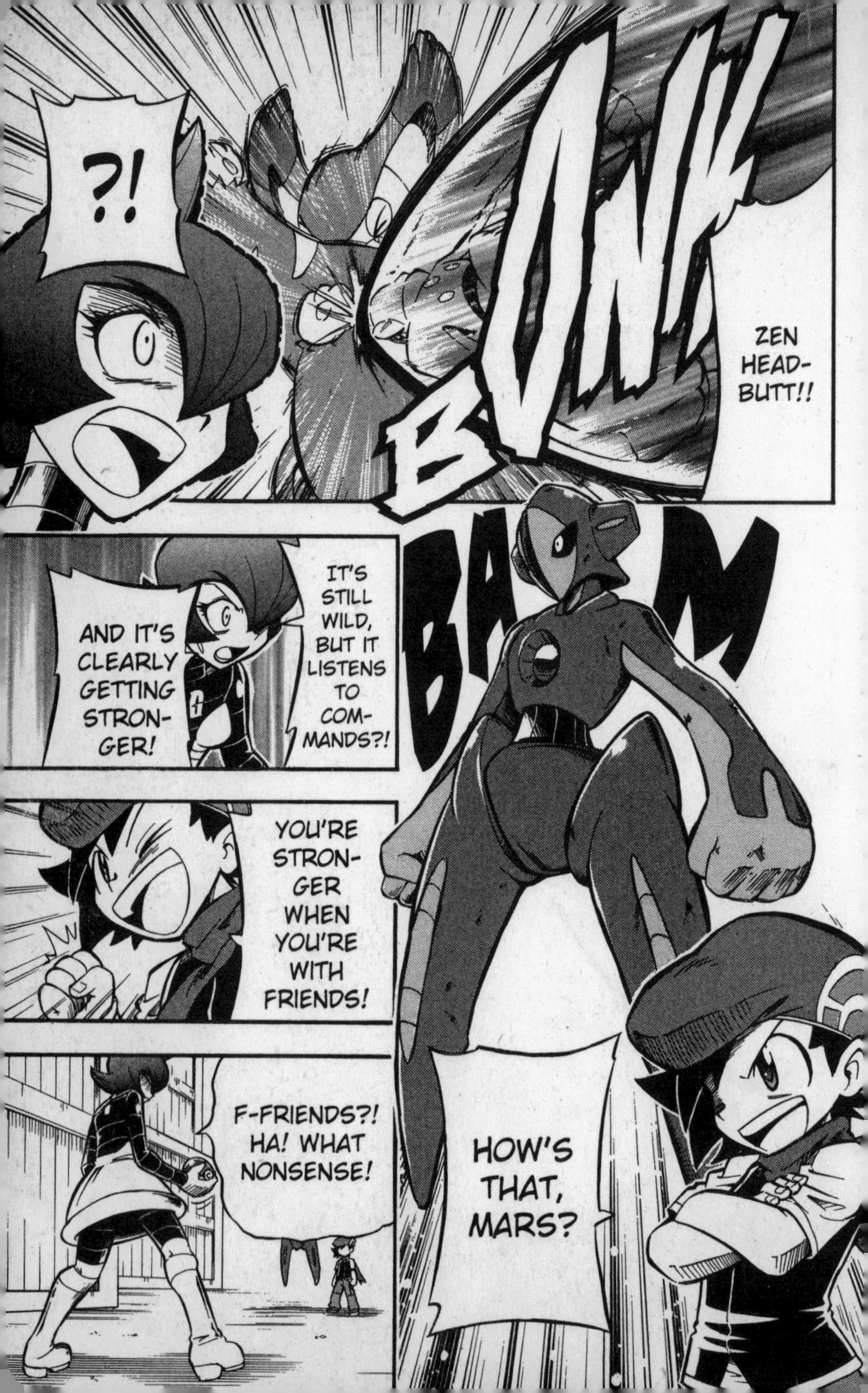
ZEN HEAD-BUTT!!
BONK
?!
BAM
HOW'S THAT, MARS?
IT'S STILL WILD, BUT IT LISTENS TO COMMANDS?!
AND IT'S CLEARLY GETTING STRONGER!
YOU'RE STRONGER WHEN YOU'RE WITH FRIENDS!
F-FRIENDS?! HA! WHAT NONSENSE!

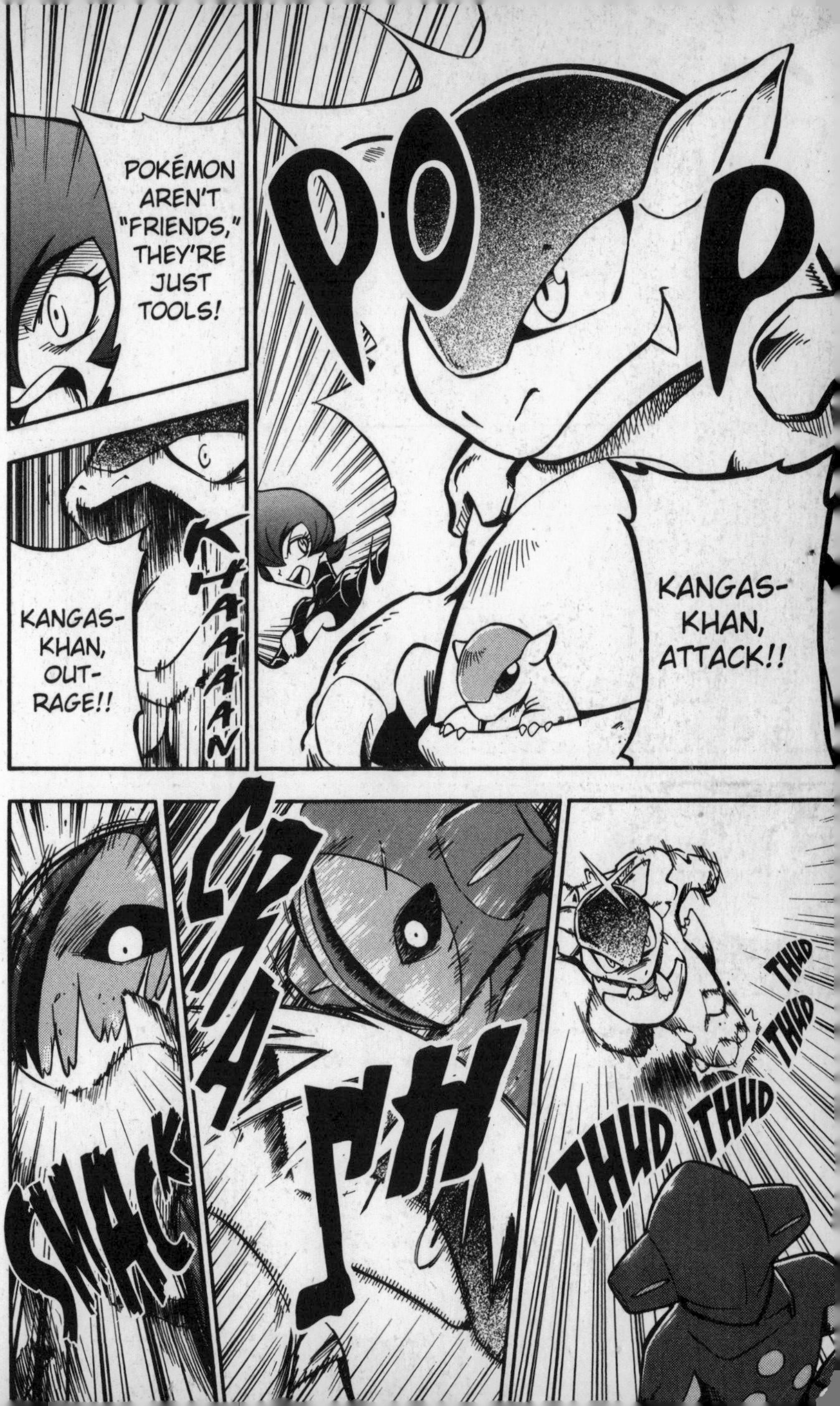

POP
KANGAS-KHAN, ATTACK!!
POKÉMON AREN'T "FRIENDS," THEY'RE JUST TOOLS!
KHAAAAAAN
KANGAS-KHAN, OUT-RAGE!!
THUD THUD THUD THUD THUD THUD
CRASH
SMACK

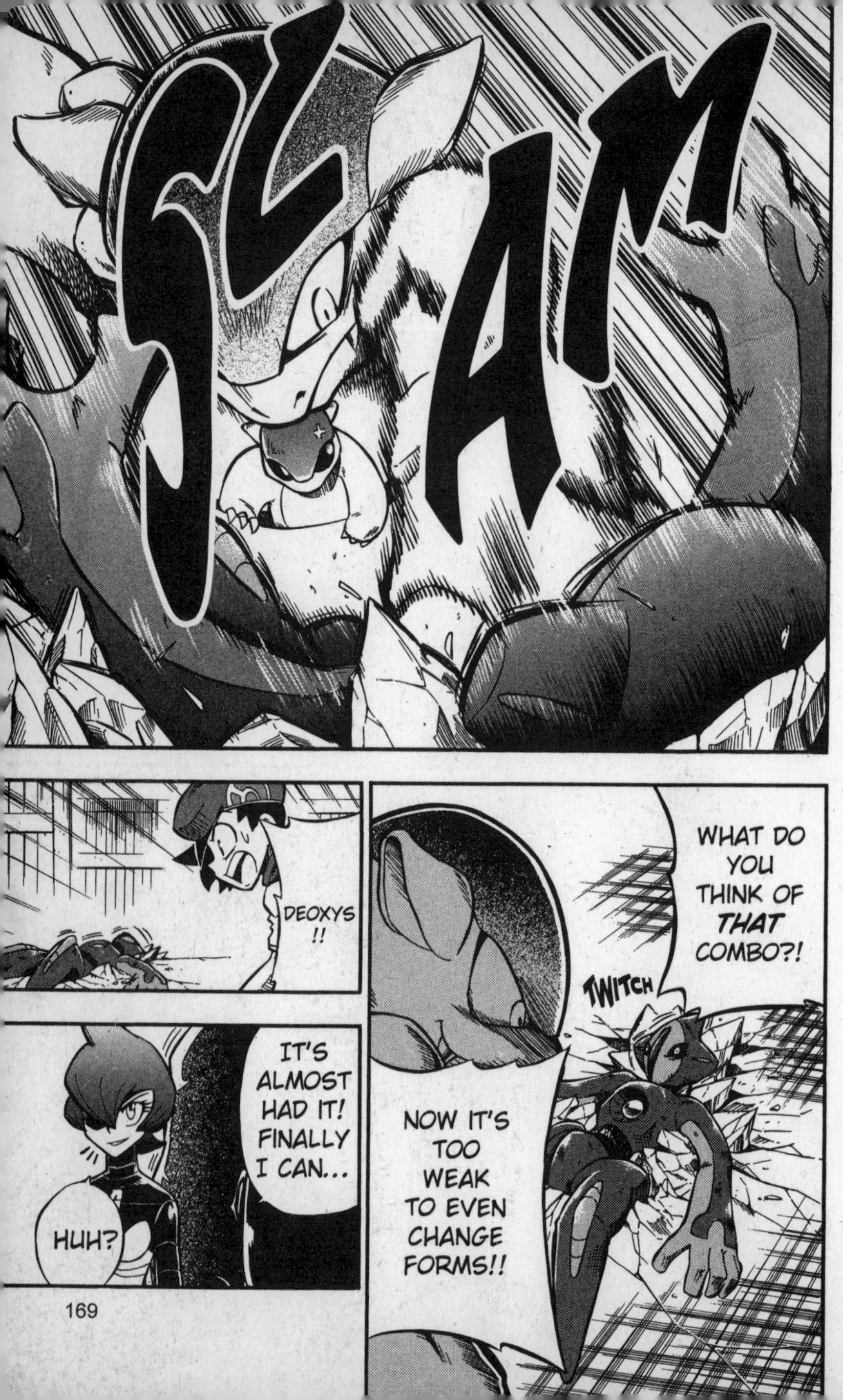
SLAM
WHAT DO YOU THINK OF *THAT* COMBO?!
TWITCH
NOW IT'S TOO WEAK TO EVEN CHANGE FORMS!!
DEOXYS !!
IT'S ALMOST HAD IT! FINALLY I CAN...
HUH?

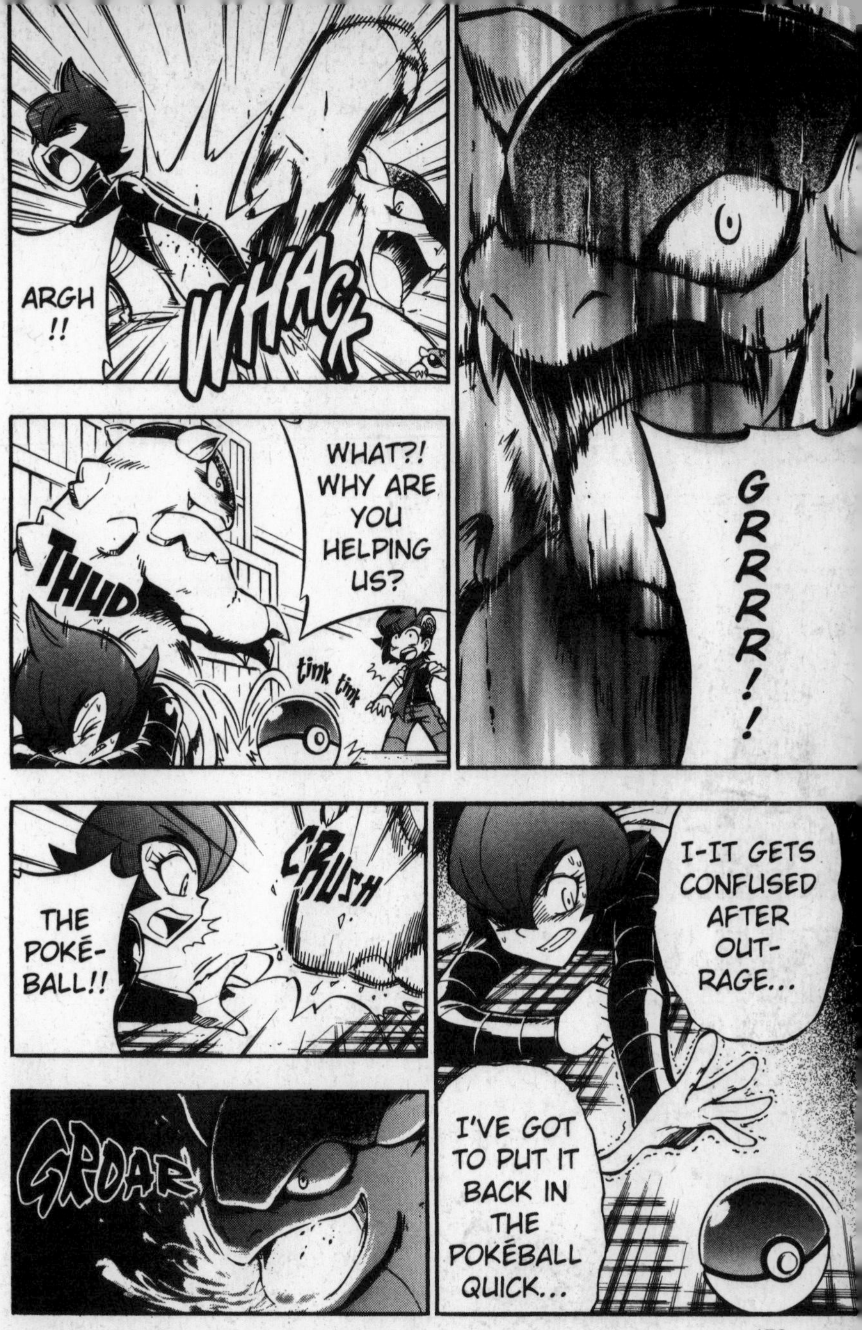
GRRRR!!
WHACK
ARGH!!
WHAT?! WHY ARE YOU HELPING US?
THUD
tink tink
I-IT GETS CONFUSED AFTER OUT-RAGE...
I'VE GOT TO PUT IT BACK IN THE POKÉBALL QUICK...
CRUSH
THE POKÉ-BALL!!
GROAR

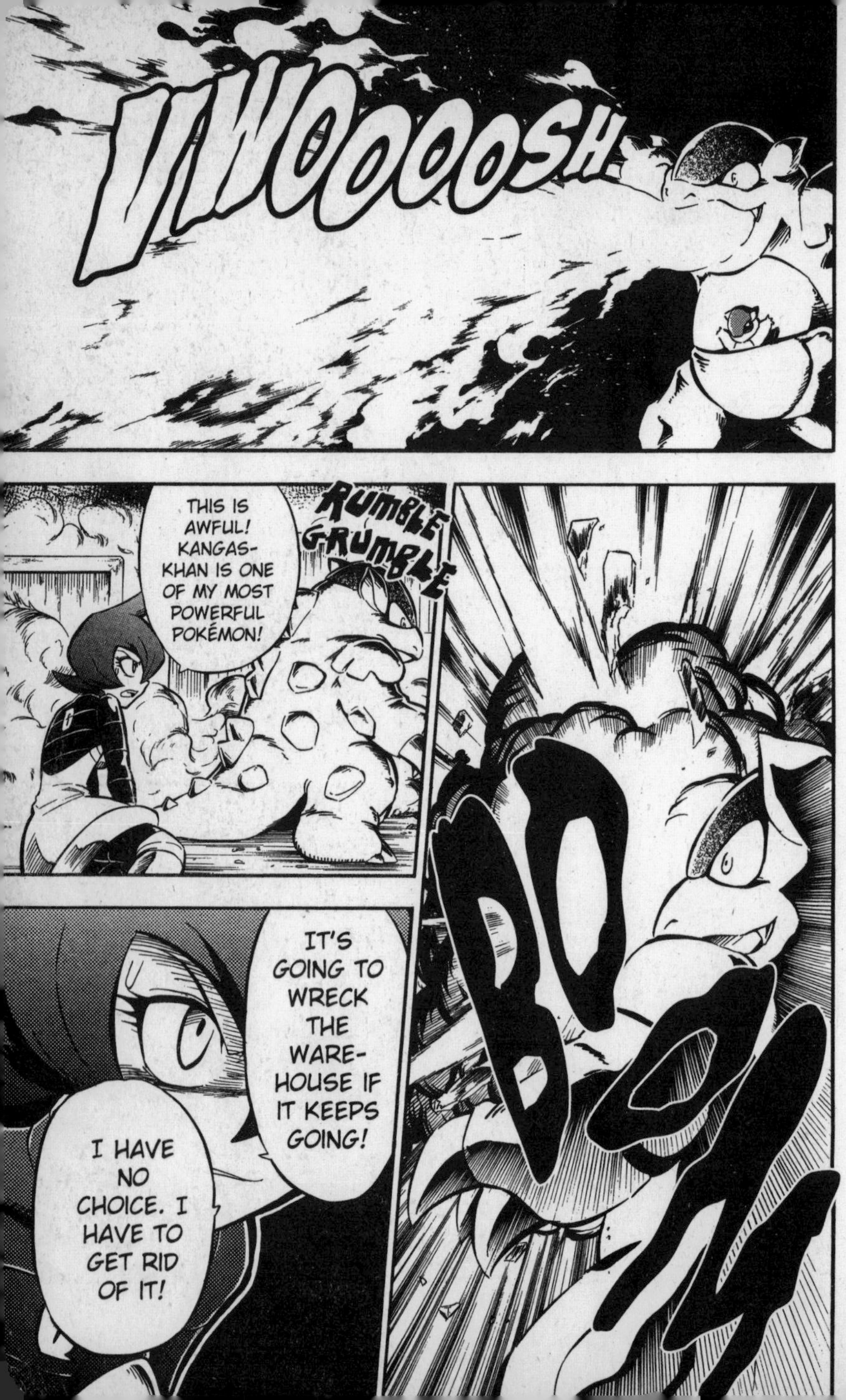
WOOOOSH
RUMBLE GRUMBLE
THIS IS AWFUL! KANGAS-KHAN IS ONE OF MY MOST POWERFUL POKÉMON!
IT'S GOING TO WRECK THE WARE-HOUSE IF IT KEEPS GOING!
I HAVE NO CHOICE. I HAVE TO GET RID OF IT!

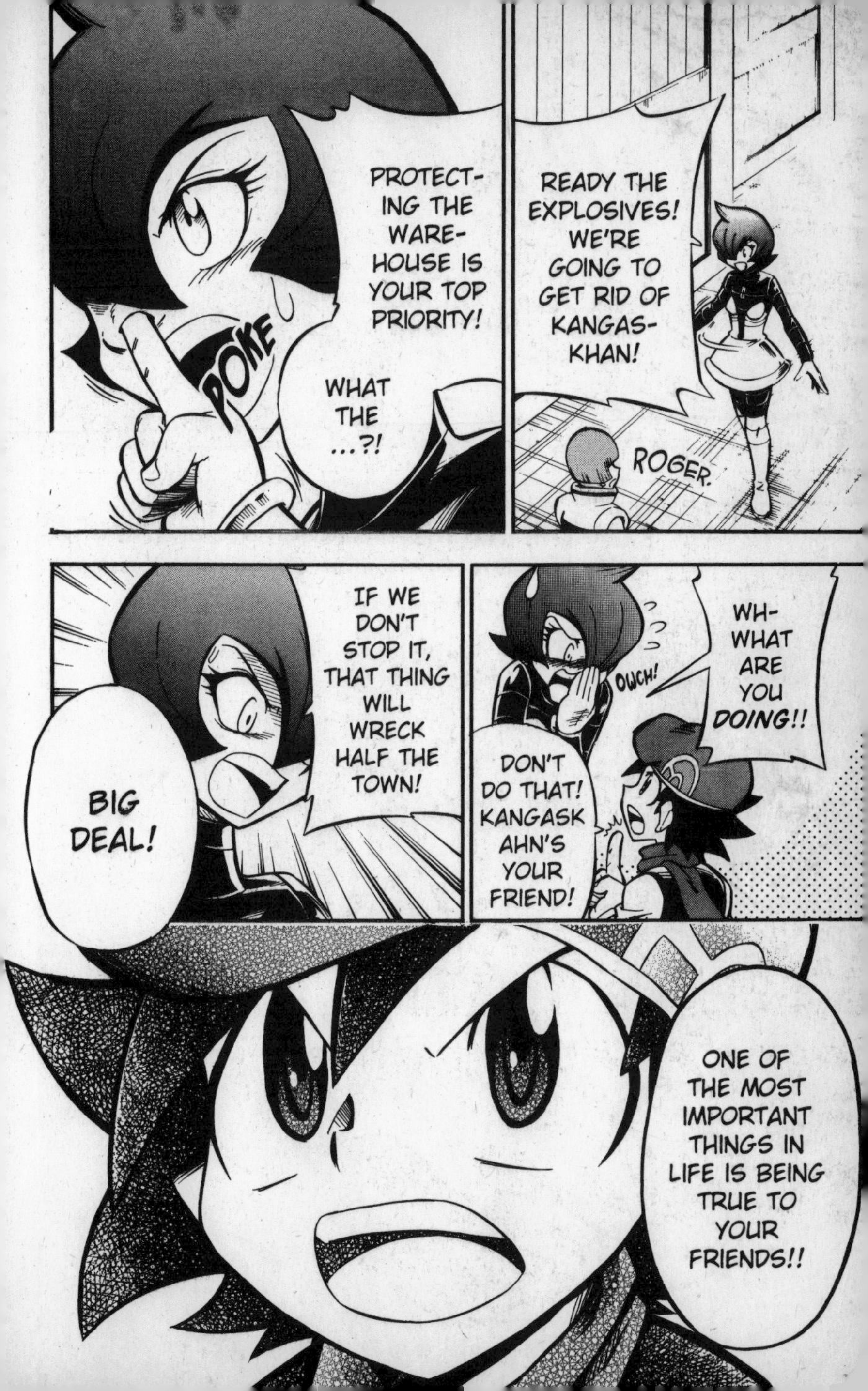
READY THE EXPLOSIVES! WE'RE GOING TO GET RID OF KANGASKHAN!
ROGER.
PROTECTING THE WAREHOUSE IS YOUR TOP PRIORITY!
WHAT THE ...?!
POKE
WH-WHAT ARE YOU *DOING*!!
OWCH!
DON'T DO THAT! KANGASKAHN'S YOUR FRIEND!
IF WE DON'T STOP IT, THAT THING WILL WRECK HALF THE TOWN!
BIG DEAL!
ONE OF THE MOST IMPORTANT THINGS IN LIFE IS BEING TRUE TO YOUR FRIENDS!!

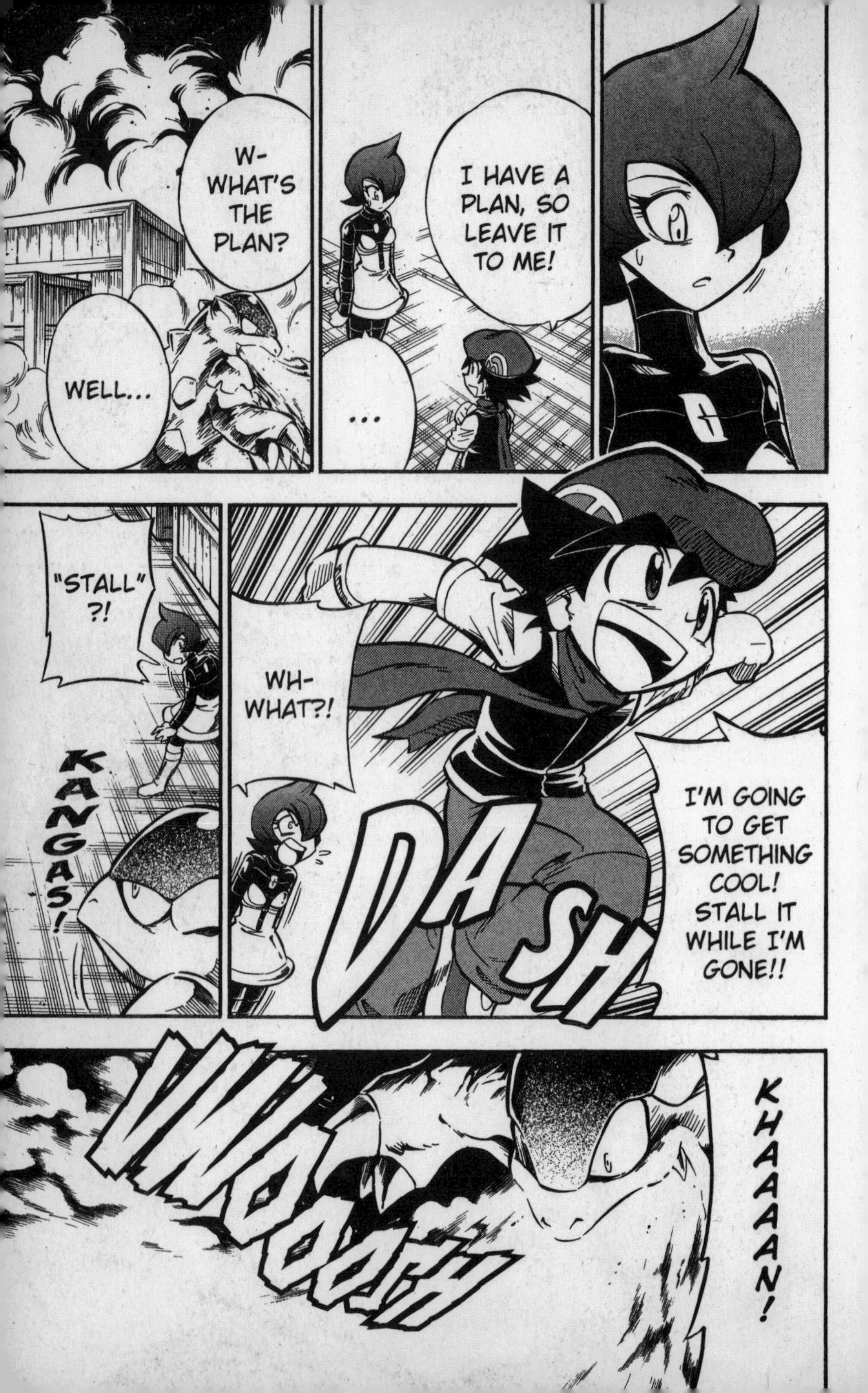
I HAVE A PLAN, SO LEAVE IT TO ME!
...
W-WHAT'S THE PLAN?
WELL...
I'M GOING TO GET SOMETHING COOL! STALL IT WHILE I'M GONE!!
DASH
WH-WHAT?!
"STALL" ?!
KANGAS!
KHAAAAAN!
WHOOOSH

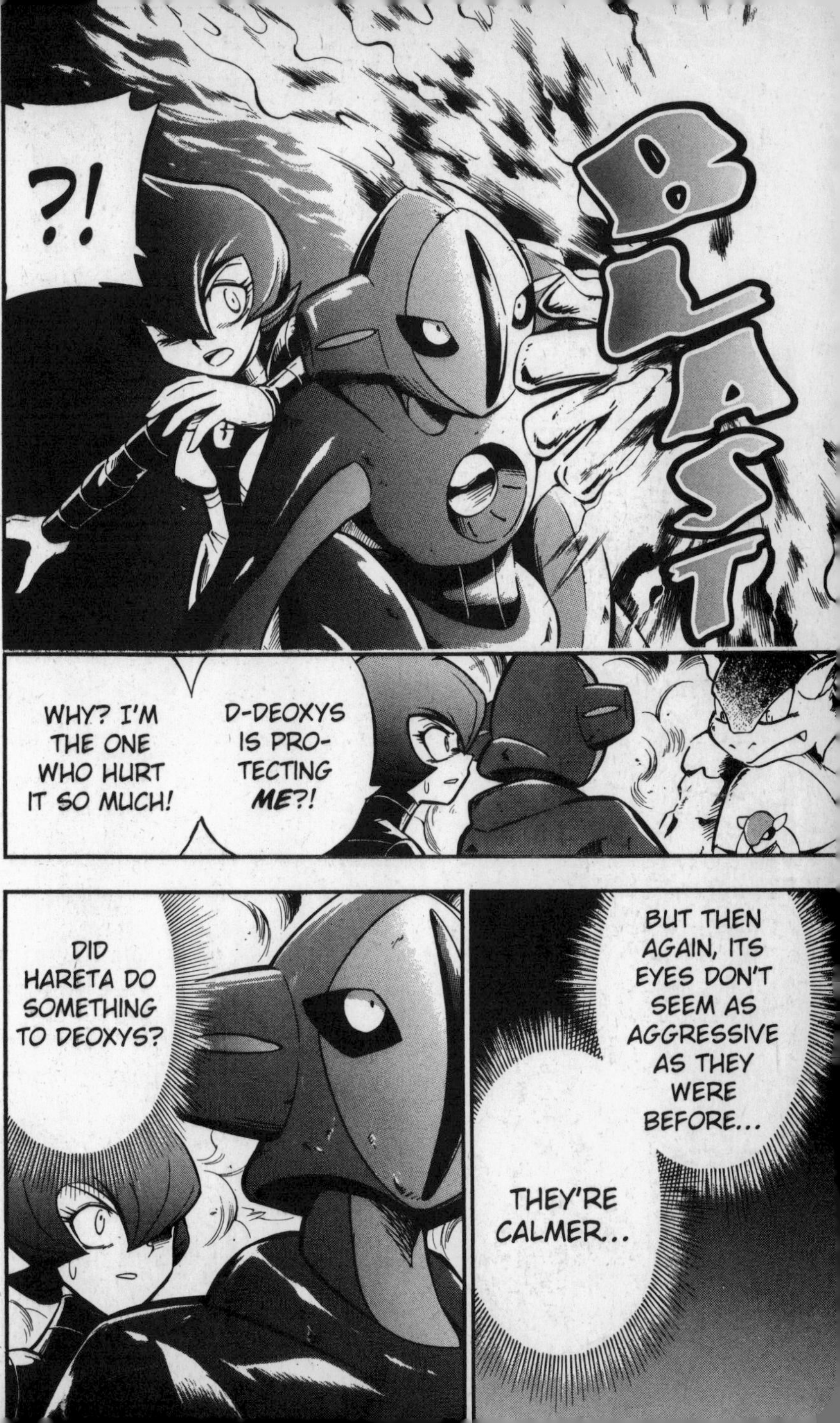
BLAST
?!
D-DEOXYS IS PROTECTING ME?!
WHY? I'M THE ONE WHO HURT IT SO MUCH!
BUT THEN AGAIN, ITS EYES DON'T SEEM AS AGGRESSIVE AS THEY WERE BEFORE...
THEY'RE CALMER...
DID HARETA DO SOMETHING TO DEOXYS?

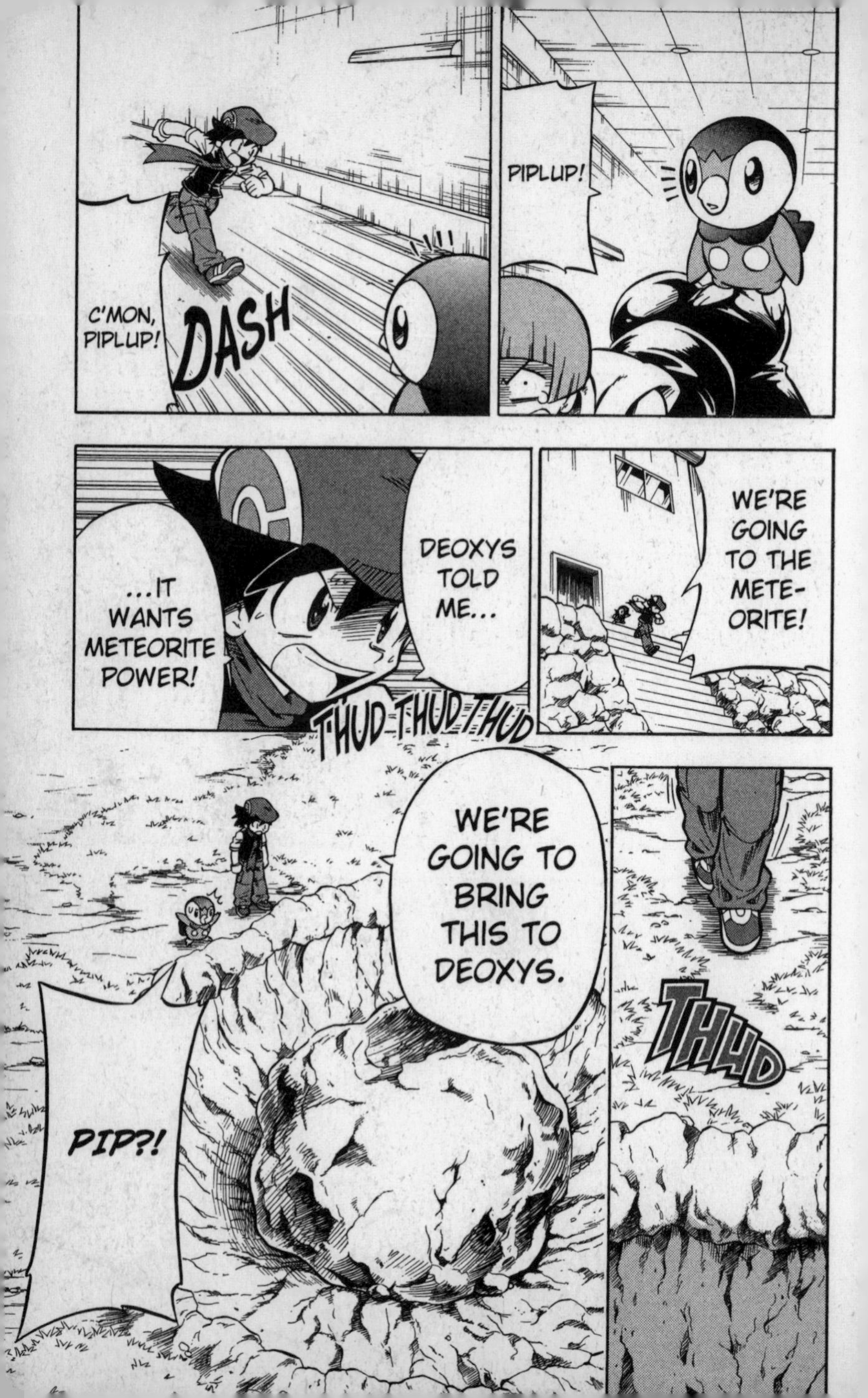
PIPLUP!
C'MON, PIPLUP!
DASH
WE'RE GOING TO THE METE-ORITE!
DEOXYS TOLD ME...
...IT WANTS METEORITE POWER!
THUD THUD THUD
THUD
WE'RE GOING TO BRING THIS TO DEOXYS.
PIP?!

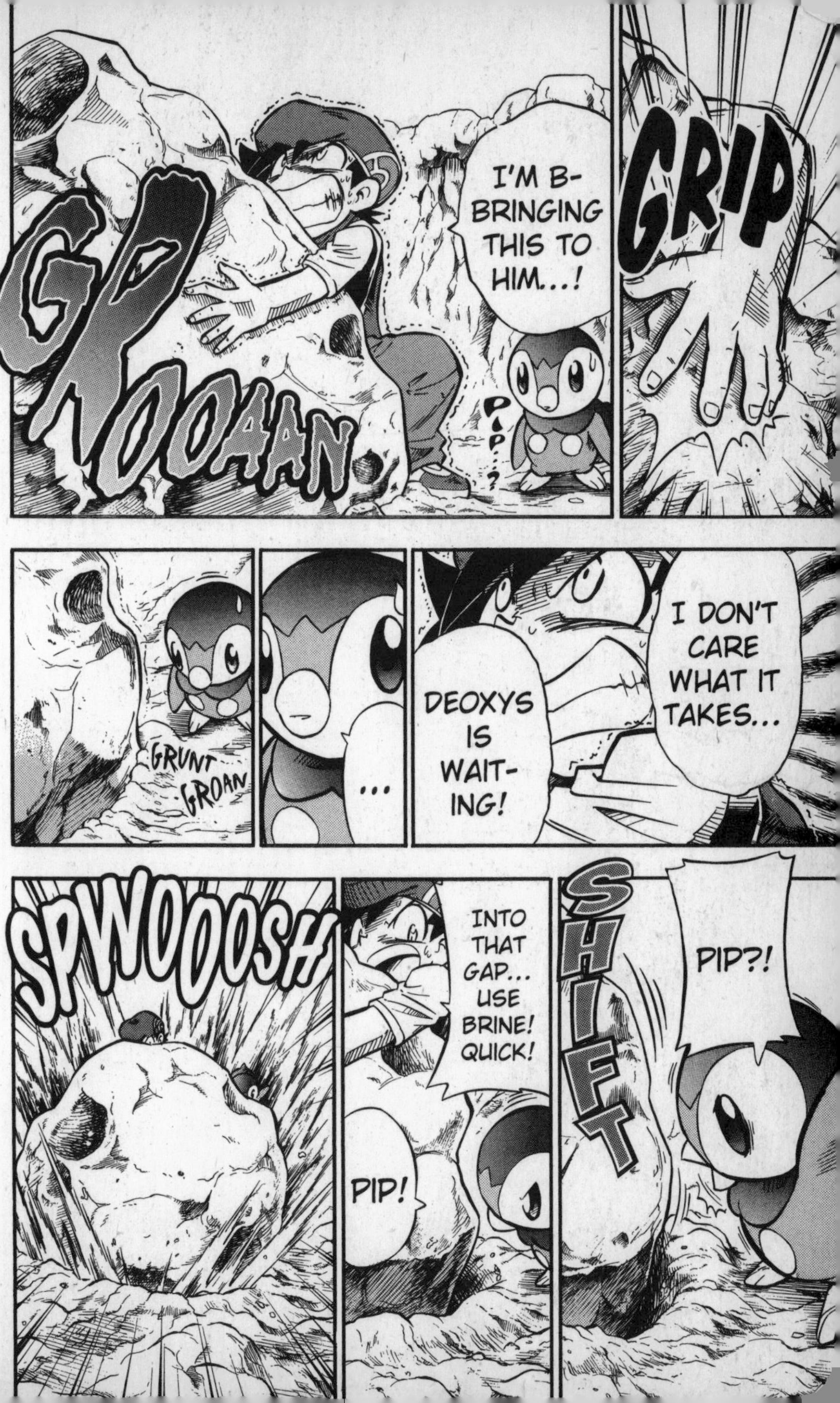
GRIP
I'M B-BRINGING THIS TO HIM...!
GROOAAN
PIP...?
I DON'T CARE WHAT IT TAKES...
DEOXYS IS WAIT-ING!
...
GRUNT GROAN
PIP?!
SHIFT
INTO THAT GAP... USE BRINE! QUICK!
PIP!
SPWOOOSH

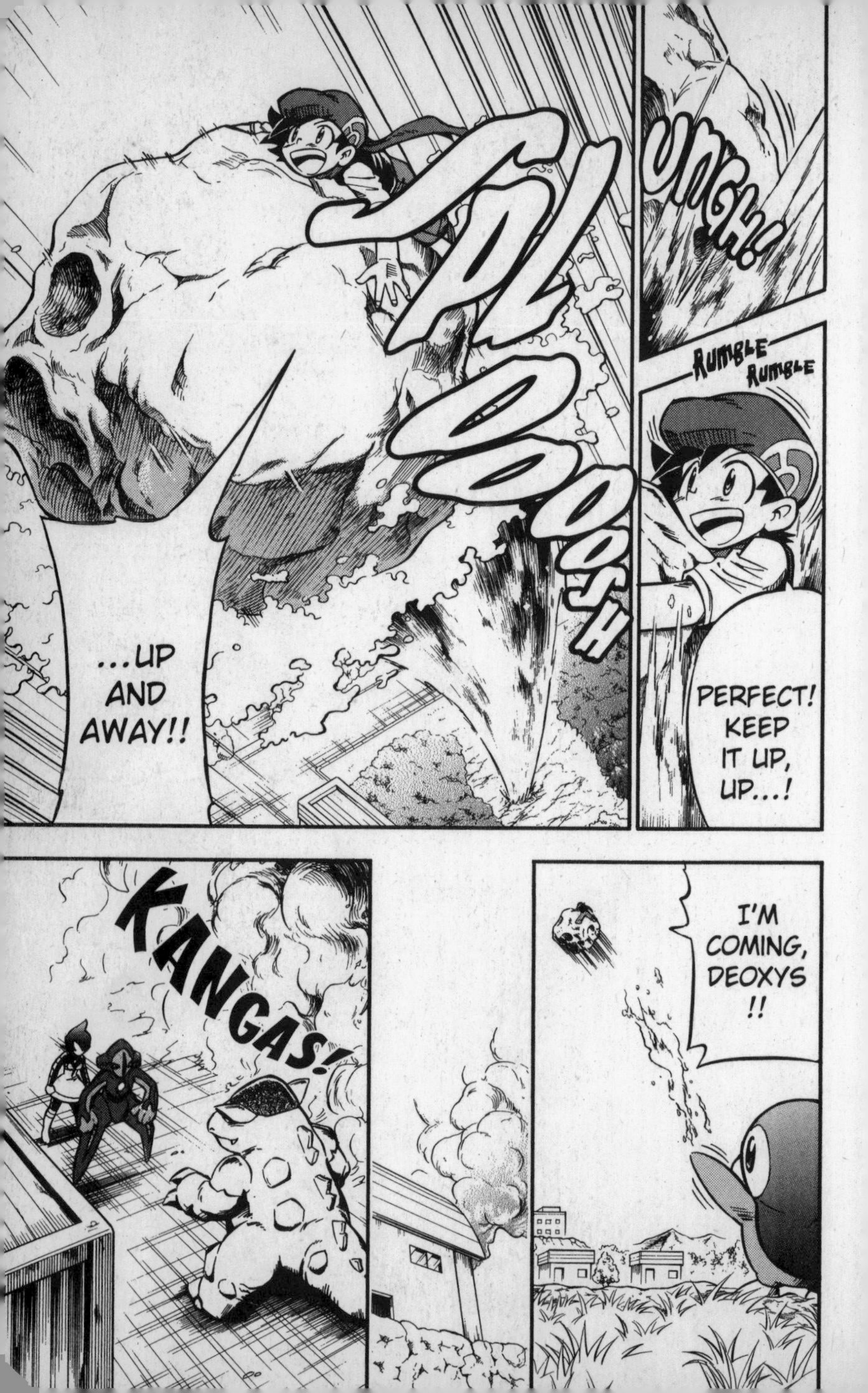
UNGH!!
RUMBLE RUMBLE
PERFECT! KEEP IT UP, UP...!
ZWOOOOSH
...UP AND AWAY!!
I'M COMING, DEOXYS!!
KANGAS!

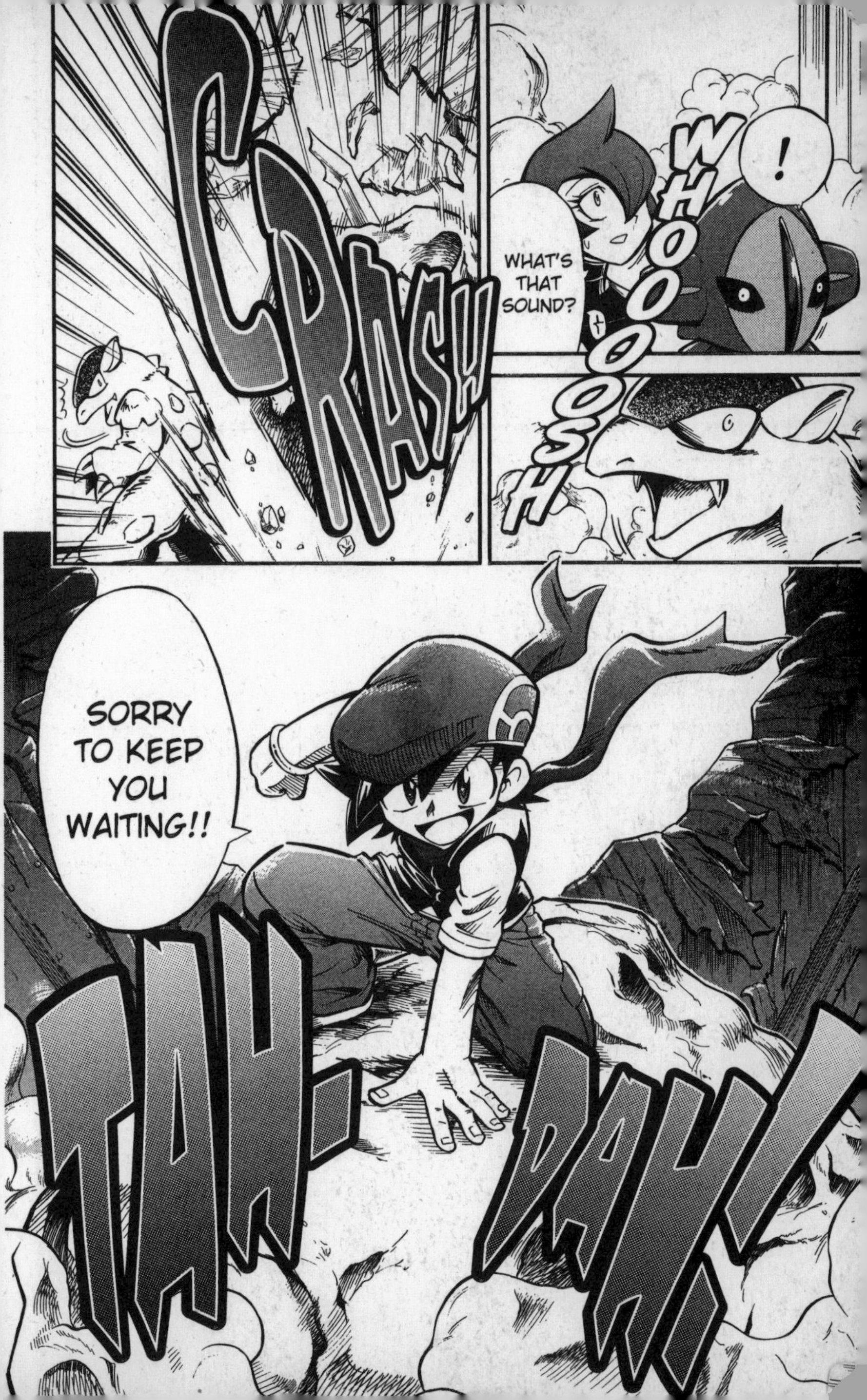
!
WHOOOOOOSH
WHAT'S THAT SOUND?
CRASH
SORRY TO KEEP YOU WAITING!!
TAH-DAH!!

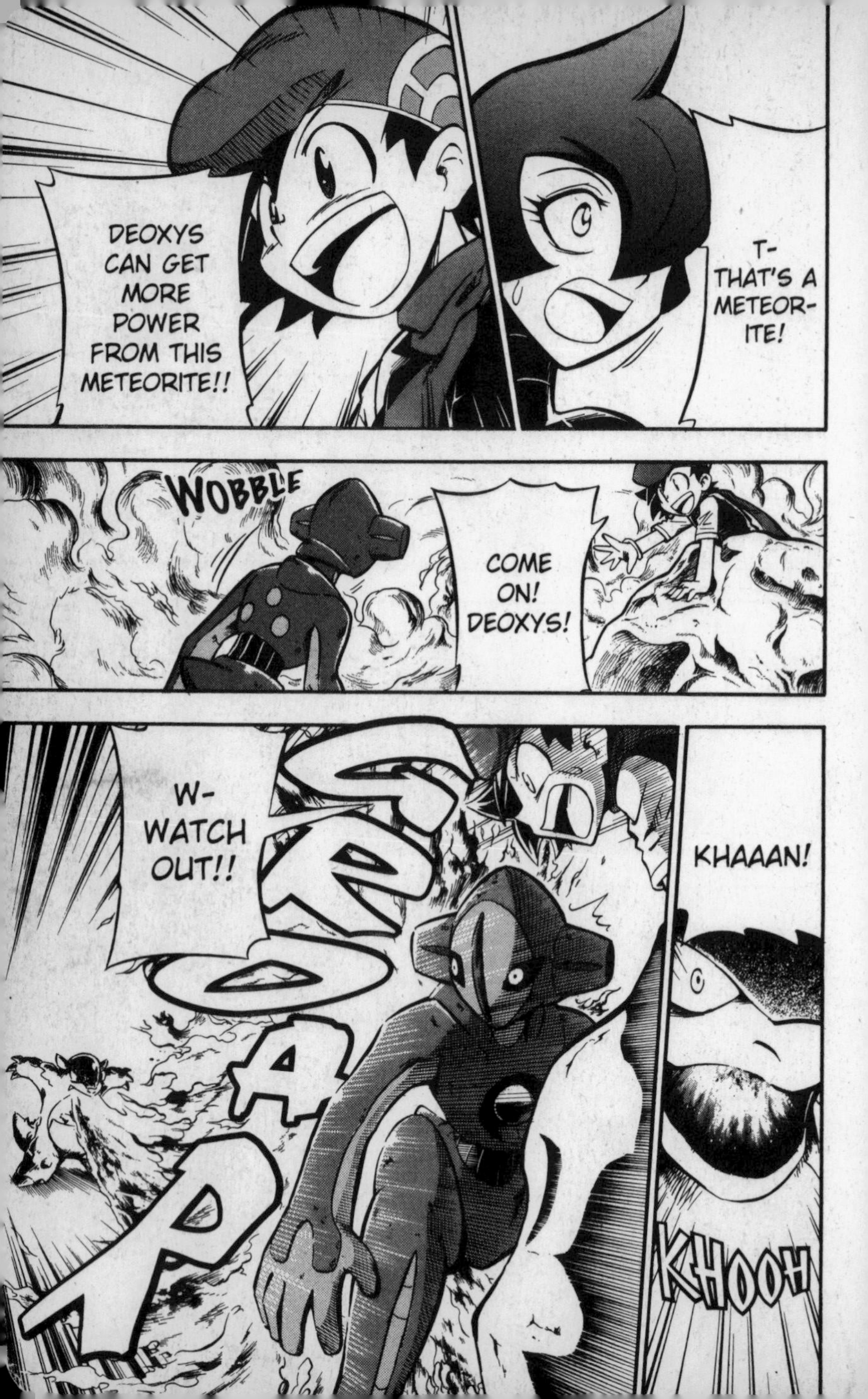
T- THAT'S A METEOR-ITE!
DEOXYS CAN GET MORE POWER FROM THIS METEORITE!!
COME ON! DEOXYS!
WOBBLE
KHAAAN!
KHOOH
W- WATCH OUT!!

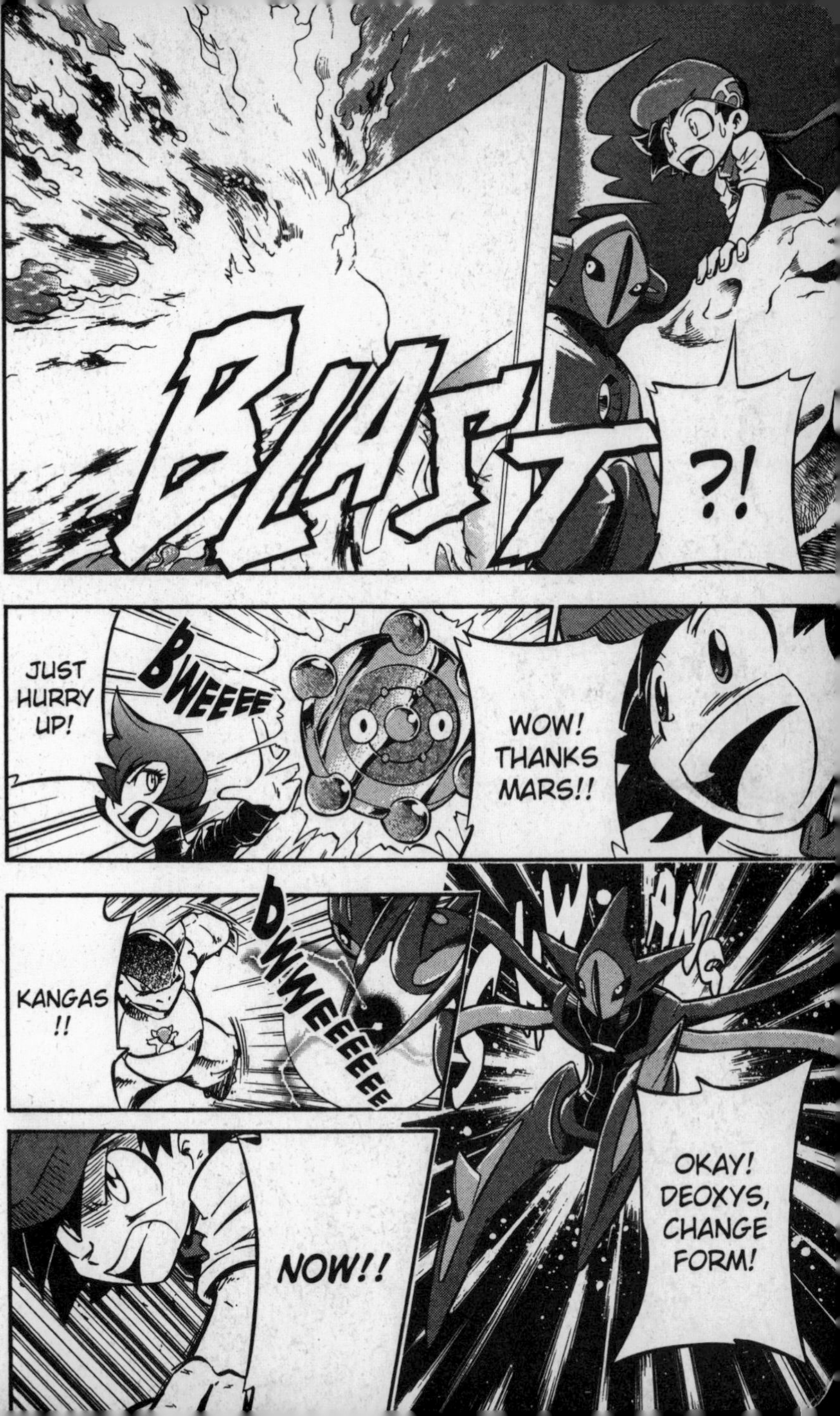
?!
BLAST
WOW! THANKS MARS!!
BWEEEEE
JUST HURRY UP!
OKAY! DEOXYS, CHANGE FORM!
DWWEEEEEEE
KANGAS !!
NOW!!

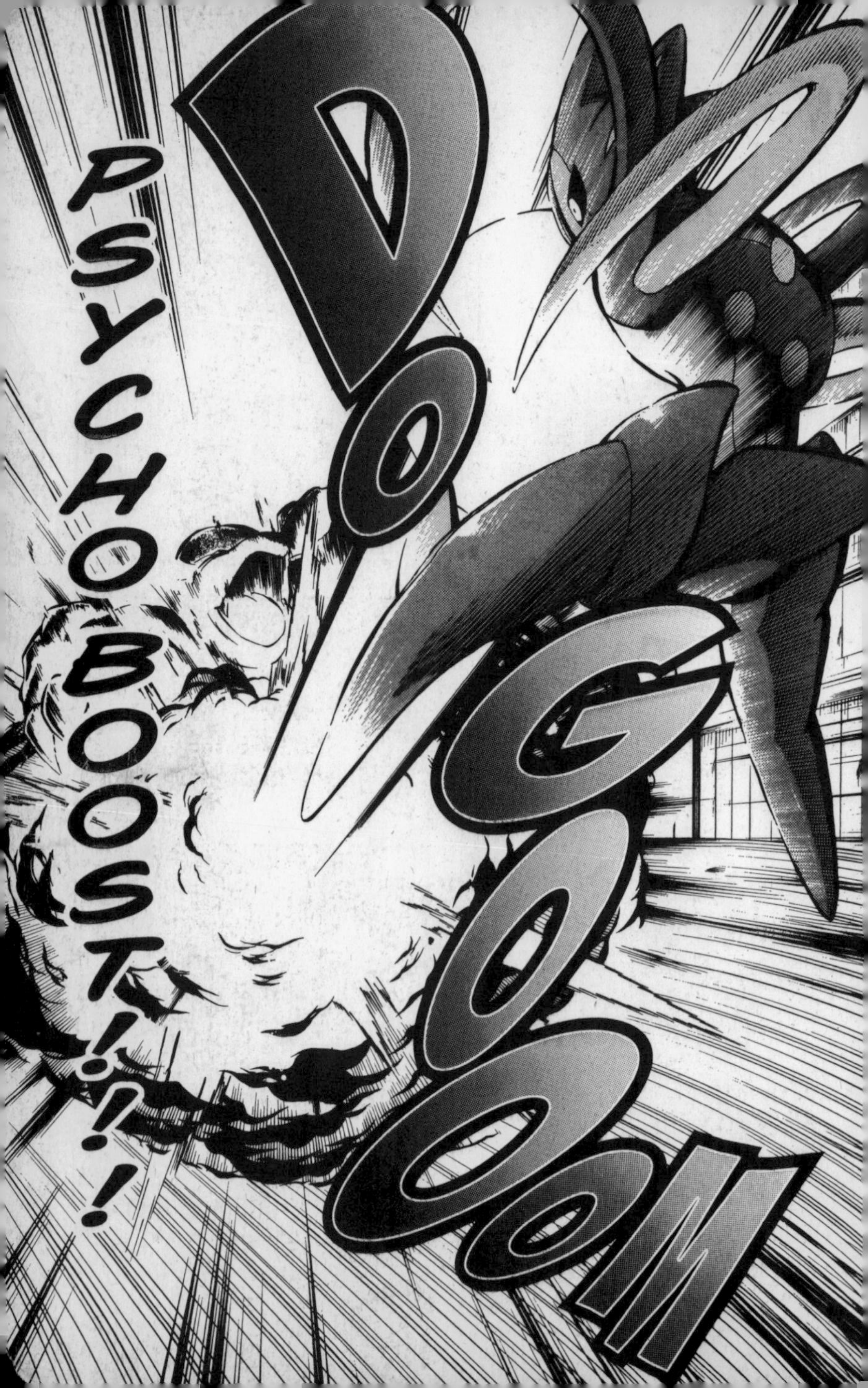
DOGOOOM
PSYCHO BOOST!!!

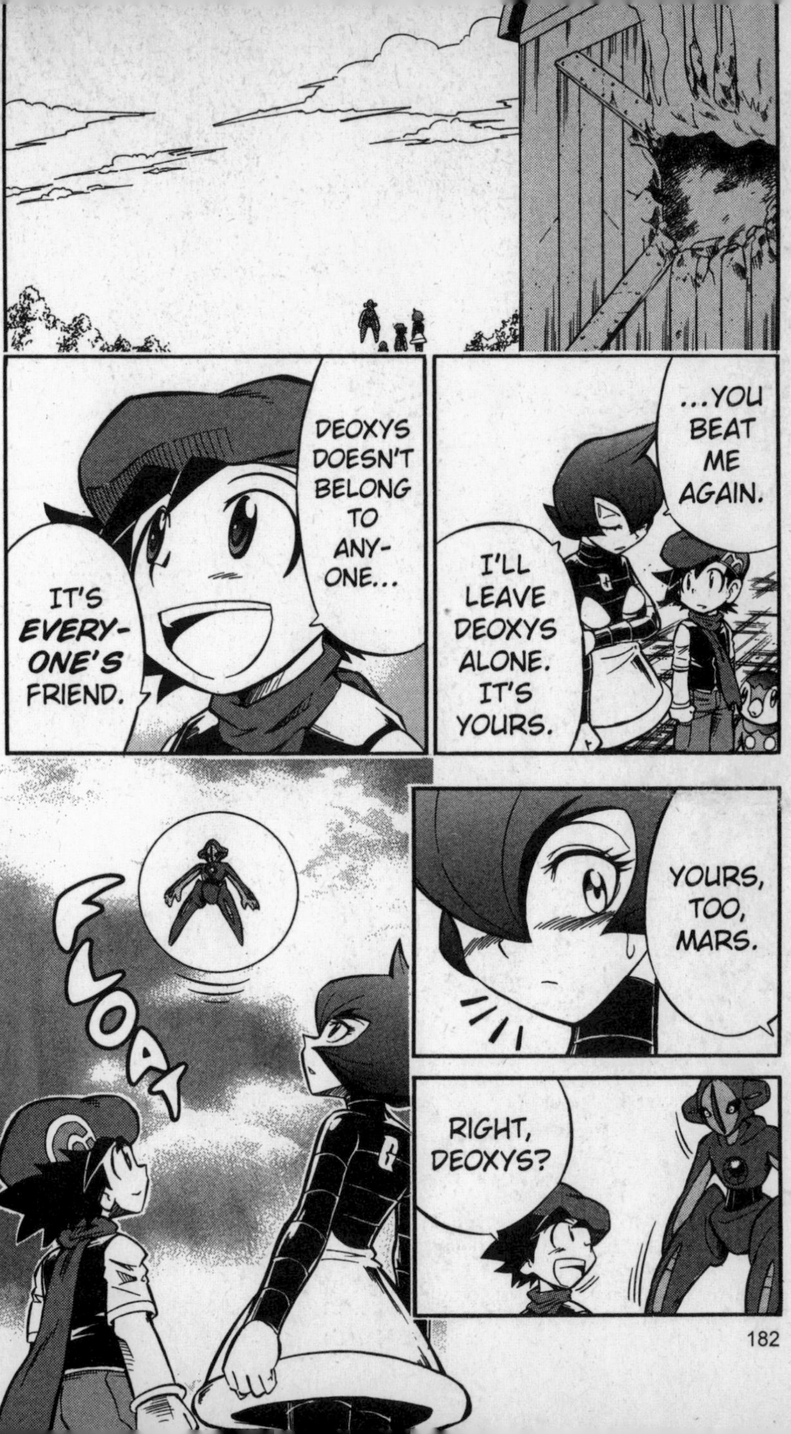
...YOU BEAT ME AGAIN.
I'LL LEAVE DEOXYS ALONE. IT'S YOURS.
DEOXYS DOESN'T BELONG TO ANY-ONE...
IT'S *EVERY-ONE'S* FRIEND.
YOURS, TOO, MARS.
RIGHT, DEOXYS?
FLOAT

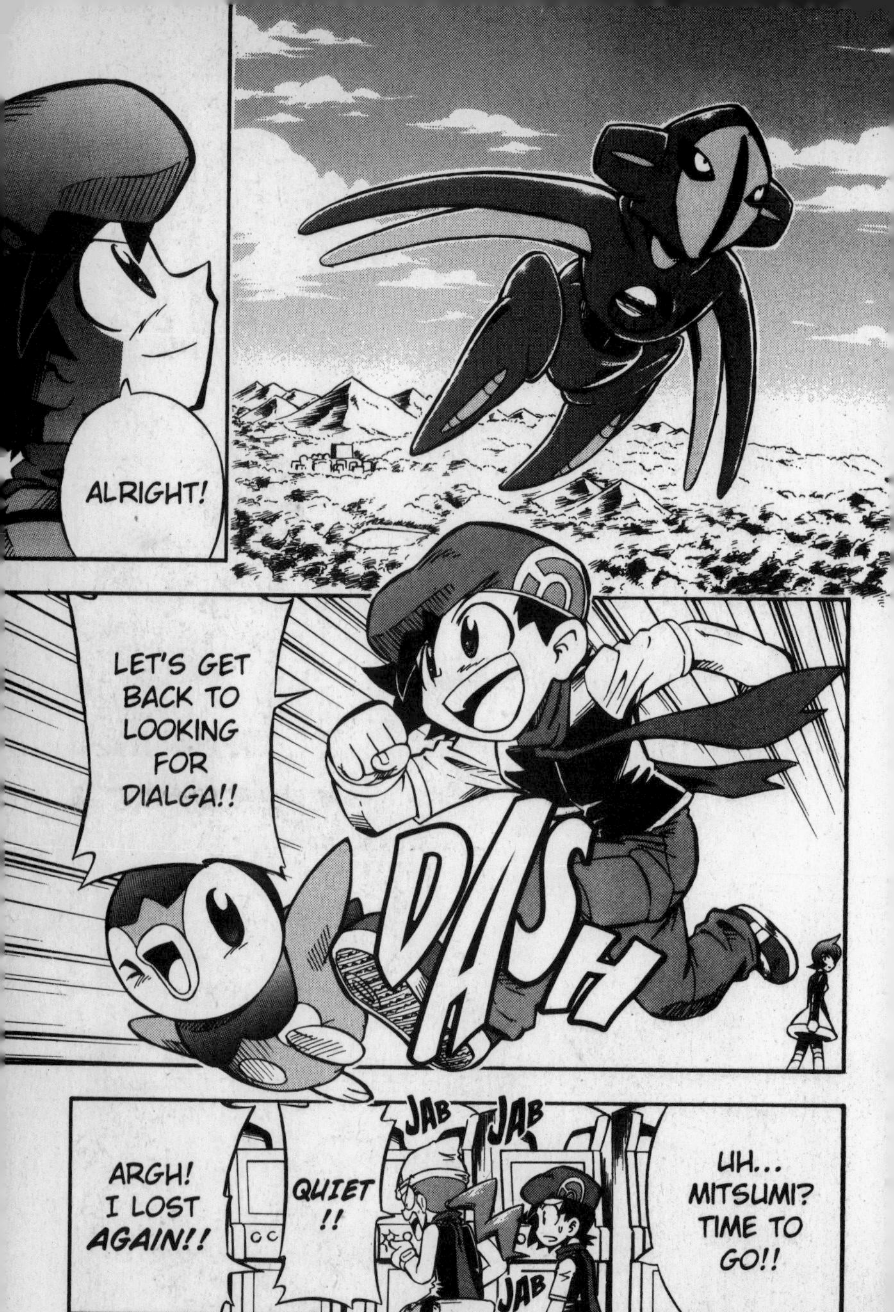
ALRIGHT!
LET'S GET BACK TO LOOKING FOR DIALGA!!
DASH
UH... MITSUMI? TIME TO GO!!
JAB
JAB
JAB
QUIET!!
ARGH! I LOST AGAIN!!

The End.

D·P SNAPSHOTS

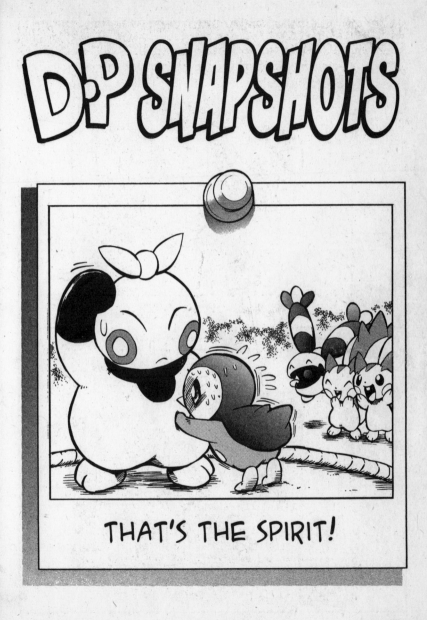

THAT'S THE SPIRIT!

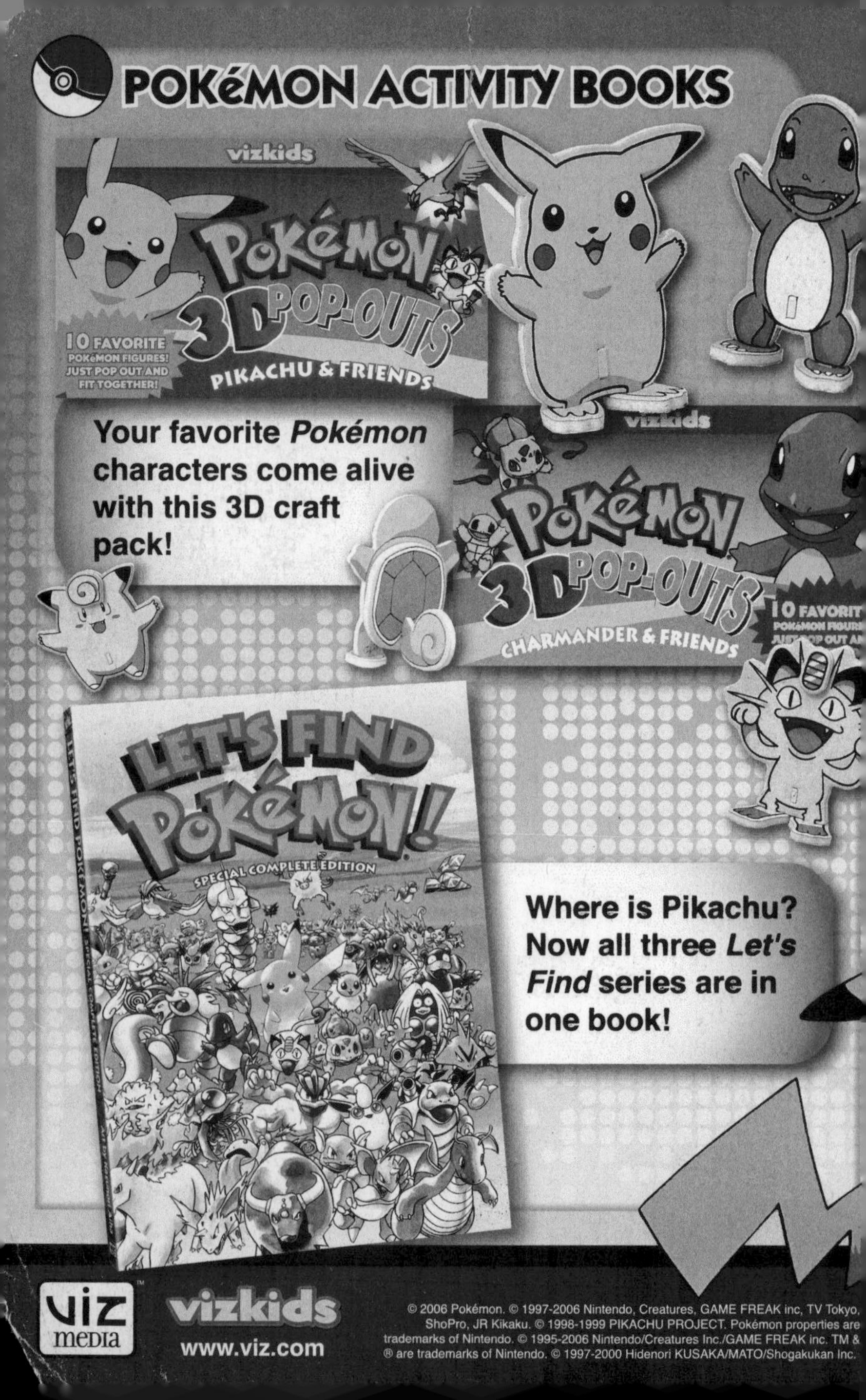
POKéMON ACTIVITY BOOKS
vizkids
POKéMON 3D POP-OUTS
PIKACHU & FRIENDS
10 FAVORITE POKéMON FIGURES! JUST POP OUT AND FIT TOGETHER!
Your favorite Pokémon characters come alive with this 3D craft pack!
vizkids
POKéMON 3D POP-OUTS
CHARMANDER & FRIENDS
LET'S FIND POKéMON!
SPECIAL COMPLETE EDITION
Where is Pikachu? Now all three Let's Find series are in one book!
VIZ MEDIA
vizkids
www.viz.com
© 2006 Pokémon. © 1997-2006 Nintendo, Creatures, GAME FREAK inc, TV Tokyo, ShoPro, JR Kikaku. © 1998-1999 PIKACHU PROJECT. Pokémon properties are trademarks of Nintendo. © 1995-2006 Nintendo/Creatures Inc./GAME FREAK inc. TM & ® are trademarks of Nintendo. © 1997-2000 Hidenori KUSAKA/MATO/Shogakukan Inc.

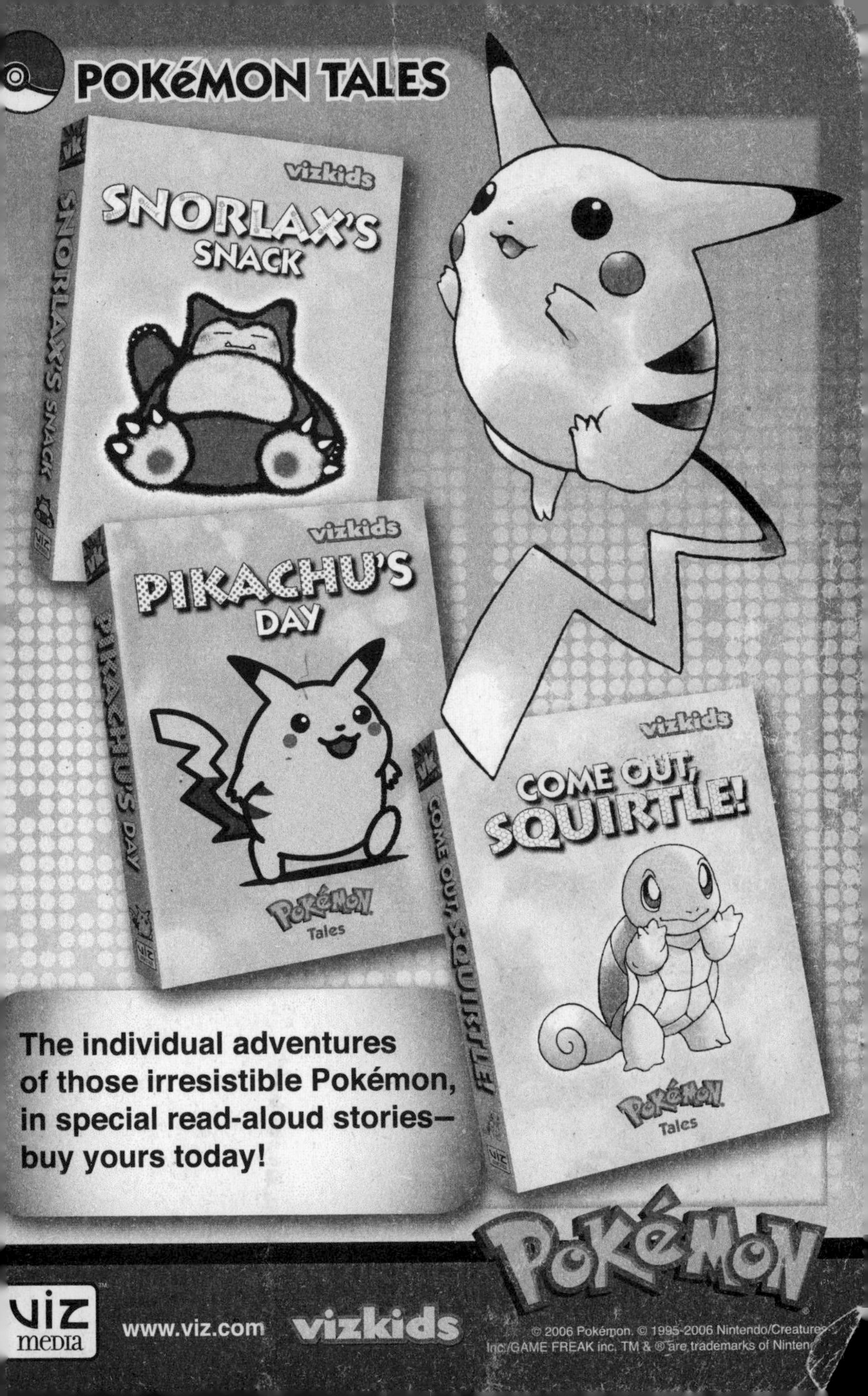
POKéMON TALES
vizkids
SNORLAX'S SNACK
vizkids
PIKACHU'S DAY
Pokémon Tales
vizkids
COME OUT, SQUIRTLE!
Pokémon Tales
The individual adventures of those irresistible Pokémon, in special read-aloud stories—buy yours today!
Pokémon
viz media
www.viz.com
vizkids
© 2006 Pokémon. © 1995-2006 Nintendo/Creatures Inc./GAME FREAK inc. TM & ® are trademarks of Ninten

WASTE BAND

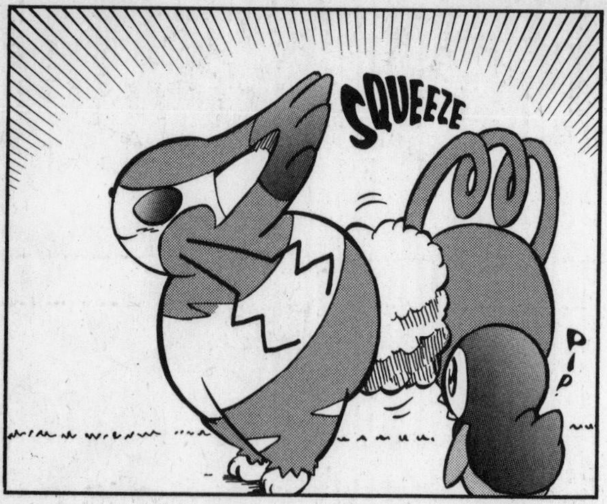
SQUEEZE
PIP!

IT LIFTS AND SEPARATES BUT...

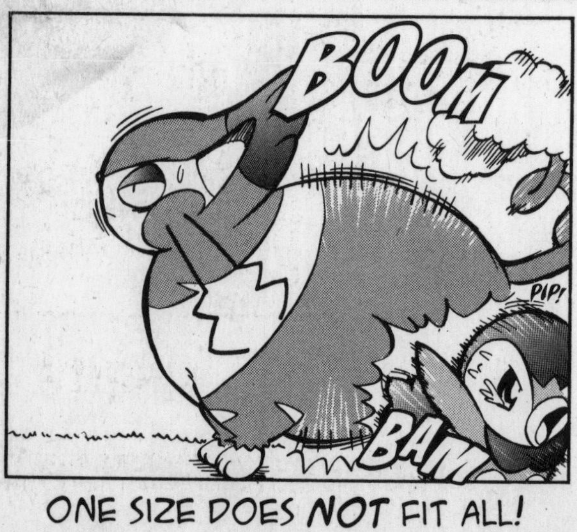
BOOM
PIP!
BAM

ONE SIZE DOES **NOT** FIT ALL!

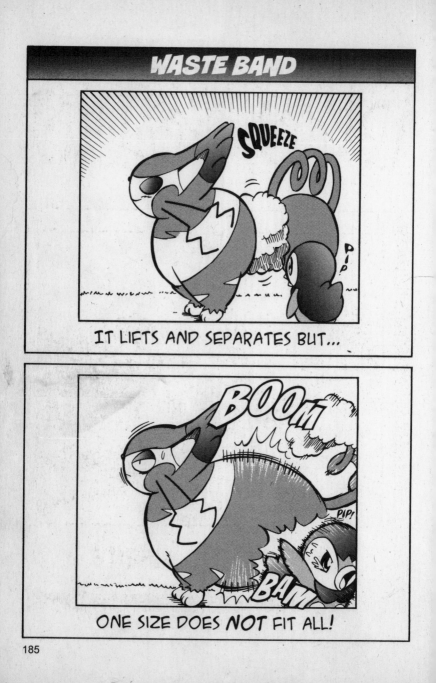

TRAINING!

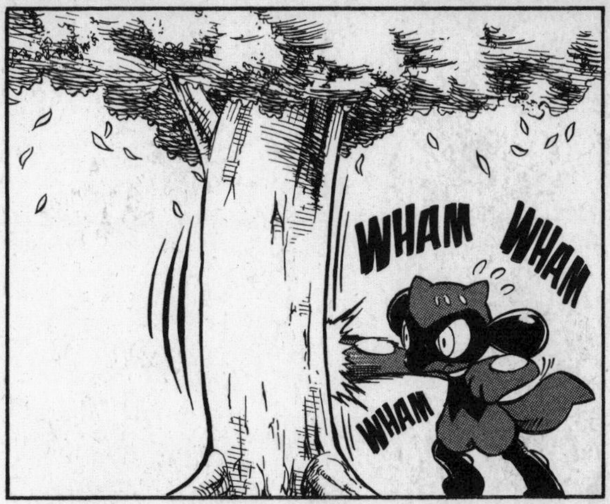
WHAM
WHAM
WHAM

GETTING STRONGER! ONE! TWO!

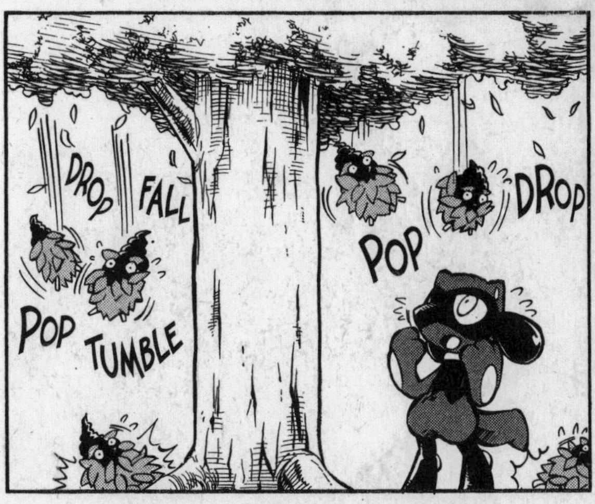
DROP
POP
FALL
DROP
POP
TUMBLE

M-MAYBE **TOO** STRONG?

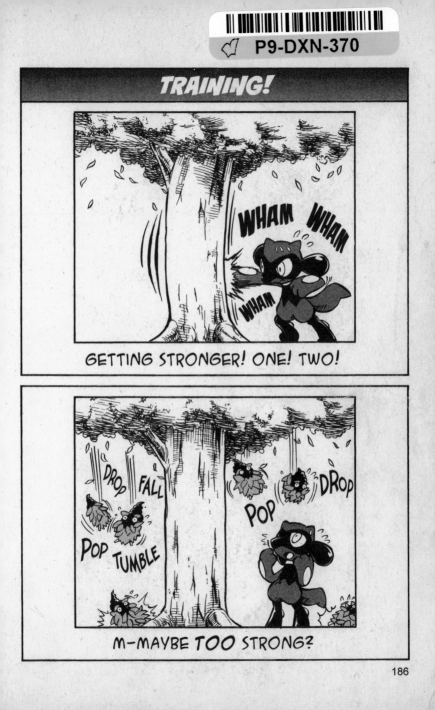